Steve Urry was born in Portsmouth, England, in 1960; he emigrated to Perth, Western Australia, with his family in 1969.

Steve joined the railways as a locomotive trainee engineman in 1981 spending the next 35 years on the railways, first as freight train driver then after some years becoming a passenger railcar driver in Perth. He then spent the last 13 years as a train controller before he retired at the end of 2020, now he is travelling around Australia with his partner.

Steve has enjoyed writing works of fiction for many years and self-published a fiction novel titled *Natasha—Queen of Matrovia*, a novel set in 1886 about a crown princess who has to fight her lunatic uncle for the crown after her father, the king, is killed.

Steve also spent a number of years as a boatswains mate in the Royal Australian Navy Reserve and his hobbies include acrylic paintings and pen-pencil sketching.

I would like to dedicate this book to all those SOE operatives who lost their lives in World War II.

Steve Urry

SOE Agent Code Name Lilly

AUSTIN MACAULEY PUBLISHERS™
LONDON * CAMBRIDGE * NEW YORK * SHARJAH

Copyright © Steve Urry 2023

The right of Steve Urry to be identified as author of this work has been asserted by the author in accordance with sections 77 and 78 of the Copyright, Designs and Patents Act 1988.

All rights reserved. No part of this publication may be reproduced, stored in a retrieval system, or transmitted in any form or by any means, electronic, mechanical, photocopying, recording, or otherwise, without the prior permission of the publishers.

Any person who commits any unauthorised act in relation to this publication may be liable to criminal prosecution and civil claims for damages.

This is a work of fiction. Names, characters, businesses, places, events, locales, and incidents are either the products of the author's imagination or used in a fictitious manner. Any resemblance to actual persons, living or dead, or actual events is purely coincidental.

A CIP catalogue record for this title is available from the British Library.

ISBN 9781398443570 (Paperback)
ISBN 9781398443594 (ePub e-book)
ISBN 9781398443587 (Audiobook)

www.austinmacauley.com

First Published 2023
Austin Macauley Publishers Ltd®
1 Canada Square
Canary Wharf
London
E14 5AA

Table of Contents

Part One: Code Name 'LILLY' — 9

Chapter One: France 1943 — 11

Chapter Two: Posey, France 1943 — 26

Chapter Three: SOE Training Camp, England 1942 — 38

Chapter Four: Posey, France 1943 — 44

Chapter Five :SOE Airfield, England The Previous Night — 48

Chapter Six: Posey, France 1943 — 51

Chapter Seven: SOE Training Camp, England — 71

Chapter Eight: Posey, France 1943 — 76

Chapter Nine: Mary's Arrival in Posey Mid-1943 — 91

Chapter Ten: SOE Training Camp, England 1943 — 94

Chapter Eleven: Posey, France 1943 — 100

Chapter Twelve: Danny's Pig Farm, Posey 1943 — 107

Chapter Thirteen: Police Station, Posey 1943 — 113

Chapter Fourteen: First Mission France 1943 — 219

Part One
Code Name 'LILLY'

Chapter One
France 1943

The small brightly lit room smelt of disinfectant, urine, sweat and cigar smoke; it was a windowless room with bare furnishings consisting of two desks, one large and ornate with a green blotter board a desk lamp and a telephone, the second was a smaller desk more of a table really with a small straight-backed chair seated on which was a Luftwaffe secretary whose hair was done up in a tight bun, giving her a severe demeanour, but the thing that caught everyone's attention when they entered the room was a large heavyset square wooden chair that was bolted to the floor in the centre of the room.

It was a malevolent looking object fitted with restraints on the legs and flat arms, the restraints were thick leather straps with large metal buckles—severe-looking and effective. It was a frightening sight for Mary Trumont who now stood trembling next to the chair, she was trembling because the room was chillingly cold and because she was standing there dressed only in her underwear and full length petticoat, she had been made to remove her blouse skirt and shoes within an hour of being arrested then brought here to the small Police Headquarters in Posey, her hands manacled behind her back, she had been thrown into a small cell for the night and now she stood here, trembling with cold and fear, waiting.

The Secretary then stood up as the door opened and two men quickly entered the room, the first was a tall thin man in an immaculate uniform with the rank of a Major, he had a thin narrow face and cold piercing blue eyes, he crossed to the desk, sat on one edge of it as he looked Mary over.

The other man she did not get to look at as he went straight behind her and her arms were quickly pulled up as he unfastened the manacles from her wrists, she moved her arms to restore some circulation.

"I am Major Eric Schrandt of the SS," the Major had paused slightly before he said SS, he smiled slightly but there was no warmth in it as he looked her up and down.

"You have exactly five minutes to tell me what your mission was, who has been helping you and what codes you are using."

"But—but there must be some mistake, Major, my name is Mary Trumont and I am a schoolteacher here in Posey. I—I have no idea why I have been arrested…" She stopped talking as the Major gave a short barking laugh.

"My dear Mary, I know you are a British agent. You were captured last night in a field ten miles East of Posey where a Lysander aircraft of the RAF had landed. Now, you will tell me who the aircraft had brought in, who you are working with and what your codes are, or I am afraid that my friend Kurt there will start hurting you in, let me see, hmmm, four minutes!" the Major consulted his watch as he said this.

"But—but Major you have it all wrong. I—I was returning home from Delmont, the chain on my bicycle broke and I had to push it home that's why I was out after the curfew and—"

"Three minutes!" snapped the Major and Mary swallowed hard.

"I…I was hurrying home when I went past this field, the next thing I knew, there was a small aircraft roaring away over my head and then searchlights lit up the night…"

"One minute!" the Major gave the briefest of nods and the man Kurt moved into her view next to her, he was a short but heavily built solid looking man with square features and short cropped black hair, his presence off to her side was very menacing.

"Then—then there were Gendarmes pointing guns at me and I was thrown into a vehicle and brought here but I—I had nothing to do with whatever happened in that field!" As Mary finished speaking, the Major suddenly stood up.

"Time's up; Kurt!" the Major snapped this out, Kurt suddenly turned and punched Mary hard in the stomach, then as she doubled over gasping for breath, he grabbed her shoulders and seemed to just fling her into the chair, knocking what little air she had gasped out of her as her back jarred up hard against the chair back; while she still struggled for breath and with seemingly practiced ease, Kurt fastened the leather restraints around her ankles and fastened her left arm to the chair arm, which seemed to bring her back to her senses as she started to struggle. Kurt backhanded her across the face which sent her reeling again, by the time she recovered, her right arm was securely fastened to the chair's flat armrest and although she kicked and bucked for a couple of minutes, the restraints had her securely strapped to the chair. Still breathing hard, she stopped struggling and looked at Major Schrandt who was smiling at her.

"You—you have no right to treat me like this, Major, I haven't done anything!"

Major Schrandt looked at the young girl who was now securely restrained in his chair. She had a slim almost boyish figure with a small bust, a round face with bright green eyes, a small, upturned nose and short chestnut hair, he knew that she was twenty-two years old and although no beauty, she was attractive but right now, her green eyes were wide open in fear, but she had a stubborn look about her. He would normally love to take the time to break her but with this one, he didn't have a lot of time as the Paris office wanted information from her and were sending transport for her to be taken back to Paris.

He didn't want those arrogant fools to get all the kudos for breaking her, he was sick and tired of being in this backwater post while those idiots with less experience were getting all the recognition for capturing British SOE agents; no, HE should be at Avenue Foche, the Gestapo headquarters in Paris, where his talents could be of better use, and he was going to prove it with this one.

"I don't want to waste time on silly stories, Mary." The Major moved until he was standing in front of her, looking directly into her scared eyes.

"My friend Sergeant Kurt Tolbek here likes inflicting pain—especially on women."

Mary felt a cold shiver go up her spine as Kurt leered at her and flexed his large muscular shoulders.

"So, you will save me time and yourself a great deal of pain if you answer my questions—quickly!"

"But…but I don't know anything, I…I'm just a schoolteacher."

"Now, we both know that isn't true, Mary. Schoolteachers don't go around in the middle of the night meeting aeroplanes and shooting soldiers, hmmm?"

Marry tried to hide her surprise from the Major, it seemed that he knew exactly what she had been doing the previous night, but how could he, unless he had captured one of the other members of the team, but surely it hadn't been long enough to get any information out of anyone even if he had.

"But…but I've never shot at anyone in my life!" The Major gave a heavy sigh and looked over at the Secretary who had been making notes of the interrogation on her pad.

"Frau Inge, the report if you please?" he said holding out his hand; the Secretary quickly stood up, picking up a manila-coloured file from her desk, she hurried over the couple of yards that separated them and handed the Major the file, then quickly returned to her desk as if she was afraid of being anywhere near the prisoner.

"Now let's see…" The Major opened the file and read the brief notes. "At 2300 hours last night, a Lysander aircraft of the RAF landed in a small field ten miles east of Posey. A woman matching your description met this aircraft, passengers were seen to have boarded the aircraft but unfortunately, an overzealous Corporal opened fire before the barriers were in place, so the Lysander was able to take off."

"We believe four suspects were in the field as well as yourself and they all scattered in different directions when the corporal opened fire, a short firefight ensued." The Major looked at her and Mary was trying to keep her face expressionless as she relived the events of the previous night.

There had indeed been four men from the local Resistance Cell, one of whom was the team leader in that field. The Lysander had landed, and a courier had jumped out and two escaped aircrew of the RAF had madly scrambled aboard before all hell had broken loose; the field had been flooded in light from a searchlight mounted on the back of a lorry and tracers from two machineguns crisscrossed the field; the Lysander pilot immediately opened his throttle and the aircraft roared away into the night with tracers following it.

The courier had been hit and had died in her arms but not before he had given her a small metal tin about the size of a cigarette lighter in which was the name and location of a scientist who was being smuggled out of Denmark with important information and blueprints that had to be taken to England; the man had desperately told her this as he died in her arms, she had to prise loose his dead fingers, which were gripping her blouse tightly, before she could move.

She had been terrified by the sudden turn of events, tracers roaring overhead and grenades going off seemingly all around and the man's death grip on her had scared her silly. Promising him that she would keep the tin safe, he had relaxed a little as he died, then she had fled for her life. The men with her had scattered in different directions, firing their automatic weapons, throwing hand grenades and smoke grenades as they went, in the confusion she had run towards the hedge near where she had left her bike, she had squeezed through the hedge but had to leap over a three-foot-wide drainage ditch filled with water and reeds which was by a narrow laneway. But she hadn't seen the soldier until it was too late. Luckily for her, he had been walking away from her when she landed on the road behind him; he had yelled "Halt" as he had spun around, raising his rifle, but she had fired her Sten Submachinegun and the short burst had riddled the soldier's chest and he had fallen back into the drainage ditch with a large splash.

She had turned and run for her life to her bicycle which was along the hedge and had been hurrying up the laneway as fast as she could pedal, she had made about a mile before she spotted a car come barrelling around a bend towards her, realising that she couldn't be caught with either the Sten or the small tin, she had thrown both into the drainage ditch, then had pulled the chain off the sprockets and kept pushing the bike. Unfortunately for her, the car had been from the local police and had come to a skidding halt alongside her; then, despite her protestations, she had been bundled into the backseat and had been brought here.

"I—I had nothing to do with any of that, Major, I…I'm just a schoolteacher."

"Now Mary, or should I call you 'LILLY'?" The Major smiled as he saw the flicker of surprise cross her face.

Mary was surprised by the Major calling her 'LILLY' for that was her code name which was only known to a few people, her handler at Special Operations Executive (which was more commonly called SOE) and the head of her Department so for the Major to know, someone must have talked but—WHO?

As far as she knew, she was the only one who had been caught in the field last night and even if someone else had been caught, it was too early for them to have talked even if they had been tortured, after all, she had been here all night and they hadn't done anything to her—yet!

"Well?" snapped the Major, bringing her out of her thoughts.

"I don't know what you mean, Major, I don't know any Lilly and I have told you my name, I can't do any more than that."

"Your name you say, well let's have a look, shall we?" The Major flicked open his file again and after briefly consulting his notes, he looked up at her; when he spoke again, it was in perfect English.

"Now let's see, your real name is Mary Alice Dupont, you are twenty-two years old and you hold the rank of a Third Officer in the Women's Royal Naval Service, you were recruited by the British Special Operations Executive where you were trained as an agent with the code name of 'LILLY' and you were captured in a field last night." He smiled at her as he closed the file.

Mary tried hard to keep her face expressionless, but it was hard work as he had completely stunned her, firstly by speaking in perfect English although she had been warned that this would happen as it was a favourite trick employed to entrap agents, but she had mainly been stunned by the accuracy of his information. How could he possibly know all that about her unless someone had either talked under duress or had deliberately betrayed them! She shook her head negatively and replied to him, still speaking in French.

"I'm sorry, Major, but you obviously have me confused with someone else."

"Ah but you DID understand my English, didn't you, so let's stop playing games, shall we?"

"Alright," Mary answered him in English this time. "Yes, Major, I speak English. I speak English because my father was English and he taught me the language, but the rest of your information is incorrect. As I said before, I do not know who this 'LILLY' is, my name is Mary Trumont and I am a schoolteacher here in Posey." Mary swallowed hard as she finished speaking, she knew that they would probably torture her, but she could not tell them anything, she had to resist for forty-eight hours, that would give the other members of her Resistance Cell time to escape.

They had scattered when the shooting had started in the field last night; they would know that they had to get out of the area fast, she had no way of knowing if they knew that she had been arrested, what she did know was that no one else knew about the mission to get the scientist out of France and to England for all the details of that were written in code and were in the small tin that the courier had given to her before he died.

She had been given sketchy details of the mission in a couple of radio transmissions a few days ago and hence why the landing had taken place and even her team leader didn't know the details of the mission, he was to have been told after she had decoded the information in the tin.

"So, who was the dead man in the field, 'LILLY'?" asked the Major.

"Man—what man?"

"We know you met the Lysander, one man got out and two men got in before the unfortunate gunfire started. I don't care about the two men who escaped; after all, I can't do anything about them, hmmm?" The Major smirked again as he said this and again Mary wondered where he had obtained his information, had he been able to observe the aircraft before the gunfire had started, but that wouldn't have given him the information that he had about her and again, she shook her head negatively.

"Who was the man from the Lysander and what codes are you using? These are my questions, Lilly, and as I said before, I don't have a great deal of time, so I suggest that you start answering me."

"I…I don't know what you are talking about, Major, as I said I am just a schoolteacher."

"Very well—Kurt, I think a little persuasion is needed, hmm?"

Mary swallowed hard as the Major went and sat behind his desk and the man Kurt took a small wooden box out of his pocket and opened the lid, taking out three gleaming metal pins, each a couple of inches long and very thin.

"What…what is he doing?" she asked nervously as Kurt took a step towards her.

"As I told you Kurt enjoys inflicting pain, he has done quite a bit of research on the subject. Take those pins, for example; they are a variation of an ancient Chinese torture method, only the Chinese use bamboo. Kurt will hammer those pins under your fingernails one at a time. It is effective and quite painful so unless you want to experience that pain, I suggest that you start answering my questions, hmm?"

The Major had spoken to her calmly as if sticking pins under people's fingernails was quite a normal daily occurrence, but she just shook her head as Kurt approached her. She was terrified at the thought of what was about to happen and found she was bracing herself, pushing back against the chair back thinking that this wasn't supposed to be happening like this as she tried to curl up her fingers, pulling against the arm restraints as Kurt grabbed her hand.

This was not supposed to happen, it had all sounded so easy when she had agreed to join SOE and then, as Kurt forced the first pin under her fingernails, she started screaming against the searing pain!

****

It had all started in England in late 1942.

Mary Dupont worked in the underground Operations Room at the Admiralty in London; as a Third Officer in the WRNS, she oversaw a section of WRNS radio operators and had been sitting at her small desk going over a sheaf of radio messages when one of her operators had knocked on the door.

"Excuse me Ma'am but Commander Harris would like a word with you if you are free?"

"Commander Harris?" she asked as he was the Operations Intelligence Officer, someone that she rarely had contact with unless there was some sort of flap on, and that had not happened for a while now.

"Yes Ma'am."

"Alright, thank you."

"Ma'am." The WRN went back to her duties, Mary put the signals into a file and then left her office, wondering what the Operations Intelligence Officer might possibly want with her as she hurried down a couple of corridors until she came to an office with a glass-fronted door that was marked simply OIO. She straightened her jacket before knocking on the door.

"Come in."

Mary opened the door and entered the small office. Commander Harris, a slight figured man in his early sixties, looked up at her and then smiled.

"Third Officer Dupont; I believe you wanted to see me, sir?" she asked.

"Yes, take a seat would you, Mary, oh you don't mind my calling you Mary?"

"Of course, not sir." Mary sat down in a chair near the desk and was a little surprised that the Commander even knew her name, she had of course seen him about the Operations room but could not remember having spoken to him before.

"Good, that's good." Commander Harris looked at her for a moment as if deciding whether to proceed and then he took a letter from his desk drawer and handed it to her. It was a neatly hand-written letter and it was in French and Mary frowned as she quickly read it.

"Are you able to understand that Mary?" he asked.

"I can sir."

"Would you mind reading it out loud for me?"

"Oh—well, it's a letter from a—" she stopped as the Commander raised his hand.

"Could you read it in French for me please, Mary?" he asked, and she frowned again and then read the letter out loud in French. It was a letter from a lawyer asking a Mr Pierre Motrin if he would be good enough to make an appointment at his earliest convenience.

"Thank you, Mary, that was very good," said the Commander as he took the letter back.

"Is there anything else sir?" she asked wondering what on earth this was about.

"Yes, can I ask where you learnt your French, Mary, was it at school?"

"Well, partly sir; you see, my mother was French and my father English. My father was a doctor, and we went to live in France just after I was born and then after my mother died, Papa brought me back to England."

"Oh, I'm so sorry, Mary, I didn't mean to bring up painful memories."

"That's alright sir. I was ten when Mama passed away, so it was quite some time ago." It still did hurt whenever she thought about her mama but there was no reason for him to know that.

"And is your father still alive, Mary?"

"No sir, Papa was killed at Dunkirk. Look sir, do you mind if I ask why, you are asking me these questions?" Thinking about her Papa was still painful, and she wondered why he was asking these things.

"A man I know needs people who can speak fluent French, now I can't tell you much about it myself as it's all rather hush hush as it were, but I've had my eye on you for some time and I think you're just the sort of person that he would be interested in."

"I'm not a translator if that is what your friend needs, sir." She wondered how the Commander had been keeping an eye on her as he had hardly ever seen him at the Admiralty.

"No, it's nothing like that but I know that he would be interested in talking to you. Now, his name is Major Alexander Scott, and this is his address, it's only a short walk from here." Commander Harris handed her a small card with a name, address and telephone number on it.

"But what is this about sir?" she asked as she took the card.

"Well, as I said I can't tell you much as it's all rather hush hush, but the Major is keen on talking to you and if you don't like what he has to say…well then, you return to us here and we forget all about it, would that be alright?"

"But what could Major Scott want to discuss with me, sir; is it anything to do with signals?"

"I think it best if the Major explains what he needs, alright Mary?"

"I suppose so, when do I meet this Major, sir?"

"Now, if you don't mind. I've squared it with your Section Department Head so collect your things and go along to that address and if you don't like what the Major has to say, well then, you can return to your normal watch duties here and no harm done, alright?"

"Well, I suppose so sir." Mary thought it was all rather strange, but she was curious to know what it was all about.

"This is a real chance to help the war effort, Mary, so off you go, the Major is expecting you," said the Commander effectively ending their interview.

"Sir." Mary put the card into her pocket then stood to attention and left the office, returning to her own office to collect her cap and gasmask, then she made her way out of the bunker to the street and ten minutes later, she was standing outside a two-storey building with a sign that simply stated "Ministry of Information".

Feeling a little apprehensive and unsure of what was about to happen, she entered the building and was confronted by a young secretary at a desk inside a small foyer. There were a few civilians coming and going but she seemed to be the only one in uniform.

"I'm looking for a Major Alexander Scott, I believe he is expecting me," she said, showing the card that Commander Harris had given her.

"Can I see your identity card please?"

"Oh yes, of course." Mary handed over her ID card and the secretary quickly read it and made a note on a list on her desk as she handed the card back.

"Major Scott is up the stairs to the first floor and room fifteen."

"Thank you." Mary moved to the stairs and made her way up to the next floor and along to room fifteen, there was no sign on the door, so she knocked tentatively.

"Come in."

Mary opened the door and entered a small office, there were a couple of filing cabinets and a large desk near a full height window at one end and there was a small table with a couple of chairs just off to one side of the main desk. A civilian in a dark suit was sitting at this table and he stood up as she entered the room.

"Uhm, I'm looking for a Major Scott, do I have the right place?" she asked.

"That's right, I'm Scott, you must be Mary, pleased to meet you," he smiled warmly as he extended his hand.

"Oh, uhm, Third Officer Mary Dupont; pleased to meet you sir," she said as she shook his hand.

"Well take a seat Mary, would you like some tea, I've just made some?"

"Uhm yes. Thank you, sir," she said as she sat down in the indicated chair at the table.

"We are quite informal here so please call me Sandy." The Major sat down opposite her and started pouring tea into a cup from a large pot that was on a tray on the table and as he did, Mary quickly looked him over. She guessed he was about forty years old with an athletic build and short black but rapidly greying hair, he had slightly chiselled features with a short moustache under a nose that had obviously been broken a couple of times and bright eyes that seemed to dance over her a couple of times as he poured the tea.

"Sugar?"

"Please." He spooned sugar into the cup and passed it across.

"Thank you and uhm, I don't want to appear rude, Major, but could I see some identification please?" she asked taking the cup.

"Can't be too careful eh, good for you." The Major took his identity book from his jacket pocket and passed it over.

Mary quickly scanned it, the ID photo was a good likeness and proclaimed him to be Major Alexander Scott, Military Intelligence SOE.

"Thank you, sir," and she handed the ID back.

"Sandy, please?"

"Alright, Sandy then, would you mind telling me who you are and why I have been asked to come and see you?"

"Of course, but before I do, would you mind reading and signing this please?" The Major pulled a file out from under the tea tray and passed it to her, it was a copy of the Official Secrets Act and she looked up as he held a pen out to her.

"I've already signed one of these when I received my Commission sir."

"Yes, I know that but unfortunately, I can't tell you anything that I need to tell you until you've signed that again, I'm afraid."

Mary hesitated for a moment and then thought that as she had already signed this once, it could not do any harm doing so again, and she was curious to see what this was all about, she quickly signed it and handed it back.

"Thank you." The Major put the file onto the floor under his seat and then pulled out another file and took a sip of his tea before he opened it.

"Your full name is Marion Alice Dupont twenty-two years of age and you are the daughter of Doctor David Dupont and Lillian Parkes. Your father was a paediatrician and he met and married your mother in London. Then shortly after you were born, your father took a post in France and then when you were ten your mother passed away from an influenza epidemic, so your father decided to return to England where you completed your education and hence is the reason why you speak fluent French as well as English; am I right so far?" asked the Major as he closed the file and looked up at her.

"Yes, but I don't understand why you have that file on me or my family. My father was a good man and a good doctor, he took the post in France because there was a severe shortage of paediatricians and he wanted to help!"

Mary felt herself getting defensive about her family as she couldn't understand why this man had that file on her; she was a little surprised as the Major held his hands up in a sign of surrender.

"Please Mary, I meant no disrespect to either you or your family, but in my line of work, you have to be thorough." And again, he smiled warmly at her.

"And just what IS your line of work, Major?" she asked as even though she had become a little defensive, she was still intrigued about this meeting and wanted to find out why she had been asked to come here.

"Before I tell you anything, Mary, I must inform you that anything I say from this point onwards is Strictly Top Secret, if you reveal anything about our conversation to anyone then you could spend the rest of your life in prison as per the Official Secrets Act that you have just signed."

"Major, I am a Third Officer in the WRNS, and I am not in the habit of discussing my work with anyone outside the service who isn't entitled to know about it and before you ask that also included my father before he was killed."

"Good, that was well said, now would you like some more tea?"

Mary did not realise that she had finished her tea, so she nodded.

"Please."

"What do you know about the Ministry of Information?" he asked as he poured them both another cup of tea.

"Until I saw the sign outside today, I'd never heard of it, Major."

"Sandy, please," he said as he stirred his tea.

"Alright, Sandy then and your ID said Military Intelligence, so I assume it has something to do with that?"

"It is but first let me ask if you have thought about how, you could do something that would make a real difference in this war, shall we say by taking a more active role than what you are doing now?"

"More active, in what way, Sandy?" she asked with her curiosity aroused as she had become a little bored with the mundane job that she did at the Admiralty, she knew that the signals section was doing an excellent job but somehow it wasn't very fulfilling.

"The Ministry of Information is a cover name for Special Operations Executive, this Department was formed by the Prime Minister at the beginning of the War; our job at SOE is to help our friends across the pond to take the war to the enemy by providing them with the equipment, training and on the ground assistance to do acts of sabotage and other things that interrupts enemy movements and their ability to fight this war." And he watched her intently as he said this to gauge her reaction.

"When you say over the pond, Sandy, do you mean France?" she asked, feeling her pulse quicken at the prospect of possibly being able to do something to the Germans who had taken her father from her.

He had been serving as a doctor in the British Expeditionary Force that had gone to Belgium in the opening stages of the war and then when the Blitzkrieg had started and the BEF had been forced back to the beaches at Dunkirk, her father had been killed by a Stuka bombing attack that had hit his Regimental Aid post. She had held a bitter hatred of the Germans ever since her father had been killed and if she had the chance to do anything to even the score, as it were, then she was interested in listening.

"That's right Mary, I'm offering you the chance to become an agent with SOE, now I can't give you all the details because of security but you would undergo a period of training and if found suitable, you may be asked to go to France to join the Resistance, it would be exciting and challenging work, but it would also be very dangerous."

"Why me, Major?"

"Commander Harris has worked for Military Intelligence for a long time, he is an old friend, and he knows the type of people that I need for this work, people who speak flawless French and he feels that your background gave you an edge."

"Because I lived in France with my family, is that it?"

"Partly and because now that your father is gone, and I am truly sorry for your loss, Mary, now that he is gone, well to put it bluntly you have no family that could cause you to be compromised if things went wrong." And the major looked at her intently here to see how she would react; he had deliberately brought up the subject of her father, this would be a sensitive subject and emotionally still raw for her and he needed to know how she was going to react to this.

"I still don't see why Commander Harris thought of me, Sandy, after all I barely knew the man."

"He thought of you because you are the sort of operative that we can use. You speak fluent French you were a qualified Radio Operator Leading WRN before you gained your commission and you are intelligent and are familiar with cyphers and codes. In short, Mary, you are the sort of person that we need. So, do you think that you would be interested in undergoing the training to become an Agent with SOE and please keep in mind that if you fail the training—and not everyone does pass it—then you would be returned to your present post but of course, you wouldn't be able to talk to anyone about what you had been doing under the terms of the Official Secrets Act."

"I understand that Sandy, and can I ask, well do I get a say in this or has Commander Harris already volunteered me?"

"Commander Harris saw your potential and recommended you to me, but this is strictly on a volunteer basis only, no one can be forced to do this, Mary."

"And do I have to decide right now, Sandy?" she asked as although it sounded interesting and it offered her a good chance to be able to do something positive to help the war effort, she thought that she really needed to be able to think it over properly and not be rushed.

"No. I've spoken to your CO, so the rest of today is yours. Go home and think this over and if you decide you'd like to give it a go then report back here at eight tomorrow morning with your suitcase packed, but if you decide that this isn't your cup of tea shall we say, then go back your duties at the Admiralty, but of course, you can't talk to anyone about today's meeting, alright?"

"And you can't give me any more information, Major?" she asked, she had about a hundred questions running through her head but did not want to sound like an idiot.

"No. Other than tell you that the training will be hard challenging work and that you will be doing things that you have never done before, and you would be making a real difference. You also must know that it is dangerous work and that you would be up against a determined and ruthless enemy, it isn't easy, and people do get killed, so please think hard and carefully, Mary, alright?"

"Alright Major, I'll give it careful thought," she smiled, and he returned her smile with genuine warmth as he stood up and extended his hand to her and Mary stood up and shook his hand.

"That's all I can ask of anyone and thank you for coming to see me."

"Thank you, sir." Turning, she left the office and made her way downstairs before leaving the building.

For the rest of the day, Mary's mind was in turmoil as she tried to think on what she should do. On the one hand, she could go back to her mundane job at the Admiralty where the only risk was from an air raid but on the other hand, she had a chance to really do something that might actually make a difference in this war even if it was dangerous, but then she thought that everything in wartime could be dangerous in one way or another. She knew that she needed to give this some serious thought, then she had to run to catch her bus as it came around the corner.

Chapter Two
Posey, France 1943

There was enough moonlight to see the full length of the small field that was ten miles to the east of the small town of Posey, and they had a few more minutes before the aircraft was due to land.

Behind her, Mary could hear the ragged breathing of the two escaped British air crew, they were breathing hard for they had to run up to this location and after weeks of being on the run and hiding in small, cramped cellars or haybarns meant they were out of condition and the sudden need to be running in the middle of the night had been taxing on them. They now lay on the ground excitedly waiting for the aircraft that would take them back to England and freedom.

Mary was also waiting anxiously for the aircraft for it was bringing in a courier who not only had some spare batteries for her wireless transmitter, but he was also bringing in some detailed instructions for her Resistance team. The last coded message that she had received from London had informed her that the courier would give her group the location and identity of a Dutch scientist who had been smuggled out of a research centre in Denmark; apparently, he had some blueprints and other information that was vital to the war effort, and he was to be gotten out of France and taken to England as soon as possible.

The location of the scientist and also details of how he was to be moved were being brought in by courier as the wireless transmissions could be intercepted by the Germans and this man was too important for that to be risked, hence why this was a very important landing and why they had gone the ten miles out of the town to minimise the risk of them being overheard or being stumbled upon by any patrols that may be out.

She turned her head as Pierre the team leader crawled over to her.

"All clear Mary, give the signal."

Mary had been laying on the ground for the last half hour with her hand poised over a Morse key fastened to a small square of wood which she now used to tap out the letters *AR Dit Dah Dit Dah Dit*, a short length of wire led from the key to a lamp attached to a post that had been shoved a couple of inches into the ground. The lamp was shielded so that it could only be seen by an aircraft flying overhead at a specific altitude, or at least that was the theory, but she had only ever used it once and that had been during training with SOE in England and that seemed like a lifetime away now.

"Do you think he will see it, Mary?" asked Pierre in a harsh whisper.

"Be a wasted trip if he doesn't."

Dit Dah Dit Dah Dit Dit Dah Dit Dah Dit slowly and rhythmically for five minutes. Mary carefully sent the Morse letters AR and then she stiffened slightly as she faintly heard the drone of an approaching aircraft flying low, now all they had to hope was that it was the RAF Lysander that they were expecting and not a Luftwaffe night fighter. Then a feeling of sheer relief swept over her as the Lysander gunned its engine twice in the prearranged signal before turning abruptly AND starting its landing run.

"Get ready, boys, you jump in as soon as he lands as he will only be on the ground for a couple of minutes," she whispered to the airmen, then as the Lysander touched down, she pulled the lamp out of the ground and quickly coiled the line around it, by the time she had done that, the Lysander had pulled to a noisy stop besides them and then, everything seemed to happen very quickly.

As the Lysander pulled to a stop, a dark figure jumped down from the rear cockpit and the two escaped airmen scrambled madly onboard.

"Mary! Where are you?" The dark figure that had just jumped from the aircraft was looking for her in the gloom.'

"Here! I'm here." The man came out of the darkness and grabbing her hand he shook it warmly.

"I'm Jones and I've a package for you, Mary, I—" Then all hell seemed to break loose as the field was suddenly flooded in harsh light from a searchlight that was mounted on the back of a lorry that came bursting onto the end of the field and two machineguns started hammering harshly with their red tracers criss-crossing the field before settling towards the Lysander.

As the men of her group started returning fire with their automatic weapons, the Lysander pilot opened his throttle and the plane roared away into the night with the tracers following closely.

"Scatter—Scatter—GO—GO—GO!" yelled Pierre and Mary grabbed the arm of the Courier and spun him around.

"This way! Run! Quickly!" she called, firing a short burst from her Sten Submachinegun as she went, her group had rehearsed for just such an eventuality, the men scattered firing their weapons and throwing smoke and hand grenades as they went in an effort to cause as much confusion as they could so as to cover Mary as she escaped from the field with the Courier in tow.

Mary threw herself to the ground as Machinegun tracers whipped just inches above her head, but she heard the Courier cry out as bullets thudded into him and he crumpled to the ground. Breathing hard and scared to death, she crawled over to him and turned him onto his back, which made him cry out in agony. she jumped, badly frightened as he grabbed her arm fiercely.

"Sorry…I…Oh God…instructions…inside…take it!" he was gasping for each breath and was getting the words out through clenched teeth as he thrust a small tin the size of a cigarette lighter into her hand, Mary grabbed the tin and was about to reply when the man groaned loudly and blood shot from his mouth as he spasmed then was still as he died. Mary stared at him wide-eyed for he was the first person that she had ever seen die right in front of her. She stared in bewilderment not knowing what to do, then the explosion of a hand grenade seemed to bring her back to her senses and scrabbling to her feet, she started running for her life.

She was heading for a row of hedges on the left-hand side of the field; she knew there was a three-foot wide water-filled drainage ditch on the other side of the hedge, indeed this was partly why she had chosen this route to arrive and leave by as this ditch would slow down anyone who may pursue her and hopefully, they wouldn't know about the ditch and this would slow them down even more, giving her more time to flee.

The gunfire and grenade explosions were still going on behind her as she burst through the hedge and jumped over the, ditch landing heavily on a pathway the other side, but unfortunately, she didn't see the soldier until it was too late, he was about twenty feet away and luckily for her, had been walking away from her when she landed on the pathway.

"Halt!" the soldier shouted as he spun around, raising his rifle; instinctively, Mary dropped to her knee as her training kicked in and raising her Sten she fired a short burst, the soldier yelled out as the burst took him across the chest, the impact threw him backwards into the ditch where he landed with a large splash but not waiting to see whether or not she had killed him, Mary turned and ran down the pathway to a style where she had left her bicycle. She pulled this out onto the pathway, mounting it, she started to pedal as fast as she could, trying to put as much distance between herself and the field.

She wondered what on earth had gone wrong! Was it just a chance encounter with a patrol that had stumbled onto them in the field, but then how many patrols were equipped with lorry-mounted searchlights?

Had someone talked? No, they could not have as they had all been in the field together, surely if someone had betrayed them then they wouldn't want to take the risk of being hit by machinegun fire when the Lysander had landed.

No! It had to have been a chance encounter.

She skidded to a halt as she suddenly realised that if she was caught now, the Germans would get the information—whatever it was—that was in the tin that the Courier had given her before he had been killed; she couldn't let that happen for the whole Operation would be a failure if she did.

Cursing herself for being a fool, she pulled up alongside the ditch and hoping that she would be able to find the spot sometime later, she threw the tin and the Sten gun into the water, making sure that they landed in the water and not amongst the tall reeds by the path edge.

"No…No…Oh no!" she cursed as she spotted a vehicle come skidding around a bend ahead, she kicked the bike chain off its sprocket as she had rehearsed many times to give herself an alibi then started pushing the bicycle again as the vehicle skidded to a halt alongside her.

"Halt…Hande…Hoch!" Mary swore to herself as she raised her hands as two Gendarmes and a Wehrmacht Corporal were now pointing weapons at her; breathing hard and feeling terrified, she knew it was now over—she had been caught!

The images of that night now came flooding back crystal clear to her as she struggled against the hand clamped to the back of her neck holding her head under the cold water, her hands were manacled behind her back and she was kneeling on the floor next to a large metal bath that was filled with water a couple of feet away from that horrid chair that was bolted to the floor in the centre of the room.

Kurt was standing behind her with one arm over her shoulder and one hand on her neck with which he was pushing her head and shoulders into the cold water, her lungs were burning with a searing pain from the need for oxygen and she struggled with the fear of drowning as bubbles poured from her mouth as she involuntarily screamed out to ease the burning pressure in her bursting lungs. She fought hard, trying to beat down the panic that threatened to overcome her rational thinking; she knew they would not let her drown, they wouldn't let her drown because they needed information from her.

She tried to tell herself this each time the panic overwhelmed her for this was the tenth time that her head had been shoved under the water and each time she had been given shorter and shorter amounts of time to gasp for air when Kurt wrenched her head up out of the water, where she would gasp and gag and cough on the water that she had inevitably gasped into her protesting bursting lungs.

Kurt had timed each dunking to perfection, holding her down against her struggling until she was on the verge of blacking out, whereupon he would yank her backwards to land painfully on the floor where she would lay coughing and gagging, getting rid of the water in her throat, laying there with her knees drawn up as she gasped for air like a landed fish. But this time was longer as she breathed out the bubbles, trying to ease the pressure and pain in her bursting lungs, this time her vision started greying out and the ringing in her ears became louder, this time he had left it too late and this time she was going to drown!

"Kurt! Kurt, get her out!" She dimly heard the Major shouting as her vision went totally black. Kurt yanked her back and she landed on the floor with a dull thud.

"You bloody fool! She's no good to me dead!" Major Schrandt rolled Mary onto her side and thumped her back then rolled her onto her back, which was a little difficult with her hands being manacled behind her, then he started pushing on her stomach.

"Ggaarwraack!" Mary vomited up what seemed like a gallon of water before taking a deep ragged gasp of air.

Slap! Slap! Slap! "Come on Mary…wake up!" The Major slapped her face from side to side until with a gasping groan, her eyes opened and she vomited up water again.

The major rolled her onto her side and then looked up at Kurt who was watching him anxiously; he knew that he had gone too far this time and had almost drowned the girl. He hadn't meant to but had just lost all control and sense of reason, he had enjoyed drowning the girl, the sense of power over the helpless victim had almost been sexual and he had only just gained control over himself when her struggles had stopped, and the Major had shouted at him.

"Take a break, Kurt," said the Major quietly.

"I…I'm sorry Major, I—"

"Get out, Kurt—NOW!"

"Sir." Kurt hurried out of the room, knowing how close he had come to disaster.

Major Schrandt knelt next to Mary and took her head in his hands; she blinked a couple of times as still struggling for breath, she tried to focus on him as the ringing in her ears faded.

"Mary—can you hear me?"

Not trusting herself to speak, Mary nodded slowly as her vision cleared and her hearing returned to normal; she felt awful, her lungs and throat were burning, and she felt close to hysterics as she thought of how close she had just come to being drowned by that lunatic!

"As I told you before, Kurt enjoys hurting people, especially women, but he went too far that time, I don't want to drown you—yet!"

The veiled threat was all too real as she knew that the only reason, they were keeping her alive was because they wanted information from her, which she mustn't give for there were too many lives at stake if she did; for the first time in her life, Mary felt incredibly scared and very alone.

"All this pain can stop, Mary; all you have to do is tell me what I want to know?"

Mary gagged a little and then shook her head as she looked him in the eye.

"I…I have nothing to tell you, Major, I am Mary Trumont, I am a schoolteacher here in Posey, you…you have me mixed up with someone else."

The Major sighed heavily as he stood up; she was being stubborn. Kurt had already pushed needles under her fingernails and had then used a pair of pliers to pull out all the nails on the fingers on her left hand—to no avail; then they had dunked her in the tub—again to no avail—but he was running out of time for he knew that those idiots in the Gestapo would be arriving from Paris and once that happened, she would be out of his hands.

He rubbed his chin in reflection, maybe he should try something new before he ran out of time? Reaching down, he hauled her to her feet and frogmarched her out of the room and down a short corridor to a row of six cells, a soldier opened one of the doors, the small cell in front of her was eight feet long and six feet wide, a bleak looking room with no windows, drab brick walls and a concrete floor.

A wooden bench was the room's only furnishing with a bucket in the corner for the prisoner to relieve themselves. The door was of heavy wood with a square barred aperture in the centre, this was the sight that greeted her as she was shoved unceremoniously into the cell with such force that she hit the far wall and fell back onto the concrete floor but before she could recover herself, Major Schrandt marched into the room,

"Get up, Bitch!" he yelled at her as he grabbed her by the hair and hauled her to her feet and tossed her onto the wooden bench; she cried out as she drew up her legs waiting for him to strike her but instead, he grabbed her by the hair again and pulled her into a sitting position.

"This is your new home, Mary, and you'd better get used to it because if you don't start talking to me, you will be here for a long time and it won't be pleasant. Now I will leave you alone to gather yourself," he pushed her away then moved over to the door where he turned and looked at her.

"I will give you one hour, Mary, and after that, if you don't tell me what I want to know, I'll have Kurt get his 'little pins' ready for your feet," and with that the Major left and the guard slammed and bolted the door.

Mary curled herself up into a ball on the bench and began sobbing; her left hand was bloody and throbbed painfully from where Kurt had forced the pins under each nail repeatedly before finally pulling all the nails off with a pair of pliers, her petticoat and underwear were saturated and her hair was plastered to her face from the repeated dunking under the cold water in the bath tub, her lungs and throat felt raw from the lack of oxygen and the screaming that she had done while struggling against being forced underwater.

The humiliation of being tortured and having involuntarily pissed herself a couple of times out of sheer terror as she was being forced under water was the worst part, now she had been told there was worse to come for Kurt would soon be forcing his 'little pins' under her toenails; she knew the agony that was awaiting her and she didn't know if she had the strength to endure it; feeling utterly alone, she drew her knees up tighter and continued sobbing.

Back in the interrogation room, Major Schrandt sat at his desk and accepted a cup of coffee from Kurt.

"She has a strong will, this one, Major," said Kurt quietly as he was still aware that the Major was angry with him for almost drowning the British agent.

"Yes, but I don't have the luxury of time to enjoy breaking her slowly, those idiots from Avenue Foche will be here tomorrow afternoon and that will be that."

"What makes them so interested in this girl sir, we've caught Agents before and they have always let us deal with it, what makes this one so different?"

Schrandt looked at Kurt for a moment deciding whether to confide in the man or not but he needed his help if he was going to break this girl quickly and if he knew what was at stake then maybe he would keep better control over himself as he interrogated her.

"A couple of months ago, one of our scientists decided that he had had enough of Hitler and his ideals and has decided to change sides, somehow, he managed to contact the Resistance and they helped him escape from wherever the hell he was working, and he has gone into hiding. I have no idea what this scientist does but it's important as the Gestapo has had a fit."

"Apparently, our little English agent was to receive vital information on his location and intended movements to a submarine that will meet him on the coast somewhere to get him to England, that was why she met the aircraft in that field, and I want US to be the ones to get the information from her. This is our chance to get out of this flaming backwater dump, Kurt, and I want to do it before those idiots from the Gestapo get here."

"So, what do you suggest we do, Major, she seems to be pretty stubborn?"

"I've told her that you will use your pins on her toes shortly, but I think we need something else to help us with this one as we don't have much time."

"Excuse me, Major, but I may be able to help there?"

Major Schrandt looked around as his Secretary Frau Inge spoke, he usually did not even notice the woman as she sat there taking her notes during the interrogations and this was the first time that he could remember her having spoken, let alone offer information.

"Oh, and how is that Frau Inge?" he asked, and he was glad to see that she swallowed hard before speaking.

"I…I think that Doctor Neuman may be able to help, sir."

"Doctor Neuman?" Schrandt frowned, they had used Doctor Otto Neuman a couple of times over the previous few months but only when one of their prisoners became sick or died during interrogation and he did not see how he could help with this English Agent.

"Yes sir, he was here helping with that French boy last week, you may recall?"

"Yes, I remember." The Doctor had looked over the boy after Kurt had beat him with an iron bar.

"Well sir, in the mess he had been saying how he thought our methods were so crude when there were drugs that could do the job so much better and I…I thought that he might know how to help, sir."

"Alright, ask the good Doctor if he would come and see me, would you, Frau Inge?"

"Yes sir." Smiling at being able to help a little, Frau Inge hurried out of the room.

"Alright Kurt, while I have a word with the good doctor, we need to keep the pressure on Mary, have Conrad use the cane on her in her cell but tell him not to break any bones and don't mark her face, alright?"

"Yes sir, and can I help with that, sir?" asked Kurt with a gleam in his eyes as he would love nothing better than to beat the girl, all to get some information, of course.

"No, I want you to get your pins ready in case the good Doctor can't help us."

"Right sir." Disappointed, Kurt made a call to Conrad.

Half an hour later, Doctor Otto Neuman knocked timidly on the door.

"Enter!" Major Schrandt looked up as a thin faced rather scrawny looking man in his late fifties entered the room in a rather crumpled uniform entered the room.

"Ah Doctor Neuman, thank you for coming so promptly," said the Major as he indicated the Doctor should take a seat in the plain wooden chair in front of the desk.

"It sounded urgent when I was called for, Major?" The Doctor sat on the indicated chair and felt very uneasy under the Major's steady gaze; he had hurried over when Frau Inge had called him because he knew that the Major wasn't a man to be kept waiting and you would need a very good excuse not to have come.

"I believe you may be able to help me, Doctor?"

"Of course, sir, is there a medical problem with one of your prisoners?" the Doctor felt uncomfortable as he said that as he knew the Major and his henchmen mistreated their prisoners as he had treated several of them. He didn't agree with the methods that they used, he thought they were crude and barbaric, but he didn't want to say to the Major as he was known to be a dangerous man and he wouldn't risk getting on his wrong side.

"Not exactly, Doctor. I have a problem with a British female agent, she has some information that I need but I don't have a great deal of time and Frau Inge tells me that you may be able to help, she tells me that you may have some drugs that could be of use?"

The Doctor looked up as the Major said this and he had a sort of gleam that came into his eye as he sat upright in the seat. It seemed that finally, someone was interested in the research that he had done in this field. For a couple of years now, he had been experimenting with the use of drugs, a so-called truth serum which he had been able to use mainly on criminal prisoners of the police and once by the Gestapo. Barbarians that still believed that they could torture the information out of their prisoners. What he really needed was someone to back his research and he suddenly felt a little excited as he thought that this moment may now have come for him.

"That's right, Major, you see for some years now I have been experimenting with certain drugs to produce a serum that has been…" The Doctor trailed off as Schrandt held up his hand.

"I don't have time to listen to your research history, Doctor, although I'm sure it would be fascinating, but I am short of time so, can you help me or not?"

"Perhaps we can help each other, Major."

"Doctor, I don't—"

"Please Major, let me explain." The Doctor had sat forward in his seat and had not seen the flicker of annoyance cross the Major's face as Schrandt wasn't used to being interrupted like this.

"I do indeed have some drugs that will probably get your Agent talking but I need help in being able to do some research so perhaps we can help each other, sir?" The Major was about to yell at the man for being a total idiot and interrupting him, but the Doctor had said that he DID have some drugs that could help get his agent talking and that changed everything.

"I warn you, Doctor, I am not a man to be trifled with!"

"I…I understand that Major, and I'm not trying to be obstructive." Doctor Neuman swallowed nervously under the Major's cold gaze.

"If your drugs can get me the information that I need, Doctor, then I expect to be transferred to Paris and if that happens then I am sure that we could work together in the future on your serum but at the moment, that is all that I can offer you."

"If you could arrange a transfer to Paris so that I can continue my research, that would be very good, Major," said Neuman smiling broadly as he felt his excitement mounting with the prospect.

"And you have this serum available now, Doctor?"

"No but—" Neuman jumped, startled, as Schrandt banged his fist down on the desk as he jumped to his feet glaring at the man.

"How dare you waste my time—GET OUT!"

"Please…Major, I…I don't have any serum now b…but I can readily make some more!" Schrandt glared at the man as he got himself back under control and he sat down at his desk.

"How long would that take you? As I said, Doctor, I don't have a lot of time."

"If…if you can have me released from my present duties, I can work on a new batch of serum this evening and you would have it by tomorrow night sir."

"And how long does it take for this serum to take effect, doctor?" The Major felt his anger subsiding and his hope rising; if this idiot could make a new batch of serum then he may be able to get the information that he needed before the Gestapo snatched Mary away from him.

"That depends on the patient sir, but so far the longest it has taken to have effect is three hours."

"Hmm, and what about side effects, Doctor, I don't want to kill the girl, not yet anyway!"

"The subject is a woman! How old is she and is she fit and healthy, Major?"

"Fit, healthy and twenty-two."

"Good, very good."

"And side effects Doctor?"

"Oh well, so far with the subjects that I have been working with side effects haven't been of consequence as they were going to be executed anyway, Major."

"Doctor, I need to keep this girl alive and in a fit mental state for further interrogation if needed so can you guarantee that or not?" The Major felt his anger rising again.

"Yes, Major I can, there may be some physiological damage but so far all my subjects have survived long enough to be executed a week or so after treatment."

"Very well then; the quicker you get started on a new batch of the serum the better, I'll make some phone calls, and have you assigned to me from now on."

"Thank you, major, I'll get started straight away." As the Doctor stood up to leave, the major picked up his telephone handpiece.

"Doctor?"

"Sir?" the Doctor turned at the door to look at him.

"If your serum kills my agent before I get the information I need, I shall have Kurt skin you alive, do I make myself clear?"

Doctor Neuman paled visibly as he had no doubts that the Major would keep his word and he nodded nervously before he hurried out of the room.

"Stupid sod!" said Kurt as the door closed.

"Possibly, but if he can get us the information that we need then I'm willing to give him a try." The Major looked at his watch and then back to Kurt.

"Conrad should be with Mary now. I'll have some lunch and then we'll get her back in here as we need to keep the pressure on until the good Doctor is ready. Alright, I'll return shortly so don't so anything until I get back, is that clear?"

"Yes Major, of course." With a brief dismissive nod, the Major strode out of the room and Kurt looked over at the Secretary.

"Frau Inge, you may as well go for a break, an hour should do I think."

"If you're sure, Kurt?"

"I'm sure in fact, I will join you I think."

"Oh, uhm yes alright." Frau Inge put her notebook on the desk and tried to avoid looking at the man for she didn't like Kurt at all; in fact, the man disgusted her, but she dare not refuse him, so she hurried out of the room.

Chapter Three
SOE Training Camp, England 1942

Mary landed on the ground with a jar that almost knocked all the breath out of her, she had managed to break her fall so she ended up sitting on the ground breathing hard, she had just jumped off a six-foot high wooden wall that was a part of an obstacle course that she had just completed. This was situated on a grassed area near a rather quaint manor house in the hills of Northumbria or at least that's where she thought she was, as after a train and bus ride she had been bundled into the back of an army truck with the canvas flap pulled down which had driven for three hours to the SOE Training Camp two weeks ago and since then, she had been doing physical exercises of one sort or another.

She was billeted in a hut with two other females whom she only knew by their first names, they had been given a bed, bedding and army battledress without rank or insignia on arrival and a hot meal, she had gone to bed very tired after the journey only to be rudely awoken at 0500 in the morning by a burly Sergeant bursting into the room, pounding on a metal rubbish can and yelling for them to get dressed and fall in outside. That was how it had been every morning for two weeks, then they had passed onto the weapons training phase where she had learnt to use a rifle, a Sten Submachine gun, a Bren gun and two pistols.

She had been surprised to find that it had come naturally to her and she wasn't a bad shot, probably because the instructors were good and the one-on-one training was better than at the recruit school when she had enlisted and had first used a rifle; the next phase had been sabotage, learning to use explosives on various targets, map reading and survival techniques and of course, wireless telegraphy and coding, which was her forte as they say.

"What the hell are you sitting there for, admiring the scenery, get up, do it again! MOVE—MOVE—MOVE!" Sergeant Moss yelled at her as he came hurrying up from behind the wall; she scrambled madly to her feet and started running again.

An hour later she was sitting on the grass with a mug of hot tea and was talking to Alice, a tall rather thin blonde whom she thought was Danish but wasn't allowed to ask for security reasons, but the girl was friendly enough.

"I must say I'm glad the PT rubbish is over, my feet are killing me," said Joan as she sat down next to them, she was the third member of their party, she was a twenty-year-old brunette with a round jovial face and bright blue eyes.

"Look out, here comes the bullfrog." Mary could not help smiling as Alice said this as the Bullfrog was what they had nicknamed Sergeant Moss, who had a canny resemblance to a puffed-up bullfrog every time he started yelling at them, which seemed to be often.

"Alright ladies, on your feet, the truck will be here shortly to take you to the RAF, God help them."

"RAF?" asked Alice as she stood up.

"Yes, they will show you how to jump out of nice little aeroplanes and if you land with them the way you have been off my wall then God help you, ah here's the truck."

"Oh dear," said Joan as she stood up.

"What's wrong, you don't like trucks?" asked Alice frowning.

"I don't like aeroplanes, I'm not really very good with heights, you see."

"Well don't worry, when you jump it will be at night and you won't see anything really, I suppose." As the truck pulled up, the Sergeant helped them climb up into the back.

"That's right, ladies, when you jump out the hole, the chute opens, and you hit the ground; all over in a couple of minutes so don't sweat it. Alright George, off you go," and the Sergeant banged the side of the truck as he walked off.

"Oh God!" The truck started to move off and Mary tried to make herself comfortable as she thought about this part of her training, she knew that parachute training would be happening as it was the main way of inserting agents into enemy occupied territory but hadn't really given much thought to it, she didn't have a fear of heights so that shouldn't be a problem but the way she had been falling off that wall worried her; what if she had a rough landing in a strange country in the dead of night, possibly surrounded by the enemy? If she broke her leg or worse, what the hell would she do then, this occupied her thoughts until they arrived at the RAF training base.

Their training was to take place in a hangar at the far end of the airfield away from prying eyes. They were issued with coveralls and a round padded helmet and were given a briefing on how to land correctly and then, as their Sergeant said, 'the fun begins'. They started jumping off platforms at first six feet off the ground and then ten feet and were jumping down onto matting, learning how to land so that they did not do themselves any injuries although Mary felt badly bruised after having landed wrong a couple of times.

"Alright Ladies, back into the truck and we'll take you off for some grub," called the Sergeant and they removed their coveralls before getting into the truck, which drove them to one of the mess halls on the airfield. They collected a hot meal and sat at a table away from everyone by themselves and were seemingly being ignored by everyone.

"Well, at least the food is good," said Joan as she sat down at the table.

"Ever had the feeling that you're being watched?" asked Alice as she gestured to people who gave them a brief look before turning away.

"Like being a goldfish." Mary chuckled as she said this but had been feeling that way as well.

"Mind if I join you, Ladies?" asked a Flight Lieutenant as he sat down at the table with a plate of food, he was about thirty, sandy-haired with a rather large protruding handlebar moustache; the three women just nodded as they continued eating.

"Keeping you busy, are they?" he asked but they ignored him.

"You must be the Polish ladies that we have been hearing about?" he asked; Mary looked up.

"What makes you say that?" she asked.

"Well, you're in army battledress with no insignia or rank showing and I know that we are expecting some Polish ladies for training, you see, so I just thought—"

"Obviously, you didn't think, Flight lieutenant!" The man looked a little surprised as she interrupted him with a sharp tone in her voice.

"I beg your pardon?"

"Well obviously, we are not associated with whatever it is that you do here so for security reasons if we don't belong to your section or whatever then we have nothing to do with you, so I suggest that you either stop asking questions about something that doesn't concern you, or you go away!"

"Oh, I say—"

"No, we say, you should go away, I think!" said Alice and the man looked at them in turn before he smiled broadly and pulled an ID card from his pocket.

"Well done, Ladies, I'm Flight Lieutenant Dawson, Base Intelligence, and I was just testing you."

"Maybe you are but we don't know you and we are on a tight schedule and are trying to have our lunch so would you please go away, Flight Lieutenant Dawson?"

"Fair enough, good afternoon, ladies," and with that he stood up and walked away.

"I told you we were being watched."

"Just as well we didn't say anything then, pass the sugar, would you?" Mary was pleased that she had listened to her trainers back at the camp who had warned her that they would always be watching for signs of a security breach, it was also teaching them to be aware of their surroundings and to be wary of everyone, which was good training for when they would be dropped into enemy territory. The rest of the day was spent in the hangar learning how to land and by the time they returned to the camp, they were tired and very sore.

Their training continued for the next three days at the airfield, they progressed rapidly from jumping off wooden platforms to the FAN where their parachute harness was attached to a wire which was then attached to a spool on a large FAN which when they dropped through a hole in a mock-up of an aircraft fuselage. The blades of the FAN spinning slowed down their rate of descent simulating a real jump, but it was still a fairly hard and, for Mary, a bruising landing.

On the morning of the fourth day, they were issued with a parachute pack from WRAF packers and were driven over to one corner of the airfield where a large square basket was suspended beneath a huge barrage balloon which would be raised a couple of hundred feet into the air by cables attached to a large, motorised drum. They had to make this jump to qualify and if they didn't qualify in this parachute course, then they wouldn't be able to continue with their training to become SOE agents.

The van pulled up alongside the balloon and as they jumped down pulling their parachute harness with them, Mary swallowed nervously as she got her first good glimpse at the basket beneath the balloon and although she didn't really have any problems with heights, it was still a daunting prospect knowing that she would shortly be jumping out of this thing and would be entrusting her life to a few feet of parachute silk.

"Mon Dieu!" said Alice crossing herself as she looked at the balloon. "We have to jump from this thing?" she asked.

"Safer than a Kite, Miss, and doesn't use any fuel. Alright Ladies, get your harnesses on and we'll get started," said an RAF Corporal as he strode over and said something to the men manning the winch.

"We are flying kites too?" asked Alice and Mary couldn't help chuckling at her puzzled expression and it was at time like these that her Danish accent seemed to come out.

"No, a Kite is RAF slang for an aircraft, come on, I'll give you a hand."

As they had been shown, they helped each other struggle with the straps of the parachute harness until they had the heavy parachute on their backs with the reserve chute in the front and held the static line over their shoulder. (This first jump would be by static line which meant that a line leading from their parachute would be attached to a cable in the basket and when they jumped, this line would automatically deploy their parachute so they wouldn't have to worry about pulling the rip cord.) They stood in a group waiting nervously.

"Alright Ladies, all aboard for the skylark." The Corporal lifted a bar in the basket opening that acted like a doorway and he stepped up into the basket where he attached a wire that led from his harness to an overhead wire in the basket as he wouldn't be jumping but there was a spare parachute in a rack just in case anything went wrong. One by one the women walked forward and took the Corporal's offered hand to help them up the short ladder into the basket and then he lowered the bar, thus closing the door.

Mary grabbed a rail on the side of the basket and swallowed again for the basket was moving slightly from side to side and seemed to be creaking a lot; she could see that her companions were just as apprehensive as she felt.

"Ready for ascent!" Mary felt her stomach turn a little as the Corporal said this into a telephone handset and the balloon started to rise. Although she was a little nervous, she found it fascinating as the ground fell away as the balloon went higher and then suddenly stopped as they had reached their jump height.

"Number One—Standby!" Mary felt her heart start to race as she would be the first one to jump, she swallowed hard as she shuffled forward, receiving a brief reassuring smile from Joan who would be jumping second.

"Equipment check!" The Corporal tugged and pulled on her harness and checked her parachute before giving her the thumbs up.

"Number One—hook up!" Mary attached her static line to the overhead wire and the Corporal checked it.

"Stand in the door! Don't forget that you will be getting directions from the ground, count as you go and if your main hasn't deployed by the count of four thousand then deploy your reserve, understood?" called the Corporal in her ear as she shuffled forward to the bar at the doorway and she nodded her understanding.

"Mind the air rushing in as I open the door." She smiled at the man's little joke and then her heart started racing again as a little red light blinked on in a box alongside the doorway, then the light flashed a couple of times before turning green.

"GREEN ON—GO!" shouted the Corporal and Mary held her breath as she stepped out of the door and felt her stomach churn as she started to fall.

"One Thousand—Two Thousand—Thr—"

Craaack!

There came a rustling crack from over her head and a jarring jolt at her shoulders and groin as the parachute deployed.

"Thank Christ for that!" she said out loud as she started breathing again and was surprised to see that the ground seemed to be coming up fast as she raised her arms and took hold of the raisers.

"Looking good, Number One. Knees together, prepare for landing now!" She realised that someone had been talking to her through a loud hailer although she hadn't heard anything until now and too late, she closed her knees together as the ground came up and smacked her hard on the backside as she landed on her side and rolled.

Then, as she regained her breath, her training kicked in as the parachute started pulling her along the ground and although she knew that she would be badly bruised in the morning, she had a huge grin on her face with the exhilaration of having made her first parachute jump.

Chapter Four
Posey, France 1943

In her cell, Mary tried not to cry out from the agony that wracked her body every time she breathed in. Fifteen minutes ago, four soldiers had burst into the cell; they had forced her to her feet and had stripped her naked before tying her face-down onto the wooden bench that served as her bed, then Conrad—a tall, very thin, hawk-faced man—had entered the cell, carrying a three-foot long thin bamboo cane, with which he proceeded to slash her slowly and methodically, working from her shoulders down to her feet with slow and brutal blows that knocked the breath out of her each time they struck, making her cry out and thrash about although she was securely bound by ropes.

The worst part of the ordeal was that Conrad hadn't spoken a word to her, in fact none of the men spoke, they didn't ask her one question for the full fifteen humiliating minutes and the only sound for that entire time was the very slow and methodical swish crack of the cane and her yells echoing off the walls. Then at the end, the ropes were untied, and her clothes were thrown at her.

"Get dressed. The major will see you shortly!" Then the men left, the door slammed shut. Mary cried bitterly as she slowly sat up and with each move being extremely painful, she put her underwear back on to give her some modesty and warmth; she curled herself up onto the bench as she cried not knowing how much more she could endure.

Exactly one hour after he had left the interrogation room, Major Schrandt strode back in with Conrad behind him.

"Well Conrad?" asked the Major as he took a seat at the desk.

"We did as you instructed sir, she yelled out a few times but other than that, she said nothing."

"You did no permanent damage, I hope?"

"No sir, we tied her face down so we didn't risk marking her face as you ordered, sir."

"Good, alright take a break as I won't be needing you for a while."

"Sir." As the man left the room, the telephone started jangling and the Major snatched up the handpiece.

"Major Schrandt," he said.

"Major Schrandt, this is Doctor Neuman, I've just been informed that the prisoner has just been given a beating, is that true?"

"What? Who told you that and what the hell does it have to do with you, Doctor?" The Major stiffened up a little as he said this for, he didn't like the idea of people telling the Doctor anything and the impertinence of the man to question him was astonishing; of all the—

"I'm not trying to interfere, Major, but for my serum to be effective, the prisoner can't be put under undue stress; she—"

"So, you want me to stop interrogating an enemy agent, is that it, Doctor?"

"Well Major, you told me you had a time constraint; I'm only trying to—" The Doctor stopped speaking as the line went dead.

"Stupid bastard!" Major Schrandt swore as he slammed the receiver down, he was angry at the nerve of the man, how dare he tell him to stop interrogating an enemy agent!

While Schrandt was seething in anger in the interrogation room, two miles away in a small garage, Pierre Blaise—a round-faced man in his early fifties—opened his garage door then quickly shut it again as Mark Deneau hurried in, looking around furtively as he did so. Mark was the local dentist, a short fair-haired man of thirty with a round pockmarked face and round wire-rimmed spectacles.

"I wasn't sure whether I should come here or not, Pierre, but I had to find out if you were alright."

"Let's go into the office, we could be overheard here." Pierre led the way into his small office and after Mark entered, he closed the glass-fronted door, it was only a small office but with the door closed, no one passing by on the street would be able to hear them.

"What will we do, Pierre, she has definitely been taken," said Mark as he looked out of the window nervously, he knew he was taking a major risk by being here as Mary had definitely been caught by the Germans; she may have already given up the names of the members of her Resistance Cell, he didn't think she would but who knew what she would do if they started interrogating her.

"You're sure she's been arrested, Mark?"

"Yes Pierre, George came to see me first thing. He saw the Gendarmes nab her at the roadway alongside the airstrip, he was about to step out of the field himself when he saw the car pull up. He also told me Mary had shot a soldier as she left the field. God, what a mess!" Mark ran his hand through his hair as he said this, he felt a little sick and was sweating badly.

"Damn!" Pierre had to think quickly for if George Buchard said he had seen Mary being arrested then he believed him as George was the third member of their cell and was a very level-headed trustworthy man and he wouldn't say anything unless he knew the facts were correct, but what should he do now? He knew that Mary wouldn't give up any information on the members of the Cell no matter what they did to her, but he also knew that he couldn't take the risk of her possibly talking; unlike the other men, he knew that Mary was to have received vital information concerning a top priority operation but obviously, that would now have to be changed.

"I'll have to contact London for directions on this, Mark."

"What! Why?"

"Because Mary was to have received information on a top priority mission and I don't know if she received it or how her arrest now affects that mission."

"But Pierre, if she talks, we—" Mark stopped talking as Pierre grabbed his arm.

"She won't talk! If she had, we'd all have been arrested by now, so get a grip on yourself!" and Pierre shook the man's arm as he spoke. Mark shook his head and swallowed nervously.

"Yes…yes, you're right, of course."

"Get the others and meet me at the farm in a couple of hours, we'll get a message off to London and see what they want us to do."

"You think that wise, Pierre? After our efforts in the field last night, they'll have the Detector vans out in force, surely?"

"We don't have a choice, Mark, so get going"

"Yes…yes alright." Pierre led the way out of the office and opened the garage door, it was imperative to carry on as if nothing had happened. He would close in an hour under the pretext of having to go for parts and in the meantime, he hoped that Mary would be able to hold out against whatever those sadistic bastards were doing to her.

Chapter Five
SOE Airfield, England The Previous Night

The pilot of the Lysander walked into the briefing hut with the two escaped aircrew by his side. Captain Elizabeth Sims was waiting at a table with a couple of Intelligence Officers and some mugs of coffee. The two aircrew were given a mug of coffee and were hurried out of the hut by one of the Intelligence officers who would debrief them in another hut.

The Lysander pilot dumped his parachute harness onto a chair and took a mug of coffee from Beth.

"Thanks."

"What happened?" she asked him anxiously as his brief radio transmission once clear of the continent hadn't sounded good for her agent.

"The approach to the airstrip went smoothly, I received the correct code letters from the reception party on the ground and the approach went well. Visibility was good, so I made a fast approach and landed. The courier jumped out and as those two airmen scrambled aboard, all Hell broke loose, a searchlight illuminated the field and two machineguns opened up."

"A searchlight, you say?" asked the Intelligence officer and the pilot nodded.

"Yes, it was mounted on some sort of vehicle and came bursting through the hedges at the far end of the field."

"And did you see our Agent?"

"Briefly. There were four men and one woman there, she had just met the courier when the machineguns opened. I saw the Courier go down but that was all as I had opened up to get the hell out of there, I just managed to clear the obstacles that they were putting up. I get the feeling that someone opened fire a bit early, another couple of minutes and they would have had those obstacles up and I wouldn't have gotten off the ground!"

The pilot took a sip of his coffee as he made his report, it had been a hair-raising experience and he knew that he had only just gotten off the ground, another couple of minutes and those obstacles would have prevented him leaving but it was a part of this job, everyone knew the risks, but he felt sorry for those Agents on the ground as he felt sure that they would have been taken.

"Did you see if our Agent went down?" asked Beth hating to think what he was going to say to her.

"I saw the Courier go down and the woman went to him but that's the last I saw, I was busy dodging the trees after that, sorry."

"Thank you, Lieutenant, let me have a written report later today, would you, and I'm glad you made it out."

"Thank you, Ma'am." The pilot picked up his parachute and hurried out of the hut. Beth turned to a Corporal standing next to her.

"Tell the WT Office to keep a good listen out on Mary's frequency, would you, while I go and see Major Scott."

"Yes Ma'am." As the Corporal hurried off, Beth closed her notebook; she just prayed that Mary had been able to get out of that field.

The following afternoon, she was sitting at her desk in her office when Major Scott entered the room.

"Mary's been arrested," he said as he strode across the room.

"Oh my God! Are you sure?" she said as he handed her a signal slip.

"Yes, that's from the second operator of her group, apparently, she was arrested as she left the field after the Lysander took off, the signal was authenticated twice!"

"Do we know where she is now?"

"Unknown, all we know is that she was arrested by the local Gendarmes."

"Oh, that poor girl."

"The worst part is that we don't know if she had the information from the Courier on her when she was arrested."

"I don't give a damn about that, Sandy, I only care about my agent!"

"I know, and I care about Mary too; after all, I recruited her, Beth, but that information is vitally important and if they get a hold of it, a lot of lives could be lost."

"So, what can we do?"

"If she is only being held by the police and isn't at the local military garrison, then it might be possible to get her back."

"What! How the hell can they do that. Mary's group is only four-strong, for goodness' sake!"

"I know but that scientist has information that is vital to the war effort, so we need to get Mary back!" Beth sighed heavily before she picked up her telephone receiver and dialled three numbers.

"Hallo Grace, Beth here. I need you to send an urgent signal to code name 'Brandon' do you have a pencil—good—send this—IMPERATIVE YOU RECOVER MARY SOONEST—have you got that—good, send it straight away," she replaced the handpiece and looked at the Major.

"We are risking a lot of lives here, Sandy, are you sure there is no other way?"

"If we knew for certain that Mary didn't have the information on her when she was arrested, it would be different, but we don't, so, for now this is the best we can do."

"I just hope you're right, Sandy." Beth also hoped that Mary had taken her L-Pill with her so if the torture that she was bound to endure got too bad then she could at least give herself a quick and painless release.

Chapter Six
Posey, France 1943

An hour and a half after her beating, Mary was brought back to the interrogation room, she was walking slowly and held herself rather stiffly; although her head was defiantly upright, she was trying her hardest not to show just how much her body was hurting for her whole body was burning, each step was incredibly painful.

"Sit down, Mary." Major Schrandt indicated a wooden chair that had been placed in front of the desk, being grateful that she wasn't having to sit in that horrid interrogation chair, she sat down groaning a little as she did so as it hurt dreadfully.

"Kurt, you can remove those manacles," the Major indicated the manacles on Mary's wrists and Kurt quickly moved forward and removed the manacles. Mary massaged her wrists as the weight was removed.

"Would you like some coffee?" asked the Major as he poured two cups of coffee from a pot on his desk, he poured some milk in the cup and spooned in some sugar, holding the mug out to her.

Mary hesitated for a moment. SOE had warned them about this approach: first hard with beatings and then the softly softly with refreshments but just then, she was as dry as dust, so she took the cup.

"Thank you," she croaked before taking a rather large gulp of the hot coffee which burnt a little, but she didn't care as it tasted and felt good just then.

"Good." The Major sat down behind his desk and took a sip of his own coffee.

Mary quickly drank the coffee then despite the pain that the movement caused, she reached forward and put the mug onto the desk.

"Is this the softly softly approach before your thugs beat me again, Major?" she asked with as much disgust in her voice that she could muster.

"Not at all, my dear. I know you have been through a lot today, so I thought you would like some refreshments, also while I pour you another cup of coffee, Kurt has your clothes for you and I'm sure you would like to get dressed?" The Major nodded and while he poured her a second cup of coffee, Kurt tossed her skirt and blouse to her. Mary didn't know what they were up to but was grateful to be able to get dressed and despite the pain that each move caused, she quickly stood up and slowly pulled on her skirt and blouse. She sat down again and buttoned up her blouse then accepted the second cup of coffee, which she sipped slowly.

This being nice to her was very disconcerting and had thrown her off balance a little and she wondered what they were going to do to her next. They sat in silence for a couple of minutes while she finished the coffee.

The Major had been studying her while she drank the coffee, he could see that Mary still had a determined look on her face, he was giving her this respite and time to rest so that hopefully, the Doctor's serum would have a better chance to take effect, he was taking a big risk for if the Doctor's magic drugs didn't work then he would lose his agent to the Gestapo and all his hopes would be ruined.

Mary placed the mug onto the desk and waited, wondering what would happen now.

"Well Mary, I trust that you understand that we mean business. You've seen what Kurt and Conrad are capable of, so I will give you some time to consider your options. You either start answering my questions or we will have to start a new round of interrogations. Hmm?"

Mary swallowed hard and shook her head negatively as she looked at him.

"I've told you, Major, I can't answer your questions as you have me mixed up with someone else, I…I'm only a schoolteacher." Major Schrandt sighed hard before he stood up.

"Mary, I can assure you that the next round is going to be far more painful than what you have experienced up to now, so I will ask you for the last time: who are your companions and what codes are you using?"

"I told you, Major, your men have mistaken me for someone else. I am a schoolteacher here in Posey, I was on my way home when the chain on my bicycle broke so that was why I was out after the curfew but the rest I…I had nothing to do with!"

"Your file says otherwise, Mary. Hmm?"

"I…I don't know anything about that, Major"

"If you continue to be stubborn, Mary, then your stay with us will be long and VERY painful!" The Major emphasised the last word, Mary shook her head negatively as she swallowed nervously, the Major gave the briefest of nods, she caught a blur of movement off to the side as Kurt quickly stepped forward, backhanding her across the face with such force that the blow knocked her off the chair.

There came a slight thud as she hit the floor but she wasn't given time to recover herself as Kurt moved forward, grabbed her by the hair and hauled her to her feet, he dragged her grimacing with pain from the tight hold of her hair to the horrid interrogation chair; tossing her onto the chair, he gave her no time to recover as he set about striking her with savage force to the left side of her face.

"Who" SLAP! "Are you" SLAP! "Working with?" SLAP! SLAP!

"What are" SLAP! SLAP! "Your codes?" SLAP! SLAP!

For fifteen minutes the blows rained down between each set of questions, always to the left side of her face, her head was reeling, and she was breathing hard through her mouth, then Kurt grabbed her by the hair again, hauling her to her feet, as soon as she was upright, he punched her hard in the stomach, making her double over in pain as the breath was knocked out of her.

He threw her back into the chair, there while she was still gasping for air, he quickly fastened the shackles to her ankles and wrists till she once again found herself totally restrained on the horrid chair, her eyes opened wide in fear as she expected Kurt to use his horrid 'little pins' at any second.

"Let's stop wasting time, Mary!" She cried out as Kurt grabbed her by the hair, forcing her head up so that she was looking directly at the Major.

"I know you are a British agent!" SLAP—Klunk! This time as Kurt backhanded her, the blow snapped her head back into the wooden chair, back making her teeth rattle.

"You work for Special Operations Executive!" SLAP—Klunk!

"You met the Lysander?" SLAP—Klunk!

"No…I—" Mary tried to answer but a blow snapped her head back again.

"You shot one of my men!" SLAP—Klunk!

"You met a Courier?" Slap—Klunk!

"What information did he give you?" Slap—Slap!

"Who are your companions?" Slap—Slap!

"Where is your wireless transmitter?" Slap—Klunk! Slap—Klunk!

"What codes are you using, Mary?" Slap! Slap! Slap! Slap!

Mary's head felt as if it was ready to explode as the Major's questioning droned on in a monotone in time with the vicious slaps, the left side of her face felt as large as a football as it swelled up and changed colour, the left eye closed with swelling, her temples ached dreadfully from the blows to the back of her head from the chair back, her mouth was as dry as dust and she could taste blood, then the room started spinning as Kurt continued to slap her, there came a dull roaring in her ears before she blacked out.

"Take a ten-minute break, Kurt," said the Major as Mary's head slumped forward.

"Sir." Kurt massaged his knuckles as he left the room, wondering why the Major had suddenly stopped; as Kurt left the room, the Major picked up the telephone handpiece and dialled a number.

"Ah Doctor, this is Major Schrandt, is everything progressing well, is there anything that you need?"

"I…I had a slight delay, Major, as I…I couldn't get one of the chemicals that I needed straight away but they are on the way, so I won't lose more than an hour or so, sir." The Doctor had cringed as he had said this as he expected the Major to rant and rave at him, or worse.

"But you will be able to have everything ready as you said you would, Doctor?"

"Yes Major, I will be ready."

"Good!" CLICK—the Major had hung up.

Mary gagged as her eyes opened, she recoiled from the horrible smelling salts that were being held under her nose by the Major who smiled as her eye came into focus.

"That's better, Mary, wake up, my dear!" he said as he waved the bottle under her nose, making her pull her head away from the smell.

"Not—" Mary shook her head to clear her senses.

"What was that?" asked the Major as he straightened up.

"I'm…I'm NOT your dear!" she said this quietly as she took a couple of deep breaths to regain her composure, the Major did a short laugh but there was no warmth in it.

"So, Mary, are you ready to talk?" he asked, and she shook her head negatively.

"I…I have nothing to say, you have me mixed up with someone else," she said stubbornly, the Major sighed heavily then looked up as Kurt re-entered the room.

"We will start over, Kurt, now that Mary is with us again!" The Major gave her an evil grin, Mary cringed as Kurt started walking towards her. This was how it went for the rest of the Morning, Kurt would slap her face for ten minutes at a time with a ten-minute break where the Major asked her repeated questions, after three hours, Kurt unfastened the buckles at her ankles and wrists, she thought that it might be over for a while but she was wrong, again she was punched in the stomach then as she doubled over in pain with the breath knocked out of her, Kurt manacled her wrists behind her back, then as she regained her breath she startled struggling against him as he was walking her towards the bathtub that was in the corner of the room, she knew what was coming, she struggled as hard as she could but to no avail, then he had forced her to her knees and she was staring at the water in the tub.

"Answer my questions, Mary, and we can forgo this unpleasantness?" said the Major from where he was sitting on the edge of his desk, smirking at her.

"I…I can't tell you anything, Major, you have me mixed up with someone else, I…I am only a schoolteacher!" She found herself tensing up, bracing herself against the shove that would force her head into that water, then she jumped as Kurt's hand clamped onto the back of her neck, then she was screaming as the water closed over her head.

So it went on for the rest of the day, she was repeatedly forced under the water until her lungs were bursting, when she reached the point where she almost blacked out, Kurt would haul her back throwing her to the floor where she spent minutes vomiting up water while she gasped for air, then after the tenth dunking, he would throw her onto the hard chair and start slapping her face again but always just the one side until she thought that her head would explode.

The Major and Kurt had an hour's break for lunch but for her there was no break and no lunch as a line was attached to her manacles; it was then pulled up over a beam in the ceiling which, with her hands manacled behind her, had the effect of pulling her arms up over her head and bending her over in the middle which gave an excruciating pain to her shoulders. Although she had to pant against the pain in her arms and shoulders, she could at least breathe as she hung there dripping wet with her head throbbing and her lungs burning dreadfully.

All too soon for her, their lunch break was over, she cried out as Kurt released the line holding her arms suddenly as he entered the room, she fell to the floor in severe pain as the blood rushed back to her shoulders.

"You can stop this any time you want, Mary, all you have to do is talk to me?" The Major knelt down by her head as he said this, Mary was sobbing from the pain in her shoulders, she couldn't do anything except shake her head, she tried to speak but it came out as a dry croak.

"Give her some water—gently!" said the Major meaning that Kurt should give her some water to drink rather than forcing her head under it. Kurt fetched a mug of water then pulled her up to her knees, holding the mug up for her to drink from which she did greedily as she was incredibly dry, she gagged a couple of times as the water went down to her already bloated stomach for she felt certain that she had swallowed gallons of water when they had tried to drown her in that damned bath tub, she cleared her throat to get her voice to work.

"Nothing to say!" she croaked, making the Major sigh heavily.

"Very well—Kurt!"

"NO—Please!" Mary started sobbing again as Kurt grabbed her by the hair dragging her to the bath, again she started screaming as her head went under.

"Ggaarwraack!" Later that day Mary vomited up water a couple of times, she had woken in her cell a little disorientated as she had blacked out again after having been yanked out of the water before waking up in her cell, she was wringing wet, cold, her head was splitting and her lungs were burning, she had no idea of the time but was just glad to be out of that room, any respite was welcome, she drew up her knees and gagged again.

"GOD, please help me!" she muttered to herself quietly as she drew up her knees trying to get some warmth, she was desperately tired but couldn't sleep because of her throbbing head and the ache in her lungs.

SHE WASN'T GOING TO SURVIVE! She knew that now; they would torture her until she broke then once they had their information, they would either drown her in that horrid bathtub or they would take her out and shoot her.

"Will it hurt?" she wondered, then she caught a hold of herself, THAT was no way to be thinking!

She had to be strong! She had to endure it until her teammates had a chance to escape, they must know that she had been taken by now. Then she suddenly had a clear mental image of Margite and Danny on their pig farm, the image seemed to steady her resolve somehow, she started thinking about herself.

No one else could help her here!

She was on her own, if she was going to survive then she would have to HELP HERSELF!

"What did they say at SOE, look for opportunities, things out of the ordinary that you could turn to your advantage." Just then as she talked quietly to herself, she looked around her cold bleak cell, she couldn't see any way out of this, but she told herself that there was always hope!

She couldn't give in! She closed her eyes and tried to curl up tighter as she started shivering. She had no idea of how long it had been since they had thrown her back into this cell but it must have been a couple of hours for her petticoat (perversely they had stripped her out of her skirt and blouse again during the dunking in the bath) had started drying out a little, then she was looking up as the door bolt rattled, the cell door opened and the soldier who had been on guard outside walked in carrying a tin mug.

"Stand up!" he shouted as he entered the cell; wearily, Mary forced herself upright, her leg and stomach muscles ached as she stood up which was a little difficult to do as her hands were still manacled behind her back.

The soldier placed the mug onto the bench before he turned her slightly to remove the manacles.

"Put your hands in front!" he snapped at her, Mary put her hands out and he quickly refastened the manacles about her wrists again before indicating the mug of water on the bench.

"Breakfast!" he said with a sneer before walking out slamming the door shut. Mary sat down on the bench and gently lifted the mug of water, she forced herself to sip it slowly although she was as dry as dust, she savoured every drop not knowing when or even if she would get any more. The soldier had said that it was her 'breakfast', so she assumed that it was morning, although with no window to look out of she had no reference point for time.

"Cup!" she jumped a little as the soldier snapped this at her through the barred aperture in the door, she stood up then slowly moved to the door lifting the mug up to the aperture where the soldier snatched it from her before moving out of her sight, she took the opportunity to take a quick peek out of the aperture but there wasn't much to see except a corridor with a couple of cell doors on each side but she couldn't see any other prisoners or guards so she assumed that she was the only one here at that time, then she was quickly jerking her head back as the soldier slammed shut the little flap on the barred aperture.

Mary went back to the bench, she was thirsty, hungry and desperately tired. Her left eye was closed due to the swelling on the left side of her face, she hadn't been able to understand why Kurt had only slapped one side of her face unless it was to make sure that she could see out of one eye.

Ten minutes later, the door rattled again, this time the soldier entered with Conrad close behind, she stood up and started backing away as he was carrying what looked like a length of black tubing; her heart started racing as Conrad grabbed her by the manacles, dragging her to the wall at the end of the room where he deftly pulled her wrists up; dropping the manacles neatly over a hook set into the wall just on six feet above the floor, which meant she was forced to literally stand on her tip toes with all her weight being on the manacled wrists.

She was now dangling from the hook with her nose pressed up against the bricks of the wall, she braced herself waiting for the first blow but nothing happened; carefully, she turned her head trying to see behind her but her vision was limited, then she stiffened as she heard footsteps behind her.

"Morning Mary," said Major Schrandt as he marched into the cell, she didn't answer as he moved up behind her.

"Now I am sure that you don't want a repeat of yesterday's unpleasantness. Hmm?" he asked, she flinched as he flicked the hair just above her neck, again she didn't answer him.

"Well?" he asked with his mouth close to her ear.

"I…I have nothing to say to you, Major."

"That WILL change, Mary, but for now you are causing yourself a lot of pain for nothing! London can't help you, neither can your companions here," he pushed her in the small of her back, causing her to move forward pressing her nose against the cold bricks.

"Tell me what I want to know, Mary, and it all stops. So, who are your companions here in Posey and what are the codes you are using, hmm?" he asked, Mary just shook her head negatively.

"Such a pity," the Major sighed heavily as he walked away, Mary hadn't seen him give the briefest of nods to Conrad, then as the Major walked out of the cell, she cried out as the first blow fell across her shoulders knocking the breath out of her but unlike the rattan cane that Conrad had used on her before, this pipe didn't cut as it landed, instead it delivered a deep stinging blow that knocked the breath out of her, leaving a foot-long bruise where it landed.

Conrad took his time, there was a big gap between each blow which left her in fearful suspense as she waited for it, tensing up trying to regain her breath after each blow landed. This time Conrad asked her the same question after each blow:

"What are your codes?" THWAACK!

"What are your codes?" THWAACK!

"What are your codes?" THWAACK!

Slow rhythmic blows after each question delivered with his full strength. After ten minutes, her jaw was aching as she had been clamping her teeth together trying to stop herself from crying out as tears of humiliation ran down her face.

It was hurting. *'Oh God it was hurting,'* she thought to herself, but she knew that she would be able to handle this. This was now a clash of wills; hers against this brute who was slowly beating her with that horrible pipe. It was incredibly painful on her wrists where the manacles were biting into her flesh as her full body weight pulled on them even though she tried easing the weight by raising up and down on her toes. For a full hour, the blows rained down on her back and shoulders, she couldn't help crying out as Conrad methodically beat her asking his question between blows.

Then suddenly, it stopped. Conrad tucked the pipe into his belt, walked forward and grabbed her by the manacles which he lifted, so they cleared the hook in the wall and then he just let go. Mary fell to the floor with a thud, screaming out in sudden agony as all her muscles seemed to scream in pain at the same time, Conrad looked at her for a moment then turned, leaving the cell.

"Oh God—Oh GOD!" Mary forced herself not to cry out as she pulled herself onto the bench lying face down as the tears streamed down her face at the agony in her back and shoulders. Her legs and arms were burning fiercely as her circulation returned, she closed her eyes feeling utterly alone and desperate, she knew they were going to kill her!

In his office, Major Schrandt was pouring himself a cup of coffee when he looked up as Conrad entered the room, he was about to say something when the telephone jangled, he snatched up the receiver.

"Major Schrandt!" he said.

"Doctor Neuman here, sir, my serum will be ready for use by eight o'clock tonight."

"You can't have it ready sooner, Doctor?"

"No Major, I had some difficulty obtaining—"

"Alright Doctor, eight tonight!" The Major hung up then looked at Conrad. "Well?" he asked.

"Not a word sir."

"Damn!" The Major rubbed his chin in thought for a moment.

"Did she react differently when you used the cane, Conrad?"

"She was a little more vocal then, sir."

"Right, giver her an hour then use the cane again. Same routine as before, don't break any bones and don't mark her face, alright?"

"Yes sir." Conrad left the office; the Major finished his coffee before he started making some notes about the interrogation of the British agent.

Later that afternoon Mary was lying face down on the bench in her Cell, her entire body was burning, each movement was agony. After her beating with the pipe, she had been given an hour's respite before Conrad and the soldier guarding the door had marched in, grabbed her and hung her from the hook on the manacles with practiced ease, this time Conrad had used the rattan cane. Her back and shoulders were still swelling with bruises from the earlier beating, this time she had screamed from the first blow as her petticoat was no protection from the searing pain on her back which was still raw from the earlier beating.

This time she felt close to breaking as each slash of the cane was slowly delivered with full force, her mind screamed out for release from this savage onslaught.

"What codes are you using?" asked Conrad between each slash of the cane.

Oh, it would be so easy to give them something, anything to stop the burning agony on her back and shoulders, to stop the breath being knocked out of her sore lungs, it would be so easy to say something!

"NO!" Mary shouted this out as the cane slashed across her back in searing heat, she shocked herself as she yelled out. She felt totally disgusted with herself for even daring to say anything! She clamped her jaws shut as she shook her head from side to side.

You can't talk—mustn't say ANYTHING! she berated herself over and over as Conrad slashed her asking his question each time.

"What is your code, Mary?"

No…mustn't say anything! she said to herself.

"What is your code, Mary?" SLASH!

NO—mustn't say anything!

"What is your code, Mary?" SLASH!

"NO!" she shouted this out loud this time as her ears started to ring.

"What is your code, Mary?" SLASH!

"NO!" she hung from the manacles with the tears streaming down her face as she concentrated on her breathing as the room started to spin as she was delirious with the pain.

Conrad stopped as he saw her head flop to the side, he knew the signs, once a prisoner reached a certain point, continuing the beating would be a waste of time, they wouldn't feel the blows so it would be counterproductive, not what the Major was looking for. Again, Mary screamed as she was released from the hook to thud to the floor with her muscles screaming out from the sudden release.

Ggrrwwraack! Mary gagged loudly as he held a bottle of smelling salts under her nose, keeping it there until her eyes opened and she focused on him, he grabbed her wrists and pulled her up to her feet.

"Uggh!" He waved the bottle under her nose until he was sure that she wasn't going to fall over, then he unfastened the manacles leaving them to dangle from one wrist, then he reached into a knapsack that he had brought into the cell with him, he pulled out her skirt and blouse tossing them at her, the garments hit her in the face then fell to the floor making her blink rapidly.

"Get dressed! Quickly!" he barked at her.

Mary reached down for her clothes, yelling out in pain as she did so as each movement was agony, then as her head cleared a little, she started dressing, wondering what the hell was happening now.

"Hands out front!" he snapped as she finished fastening her blouse buttons, she lifter her hands slowly in front of her, Conrad quickly refastened the manacles again.

"We will collect you shortly!" said Conrad as he turned to leave.

"Wh…where are you taking me?" she croaked at him through incredibly dry lips.

"You will find out soon enough!" The door banged shut and the bolt was rammed across.

Mary cried out as she lay herself down on the bench, her mind was racing, where were they going to take her? Were they just trying to throw her off guard? Her biggest fear was that they would hand her over to the Gestapo, was that what was about to happen?

"You have to get out, Mary, somehow you have to get OUT!" She curled herself up into a ball and tried to fight down the panic racing through her mind.

Mary curled herself into a tighter ball on the bench, trying not to cry out from the pain that was wracking her entire body, hugging her knees seemed to help a little but she was scared, not only wondering what they would do to her next but she was also scared stiff that they were about to hand her over to the Gestapo, she knew that if they did that she was finished!

She was struggling to deal with what the Major had done to her so far, but she knew the Gestapo would be worse, she knew she wouldn't survive in their hands! Then she jumped as the door lock rattled then the Major strode into the cell with Kurt by his side.

"Get up!" snapped the Major as he came in.

Painfully, Mary forced herself up then she slowly got to her feet, she cried out as Kurt moved up pulling her around as he unfastened the manacles from one wrist before moving aside.

"This is your last chance, Mary, your last chance to talk to me. Answer my questions and all this unpleasantness will end?" The Major raised a quizzical eyebrow as he said this waiting for her to reply. She swallowed hard to get her dry vocal cords to work.

"I...I can't tell you anything, Major, as I said you have me mixed up with someone else," she croaked at him quietly.

"Still persisting with the silly story of being a schoolteacher isn't going to help you, Mary, we know you are a British agent, talk to me now and all the interrogations will stop, all the pain will stop!" The Major folded his arms as he looked at her, for just a moment Mary felt disgusted with herself as she thought of how easy it would be to say something, ANYTHING, just to stop the pain and humiliation of the interrogations, of having that bastard Kurt forcing her head under the cold water, no more pain from Conrad's slashing cane.

Then she thought about how many lives were at stake if she uttered a single word, it made her feel sick thinking about it.

"Well!" Mary jumped as the Major shouted at her.

"I...I can't tell you anything, Major, I...I'm just a schoolteacher." She clamped her jaws together as she looked at him stubbornly knowing that she would pay for this dearly. The Major sighed heavily as he shook his head.

"You are a fool and I have had enough of this. Take her out!" with that the Major turned, leaving the cell.

"Follow me!" Kurt then turned and strode out of the cell, the guard moved towards her raising his rifle and giving her no choice but to follow him out. Leaving the cell, they turned left walking down a short corridor with Mary wondering where they were taking her and why. At the end of the corridor, there was a solid wooden door which Kurt unlocked, he opened the door then stood aside, Mary could see a small courtyard surrounded by three high brick walls, there was no roof as she could clearly see the sky, but the thing that caught her attention made her stop dead in her tracks, it was a flat-sided post six feet tall set into the ground a couple of feet from the rear wall, it had four sandbags at its base, the wall behind was pockmarked. Mary felt the bile rising in her throat, those pockmarks had been caused by bullet strikes, this courtyard was used for executions!

The breath caught in her throat as she realised what this place was, she looked at the post as her heart started racing, she felt suddenly numb all over, this was very real, it was no longer just a possibility, something that could happen, this was going to happen—they were going to shoot her! She jumped as Kurt grabbed her arm.

"Move!" he snapped then Mary was pulling against him, digging her heels in as he dragged her into the courtyard, then she felt like vomiting as her back jarred up against the post, Kurt gave her no time to think as he unfastened the manacles, yanked her arms behind the post then quickly refastened the manacles, she looked up wide-eyed as Kurt straightened up, she tried swallowing but her mouth and throat were bone dry.

Now she stood with her arms manacled behind the post with her back pressing into the wood with her heels on the sandbags at the base of the post, she swallowed hard as Kurt stepped back.

"This is your last chance to talk?" he said as he pulled a Luger pistol from the holster on his belt. Not daring herself to speak and feeling close to vomiting, Mary shook her head negatively.

"What codes are you using, where is your transmitter and who are your companions. Tell me these things and this will all be over." said Kurt as he raised the pistol and cocked it with a loud menacing click! With her heart thudding loudly in her ears, Mary shook her head.

"Damn it girl, this is real! Tell me your codes or I will shoot you!" Kurt raised the pistol so she could watch wide-eyed as he thumbed off the safety catch.

"I…I am only a schoolteacher, you have me mixed up with someone else," she said quietly.

"You stupid bitch!" Kurt snarled at her then turning he walked off for a few yards, for Mary the next few minutes seemed to happen in slow motion as Kurt walked off then turned side on to her then slowly raised his arm, pointing the pistol at her. Her bowels turned to water and the vomit rose hotly in the back of her throat as she stared at that pistol as she was about to DIE!

"Oh GOD! Please let it be quick!" she cringed not daring to breathe as she waited for the pain, then she jumped and cried out in fright as the pistol went off with an alarming Bang! she heard the bullet thudding into the brick wall behind her but there was no pain!

Then she heard it! A deep snarling laugh, it was a humourless laugh, and it was coming from Kurt as he holstered his pistol walking towards her.

"My god!" The reality hit home suddenly! They had been playing with her!

They had no intentions of shooting her! The heat in her stomach rose up and turning aside as best she could, she was violently sick.

"Uggh!" she cried out as Kurt grabbed her by the hair lifting her head up so she could look at him.

"Start talking you, stupid bitch! The next time I won't miss!" he dropped her head then walked out of the courtyard.

Mary dry heaved a couple of times then slowly slid down to her knees as she started crying bitterly.

"Oh god! Help me!" On her knees she hung from the manacles, leaning forward crying bitterly feeling terrified and utterly alone. She couldn't believe what had just happened. How could someone play with another human being like that, as if they were nothing, just an object! She threw up again as the tears continued to stream down her face.

She hung there on her knees hanging from the manacles on her wrists, not feeling the pain, totally despondent for fifteen minutes before Conrad marched in, unfastened the manacles, pulled her away from the post then refastened the manacles with her hands behind her back again. Mary could barely walk on badly trembling legs as he dragged her back to her cell where he shoved her through the door, she came up hard against the rear wall where she dropped down to her knees leaning against the wall, she felt incredibly numb, they had just been playing with her this time, next time she was certain that she would die!

****

On a small farm ten miles from Posey, Pierre sat at the kitchen table trying to remain calm while Danny Duguay the sixty-year-old owner of the farm and the fourth member of their Resistance Cell laboriously decoded a reply to the message that he had sent to London earlier that day.

"Mon Dieu! They've gone mad!" exclaimed Danny as he handed Pierre a piece of paper that he had decoded the signal on.

"You sure this is right, Danny?" asked Pierre as he quickly read the message.

"Mary is the expert with these cyphers, Pierre, but I've checked it three times and it is right." Pierre smiled as he patted the old man on the shoulder, Danny was a sixty-year-old pig farmer with short cropped grey hair and sparkling blue eyes, but he was also ruthless when it came to killing enemy soldiers, he had fought them in the last war and had already lost a son in this one and had tried to fight them by himself before Pierre had recruited him.

"I'm not doubting you, old friend, but this is unusual." Pierre reread the message again which simply said, 'Imperative you recover Mary soonest!'

"They've gone mad, Pierre, how the hell do they expect us to get Mary from that police cell, there are only the four of us for Christ sakes?"

"They know that Danny, and for them to have sent this means that whatever the information was that Mary received in that field must be very important!"

"Do you think the Boche know, Pierre, if they do, they'll stop at nothing to get it out of her."

Pierre shook his head as he had been thinking along the same lines, he knew Mary was a brave girl, but she was only human and as Danny said if they wanted the information from her then they would stop at nothing to get it and they would be ruthless in their methods, after all to them it wouldn't matter if she died under interrogation, as they would only execute her later anyway. He took a pencil from his pocket and quickly scribbled a note on a piece of paper before passing it to Danny.

"Code and send this, Danny, and then stay by the receiver."

"Alright Pierre, and where are you going?"

"Well, before we can get Mary, we have to know where she is, eh?" and he smiled at the old man who just shook his head and then Pierre hurried out of the farm, if he had any hopes of rescuing Mary then he would need information and to get that he had to play a dangerous game.

****

In her cell later that day, Mary lay curled up as best she could on the narrow wooden bench that served as her bunk, she was shiveringly cold and thirsty and her body ached dreadfully, she had curled up and tried not to move as each movement was agony, the beating she had received from Conrad was still throbbingly raw and the only blessing from this was that it took her mind off the constant throbbing pain from her ripped out fingernails.

She was grateful for the respite that they had given her after the episode in the courtyard although she was uncertain as to why they had stopped the interrogation, but it had given her time to gather herself and although she was shiveringly cold having been given her blouse and skirt back had helped to warm her a little and she now retained some of her dignity.

She knew that if she was going to survive then she had to help herself somehow as there was no-one else here who could help her. She knew the interrogation would start again shortly and would probably intensify until she told them something, she was just grateful that she hadn't had the time to be able to read the information that the courier had brought her on the airfield the other night—Hell she had only been here for two days and yet it felt like a lifetime, but she knew that somehow she had to help herself to get out of here, even though it seemed impossible she knew that if she didn't get out then she would die! She knew that the next time they took her to that courtyard it would be for real; they WOULD shoot her.

She jumped a little startled as the air raid siren started wailing, there were raised voices outside and moving slowly, she crossed to the door where the aperture in the centre of the door was open and she heard the Major shouting instructions to the police officers to get everyone down to the air raid shelters, then she heard footsteps coming towards the cell so she moved back to the bench and had sat down when the door bolt was drawn back.

"Get up, Bitch!" shouted Kurt as he opened the door and Mary got to her feet and gasped as pain shot through her back and upper legs then as Kurt moved aside for her to move towards the door, she noticed that the soldiers who normally were outside the door weren't there and her heart started racing as an idea formed, it was completely mad and probably had no chance of succeeding but she had to do something and it was now or never!

"No shelter for you, Bitch!" snapped Kurt as he entered.

With a very loud groan, Mary doubled over clutching at her stomach with her manacled hands groaning loudly.

"Get up!" As Kurt turned slightly and reached out to grab her hair, Mary swung around with all her strength, the manacles attached to her wrists caught Kurt squarely on the nose which cracked loudly with a shower of blood as his nose broke, as Kurt yelled out, Mary swung around and caught him with a savage blow to the side of the head and he crumpled to the floor groaning.

Mary was momentarily stunned by her success, she couldn't believe that it had worked, then as Kurt groaned again, she pulled herself together, kicking him in the side of the head as hard as she could. She ran out of the cell and slammed the door shut, she pulled the bolt across then reached up and closed the small flap on the aperture in the centre of the door; now any yells that Kurt made would be muffled by the door and hopefully, this would give her some time. With her heart beating madly, she looked around for a couple of seconds not quite sure of what to do. She was in a small corridor with six cells on each side and now there was no-one else around; if she went left, she would come to the interrogation room with its horrid chair, so she turned right and hurried up the small corridor, not really knowing where she could go.

At the end of the corridor was another door with a small window which she noticed had no lock and looking through the window saw another corridor between some offices and again she couldn't believe her luck as there seemed to be on-one around as everyone had been sent to the shelters. She slowly opened the door trying not to make any noise and although she could hear voices she couldn't see anyone so without running, which she thought would attract attention, she walked as fast as her beating heart would allow to the main door and out onto the street and then moved fast down the road and then started running slowly at first and then faster and faster putting as much distance as she could between herself and police station, then at the end of the road she ducked into a side street.

She paused leaning against a wall as she regained her breath with her heart racing madly, she couldn't believe that she had managed to get out of there without raising an alarm, but she had! She jumped badly as anti-aircraft guns started barking in the distance, she knew she had to keep going and fast but where!

She pushed herself off the wall and started running again, she had to get off the streets and find somewhere to hide before they found Kurt and that wouldn't take long. She came to another corner and having a quick glance around it first she saw a laneway a short distance away, she hurried over to it and made her way down the lane, madly looking for somewhere to hide but there was nowhere here.

She was close to tears in her desperation, she knew she could only have minutes before an alarm was raised, with her hands manacled in front of her and in bare feet, she stood out badly. At the end of the laneway was a short street, she hurriedly jumped into a doorway as a small truck drove up the street and past her slowly. She ran up the street and into another laneway, then started pulling on latches on gates desperately looking for somewhere to hide for if she could hide herself until nightfall then she might have a chance to get to Pierre.

A double wooden gate was slightly ajar, peering through the gap she saw an overgrown courtyard high with weeds outside an old factory building, the factory windows were boarded up and in one corner of the courtyard was a derelict old car. The wooden gates had a chain through two holes near the latch, she pushed on one of the gates which gave a little and with a lot of scrabbling she managed to squeeze herself through the gap into the yard.

She hurried over to the derelict rusted vehicle that rested on tyre less wheels, the right-hand passenger door was missing, every window except the windscreen had been smashed out at some time and tall weeds were growing up through the rusted floor. She moved to the rear of the vehicle where the boot lid was stuck halfway open, there was a length of old smelly canvas in the boot.

She pulled this out and looked around in alarm as tins banged and rattled as she pulled the canvas and a dog started barking but no-one else seemed to be around. Then, as she moved towards the rear of the vehicle, she spotted a pile of stacked bricks near the rear fence, like the car the bricks were surrounded by tall weeds but there was a gap between the bricks and the fence.

At first, she had thought about hiding in the boot of the derelict vehicle with the canvas to cover her but she thought that when they started searching for her, they would look into this obvious hiding place so she hurried over to the pile of bricks, it was a high stack and she had to squeeze herself into the gap between the bricks and the fence but with a little difficulty she was able to lay down with her back to the fence. The manacles on her wrists made it very difficult but she was able to cover herself with the canvas from the vehicle and with her heart pounding in her ears, she pulled the canvas over herself and prayed to God that no-one would stumble upon her if they searched the factory yard, it was risky being so close to the police station, but she had to hide and she had to rest.

****

Kurt groaned loudly as he sat up groggily, he was covered in blood from his broken nose and his head throbbed painfully, he looked around a little disconcerted and then his senses cleared rapidly as he saw the closed cell door. He pulled himself to his feet and staggered to the door and stared in disbelief as he tried to open it and found it was bolted, he shook it a couple of times, but it was bolted shut.

"Bloody bitch!" He couldn't believe that the British Agent had overpowered him and had managed to get out of the cell and then the meaning of those words hit him—she had gotten herself out of the cell—had she also managed to get out of the station?

He pulled a whistle out of his pocket and putting it between his teeth he started blowing it loudly as he pounded on the cell door with both fists, he felt slightly sick not only because of his broken nose and the bash he had received to the side of his head but mainly because he was scared to think of what the Major would do if Mary had indeed managed to escape from the police station. Five minutes after he had started pounding on the door, the small hatch over the window was opened and a soldier peered in at him, it had been the shrilling of the whistle that had attracted the man's attention.

"Don't just stand there, get this BLOODY DOOR OPEN!" Kurt shouted, and the man quickly unbolted the door and opened it.

"Sound the alarm and search the building, that British bitch has escaped!" Kurt shouted this at the man as he ran down the corridor and a moment later burst into the interrogation room. Frau Inge gasped as she saw the state, he was in. Major Schrandt was on the telephone as Kurt burst into the room and he held his hand up to silence the man.

"So, you'll be here in two days then, yes splendid I'll have the prisoner ready for you to take back to Paris—yes thank you for the call—Heil Hitler!" The Major slowly put the receiver down as he looked at Kurt's bloody state and thought that whatever had caused this could not be good.

"Tell me," he said quietly, and Kurt swallowed hard.

"When—when I went to collect Mary, she doubled over as if she was in pain and when—I—when I went to see what was the matter she—she used the manacles to break my nose and—and then hit me in the side of the head and then when I came to—she was gone, sir."

"Gone!" The Major jumped to his feet and within two strides was standing in front of Kurt, glaring at the man.

"Yes sir, I've sounded the alarm and have men searching the building." The Major grabbed Kurt by his shirt and gritted his teeth as he spoke.

"I've just gotten off the phone with our Gestapo friends in Paris, they've been delayed and have just told me that they can't get here for two days and now you are telling me that you have let our Mary escape!" The Major had spoken quietly as he said this, and Kurt paled visibly as the Major spoke to him for he knew how dangerous Schrandt could be when he was angry and he was livid right now.

"Ye…yes sir." The Major closed his eyes as he got himself back under control, he let go of Kurt's shirt and went back to his desk.

"Organise a search, I'll get you some men from the garrison, but I want every inch of this Town searched, do you understand?"

"Yes sir." Kurt turned and hurried towards the door.

"And Kurt?"

"Sir?" Kurt turned at the door and swallowed hard as the Major glared at him.

"If you don't find Mary and quickly, I'll have you shot!" Kurt swallowed hard again and not daring to speak, he hurried out of the room.

Chapter Seven
SOE Training Camp, England

"Again—what is your name?" Captain Elizabeth 'Beth' Sims asked for the umpteenth time that day as she looked at Mary who was dressed simply in a plain blouse and skirt, she was sitting at a small desk in the library room of the Manor House. Her parachute jump had been two weeks ago and for the past week now she had been studying and rehearsing her new identity with 'Beth' who would be her 'handler' and who had been coaching her for she would shortly be dropping somewhere 'over the pond' on her first operational mission so she had been living and breathing in French.

Everything she now wore, ate or drank was French. She only spoke French and with her handler's help she had been studying hard for her new role as a schoolteacher.

"I am Mary Trumont and I have been sent to Posey as a relief teacher. I was sent there because they are short of teachers and because my school was recently bombed."

"Good. Now I have your code name and details for this operation." Beth held up a small file and Mary sat up a little for that meant that the operation was getting close.

"How soon before I go, Beth?" she asked as she took the file.

"You've done our homework well, Mary, and you are more than ready. All you must do now is memorise the details in that file and for that I'll have to lock you in your room, the only contact you'll have with anyone is me I'm afraid. Once you have memorised that and destroyed it, you'll be ready for your drop in two days." Mary nodded and picked up her bag that was on the floor by the table, the prospect of the forthcoming operation was both exhilarating and frightening at the same time, all the hard work that she had been doing had led up to this moment.

"Let's go then" Beth stood up and led the way up to the second floor to the row of rooms that were being used by the Agents and she opened the door for Mary.

"Take your time memorising that file, Mary. You have two days to do it and once you know it, destroy it but make sure you know it before you destroy it as some of it could save your life."

"Alright, thank you Beth."

"I'll send your dinner up later, if there is anything else you need then just call me on the phone, alright?"

"Yes, thank you." As Mary entered the room Beth closed and locked the door, for a moment Mary felt as though she was back in school being punished for some misconduct or other. She put the file down onto the bed and crossed the room to look out of the window, it was overcast outside and threatening to rain, as she looked out over the grounds, she wandered what was going to happened over the next couple of days and not for the first time she wondered if she had indeed done the right thing by volunteering for SOE. Sighing heavily, she went back to the bed and making herself comfortable she started reading the file.

2200 hours (10 pm) two days later found Mary standing in a small wooden shack at the side of an airfield that was used by SOE to deliver Agents and supplies into enemy territory. Earlier this evening she and Alice had shared a meal together and then went with their Handlers to two different shacks for Alice would be dropped one hour earlier than Mary for her mission and although they would be using the same aircraft to take them to their drop zones, they had no idea of the details of each other's mission and would be kept separate until they boarded the aircraft.

Mary had dressed in a skirt, blouse and cardigan and was now donning a pair of coveralls, on the table next to her was her documents and a silenced 9 mm automatic pistol, on the floor was a small suitcase containing her travelling clothes, her code book which was hidden inside a bible and a small lightweight wireless transceiver of a new type, which was to replace the old set that her Resistance Group had been using.

"You need to sign for this, Mary," said Beth as she held up a small vial in which was a small white pill, this was known as the L-pill which was cyanide and the theory was that if you were captured and were being tortured then before you gave up any information that might lead to the other members of your Group being arrested, you could take the L-pill and cease your suffering but Mary shook her head negatively.

"No! I...I can't take that." Each Agent was offered the L-pill and a small hidden pocket was sewn into a part of their clothing for easy access.

"I know it sounds a little melodramatic now, my dear, but if they arrest you, it...well, it won't be pleasant, and this could give you a way out."

Committing suicide was a mortal sin and Mary couldn't conceivably see a situation that would make her commit that sin and so she shook her head again.

"No, I...I can't, sorry, Beth."

"That's alright my dear, it is strictly your choice," and Beth tucked the Pill into her pocket.

"Thank you." Beth then ran through each of her documents and then helped her don her parachute harness and finally it was done, she had sweaty palms and a rapid heart rate, then she was looking up as she heard a clink of glasses as Beth poured out two measures of cognac passing one to her.

"To a safe journey, my dear."

"Thank you, Beth." Mary downed the cognac and coughed as the fiery liquid burned her throat, then as she passed the glass back, she was a little surprised as Beth stepped forward and hugged her warmly.

"I look forward to hearing from you tomorrow night, good luck, Mary."

Mary returned her hug then followed her outside to a waiting van, Beth helped her into the back and passed in her suitcase and a minute later, Alice climbed in awkwardly and gave her a small smile as she was visibly nervous as well, and then the doors banged shut and they were given a final wave as the van moved off.

It was only a short run down a perimeter track to where a twin-engine Wellington bomber stood waiting with its engines running. They pulled up alongside the aircrafts tail and they clambered out of the van and walked through the turbulence from the propellers to a small door in the fuselage where helping hands helped to pull them up a small ladder into the dimly lit fuselage, then they walked uphill to a couple of seats in the aircrafts side. As they sat down the door banged shut and the aircraft started to move. It jolted down the track groaning and bumping before turning right and then as they straightened up out of the turn the engines started roaring and they began moving down the runway gathering speed. One of the aircrafts crew was sitting next to them and he gave them a broad grin and a thumbs up sign and Mary's stomach dropped a little as they took off.

Alice gestured to the airman and as he leaned over, she spoke into his ear, she had to shout to be heard and the airman turned and fetched a small metal pail which Alice gripped firmly as she was feeling very sick. Mary thought that it was probably more nerves than airsickness but a few moments later felt her own stomach turn a little queasy as Alice started throwing up into the pail.

It wasn't a very nice flight as it was cold, noisy and bumpy and she tried to make herself comfortable on the small seat which wasn't easy wearing the parachute with the reserve chute pressing into her chest but mercifully Alice had only thrown up a couple of times. Then two hours into the flight the airman came over with a steaming mug of tea for them which Mary gratefully accepted for it was hot and sweat and helped her to relax a little. She looked over at Alice and the girl gave her a feeble smile and a thumbs up as she also drank the tea.

Not being able to see where they were going was the hard part and she kept going over everything in her mind, who she would be meeting once she landed and what she had to say, she reached down and touched the reassuring bulk of the Automatic in her pocket, she hoped that she would never have to use the thing but the bulk in her pocket was somehow reassuring.

Then suddenly there was a little red light blinking and the airman went over to Alice and helped her to stand and move to a circular hatch in the centre of the fuselage where he removed a large circular plate from the hole in the floor that they would be dropping through. As she stood up Alice held out her hand and Mary shook it and mouthed the words 'Good Luck' and Alice gave a broad smile as she staggered down the fuselage to the hatch and awkwardly sat down on the floor while the Airman attached her static line to a hardpoint, then he said something into his facemask and then held up two fingers to the waiting woman who nodded her understanding.

Two minutes later the little light in the box on the fuselage wall suddenly blinked red a couple of times then went to a steady green.

"GREEN ON—GO!" The airman's shout was clearly audible to them both, but he tapped Alice on the shoulder, she immediately tipped forward as she stiffened and suddenly was gone. The airman pulled in the static line and closed the hatch as the aircraft banked steeply and he gave Mary a cheery thumbs up as he staggered past her to his own position.

It seemed a little funny to Mary but with Alice gone, it seemed a little bit colder in the aircraft as she sat there feeling nervous; she went through everything in her head again, she just hoped that everything went well with her drop.

The next hour seemed to fly past incredibly fast and after a short left-hand turn, the airman staggered down the fuselage and opened the hatchway again. Mary's heart started racing as there was no turning back now. Then the airman was gesturing to her to come forward, she stood up, clutching the small suitcase to her chest she staggered unsteadily down the fuselage, the Airman smiled at her as he helped her sit down at the hatch with her legs dangling into the hatch as the little red light started blinking.

"EQUIPMENT CHECK!" The Airman shouted into her ear and then he started tugging on her harness, checking the parachute and the line that attached her suitcase to her harness, once the parachute deployed, she would lower the case down on this line to get it out of her way for the landing.

"HOOK UP!" Mary attached her static line to the hardpoint and gave it a couple of sharp tugs before she gave the airman a thumbs up.

"Good luck Miss!" he shouted to her and then said something into his facemask and then the little red light stopped flashing and remained steady red.

"STAND BY!" Mary's mouth suddenly went bone dry.

"God please let my chute open cleanly!" she said to herself and then the light went from red to a steady green!

"GREEN ON—GO!" shouted the airman as he slapped her on the shoulder, without thinking Mary stiffened as she shoved herself forward through the hatch and out into the night.

Chapter Eight
Posey, France 1943

Pierre climbed the rather dingy stairs to an apartment on the second floor of the building in a rather seedy part of the Town, he made sure his Automatic was easily accessible in his pocket as he knocked on a door. He knew the occupant of the flat was home as he had been watching the place for a couple of hours and he had just seen the man come home carrying some bread and a bottle of milk. He stiffened slightly as he heard the door being unlocked and then as it started to open, he kicked the door open which sent the man flying backwards and as he fell to the floor Pierre entered the room closed the door and pulled out his Automatic in one swift move.

The man on the floor scrambled to his feet and made to run towards an open window a few feet away but Pierre kicked him in the stomach which rolled him doubled over to the floor gasping for breath.

"Morning Martin!" Pierre quickly locked the door and then started screwing a silencer onto his automatic pistol while he looked at Martin Radford, a very thin scrawny man who was wearing the uniform of a local gendarme, the man had been recruited at the beginning of war and he was a known collaborator, he was also a bad gambler and a drunkard but Pierre had used him to gain information on a number of occasions as the man thought that he was just a petty crook and had made a lot of money from Pierre so the acquaintance had mutual benefits, but this was a dangerous game as the man could easily denounce him to the Germans at any time.

"Pierre, why the rough stuff, I thought we were friends?" Radford hastily stood up eying the pistol that now pointed directly at him.

"I don't have time for pleasantries, Martin, I need information and you are going to give it to me."

"I…I've always helped, Pierre, there's no need to get rough you know that" said Radford as he smiled ingratiatingly at Pierre, he was wondering what was wrong as he had always cooperated with Pierre, after all it was a good way to make some extra money on the side, but he had never seen the man with a pistol before and that had him worried.

"Do you want a drink, Pierre, I was just going to make some coffee, or we could have something stronger if you'd like?" and Radford started edging his way towards a small kitchen off to the side of the room.

"Sit down, Martin!"

"Alright," Radford moved to a chair not far from the window and sat down, wondering what the chances were of making it out of the window before Pierre could get a round off and then that hope was dashed as Pierre moved so that he was standing between him and the window.

"I don't have a lot of time, Martin; all l want is some information and then I'll go, alright?"

"Well, there was no need for the rough stuff, I've always helped you, out, haven't I?"

"Yes—for a fee!"

"Well, there is no harm in making a little cash on the side is there? Times are hard for everyone."

"As I said I don't have time for pleasantries. Now were you on duty last night?"

"Yes, we all were."

"And were you involved in an arrest in a small field outside of Posey?"

"How on earth—?" Martin stopped talking a little surprised that Pierre knew anything about an arrest concerning members of a Resistance Cell, surely if he knew anything about that meant that he was involved somehow and that meant that he was more than just the petty crook that he had always thought he was, and then his heart started racing as he thought that he would be able to make a tidy sum if he could somehow turn the man in.

"Are—are you with the Resistance, Pierre?" he asked quietly for even just talking about such things was dangerous and he didn't want them to be overheard.

"And what if I am; thinking about making a tidy sum by turning me in, Martin?"

"I…I would never do that!"

"The hell you wouldn't! but as I said I don't have a lot of time so what do you know about the operation in the field?"

"As I said I was on duty when the Germans mounted a full-scale operation at about eleven o'clock, Major Schrandt was in command, and he had everyone running about all night."

"And this Major, is he still at the police station?"

"Yes, he is stationed there with a small group of—" Martin suddenly stopped talking as he realised that he had said too much already.

"A group of what?"

"Nothing—I can't tell you anything else, Pierre, that is police business, and I shouldn't have said anything at all."

"You'd better tell me everything, Martin, or this pistol might just go off!" and Pierre waved the pistol at him to emphasis his words.

"You—you can't be serious Pierre, I'm a policeman and—"

"You're a collaborating little shit and I should shoot you for just working with Germans, Martin, so start talking—or else!"

"I can't tell you anything…I—"

PHLAAT! The pistol in Pierre's hand fired almost noiselessly and a 9 mm round was ejected across the floor and a lamp on the side table shattered, making Martin jump.

"The next round goes through your knee then the next in your head, now start talking!"

"Wh—what do you want to know?"

"You said this Major is stationed at the Police station and that he organised a full-scale operation the other night?"

"Yes, he has a small group of soldiers with him at the station, he arrived a couple of months ago and has been hunting members of the Resistance, he has caught a couple who he uhm Interrogated and then arrested the people that they denounced. Two nights ago, he mounted a full-scale operation after getting some information from the Paris office. The Major was annoyed because the group that were supposed to be meeting an aircraft in that field managed to get away and they only caught one suspect, apparently some idiot Corporal opened fire too soon and the aircraft was able to get away."

"And the person they caught?"

"A woman, they have been interrogating her."

"They were interrogating her at the police station?"

"Yes, I heard her screaming a couple of times but—" Martin stopped talking afraid that Pierre might shoot when he found out that this woman was no longer at the station.

"But what? Come on Martin!"

"I…I was just finishing my shift today when one of the Germans came running out of the cells, he was covered in blood from where this woman had apparently broken his nose. God knows how she managed it, but she escaped from the cells and because everyone was out during an air raid she managed to get out of the station as well, they've mounted a full-scale search for her, the only reason I'm not there is because they need people for the night shift."

Pierre felt his hope rising as he listened to Martin's story, if what he said was right then Mary had somehow managed to escape and was now on the run.

"How long ago was this and are you sure that it was the woman from the other night?"

"I'm sure Pierre. I finished my shift a couple of hours ago and it had to be her as she is the only person that we are holding in the cells now."

"And you are sure the Germans are looking for her now?"

"I'll say. The whole place went crazy after she escaped. I wasn't involved because—"

PHLAAT! PHLAAT! The pistol in Pierre's hand jumped twice and Martin stopped talking with a surprised look on his face as the two rounds took him squarely in the heart, a large red patch opened on the front of his shirt and his mouth opened and closed a couple of times before he slumped forward in the chair dead!

"That was too quick, you traitorous bastard!" Pierre unscrewed the silencer and tucked the pistol into his pocket then went to the man's wardrobe and took one of his uniforms before he hurried out of the flat, he had to warn the others to start searching for Mary, but he had no idea where to start.

****

Mary jumped startled as something was snuffling near her head on the other side of the piece of canvas that covered her body, she groaned as pain wracked through her stiff body as she moved and the dog that had been snuffling around her ran off into the night barking.

Carefully, Mary pulled back the canvas and investigated the darkness of the night, she had no idea of what the time was but guessed that it was late as it was pitch black and very damp. She had heard pounding footsteps and shouting voices a couple of times during the day, she had pulled her legs in tighter under the canvas but despite being terrified at possibly being discovered she had fallen into an exhausted sleep until the snuffling of the dog had startled her awake and now, she felt incredibly stiff and very dry.

Slowly, she pulled back the canvas and sat up looking around tentatively, but she couldn't see or hear anything, so she stood up and groaned as her muscles protested after her having been curled up tense all day. She knew roughly where she was and thought that her best bet would be to go to Pierre's Garage, but she had to be careful as the normal patrols would be out and she could guarantee that others would also be searching for her. She made her way to the wooden gates and after listening intently for a couple of minutes she squeezed her way through the gap and made her way slowly down the laneway and out into the night.

For four long hours, she made her way through the outskirts of the large town hiding in alleyways and keeping to the shadows as much as she could and straining her ears to hear the first signs of anyone approaching her. Then with dawn rapidly approaching as she rounded a corner, she gave a heavy sigh of relief as Pierre's garage came into view.

Out the front of the building was a pair of large wooden doors and in front of this and just off to the side was a junk pile where Pierre kept odds and ends that 'might come in useful' as he often said which it did now for her as she was able to move aside a large sheet of tin and moved it to the doors and propped it up so that there was just enough room for her to be able to lay down with her back against the door with the tin over her, now all she had to do was wait for Pierre and hope to God that no-one had noticed her.

It must have been a couple of hours later that Mary stiffened as she heard an approaching engine, she couldn't see the vehicle, so she stiffened under her piece of tin and prayed that it would indeed cover her from prying eyes. The vehicle pulled up near the doors and a couple of seconds later the engine was shut off and the driver got out walked up to the large doors and the lock rattled as he used the key.

"Pierre!" she croaked quietly but he hadn't heard her over the noise of his rattling the padlock.

"Pierre!" she whispered more urgently and at first Pierre thought that he was hearing things but then as he removed the old-fashioned large padlock from the door, he heard the whisper again, he looked around then couldn't believe his eyes as he saw Mary's hand under a sheet of tin by the door. Quickly, he opened the left-hand door then moved to the right-hand side one.

"Can you move, Mary?" he whispered as he looked around making sure no-one was approaching the garage.

"Yes," she croaked.

"When I open this door, go straight to my office fast as you can, no-one watching will be able to see you as the door will cover you, alright?"

"Yes."

Pierre opened the door fully making sure that he bent over longer than he normally would with the bottom bolt, hoping to block Mary from view, he saw the sheet of tin move and then a blur as she hurried into the garage and over to the office. Slowly, he moved into the garage and over to the office and as he entered, Mary flung her still manacle hands over his head so that she could hug him tightly as she started to cry out of sheer utter relief.

"Oh God Pierre, I never thought I would see you again," she sobbed onto his shoulder as he held her.

"It's alright girl, you're safe now." It took Mary a couple of minutes to get herself back under control.

"I…I need to sit down," she said as she brought her hands down from around his neck and he helped her to sit in the offices only chair.

"My God, girl! You're a mess," he said as he saw her properly for the first time. Here hair was lank and plastered unruly to her face, her eyes were black with fatigue, and one was closed from heavy dark bruising on the left side of her face, her clothes were filthy and then he saw the blood encrusted on her left hand.

"My God, Mary, what did those bastards do to you?" He went to touch her hand, but Mary pulled it back out of fear that his touch would hurt her, and she shook her head.

"That bastard! He ripped my fingernails out, Pierre, and tried to drown me but—but I swear I didn't tell them anything!" She shook her head violently as tears ran down her face, but she pulled back as he made to comfort her.

"Later, for now I need some water and you need to hide me—please!" she tried to force a smile as she said this, and his heart went out to her, it was obvious that the girl had been tortured and yet she was still trying to put up a brave face.

"Yes, you're right, I'll get some water and a hacksaw, and we'll get those manacles off." He hurried out of the office and a few minutes later he returned with a mug of water and as she greedily drank that down, he got a hacksaw from his tool bag and set about getting the manacles off which proved harder than he thought.

"We'll get you to the farm. I'll get the van alright?"

"Yes, thank you." Pierre hurried out and a few minutes later he had backed the van into the garage, and he opened the rear door and moved things about in the back, making a place to hide her.

"I'll cover you with some of the spare parts, Mary, in case we are stopped by any roadblocks and if we are, I will bang on the side of the van as a warning, alright?"

"Yes, thank you Pierre and it is so good to see you again," he helped Mary to climb into the back of the van and then she curled up in the small space that he had made, then he covered her in a short piece of canvas and moved some of the parts to cover her.

"Alright Mary?" he asked quietly.

"Yes." Pierre moved the van outside and then closed the two wooden doors and fastened the padlock and then they set off towards Danny's pig farm. Twenty minutes after they set off as he had expected he was being flagged down by a soldier at a roadblock and he banged on the side of the van as a warning.

"Roadblock, Mary, be ready!" Then he changed gears and brought the van to a stop.

"Papers!" ordered the soldier peering in the window at him holding out his hand. Pierre pulled his papers from his pocket and handed them over.

"What are you doing here?" asked the soldier as he handed the papers back.

"Pig farmer up the road needs some spare parts for one of his machines, I'm a mechanic."

"Open up!"

"Oh, come on, I'm only carrying spare parts, for goodness sakes!"

"Open up—Now!"

"Alright—alright." Leaving the engine running, Pierre moved to the rear of the van.

"It's bad enough that I have to spend all day on a flaming Pig farm, do you really have to delay me like this?" grumbled Pierre as they moved to the rear of the van.

"The quicker you open up, the quicker you can go!" Pierre just shook his head as he opened the rear door of the van and held his breath as the soldier peered into the interior.

"Spare parts alright." The soldier moved a couple of items around but didn't get near to Mary's hiding place.

"Alright, you can go." Pierre closed the door and walked slowly back to the cab still grumbling about being delayed, he closed the door and then moved off slowly. He watched the soldiers in the wing mirror and when he was sure that they were far enough away from them, he banged on the side of the van again.

"All clear, Mary!"

Huddled up under the piece of canvas and spare parts, Mary slowly exhaled, she had been breathing very slowly so as not to be heard, she had hunkered down as best she could at Pierre's warning and had been laying almost rigid afraid of betraying here position with the slightest movement that may have been seen by the searching soldier at the roadblock. She had been petrified at the possibility of being discovered and had cringed as the soldier had moved some of the parts in the van.

If he had discovered her, she didn't know what she would have done, all she did know was that she couldn't go back to that interrogation room with its horrid chair and bathtub and she had started trembling badly just as Pierre had closed the van door and was still trembling and had started sobbing as they left the roadblock. Ten minutes later as they pulled up outside the farm, Danny came out of the farmhouse frowning.

"What's up, Pierre, you didn't call ahead, I wasn't expecting you so soon?" asked the old man with a worried look on his face.

Pierre had a quick look around in case they had been followed but being sure that they hadn't, he quickly moved to the rear of the van.

"Mary escaped from those bastards, Danny; I've got her in the back!"

"What—Oh my God!" Pierre opened the van and quickly moved the gear aside, he could see the distress on her face as she sat up, she was crying from each move.

"My God Mary, come on, girl, let me help you." Danny helped her out of the van and as she straightened up, all her resolve crumpled and she burst into tears flung her hands over his head and cried bitterly onto his shoulder as the emotions came flooding out of her, she had been on her own and hadn't known for how long her resolve would last, now feeling safe with the old man and Pierre, the sudden release was too much, with a loud groan she went limp as she passed out.

"Bloody Hell!" As Mary passed out, Danny scooped her up and carried her into the farmhouse.

"Oh, my goodness! Quickly put her on the bed, Danny." Danny's wife Margite had been shocked to see Danny carrying Mary into the room, she quickly gathered herself as she hurried into the bedroom ahead of Danny, she pulled back the bedcovers as Danny gently laid the girl down.

"Pierre, this girl needs a doctor!" said Margite as she saw the state that Mary was in.

"We can't risk a Doctor, Margite, he would ask too many questions."

"Then call Mark!" snapped Margite as she moved to Mary's side.

"Mark! But he's a dentist!"

"He's had medical training and will be able to help, make sure he brings some medication with him, now get out so I can tend to her!" Margite then ushered them out of the room and closed the door. In the other room as Pierre picked up the telephone receiver to call Mark, Danny moved to the stove.

"I'll make some coffee and soup, Pierre, I'm sure she will need it.".

Two hours later, Mark Deniau came out of the farm's bedroom, wiping his hands on a cloth.

"I've given her a sedative, so she can sleep, she really needs a proper doctor, Pierre!"

"I know but we can't risk it, if he isn't one of us or someone that we can trust then it's just too risky, you know that."

"I know but I wanted you to know what she really needs."

"I know that Mark, how is she anyway?" Mark sat down at the kitchen table and nodded his thanks as Danny passed him a cup of coffee.

"I can only try to guess at what they actually did to Mary but from the wounds that I dressed; I can tell it was severe. All the fingernails on her left hand have been ripped out and I would say that something had been shoved under them first as there were puncture wounds on each finger, I think that she must have been strapped down or restrained somehow as there was severe and very deep bruising on her wrists and ankles."

"Bloody Hell!" Danny was gripping his cup very hard, he knew the Germans used torture in their interrogations, but this was the first time that he had seen the results up close and he would very much like to get a hold of the bastard that had done this to that young girl.

"That's not all, she has deep and bloody welts on her back where she has been beaten from head to foot, most of her body is black with bruising and there are a few nasty lacerations that I have treated, the risk now is infection, but Margite will look after that. What Mary needs now is sleep and time to recuperate from her ordeal, that's the best I can do, Pierre."

"You've done well, Mark, now how long before we can move Mary?"

"Move her! I just said that she needs rest."

"Listen Mark, Mary escaped from those bastards, God knows how she managed that, but she did so; it's only a matter of time before they start searching outside the town, so we have to move her as soon as we can!"

"Hell, I hadn't thought of that." Mark took a sip of his coffee before continuing. "Mary will need at least forty-eight hours to give those wounds a chance to heal and stave off the risk of infection, it'll also give her time to get a little rest as the girl is mentally exhausted."

"Thank you, Mark, and I do appreciate what you have been able to do for Mary."

"If you don't need me anymore, I'd better get going, I'll come back tomorrow afternoon and check her wounds." Mark nodded to Danny then hurried out to his vehicle and left the farm.

"Danny, get your ciphers ready; I'll write out a signal for you to send to London, they need to know what has happened."

"You think it wise to transmit so soon after Mary's escape, Pierre? They're bound to have the detector vans out?"

"Probably not but it has to be done."

"Alright but keep it short as possible, will you, don't forget I'm a hell of a lot slower at this than Mary!"

"Alright, old friend." Pierre couldn't help smiling at the old man as he sat down and started jotting down what he wanted to send to London.

Later that evening, Pierre returned to the farm and Danny gave him a brief signal from London that he had decoded a couple of hours earlier.

"Doesn't make sense to me, Pierre!"

"What is Lilly's condition, and does she have the information?" Pierre read the signal out loud and then frowned.

"Who the Hell is Lilly?" asked Danny.

"That would be me." Pierre turned and looked at Mary as she moved painfully from the bedroom door towards the kitchen table.

"You should be resting, Mary, you shouldn't—" Margite stopped talking as Mary held up her hand and smiled at the old lady.

"I'm alright, Margite, honestly!"

"I'll get you some soup." Mary nodded as Margite went over to the stove to get the soup ready.

"Lilly is my code name, Danny, which is only to be used for important reasons and I thought until the other day that I was the only one who knew it but—but HE knew, Pierre!"

"He—whom do you mean, Mary?"

"HIM—that bastard Major Schrandt, he's the one who ordered…" Mary paused as she took a deep breath being on the verge of tears as she thought about what the Major had ordered Kurt and Conrad to do to her, she fought hard to get herself back under control.

"It's alright Mary, he can't hurt you here—you're safe with us." As Pierre stepped forward to put a comforting hand out to her, she seemed to cringe a little as she took a step backward.

"Here Mary, come and have some soup," Margite spoke to break the sudden tension in the room, she had seen the fear flicker across the girl's face as Pierre stepped towards her and her heart went out to her, she could only imagine what those horrid men had done to this girl. She knew that they all risked interrogation if captured as members of the Resistance but until now, she had never actually seen the results of it, she knew that Mary would be scarred for life not so much physically for those wounds would heal but mentally, as she had just seen that for herself.

Mary sat down slowly at the table, her entire body ached, and she felt incredibly tired and not only from the effects of the sedative that Mark had given her, but she felt emotionally exhausted, and she hadn't meant to flinch from Pierre, but she couldn't help it, she picked up a spoon and tasted the soup.

"So, Mary, this Lilly?" asked Pierre, he had seen the flicker of fear in Mary's eyes as he had approached her and he didn't really know how to handle it, he wanted her to know that she was safe now that she was back with them but he didn't know how to get that across to her.

"Lilly is my code name and was given to me before I was inserted into France, it would only be used by London." Mary said this between mouthfuls of the excellent soup, and she found that now she had started eating, she was ravenously hungry.

"So, the landing in the field the other night wasn't just a routine drop then?" asked Pierre and she nodded.

"I couldn't tell you before, Pierre, as I was under orders."

"It's alright Mary, I understand, and I don't blame you as London does things their own way, we know that."

"Well, I have to tell you now, Pierre, in case—well in case something happens to me."

"And what about London, surely, you're still under those orders?" he asked, and she shook her head.

"No, London doesn't know the full story of what happened at the landing and neither do you but before I can tell you, I have to be extremely rude and ask Danny and Margite to leave the room, I'm sorry," and Mary looked a little sheepish as she said this.

"Alright, Danny, would you leave us for a while?" As Danny and Margite stood up, Mary held up her hand.

"Please don't think that I don't trust you because I do—I trust you both with my life! But if you don't know what I am about to say then that bastard can't make you talk, alright?" Margite patted her on the shoulder as she stood up.

"It's alright, my dear, we do understand—really!" She gave Mary a warm smile before they left the room.

"I hope I haven't offended them, Pierre, as they have both been very good to me?"

"No, they both know how this works, Mary."

"I really did want to tell you, Pierre, but London forbade me to do so and they probably won't be happy with my telling you now but the situation has changed drastically and London doesn't know and they won't be happy when I send my next message."

"Now I am curious." Pierre moved his chair a little closer and waited.

"I don't know the full details yet as I have only been given a partial briefing. Apparently, a few months ago a Dutch scientist who has been working for the Germans somehow contacted the Resistance as he wants to defect. This man has been working on some sort of new terror weapon, I don't know much about what that concerns, all I do know is that London has been bending over backwards to get this man out of the country."

"So, where do you come into all of this, Mary?"

"This scientist has been moved quite a few times to keep him out of the way of the Gestapo and will be passed onto us. You remember the Courier that landed with the Lysander the other night?"

"I know someone had just met you from the Lysander when all Hell broke loose, and we lost you in the firefight."

"What you don't know is that he gave me a small tin in which were all the details of how we are to get this scientist out."

"My God! The Boche didn't find it when they caught you?"

"The Germans didn't catch me, Pierre, the bloody gendarmes did!"

"And did they confiscate that tin?"

"No, luckily I saw the vehicle coming into the lane and I was able to throw my Sten and the tin into the drainage ditch."

"The drainage ditches?"

"Yes, I couldn't be taken with it, so I thought best to throw it into the ditch and if…if I hadn't after what happened then it would have been found."

"Hell, if it's in the drainage ditch then we'll never find it, you'll have to tell London to use another group for this scientist fellow."

"I…I think I can find it again, Pierre, but do you think we can risk going back to that field for a while, I'm sure that bloody Major will be looking for me still, but we need to retrieve that tin!"

Pierre thought hard for a moment, he didn't like the way those idiots in London had done things behind his back and he knew that Mary had felt awkward having to tell him, but if those idiots had told him in the first place, then he would have arranged things differently and maybe Mary would not have been caught and she wouldn't have suffered the way she had.

"I don't think they will be watching the field, Mary, I think with you having escaped, the Major will be thinking that you would be getting out of the country as fast as you can with the rest of your Resistance Cell, but are you sure that you can find this thing if we do go back? After all, it was very dark that night and with all the shooting that went on…well, it might be hard to find?"

Mary nodded and bit her lip as she thought back about that night, she knew she would be able to find that drainage ditch, she would never forget it because of the soldier that she had to shoot as she could clearly see the look on his face as she fired her Sten.

"I know exactly where it is because…because I had to shoot a soldier, Pierre, he…he took me by surprise, and I had to shoot!" Mary wiped a tear from her eyes as she spoke.

"Mary, they are the enemy!"

"I…I know but I will have to live with that, Pierre."

"Well, just remember what the bastards have just done to you, Mary, they wouldn't hesitate in killing you!"

"I know," she tried to force a smile as she said this.

"Mary, can I ask you something while we are alone?"

"Of course."

"Your escape—I was wondering, well…?"

"It was sheer luck, Pierre. Major Schrandt was trying to get information out of me before the Gestapo turned up from Paris."

"The Gestapo! are you sure?"

"Yes, I heard the Major talking to Kurt, he kept saying he didn't have much time and that he wanted to get the information out of me before they arrived. In a way, I'm grateful that the Major was handling things, Pierre."

"What on earth makes you say that after the way he treated you?"

"I know that I would have had no chance at all to get away from the Gestapo, Pierre; if they had taken me then I wouldn't have survived."

"Yes, I can understand that." They had all heard of how the Gestapo treated their 'guests' at Avenue Foche in Paris but there were very few survivors able to tell the tale.

"It was because the Major was in such a hurry that I was able to get away. He had most of the Gendarmes and his own men out looking for the rest of you, he knew there were four of you plus me on that airfield and it was just a stroke of luck that I was able to overpower the man Kurt during an air raid. Believe me, I was stunned when I was able to do it, I…I think it was sheer desperation that enabled me to do it." Quickly, Mary described how feigning an illness, she was able to break Kurt's nose with the manacles on her wrists and knock him out then lock the cell.

"I could have cried with sheer relief when I was able to just walk out of the police station, from what I could hear the majority of the gendarmes had been called out for the air raid."

"Well, I think that it was a miracle that you got away, Mary, but I am so glad that you did."

Mary nodded but was reliving her escape in her mind, she knew that she had been damned lucky to have been able to escape but everything had just seemed to fall into place at the right time, but she had heard the guards talking about the imminent arrival of the Gestapo officers from Paris. She had been terrified at the prospect of being handed over to them, she knew that she wouldn't have survived under their torture methods and God alone knew how many people she may have denounced and this was the one time that she wished she had taken Beth's L-pill which would have been sewn into one corner of her blouse, she knew that she would rather have committed suicide than give up the names of her friends.

"There is more, Pierre, the Major, he…he knew who I am!"

"What? That you are with the Resistance?" Pierre asked, and she shook her head.

"No Pierre, he knew my code name and what I did in England before I joined SOE!"

"My god! How the Hell does he know that?"

"I don't know but I do know that no-one could have betrayed us here because no-one here knows those details, not even you, Pierre."

"Christ! I think you had better contact London and let them know what has happened and see how they want us to proceed."

"Yes, I suppose so. Would you mind asking Danny and Margite to join us while I make out the cypher?"

"Alright but keep it as brief as you can you, I know the Detector vans are operating in this area."

"I will."

A couple of minutes later, Danny and Margite re-joined them and as the old lady went about making some fresh coffee, Mary made out her cypher for Beth in London and she knew she wouldn't be happy with it.

Chapter Nine
Mary's Arrival in Posey Mid-1943

CRAAACK! The parachute canopy deployed with its familiar jarring crack and Mary lowered the suitcase down on its strap, there was enough moonlight to make out features on the ground and it looked as though she was heading into a small field between some trees, then her heart gave a jolt as she saw figures moving about, she just hoped that it was the people that were supposed to be meeting her and not enemy soldiers.

She touched the reassuring bulk of the pistol in her pocket and prayed to God that she wouldn't have to use it, then she was preparing for her landing, suddenly the ground came racing up, giving her a resounding smack in the backside as she rolled on landing, then getting to her feet she started reeling in the parachute canopy, then was fumbling in her pocket for the pistol as figures were approaching her from the direction of the trees.

"Cricket!" someone called softly out of the night.

"Green!" she called softly back.

"Mary?"

"Yes," she answered with some relief as it was the welcoming party.

"I'm Pierre, welcome to Posey," and she was surprised as the man hugged her.

"Thank you, what now?" she asked as willing hands helped her out of her parachute harness and gathered up the parachute as she pulled in her small case.

"We have a small van, this way." She hurried after the man and climbed into the back of a small van that held machine parts, Pierre closed the doors behind her then they were bumping down a badly rutted road, she thought that this man must be fairly certain that they wouldn't run into any road blocks or patrols as they hadn't tried to hide her in the back of this van in any way, she made herself a little more comfortable making sure that her pistol was readily accessible.

Fifteen minutes later the van came to a halt, as the doors were opened, she saw that they were in the yard of some sort of farm.

"This is our safe house, Mary, run by Danny and his wife Margite, she will take the parachute and I will salvage what I can from the harness and dispose of the rest, alright?"

"Fine yes." Mary found conversing in French refreshing; she also found that although she was a little bruised from her landing, she was also excited about finally being here in France.

Pierre led the way into the farm then as the door was closed a lamp was lit and she found herself being greeted by an old man and his wife who came over and hugged her warmly.

"I'm Margite and this my husband, Danny. You must be very tired after your trip; would you like some coffee, my dear?"

"That would be very nice, Margite, thank you."

"Put your case on the table, the water is almost boiled."

"Thank you"

"Did you bring some spare wireless batteries, Mary? Ours have just about, had it?" asked Pierre as he crossed the room to sit at the table.

"Give the girl a chance, Pierre, after all, she's only just arrived," said Danny as he crossed over to join them and Mary felt herself warming towards the old man.

"That's alright, Danny." Mary put her suitcase onto the table and opened it.

"I've brought you a new set with some spare batteries, do you keep the set here or do I have to hide it myself?"

"Well, if you have a new set, we will keep it here and you can visit when you need to contact London. As far as the Germans are concerned, Danny and Margite are relatives but there is a curfew, so you will have to be careful."

"Fine."

"I'll show you where to hide the set, my dear." Danny led her into another room and showed her the hide that he had prepared behind a wall panel.

"Are there many changes to the set, Mary, I'm the second operator, you see."

"No Danny, it's just a smaller version of the set that you have been using with a longer battery life."

"Good." They tucked the transceiver into the hide with a spare battery then went back into the kitchen where Margite passed her some coffee with some bread and cheese, Mary started eating as she found that she was quite hungry after her trip in.

"You'll sleep here tonight, Mary, then in the morning Danny will drive you into town and if anyone asks, he met you at the train station, he'll take you to the school where they will give you the key to a small cottage which is just up from the school, I'll come by in the afternoon with some supplies before you take up as the new teacher."

"Thank you, Pierre, that will be good, and I need to contact London tonight to let them know I have arrived safely, and I hope I won't be putting you out, Margite?"

"Not at all, my dear, it'll be nice talking to another woman instead of this old goat," and Margite smiled at her husband as she said this, and Danny just raised his eyes.

"I have a small garage in town, and I'll give you the number, Mary, but please remember that all the lines are monitored so be careful, alright?"

"Alright, thank you Pierre." Mary sipped her coffee and thought that her new life in France with these good people was off to a very good start.

Chapter Ten
SOE Training Camp, England 1943

Captain Beth Sims was sitting at her desk at eight P.M. when she looked up as Sergeant Rogers knocked on the door and not waiting for a reply entered the office with a signal on a clipboard.

"Sorry Ma'am but I have a priority level two signal from code name 'LILLY'," the Sergeant crossed to the desk and held out the clipboard.

"Thank you, Sergeant." Beth signed for the signal then as the Sergeant left the office, she went to her safe, a priority level two meant she had to decode this one herself, she retrieved a small signal code book then sitting at her desk she quickly decoded the priority signal from Mary, when she was done she read it through twice before reaching for her telephone handpiece but the telephone rang before she could pick it up; she lifted the receiver.

"Captain Sims," she said.

"Ah Beth, you are still there, could you come to my office for a moment please?" asked Major Scott.

"I was just about to call you sir; we have just received a priority level two signal from Lilly!"

"Bring it with you please." Beth was surprised when the line went dead and wondered what the Major wanted, there was nothing on the training syllabus that needed to be discussed but whatever it was would change once he saw the signal from Mary, she quickly left her office and made her way through the manor house to the Major's office where she knocked on the door.

"Come in!" Beth entered the office and was surprised to see a tall and rather handsome man sitting in an armchair by the window with a glass of brandy in his hand, he was dressed in a civilian pin striped suit but by the short haircut and the way he held himself she took him to be military of some sort.

"Ah Beth, come in and close the door, would you," said Major Scott as she entered the room, she closed the door and crossed the room to the desk where Scott was sitting.

"Beth, this is Lieutenant Colonel Winters of MI5, and we have a major problem," said Scott as he introduced the man.

"Nice to meet you, m'dear" said Colonel Winters as he extended his hand to her.

"Nice to meet you sir" Beth's curiosity was raised as she wondered what MI5 the Secret Service wanted with them here.

"Take a seat, Beth, would you like a brandy?" asked Major Scott.

"Thank you, sir." The Colonel indicated the seat that he had just vacated for her and she sat down wondering what was up.

"You said we had a problem sir?" she asked as the Major handed her a glass of brandy and he nodded.

"Yes, a bloody big one, m'dear, do you recognise this woman?" asked the Colonel as he pulled a small photograph out of his pocket and handed it over. Beth looked at it and was quite surprised as it showed a young woman who had had her throat cut, she had been dumped in a wood and had been partially covered in dirt and leaves.

"No, she doesn't look familiar, sir."

"That is Alice Maxine, she was found murdered a couple of months ago, you would know her as Alice Ferron," said the Colonel as she handed the photo back and Beth looked up in surprise as Alice Ferron was one of the Agents that she had trained and had just sent off to France.

"That's the real Alice, Beth, the one we have been training is a bloody imposter!" said Major Scott a little heatedly and Beth could understand why, as they had just spent six weeks training an imposter, but who the hell was she?

"We believe that your Alice was actually Greta Mayer, an enemy agent, Christ knows how they managed it, but it seems that the Abwehr planted Alice with us and now—"

"My God! Now we have obligingly dropped her into France, she could have denounced dozens of the Resistance People by now!" said Beth, it was incredible that an enemy agent had been able to penetrate SOE, been trained by them then sent on a mission into France—no wonder the Major looked angry.

"No Beth, that hasn't happened," said Major Scott as he refilled their glasses.

"But surely that would be the whole point of infiltrating someone into SOE, to make it easier for them to catch the Resistance?"

"Normally yes, but thanks to a rather talkative diplomat at the Spanish Embassy, we know that Greta Mayer was able to take the place of Alice Ferron so that she could come here for training. Now we have arrested the Major whose inept security checks allowed this to happen." The Colonel paused while he took a sip of this rather good brandy.

"We also know that while she was here, Alice was able to photograph the dossiers of three of your agents, a Mary, Joan and one other who recently washed out…?"

"That would be Margaret Brennon, sir; she opted out after breaking her leg in training. Oh, my goodness! I'm sorry Colonel, but with all this I forgot about the signal that we have just received from Mary." Beth held out the signal, the Colonel took it and quickly read it.

"So, the SS knew Mary's code name and her details of before she joined SOE, seems like Alice didn't waste any time when she arrived in France."

"I bet that was the reason that Mary was ambushed and arrested sir."

"This Mary seems to be a remarkable woman; after all, it isn't everyone that manages to escape from the SS." Beth looked up as the Colonel said this, wondering how on earth he knew about Mary; after all, they had only recently found out this themselves.

"Mary is proving to be one of the best, Sir." Major Scott hadn't been at all surprised about the Colonel knowing about Mary as it seemed that MI5 knew everything about everyone all the time.

"She'll need to be if we are to stand any chance of catching Alice."

"Catching her! Surely, we would be risking too many lives to try to attempt that, sir, I'd like permission to send a shoot on sight Emergency signal to all our operatives in France." Major Scott put his glass down as he said this as his first concern was for the safety of his operatives of which there were over a hundred on his list in France alone.

"Denied! Believe me, Major, I would like nothing better than to shoot the lady myself before she can do any real damage, but we believe that she is after bigger fry than just the Resistance."

"Bigger fry? I'm afraid I don't follow, sir." Beth just wanted to warn their Agents before any of them were arrested.

"Do you know what information that Courier was taking to code name 'LILLY'?" he asked but Beth shook her head.

"No sir it was a 'FOR YOUR EYES ONLY' detail and Mary was the recipient."

"Major, would you elaborate please?"

"Beth, a couple of weeks ago a Dutch scientist by the name of Linus Kruen was working albeit reluctantly for the Germans on a new terror weapon, apparently they had threatened to intern his family in a concentration camp if he didn't co-operate, anyway a short while ago his wife, mother and father were all killed in a freak accident and after the funeral this professor was somehow able to contact the Resistance."

"An inexperienced cleaner was trying to steal some blueprints from the research facility when the Professor caught him and instead of handing him over to the Gestapo, he asked the lad for help," said the Colonel and Scott nodded.

"Anyway, for the past couple of weeks the Professor has been passed through one Resistance Cell after another all across France, Mary's group was to be the last contact before he was extracted from the continent by submarine," said Scott and Beth nodded her understanding.

"They still will be. We are going to get Alice to go to Mary's assistance, we are hoping to kill two birds with one stone as it were, we get the professor, a traitor and one of our agents back at the same time."

"You can't be serious sir? Mary has already been arrested, she was tortured by those bastards and now you want to try to catch this traitor who has already killed one woman and goodness knows how many others!" Beth was stunned at the mere thought of it, surely Mary had already been through enough but to do this meant risking further capture and goodness knows what else.

"I know it isn't pleasant, Beth, but this is our best chance of neutralising this traitor. If we issue a shoot on sight signal, she is bound to get wind of it, then she will not only disappear, but she will also denounce all the members of the Resistance that she has met over the past few months," said the Major and Beth shook her head again.

"I don't like it, sir, I think you are asking too much of a young girl who has only recently been tortured, if they catch her again, they will show no mercy!"

"I know it is unpleasant, m'dear, but it will be done. Now I must get back to London, so I will leave it with you, Major," said the Colonel as he stood up and put his coat on.

"I'll show you out, sir."

"It was nice meeting you, Beth." Beth stood to attention as the Colonel left the office with Scott, she sat down again and took a big swig of her brandy as she felt quite disgusted with the colonel's plan but knew she would have to follow orders then she stood up again as the Major came back into the office.

"Sit down, Beth, have another Brandy, I know I can bloody well use one." Beth shook her head as the Major went to refill her glass.

"I know we have done some nasty things in this business, Sandy, but this one really stinks!" she said as he refilled his glass.

"I know but this one is really important, Beth. I shouldn't be doing this but I need to show you something, please sit down?" As Beth sat back down in the armchair the Major took a key out of his pocket and crossed over to a small wall safe which he unlocked and removing a large folder he relocked the safe then crossed over to where she was sitting.

"What I'm about to show you is top secret and doesn't leave this room and you can't discuss it with anyone but me alright?" he said as he handed her a red coloured file.

"Of course, sir."

"That file will give you a briefing on the weapon that the Professor has been working on and it will give you an idea of this man's importance otherwise I wouldn't be doing this." As Beth nodded and opened the file the Major sat down in the other armchair opposite her and sipped his brandy, strictly speaking he was breaking regulations by showing her the file but he needed her help and understanding and reading that file would show her the importance of the man that they needed to extract from France and why they needed to put Mary to work again.

For ten minutes, he sat in silence as Beth read the brief summary on Professor Kruen and the V1 flying bomb that was to be launched against England, as she read it Beth's eyes widened as she saw the impact that this weapon would have as it was faster than their Interceptor Fighter aircraft and it would be dropping indiscriminately when its fuel ran out; no wonder that it had been labelled a terror weapon.

"This Professor has information that will let us defeat this weapon, Sandy?" she asked as she closed the file, and the Major shook his head.

"The Professor has some blueprints and a roll of film, but these things will be impossible to defeat until we invade the continent."

"You're not serious surely?" It seemed impossible to her that they wouldn't be able to defeat a weapon that would drop nearly a thousand kilograms of explosives onto unsuspecting civilians. The Major took the file and locked it away in his safe before returning to his seat.

"At the moment these things are faster than any aircraft that we have but the information that this Professor has will enable us to defeat these things at their launch sites but it's all above my pay grade I'm afraid, so I would be guessing the rest."

"What about Mary?" she asked.

"I understand why the Colonel wants to try to capture Alice. While she is trying to get her hands on the Professor, most of our Agents that she has met aren't in danger, but I intend to forewarn Mary so that she knows exactly what she is up against." Beth looked surprised as he said that as it meant that he would be going against orders, and he would definitely be getting himself into deep trouble.

"Sandy, I think that MI5 are monitoring our radio traffic. If you try to warn Mary, then I think the Colonel—"

"He won't be happy, I know. I am also certain that MI5 monitors our radio traffic, but they don't have access to our emergency codes, so I intend sending Mary a detailed cypher warning her about Alice but if she can capture her all well and good, but I will tell her to eliminate her if she can't!"

"I think you are taking one hell of a risk with the Colonel, Sandy, but for what it's worth, I will support you all I can."

"Thank you, Beth, that means a lot," said the Major sincerely. They had worked together for some time now and had a few disagreements in that time, but he respected her work, and it meant a lot to him when she had said that.

"Let me know when you have the Cypher for Mary ready and I will send it myself sir," she said as she stood up.

"Thank you, Beth."

"Sir." Beth came to attention then left the office.

Major Scott poured himself another brandy and pulled a pad towards him, they were his agents, and he was damned if he would risk one of their lives needlessly. He took up a pencil and started drafting a detailed cypher for Mary.

Chapter Eleven
Posey, France 1943

Professor Linus Kruen was a small man at just on five feet tall, he had a slight build with a round face, squinty eyes that blinked rapidly every time he removed his round wire-rimmed spectacles and what little hair he had remaining, almost pure white, at that moment was covered in sweat for it was nearing midnight and the vehicle that he was hiding in had just been stopped at a roadblock. The driver had warned him that this may happen telling him that if it did that he should remain still trying not to move so as not to attract any attention, not that he could move even if he had wanted to for he was crammed into a tiny space between crates of vegetables with a smelly sheet of canvas having been thrown over him, now he lay as still as he could hardly daring to breath as one of the soldiers manning the road block asked the driver for his papers.

"What's with all the questions, Hans? You don't normally detain me," said the driver as the soldier quickly read his papers.

"Yes, I know, Gabin, but we have orders to search everyone tonight with no exceptions."

"What? Do you think I am smuggling or something! Christ, chance would be a fine thing, I wouldn't mind being able to make a few francs on the side but who has the bloody time these days eh?" The soldier chuckled and handed the papers back.

"Alright, off you go!"

"If you delay me on the way back, Hans, I might have some cheese for your mess eh, for a few francs, of course?" said the driver as he tucked his papers back into his pocket and put the van into gear.

"Don't let the Feldwebel hear you say that, but I'll see what we can do, Gabin."

"Right oh." As the van started moving again, the Professor gave a sigh of relief trying to move his cramped legs as he did so, for weeks now he had been moved from one hiding place to another as he was passed from one Resistance Cell to another as they tried to get him out of the country, each time he wondered if he had done the right thing, but he knew that he had only thought this way because he was scared, he was scared of what they would do to him if they caught him, he knew he would be shot because he had escaped from their testing facility with some blueprints and other information on the German Vergeitungs V1 or Vengeance Weapon 1 which was a pilotless flying bomb powered by a pulse jet engine with a payload of 800 kilograms of Amatol.

In effect, the V1 was an unguided flying missile that would be aimed in the general direction of London where it would fall indiscriminately when its fuel load ran out. He could not in all good conscience continue working on this terror weapon. Oh, in the beginning, he had justified his actions by saying that he had no choice, the Germans had threatened to intern his entire family in a concentration camp if he didn't cooperate then about a year after he had started work on the project, he had been told that his family had been killed in a freak accident. Apparently, a training aircraft had gotten into difficulties just after take-off and had crashed into a house trying to return to the airfield, it had been his parents' home and his wife had been with them at the time.

He had been devastated at the news and had been given leave to attend the funeral, he snorted in disgust at the memory of that 'leave'; two Gestapo men had accompanied him to and from the funeral and it had been while laying a wreath on his wife's gravestone that he had decided he could not in all good conscience continue working on the project, then having been returned to the research facility, he had accidentally caught one of the cleaners trying to smuggle out blueprints and instead of turning the young man into the Gestapo, he had asked him for help. It had taken three very long tense days to convince the lad that he was genuine and wasn't just trying to catch his friends before the lad decided to help him, then within a week the Resistance had arranged for his needing to go into town to see the dentist so they could get him away from the research facility.

It was a day that he would never forget, he had been driven into town by the two usual Gestapo men, he had put a copy of blueprints and a small roll of film into a leather satchel which he carried with him at all times, then as they had entered the dentist's room and the door closed, the two Gestapo men had been shot dead by a silenced pistol that was being held by none other than the dentist himself, it had been absolutely terrifying and he had been scared and on the run ever since.

He swore silently to himself as the van hit a bump and he hit his head on one of the crates, then he held his breath again as the van came to a stop, the rear doors were opened, and the crates were pulled aside making him blink rapidly as the canvas was pulled off his head.

"Jump out Professor, quickly!" ordered the driver and Linus scooted himself down the van then groaned as he stood up as he was very stiff from being cramped up in the small space.

"This way…quickly!" He hurried to keep up with the driver who led him through a hedge and onto a small pathway that led down to a stone walled church, a door in the end of the wall opened and they ducked inside into a small kitchen that was in an outbuilding attached to the church, the door was closed behind them then a lamp was lit.

"He's all yours, padre, I'll see you in a couple of days," said the driver talking to a tall man in the dark robes of a priest who grabbed his arm as George turned to leave.

"No Gabin, wait—please!"

"Why, what's wrong, Padre, you know I have to complete my deliveries otherwise they will get suspicious."

"I know but there has been a change, something has gone wrong up the line and we've been asked to keep him here until further notice"

"What the Hell are they thinking of, Padre, they know we can only keep them for a couple of days at the most!"

"I know Gabin, but this is important, I'll need your help with some supplies, can you do that?"

"Oh Christ!" muttered Gabin then realising what he said, he apologised to the priest.

"Oh, sorry Father, alright I'll see what I can do but I won't be able to come back until the day after tomorrow at the earliest."

"We can manage until then. Bless you, Gabin."

"Alright Father but be careful alright?" Gabin then turned to the Professor.

"I have to leave, Professor; the Padre will hide you now so do as he tells you, alright?"

"Yes, thank you for what you have done for me, Gabin."

"You just get whatever it is that you have to England and keep safe." Gabin patted the man on the arm then nodded to the padre before hurrying out of the building.

"Professor Kruen, my name is Father Cole and I'm afraid that you will be stuck here for a few days."

"Pleased to meet you, Father, can you tell me what is happening exactly as Gabin didn't tell me much."

"Follow me, would you, Professor and I'll explain?" As the professor nodded, the priest turned leading the way out of the room, they entered the small church then were climbing up a ladder leading to the belfry.

"Gabin didn't tell you much for your own safety, the original plan was for you to arrive tonight then be passed on to the final group tomorrow night, they would have arranged for your ongoing passage to England." As they entered the belfry the priest turned kneeling down at a small hatchway built into a panel of the wall, it was well concealed and was barely big enough for a man to squeeze through.

"But something has gone wrong, is that it, Father?" asked the Professor.

"Yes, I don't know what has happened, but we have been told to keep you here until further notice."

"Do you…do you think something has happened to the next Resistance Group, Father, has someone been arrested?" asked the Professor anxiously, he knew they were playing a dangerous game and if someone had been arrested and they talked then they were all as good as dead!

"I don't think so, but I don't know. Now I'm afraid that you are going to be rather uncomfortable as this is only a rope locker. We used it to stow spare ropes and things for the bell tower. There is a small window letting in some light but that's about all."

"Thank you, Father, I am sure that I will be fine."

"I'll knock on the hatch a couple of times so that you know it is me when I come up with something hot later, there is some water, a blanket and a bucket for the…uh…necessary so try to make yourself comfortable."

"Thank you, Father, I know the awful risk that you are taking and I'm sorry to be such a burden on you."

"Nonsense, we must all fight the evil that has been thrust upon us."

"You might not feel the same if you knew what I have done, Padre!" The Professor couldn't look the man in the eye as he said this.

"From what I have been told, you were being forced to cooperate with threats against your family if you didn't, isn't that right, Linus?"

"I'd convinced myself that it was the reason in the beginning, Father, but I'm not so sure." Linus swallowed hard as he said this for he had enjoyed the kudos that he had received from the Germans in the beginning and had thought that it was only a veiled threat against his family, but then over a period of time a couple of the scientists had 'gone missing' because they had refused to continue working on the V1 Project and he had seen how the Germans treated the few Jewish members of the staff and had heard rumours about other families suddenly vanishing and then he had known for certain that the threat against his own family had been only to real, then he had started to seriously worry about them.

"Well, whatever the reason, Linus, you are doing the right thing now aren't you by taking whatever it is that you have to England?"

"Yes, I…" Linus looked around anxiously. "Can we be overheard, Father?"

"No, we are alone."

"Father, in this satchel," Linus patted the leather satchel that he had been clutching against his chest, "I have some blueprints and a roll of film about a new terror weapon, it's a type of flying bomb that will fall indiscriminately on England and—and it will kill many innocent people. That is why I must get to England, so they can set up their defences against this terrible thing that I have helped develop, Father!" Linus was almost in tears with guilt as he said this, and he jumped badly as the Priest put a hand onto his shoulder.

"You are making amends for your wrongdoing, my son, and the Good Lord will forgive you."

"He might, Father, but I won't!"

"Each man must come to terms with his own conscience, Linus, now I really must go!"

"Of course, thank you Father." Linus turned and pushed his satchel through the small hatch in the wall then had to get down onto his belly to wriggle his way into the small space, it was really only a cupboard holding some spare ropes and parts for the belfry, there was very little room and very little light coming in through a pane of glass that was set between a couple of tiles in the sloping roof, it was one time that being only five feet tall had come in handy. There was a shelf on one wall on which was a jug of water with a mug, he sat down in one corner drawing up his knees and wondered how long he would have to endure this pokey room.

For three very anxious days, Linus tried to make himself comfortable in the tiny space, the Priest had been very good to him coming up each morning with some hot coffee, bread and cheese to get him through the day and in the evenings had managed to bring up something hot. He had managed to scrape off some of the grime in the single pane of glass set into the tiles to give the room a little light, he had been doing this on the third day when the Germans had arrived.

He had been standing on a pile of old rope trying to peer out of the glass when he had seen the two vehicles pull into the courtyard. One was a small Volkswagen holding an officer with three men with the other vehicle being a truck holding soldiers, he had almost fallen off the ropes in fright. Quickly, he had scrambled onto the floor and had tried to hide himself under some old ropes that littered the floor so that if anyone did open the hatch then they would only see the ropes, for over an hour he had lain there sweating badly and hardly daring to breath as he listened to harsh commands and the soldiers moving about in the church, then everything went suddenly quiet.

He jumped badly again as he heard footsteps before there came the familiar knocking on the wall then the hatch was opened.

"Are you alright, Professor?" asked the Priest.

"Yes Father, but what happened? There were soldiers."

"Even soldiers need to pray sometime, Professor. Now I've brought you some fresh bread and some news. You will be moved tonight!" The Professor breathed a hefty sigh of relief as he took the bread.

"Thank you, Father, that is good news."

"It will be at ten or eleven tonight so be ready, alright?"

"I will be, Father, thank you." The Priest gave him a reassuring smile before closing the hatchway, this time Linus didn't mind as he would be leaving in a couple of hours, so he sat down on the ropes and started eating his bread.

Linus slept fitfully during the rest of that day, at six the Priest brought him some hot soup and reminded him to be ready to move at ten that night. For the rest of the day Linus felt restless, anxious to move yet worried as to what might happen when he was passed onto the next Resistance group, always with the fear of discovery foremost in his mind.

TAP! TAPTAP! TAP! He jumped a little startled as the Priest tapped his signal before opening the small hatchway.

"Professor—time to go!" Linus squeezed himself out of the hatch and straightened up stretching his cramped legs.

"Gabin is waiting in his van at the end of the pathway, if you are ready, Professor?"

"Yes, Father I'm ready."

"I've put together some bread and cheese, it isn't much, but it might get you through, eh?" The Priest passed him a small bag.

"I can't thank you enough for everything that you have done for me, Father." Linus extended his hand, and the Priest shook hands warmly with him.

"Take care of yourself, Professor, and may God protect you."

"Thank you, Father." Linus turned making his way down the ladder from the belfry then outside till he was on the pathway and then he hurried towards the waiting van where Gabin had the rear doors open waiting for him.

"Good to see you again, Gabin," he said as he hurried over.

"Likewise, my friend, I'll hide you as before, but I don't think there will be any roadblocks but be ready all the same, alright?"

"Yes." Linus climbed into the back of the van into the tiny space that George had prepared for him and once again he was covered with the scrap of canvas, the rear doors were banged shut and with a slight jolt they started moving. For the next four hours, he sweated in the confined space cringing and wincing at every bump in the rear of the van trying to stretch his limbs without disturbing his hiding place with his ears strained for any unusual sounds that might warn of an approaching roadblock, then the van was slowing, it made a left hand turn then stopped, he could hear voices so scrunched himself down lower into his hide waiting.

Chapter Twelve
Danny's Pig Farm, Posey 1943

"I think you're bloody mad, Mary!" Pierre couldn't help pacing the room as he said this as Mary had been in contact with London and they had told her to retrieve the information that the Courier had brought in as the mission was still on.

"I know it's risky, Pierre, but—"

"Risky!" Pierre stopped pacing and went to sit next to her at the table.

"Look Mary, I applaud your professionalism for wanting to complete the original mission, but I think you are crazy! This Major Schrandt desperately wants to get his hands on you, so he is bound to be having that field watched and even if he isn't, I know there are extra patrols out and every vehicle is being stopped."

"I know that Pierre, but this information is very important, the Courier gave his life to give it to me, the least I can do is try to retrieve that information."

"Jesus Mary!" Pierre ran his hands through his hair as he looked at her trying to gauge the risk of possibly being arrested against the chance of even being able to find the tin that Mary had tossed into a drainage ditch in the middle of the night.

"What about your wounds, Mary? Mark said that you needed at least forty-eight hours before we moved you."

"Both Mark and Margite have both been very good to me and I know the risks, do you really think that I would risk being caught again if I didn't think this mission was of vital importance, Pierre?"

"Everything is 'vitally important' to London when they order us to do things, Mary, how can you be sure that this isn't just another mission for them?"

"Before the Courier arrived, I had been told that there is a scientist who has escaped from a testing facility somewhere in Denmark who is carrying vital information on some sort of new weapon that will be used against England, I won't know anymore until we retrieve that tin, then we will know how to get this scientist to England and that it is of vital importance that we do this and…and, Pierre, it means that what I have gone through was for a good reason!" Mary was almost pleading with him as she said this, and he could see that it meant a great deal to her.

"Alright Mary, but we do this MY way, alright?"

"Alright Pierre and thank you." Mary knew that she was taking a major risk by going back to that field, if the Germans were watching it then she risked being arrested again, she knew that she couldn't go through that torture again, she didn't have the fortitude for that, to be honest the thought of Kurt and his 'little pins' terrified her.

"I have some arrangements that I will need to make so I will come back this evening, alright?" said Pierre as he stood up.

"Alright Pierre."

"You get some rest!" He nodded to Danny then left the room and a minute later his van pulled out of the farm.

"He's right, Mary, you need to rest," said Margite and Mary nodded as she stood up.

"I think I will lay down." Mary left the room.

At four o'clock that afternoon, she was woken from a restless sleep by Danny hurrying into the farmhouse.

"Mary! Get into the cellar quick soldiers coming!" he shouted as he hurried in as he had seen a truck and another vehicle approaching up the road, which meant that they would be here within a few minutes.

Mary ran from her room as Margite pulled aside the kitchen table so that they could open a small hatchway in the floor, then with her heart pounding madly in her ears, Mary scrambled down the six steps into the cellar which held all the farms supplies. Hurrying to the far wall she pulled aside a heavy flour sack behind which was a panel, pushing the top of this board there came a loud click and the panel opened inwards, Mary scrabbled into a small space and pushed the hinged panel shut then reached up to a metal lever which then locked the panel; now this could only be opened from the inside.

On the other side, Margite pulled the heavy sack back into place then hurried up the steps into the kitchen where she shut the hatch in the floor and pulled the table back into place before she sat at the table and pulled a pot towards herself, starting to peel the potatoes that she would be using in a soup later as she quickly scanned around the kitchen, making sure there was nothing in sight that might give them away; as she did so, a vehicle pulled up outside.

Danny went outside and as he did, a young Lieutenant stepped out of his vehicle.

"Name and papers!" snapped the Lieutenant as soldiers started jumping down from the back of the truck.

"I'm Danny, this is my pig farm. What do you want?" he asked as he wiped his hands on a piece of cloth in his belt.

"Where are your papers and how many people are on this farm?"

"There is just my wife Margite and myself here and our papers are in the kitchen." Danny gestured to the farmhouse as he said this, the Lieutenant turned and barked some orders to his Sergeant who then shouted orders to the men who started to spread out through the farm.

"Don't startle my pigs! They're temperamental enough buggers as it is."

"Enough of that, old man, show me your papers!"

"You'd best come in then." Keeping himself as calm as he could and trying to appear casual, Danny led the way into the farmhouse.

"Madam," said the Lieutenant to Margite as they entered the kitchen.

"What's wrong? We haven't done anything!" she said as she stood up.

"Just a routine search, I assure you my men will be careful not to disturb things too much, madam," said the Lieutenant as Danny pulled their papers from the table drawer and handed them over.

"There is just the two of you here?" asked the Lieutenant as he read the papers.

"Yes, apart from the pigs of course!" Danny glared at the young Officer. If he had his way, he would shoot the lot of them, but he was keeping himself under control because of his wife and for Mary and what she had to do; he knew that whatever it was that she was doing was important and that he would still have time to kill all these swine before this war was over.

Danny and Margite stood in the kitchen as the soldiers searched their farm for fifteen minutes. In the cellar in her small hide, Mary sat in the confined space with her knees drawn up and her arms hugging her knees, she had her eyes closed as she couldn't see anything in the dark anyway, she was breathing slowly so as not to make any noise and tears rolled down her cheeks as she hugged her knees in fear as she listened intently to the soldiers searching the farm petrified that they might stumble over her hideaway.

"All clear sir." The Sergeant reported to the Lieutenant in the kitchen and the Lieutenant handed Danny his papers.

"We shan't disturb you further; Heil Hitler!" The Lieutenant gave the Nazi salute which made Danny clench his fists together to keep his control.

"Goodbye!" he said between clenched teeth as the young Officer turned and left then amidst much shouting from the Sergeant, the soldiers got back into the truck and the vehicles pulled out of the yard.

"Bastards!" growled Danny then he calmed down as Margite hugged him.

"Well done, Danny. I'm very proud of you for the way you handled that, I know how hard it was," she said as she hugged him hard.

"Thank you, my love," he returned her hug as he got himself fully under control.

"Shall we let Mary out now?"

"No, we'd better wait ten minutes in case they double back."

"Alright Danny, I'll make some coffee as I'm sure she will need it by then."

"I know it's cramped in there but at lease she is safe." Danny looked at the clock as Margite went to fill the kettle, he knew that Mary would be scared in her little hideaway, but he had to be sure that the soldiers didn't double back before he dare let her out.

Later that evening Pierre returned to the farm and Danny filled him in on the earlier search then he joined Mary at the table, the girl still looked stressed with black rings around the eyes, but she gave him a warm smile as he sat down next to her.

"That from London?" he asked, Mary nodded as she finished decoding the cypher and she felt a little guilty as she had felt extremely relieved when she had read the first part of the signal.

"The operation is still on as planned unless we can't recover the Courier's information."

"Damn! I was hoping they would alter things."

"There is something else, Pierre."

"Oh, what do they want now?" he asked.

"Me."

"What?"

"Message reads 'operation as planned plus two date'—that means we act two days later than the info said."

"Yes, that makes sense I suppose."

"Extraction of package and Lilly plus ten time—message ends. So, they also want me extracted which will take place ten hours later than stated."

Pierre sat there quietly for a moment while he took that in, he could understand London wanting to extract Mary or Lilly as her code name was as she had been captured once and by some miracle had managed to escape but while she was still here not only was she in danger herself, but she was putting the others in danger as well. He would miss her as he had become fond of the girl, she was a damned good radio operator who had proved her capabilities on a couple of operations with them and he was going to miss her.

"I'm sorry Pierre." He looked up as she said this quietly.

"Sorry! What on earth for?" he asked frowning.

"For being arrested—I…I have messed up everything, haven't I?" she said as tears ran down her face and Pierre turned to her and hugged her.

"Oh my dear girl, you have nothing to be sorry for and it certainly wasn't your fault that you were arrested. It was no coincidence that they just happened to pick that field that night, Mary, it was a well-planned and determined attack and with everything that you have been through, you have proven yourself to be a very strong and worthy person and I for one are glad to have had you with us so don't think like that, eh?"

"Hear hear!" said Danny as Margite wiped a tear from her eyes.

"I'm sorry I have put you all in extra danger like this. I will be sorry to leave although I understand why they want me out."

"Well, we had better go and get that tin then, Mary, are you definitely sure you know where it is?" asked Pierre, Mary wiped her eyes as she nodded.

"Yes, if I can go back to that field and leave the way I did on that night then I'm certain I can find it."

"Right then, we go tomorrow night. I've arranged for a couple of diversions so that we should be able to get into and out of that field quickly."

"What time will we go?" she asked.

"Ten P.M. I'll pick you up here so be ready, and Danny, I'll be using Henry's Citroen."

"Why the Citroen, Pierre?"

"Because it's faster than my van and because I will be dressed as a Gendarme, I've loaned a friend's uniform."

"Oh right, Pierre, so it's just a small Op then?" asked Danny a little disappointed at being left out of the action.

"This time yes but be ready in case I need any help, old friend."

"Always." Pierre stood up and looked at Mary.

"I'll see you tomorrow night, make sure you are armed with a pistol and a couple of hand grenades in case we run into trouble."

"I'll be ready, Pierre."

"Oh, and you had better pack a small bag as well just in case we have to be on the move for a while."

"I will be ready, Pierre."

"Of course, you will." With that Pierre hugged the girl warmly then hurried out of the farmhouse.

"He'll miss you, Mary," said Margite and Mary swallowed back the emotional lump in her throat.

"I'm going to miss all of you, Margite."

"I know, Dear. Come on, I'll help you get ready, eh?"

"Alright, thank you." Danny watched the two women leave the room, he knew that Margite was going to miss Mary as she had grown quite fond of the girl as indeed, he had himself, it would be strange not having her warm smile around the place, she had always been willing to help him whenever he needed it, yes it was going to be quieter that was for certain.

Chapter Thirteen
Police Station, Posey 1943

At 9 A.M. the following morning, Major Schrandt was sitting at his desk and was glaring at Kurt who was standing at attention in front of the desk, Kurt was sweating badly as he knew the Major was furious, for a couple of days now his men had searched the town and outlying farms in an effort to find Mary but so far they had found nothing at all, even their usual informants had gone quiet but he thought that had more to do with the fact that one of their own had been found dead in his flat with two bullets in him rather than anything to do with Mary, then he jumped as the Major banged his fist down on the table.

"Well man!"

"Sir?" Kurt realised that Major had said something, but he hadn't heard him.

"Christ! Are you entirely stupid, man? I said did you have all the roadblocks up in time or has she managed to slip through the net!"

"No sir, all the roadblocks were up within minutes of her getting out of this station, I…I believe she is still somewhere in Posey, sir." The Major was about to yell at the man when the telephone jangled, and he snatched up the receiver.

"Schrandt!" he snapped.

"This is Colonel Eric Brehmner Gestapo, is this a secure line?" The Major put his hand over the mouthpiece and gestured for Kurt to pick up the small earpiece attached to the telephone stand as he mouthed the word Gestapo, Kurt quickly moved forward and carefully lifted the earpiece.

"Good morning, Colonel, yes this is a secure line."

"Good. Have you found the English Agent Lilly yet?" asked the colonel and Schrandt swallowed hard, wondering how the Hell they knew about Mary.

"Not yet sir, but—"

"But nothing, Major, I will be with you in two hours, and I will give you a full briefing then but for now I want you to stop looking for Mary, we don't want to make her run—"

"But Colonel, I don't—"

"Don't interrupt, damn it, I said I will give you a full briefing when I arrive, for now reduce your searches but don't make it look like you are. In the meantime, you may be contacted by an Abwehr Agent, her code name is Blackbird, if she does contact you, don't ask questions; just note down what she says and if she wants anything, you do it immediately, do you understand?"

"Wind back the search for Mary and if contacted by code name Blackbird, do whatever she wants, I understand sir."

"Good, if you act well in this, Major, I might just be able to stop them shooting you." CLICK, the line went dead and the Major swallowed hard for the Gestapo didn't make idle threats.

"Jesus, Major," said Kurt as he hung up the earpiece, he knew that if the Gestapo were threatening the Major, then he was also in real trouble.

"You heard the Colonel, wind back the searches for Mary but don't make it look like you are and keep up the pressure on our informants, someone has to know something, the little bitch couldn't just drop off the planet, get going!"

"Sir." As Kurt hurried out the Major opened his desk drawer and took out a bottle of whiskey and poured himself a glass which he drank in one gulp, for the first time he was worried about his own safety.

Two hours later he was still at his desk when the door opened and a short squat man in an immaculate grey uniform of a Colonel of the Gestapo entered the office, he wore a blue cape over his shoulders, he removed his cap as he entered the office revealing pure blond hair, Schrandt put his age at about fifty, but he didn't look it.

"You Schrandt?" asked the Colonel as he crossed over to the desk as the Major stood up.

"Yes sir."

"Have you heard from anyone since my call?"

"No sir." Schrandt came out from behind his desk and motioned for the Colonel to take his place but the man shook his head as he went to the chair in front of the desk and sat down.

"No, this is your office, well, seems that this English bitch is quite good, eh?"

"Uhm yes sir, we believe she met a courier from a Lysander but unfortunately, he was killed, we don't know if he passed information onto her or not, she…uhm managed to escape from the police cells here before we could get any information from her." And Schrandt swallowed hard under the man's steady gaze.

"Quite some feat, wouldn't you say?"

"Yes sir, but I want to say that the man she overpowered is a good man and has never let me down before, she took him by surprise breaking his nose and knocking him out before she escaped the cells."

"I don't care, Major, I'm not here to lay blame but I think you should have this man here for the briefing, I take it he is your right-hand man?"

"Yes, sir he is."

"Then fetch him in and we'll get started."

"Sir." The Major picked up his phone and made a quick call then a few minutes later Kurt knocked on the door and entered the office.

"You wanted me sir?"

"Yes, pull up a chair, Kurt, the Colonel wants to brief us."

"Sir." Kurt grabbed the secretary's chair and pulled it up to the end of the desk near the Major, sat down and waited.

"Firstly, what I am about to say is strictly confidential and no-one outside this room is to hear of it, if I find out that you have talked to anyone but yourselves, I will have you shot, is that clear?"

"Yes sir," the Major spoke for them both and Kurt swallowed hard again.

"This British girl…what was her name?"

"Mary sir and I believe her code name was 'LILLY'."

"Ah yes, well for your information, Mary's Resistance Cell was the last in a link whose task it is to extricate Professor Linus Kruen out of France to England."

"Christ! I thought that she was just a British Agent sir, who is Professor Kruen if I may ask?" asked the Major.

"Professor Kruen is a Dutch scientist who until recently was working at the Peenemunde research facility, do you know it?"

"No sir, I'm not familiar with that facility."

"No reason you should be as it is top secret, this Professor was recently moved from Peenemunde to another facility in Denmark, then a couple of weeks ago his family were killed in a freak accident and he decided to change sides, somehow he managed to contact a local Resistance Cell and asked for their help to get out of the country and they obliged, he has been on the move ever since."

"And this man is important how sir?" asked the Major.

"All you need to know is that he is working on a new terror weapon that will shortly be launched against England, he has stolen a roll of film and some blueprints which if they fall into enemy hands could prove disastrous for that weapon."

"Are we to try to get this man back, sir, is that it?"

"Yes and no. Admiral Canaris and his Abwehr have managed to infiltrate SOE in England, they managed to get an Agent into the training facility and that Agent has now been sent to France, she is the code name Blackbird."

"My God sir, that is some feat—"

"Never mind that!" snapped the Colonel and Schrandt swallowed hard, he had forgotten how the Gestapo despised the Admiral and his Abwehr, he was surprised that the Gestapo even knew what was going on.

"The important thing is that this Agent is now in France and the Resistance is obligingly informing her of the Professor's movements, she will get herself into a position where she will be able to get a hold of this man and return him and his information to us, that is where you come in, Major!"

"How can we help, sir?" asked Schrandt dreading the response as it now meant that they were under the control of the Gestapo, not a good place to be.

"You have a fair amount of autonomy in your present position here Major, I want you to have two other men on constant standby who will join you in a vehicle for whenever our Blackbird contacts us, another twenty men will be ready to move at a moment's notice as reinforcements. As you can understand this Blackbird is playing a dangerous game and may only have minutes to get a message to us here, so you will have two reliable people manning the phone twenty-four hours a day from now on and you will be ready to move at a moment's notice, is that clear?"

"Yes, sir I will see to that straight away."

"I've already done so; your Secretary and another Luftwaffe Secretary will man the phones. This is your last chance to prove yourself, Major, if you succeed with capturing the Professor and possibly your 'LILLY' at the same time then I will see to it that you are transferred to my command at Avenue Foche in Paris but if you fail then even, I won't be able to help you, is that clear?" Major

Schrandt swallowed hard as the Colonel looked at him with a steady gaze, it was obvious what would happen if they failed this time—they would both be shot!

"I understand, sir."

"Good, then that's all settled, now I shall go to my hotel to freshen up and will re-join you later, let me know at once if you hear from our Blackbird!"

"Sir." Both men stood to attention as the Colonel stood up then left the office.

"You heard him, Kurt, this is our chance to get to Paris, organise Conrad and another man to be with us in a vehicle if we get word from this Agent and make sure there is a reliable Lieutenant ready with twenty men as a backup, we can't afford to foul this up."

"Sir." As Kurt hurried out of the room the Major picked up his phone and ordered some coffee, he was feeling quite elated at the possibility of finally being able to get to Paris where his skills could be of more use to the Third Reich, he only hoped that this Blackbird had more luck in finding Mary than he had so far.

****

The blacked out Citroen moved slowly down the laneway then came to a stop, Mary got out of the passenger side and made her was slowly along the lane close to the edge of the drainage ditch, she had seen where she would have come out of the field on the night that she was arrested and slowly made her way along the ditch as she relived that night in her head, she jumped badly as Pierre came up alongside her.

"Are you sure this was the area, Mary; we don't have much time!"

"Yes, I am sure, that was where I came out of the hedge…" she said as she indicated a spot in the hedgerow, and she quickened her pace a little.

"There—it has to be there, Pierre!" she said pointing to a patch of reeds. Pierre moved forward and gingerly lowered himself into the murky and very cold water, he dare not use a light in case it was seen by anyone nearby so he felt around with his feet in the cold water, he figured that as she had thrown her Sten and the small tin into the water then they might have hit the reeds before settling down to the bottom so he would start feeling at the edge of the reeds and work outwards and although Mary seemed to be fairly certain that this was the area, he had his doubts for it had been fairly dark that night and with all the confusion that had been going on it could have been anywhere.

Feeling around with his foot for twenty minutes, he was starting to think it was a wild goose chance when he suddenly felt something, so reaching down with his hand he was almost up to his shoulder in the murky water and much to his surprise he felt something metal, grasped it and pulled up a very waterlogged Sten submachine gun.

"Yes—I knew it was the right place!" said Mary excitedly as Pierre started searching around with his hand in the water trying to find the small metal tin but it was only the size of a cigarette tin and he thought it would be impossible to find, it could be tangled in the reeds or submerged in the mud at the bottom of the ditch, he was moving his hand slowly so as not to disturb that mud too much as he didn't want to bury the damned thing if it was there at all.

For another five minutes, he slowly searched in a circle from where he had found the Sten and then he felt his excitement mount as he felt something small nudge against his hand, he gripped it and pulled it up out of the water with a big smile on his face as he turned towards Mary and saw her grinning at him.

"Damn girl, you're good, now let's get the hell out of here before a patrol comes along!" He climbed out of the ditch and they hurried to the car then started off down the lane, while he was concentrating on driving without any lights to help, Mary dried off the tin with her skirt, she had been overjoyed when she had seen Pierre pull the Sten out of the water and then her heart seemed to skip a beat when she saw him lift the tin up, she had thought that it would be impossible to find, but there it was in her hand and she could almost cry with sheer joy, she carefully put the small tin into her pocket.

For half an hour, Pierre drove slowly and carefully until he was out of the lane and onto a decent road, then he sped up as he turned his lights on, then breathed a sigh of relief as forty minutes later he pulled into Danny's farm.

"Take the tin and gun into the farm, Mary, I have to return this car, so I will see you in the morning, alright." Much to his surprise, Mary leaned over and kissed his cheek.

"Thank you for believing in me, Pierre," she said then she was out of the car and heading into the farmhouse. He shook his head then pulled out of the farm heading back to town to get rid of the car, hoping that he didn't run into any patrols on the way.

In the farmhouse as Mary entered the kitchen and closed the door, Margite turned the lights on filling the room with harsh light.

"You found it, Mary?" she said as she saw that the girl had the Sten gun in her hand.

"Yes, Pierre had to feel around for quite a while, but we found both items." Mary sat at the table and fiddled with the small tin until after a few minutes she was able to get it open and much to her relief, the contents were in greased paper so hadn't been damaged by being submerged in the water for so long, that had been one of her fears, that the water would have damaged whatever information was in the tin. She opened the greased paper wrapping, as she though there was a small microfilm on a short card.

"Margite, could you get the Bible that is beside my bed please?" she asked, the old lady hurried into the other room returning with the Bible which she passed to Mary then watched fascinated as Mary opened the rear end of the Bible and took out what looked like some sort of eyeglass.

"Do you have your torch, Danny?" asked Mary, Danny reached into the table draw and took out his flashlight which he passed over to her.

"Thank you." Mary switched it on, shone it onto one end of the eyeglass, she had set out a notepad alongside the Bible and started jotting down the letters that the light was revealing. Mary worked on the cypher for another ten minutes then sat back once it was complete.

"We only just got this in time, the package will be delivered day after tomorrow!" She was very relieved that they had managed to find the tin otherwise the operation would have to have been put back a few days and that put more people at risk, also she knew that the next move was to get the package—or the Professor as she should start saying—to a place where they would meet the submarine and get him finally out of the country and eventually to England.

"Danny, could you set up the wireless while I go over this once more, as I will have to call London?"

"Of course." Danny quickly took the wireless set from its little hideaway and set it up for her, then Mary quickly sent a signal to London then waited, within a few minutes she was getting a signal back and she frowned as it was quite a long one and it was being sent on an emergency code which was odd, with the cypher in she quickly signed off and then set about decoding the cypher which took her a good fifteen minutes because of the emergency code.

"Are you alright, Mary, you've gone quite pale?" asked Margite suddenly as Mary's colour had changed visibly, she was still worried about the girl as even though she wasn't saying much, she knew that she was still in severe pain from her torture.

"I'm just a little tired, Margite, it's been a long day." Mary forced a smile for the old lady, she wasn't about to worry her by telling her how nauseous she had suddenly felt as she decoded the cypher which informed her about Alice being an enemy agent, it also stated that she was being sent to her group, the cover being that Mary needed help with her cyphers due to being injured, the most worrying part had been the last part of the cypher which stated that she was to arrest Alice or if she couldn't safely do this, she was to eliminate her!

My God! Why do they always say eliminate when they mean kill! she asked herself as she tried to digest the message, it had come direct from Beth, she had recognised her signature on the Morse key, she had been quite stunned when she had decoded the cypher, she had always thought that there had been something strange about Alice, but she had never thought that she could have been an enemy agent, that was beyond belief and if it hadn't come from Beth then she wouldn't have believed it.

"Well, why don't you get some rest, Mary; Pierre will come back tomorrow so I'll call you at breakfast if you like?"

"Yes, I think I might turn in if you don't mind?"

"Would you like some hot milk, dear?"

"Yes, thank you Margite." As Mary left the room Margite went over to the stove, she would make some hot milk and she would also put a sedative into it for Mary, she knew the girl was still suffering despite trying to put a brave face on things.

"She alright, Margite?" asked Danny as he had seen the concern on his wife's face.

"She's still in a lot of pain Danny even though she is trying to hide it, she really needs to rest."

"I don't think she will be getting much of that, dear."

"So, I will give her some help" she said, and Danny smiled.

"Thought you might." Margite made the hot milk and took it into Mary before she returned to the kitchen to have some with Danny. In her room Mary drank the milk and within a few minutes the sedative took effect, she fell asleep before she had finished the milk.

****

Later that evening in a small doctor's surgery in the town of Delpeche, Alice sat at a wireless set which had been set up on a table in the doctor's office, no one would question the doctor being in his office at this time of night as the doctors often worked back late to catch up on their paperwork after visiting their patients during the day. Now, Alice was to all intents sending and receiving a signal from London; she was in fact sending a signal to her handler at the Abwehr Headquarters in Paris, she was able to do this as the doctor himself wasn't a wireless operator and didn't understand morse code nor how the transmitter worked, it was still risky but it had to be done, she had in fact been in contact with London who had informed her that Mary needed her help.

They had given her details of how to contact a member of Mary's cell who would take her to join Mary before they moved on to 'pick up the package', she had become really excited when she heard this and had quickly changed frequencies to send this on to her handler who had then given her the phone number of Major Schrandt whom she would contact at the earliest possible time when she knew where the Professor was going to be so that they could assist her in arresting him and all the members of Mary's Resistance Cell. So far it was all working out very well. Having finished transmitting, she took the aerial out and rolled up the wire to the Morse key and put it all back in its box so that the doctor could put it all away.

"Thank you, Doctor," she said, the man quickly put the setback in its hideaway and as he did, the door burst open and two armed men rushed into the room.

"Stand still—don't move!" they shouted as they moved into the room quickly followed by a young Officer brandishing his pistol.

"How dare you burst into my examining room, who the hell are you!" demanded the Doctor as he tried to buy some time, they all knew that they could be discovered at any time and he was just grateful that they hadn't entered when Alice had been transmitting, as it was, he might be able to bluff it out if they were lucky.

"I am Major Hans Meyer SS, and you are under arrest, Herr Doctor!"

"Arrest! What the hell are you talking about man, I'm a doctor and I have been examining a patient."

"You are a member of the Resistance; we have intercepted wireless transmissions coming from this room, Doctor! Take him out while I question this woman," said the man, leering at the woman, the Doctor started to protest but was quickly bustled out of the room then when he was safely out of the room, the Officer went over to Alice, grinning broadly he hugged her warmly.

"It's so good to see you, Greta."

"That was good timing, Hans, a few seconds earlier and you would have caught me transmitting." Alice returned her brother's hug then stepped back a pace.

"I was listening outside, the good Doctor will be taken to headquarters for questioning, I'll have to handcuff you in case anyone is watching," he said as he took some manacles from his coat pocket, but she shook her head.

"No, you can't, they would let everyone know that I have been arrested and I need to move tonight, I've just been told to join another group that will be moving the Professor shortly."

"Damn, I wish we had known that before we took the Doctor, what do you suggest?"

"I don't think that anyone else knows I am here, give me ten minutes to get to another room on the next floor before you leave, I'll wait ten minutes then I will move on to where I am supposed to be joining the next group, I'll tell them that I saw you arrive at the Doctor's before me and that I saw you arrest him, they will put out the word and we will be unable to get the rest of this group but if we can get the Professor then it will be a small price to pay, don't you think?"

"Yes, I think that sounds very plausible but be careful, you are playing a very dangerous game, Greta!"

"Alice please, I must stay in character, Hans."

"Sorry, alright we will get going, be careful and I will be waiting for the next call," he said, but she shook her head again.

"No, go to Posey, there at the police headquarters contact a Colonel Brehmner of the Gestapo, he is working with Major Schrandt, tell them that Blackbird is meeting the next cell and be ready to move, you can join them as a reserve force, alright?"

"If you're sure, but please be careful alright, they won't mess about if they discover who you are!" Alice reached up and patted his cheek affectionately.

"Always the caring brother, Hans, I'll be careful; now get going."

"Alright, let's go, men!" The Major hurried out of the room with his men following, Alice looked around making sure that she hadn't left anything incriminating behind then she too hurried from the room but while the soldiers hurried out to their waiting vehicles she hurried upstairs and his in a hallway where she waited for ten minutes before she hurried out of the building and keeping to the shadows she moved a couple of miles from the doctor's office before she found a telephone where she put a call through to Pierre.

Pierre had just finished his meagre dinner and was thinking about turning in when the telephone jangled three times then stopped, then rang another three times and stopped and then rang again, this time he snatched up the receiver as this was a prearranged signal for any Resistance member calling.

"Pierre!" he said simply and waited.

"Pierre, call Delpeche 417!" CLICK, the line went dead, Pierre had stiffened as the scared female voice had spoken on the line before ringing off, this was also a prearrangement, it meant that the person on the other end of the line had been calling of their own free will and not under duress, it was a simple way of saying that the person calling wanted to make contact and they weren't being made to do so. He waited a couple of minutes before calling the number he had just been given, the receiver had been picked up straight away.

"Pierre, my name is Alice, I need your help! Doctor Reeves has just been arrested. You must warn the rest of his group…do you understand?" Alice had sounded almost hysterical as she said this, he stiffened as he listened, he knew that she must be scared to be talking like this on a line that was probably being monitored, he didn't think they had been listening to him, but you just never knew.

"Do you know the bridge?" he asked, there was a bridge at the Eastern end of Delpeche over a small river.

"Yes, I know it."

"Two streets to the left on the far side, I'll be there in forty-five minutes."

"I'll be waiting." CLICK, the line went dead. Pierre then dialled another number, let it ring three times, hung up and repeated it twice.

"Hello, this is Martin?" said a hesitant male voice on the other end of the line.

"The doctor is delivering triplets!" Pierre said this with his heart pounding in his ears, he had dealt with the six members of the adjacent Resistance Cell for the last three years, he knew them all intimately and now his simple message would have them all running for their lives.

"Thank you, I will pass that on to the family." CLICK! The line went dead.

"Good luck, my friend!" Pierre replaced the receiver; he grabbed his jacket feeling slightly sick as he hurried out to his van. If they were lucky, they would have twenty-four hours before the doctor started giving up their names under torture; having seen what they had done to Mary, he knew it would only be a matter of time.

The forty-five-minute drive through the night was a little nerve-wracking, normally all his trips were planned so that he knew the routes he would take and what shortcuts he could use if things went wrong so having to do a trip ad hoc didn't sit well with him but this couldn't be helped this time as one of their own was in trouble and needed help but it did mean that he was only armed with his 9 mm automatic and a couple of hand grenades.

Arriving in Delpeche, he moved to a position near the bridge and pulled over checking the small amount of traffic that was out at this time of night, but it only looked like delivery vehicles, nothing that looked like patrols, he wasn't taking any risks though and fixed the silencer to his automatic and tucked into his pocket making sure that it was easily accessible before he moved the vehicle out across the bridge and into the side street, then he was standing on the brake as a woman stepped out from the shadows in front of him, giving him a fright as he almost hit her.

"Jesus, I almost hit you!" he said as she opened the passenger door and got into the van quickly.

"Sorry but I wanted to get in before we are seen, you are Pierre, I hope?" said the young woman and Pierre nodded.

"Did…did you manage to warn the rest of the group?" she asked anxiously and as he nodded, she started weeping quietly.

"Yes, I got a message out, so they should be safe."

"Oh, thank you Pierre, I…I was so worried, oh that poor man," she said, and he passed her a handkerchief.

"What happened?" he asked as he started moving away from the curb.

"I…I had just finished a routine cypher with London and as I left, I was about halfway down the street when I…I saw the car tear in and—and then I saw the Doctor being dragged out. Oh, Pierre I…I didn't know what else to do but call you," and Alice continued her feigned emotional outburst and he nodded in sympathy.

"You did the right thing, Alice, and by being quick you enabled the rest of the team to get out of town."

"You—you really think so, Pierre?"

"I know so."

"Oh, thank goodness!" Alice turned to face the window as she continued to sob knowing that her story had been believed, everything seemed to be going well so far. She sat there feigning the emotions for about ten minutes before she looked up at where they were going.

"Where are we going, Pierre?" she asked quietly.

"I'm going to see a fisherman, it'll take us about twenty minutes to get to the fishing harbour, hopefully we won't run into any patrols but be ready to act if we do, alright?"

"Alright but why are we going there, I thought we would go to your group so I could help Mary, London told me I was to join her as she has been injured, isn't that right?" she asked, she had hoped that they would go to wherever Mary was, she was hoping to be able to find out something regarding the Professor's location.

"Mary was arrested and tortured."

"What!"

"That's right, she was arrested when we had a Courier come in by air, unfortunately there was a trap set up, the Courier was killed, and Mary was arrested."

"Hell, London didn't tell me any of that, they just told me I was to help her as she had been injured."

"Oh, she was injured alright. The bastards tortured her, Alice, they ripped out her fingernails, beat her, but she managed to escape."

"She escaped, hell that is unusual, it must have been something to get away from the Gestapo, Pierre!"

"She wasn't being held by the Gestapo, thank goodness, just by an SS Officer at the local police station. Anyway, we will get to her tonight but first I want to see the fisherman, we are going to need his help if we have any chance of getting our 'package' out of the country."

"Our 'package'?" she asked, trying to sound a little bewildered where in fact her heart had started racing as she thought that she might be able to find out where the Professor was, she might not need to go near Mary and the rest of the Resistance Cell, she may yet be able to get her hands on the Professor without outside help.

"Yes. Has London told you anything about that?" he asked, and she shook her head, she had to be careful here otherwise he could become suspicious.

"No. All I was told was that Mary had been injured and I was to join your group to assist in the cyphers, that was of course before the doctor was arrested so I…I guess that changes everything!" she said but Pierre shook his head.

"No, it doesn't, in fact it just means we have to speed things up a little. We have to get a man out of the country, he has been on the run for some time now."

"A man?"

"Yes, some sort of Professor, anyway he is coming to us, so we have to get ready for the next move."

"And that is where this fisherman comes in?"

"Yes, George is a fisherman, his small group moved the downed Allied aircrew out of the country, I'm not really sure how they do that as all we need to know is that he can help us but I haven't had time to meet the man before this so I thought tonight would be just as good a time as any, especially after what has happened with you."

"How do you know this man will be wherever we are going?"

"You know what it's like, Alice, you get told things!" he said, and she nodded but she could see that he wasn't going to tell her anything more and she could understand why; after all, he had only just met her under somewhat trying circumstances and she had to be careful.

Pierre knew that he was taking a risk being near the fishing harbour at such a late hour but he needed to meet the old fisherman George Aubin who was a member of a small local Resistance Cell whose sole job was to get downed Allied aircrew out of the country, this meeting was a couple of days earlier than he had planned for but the old man had been warned that he would be contacting him at some stage and although they had never met he was expected. Twenty minutes later he pulled the van up outside a row of small cottages.

"This is it, come on." They got out of the van and went up to one of the cottages where he knocked on the door, it took a couple of minutes before the door opened a little and an old man looked at him through the gap, there was no light because of the blackout so it was hard to make out his features.

"Yes, what do you want?"

"I'm Pierre from Posey and I believe your fishing boat needs a new compressor?" asked Pierre slowly for if the old man didn't believe that he was who he said he was then their trip would have been for nothing.

"Just a moment!" the door was closed for a couple of seconds before being opened fully.

"You'd better come in." Pierre stepped into small hallway then as the door was closed a lamp was turned up filling the place with a subdued light and they found themselves looking at a white haired scruffy old man who was holding a revolver.

"Who sent you and it had better be the right answer?" said the old man as he gestured threateningly with the revolver.

"Father Cole sent me to discuss the package!" said Pierre and the old man seemed to deflate a little, he had been tensed ever since the knock came at the door and he hadn't been expecting anyone let alone two people, so he had become nervous and was prepared to shoot straight away if they hadn't given him the answer that he wanted to his question.

"Sorry about the pistol but I wasn't expecting you today and I certainly wasn't expecting a woman, I'm George," said George as he lowered the pistol and extended his hand and Pierre smiled as they shook hands.

"There has been some trouble, George, that's why I'm early, earlier today Doctor Reeves was arrested, Alice here saw it happen, if it had been a couple of minutes earlier then she would have been arrested as well."

"Well, I'm pleased to meet you at last, Pierre, as I have heard a lot of good things about you and your group but now, I have two questions for you?"

"What do you want to know, George?"

"Did you manage to warn the rest of the doctor's group, I can make some calls if you didn't have time?"

"As soon as Alice told me what had happened, I called 459 and told Martin that the doctor was delivering triplets." As soon as he said this, the old man gave him a broad smile as he knew that code word would have made the doctor's 'friends' scatter quickly with no hesitation which meant that lives would have been saved.

"That's really good, Pierre, now my second question is who the hell is Alice?" As George said this Pierre couldn't help chuckling at the slightly hurt look on Alice's face.

"This is Alice, she was the doctor's wireless operator."

"And you saw him being arrested?"

"Yes, we had just made a routine signal to London, and I had left his office when I saw the car arrive, then he was carted off." And Alice looked close to tears again as she said this.

"God help the Doctor then but at least you were able to warn the others, so they should have scattered before he starts talking!"

"You think he will, George?" Pierre had been a little surprised when the old man said this as if he believed it was a matter of 'when' and not 'if' the Doctor talked.

"The Doctor is a very good man, Pierre, but you know what those bastards are like, it's only a matter of time before they break him."

"You know, George, a little while ago I would have argued that point with you, but my wireless operator Mary was recently arrested and tortured by those bastards, she managed to escape and I have seen what they did to her in a very short period of time so I know that it is best never to let yourself be taken!"

"We think the same way then, that's good; now what about the 'package'?" George had patted his pocket when he had been speaking as if to reassure himself that his pistol and hand grenade were still readily accessible, he had no intentions of ever letting himself be taken by those Gestapo pigs!

"I don't know what else happened but there was another delay somewhere, so the 'package' will now be delivered tomorrow night."

"That delay was my fault, Pierre, last time out I hit a submerged object and damaged my propeller and I had to wait for a new one."

"That's all fixed now, George?" Pierre was worried for if the fishing boat wasn't operative then they would have to figure out another way of getting the 'package' out of the country and that wouldn't be easy right now.

"Yes and no! My Propeller is fixed but my deckhand broke his bloody leg helping me and is now in the hospital, the worse thing is that I can't work my boat without him as the Germans do spot checks and I have to be able to work my boat normally to be able to blend in with the fishing fleet when needed."

"Hmm." Pierre rubbed his chin as he thought for a moment.

"Does the deckhand have to be a male, George?" he asked, and George looked at Alice.

"I see what you are thinking, Pierre, it could work as a few of the boats have young girls onboard due to the lack of men in the villages these days, yes that could work," said George as he warmed to the idea, a lot of the boats did have young girls helping as deckhands due to the shortage of manpower in the fishing villages now so that shouldn't be a problem, after all they wouldn't actually be fishing, they would only have to pretend if any nosy patrols happened to make him heave too.

"I...I don't know anything about boats, Pierre," said Alice hesitatingly as she looked at them both, she wanted to be taken to where Mary was so that she would be on hand when the Professor arrived, but she felt that Pierre had other ideas, she needed to change his mind without arousing his suspicions.

"You won't need to, Alice, it's only in case a patrol boat stops the boat, you won't actually be fishing and I'm sure George will be able to give you a brief tuition while you are here."

"While I'm here?" she asked him.

"Yes. I need to get the 'package' to the boat after he is delivered to us tomorrow night, but I don't want all of us to be together not after the Doctor being arrested."

"You think he will talk that quick, Pierre?" she asked but he shook his head.

"No, but after his arrest there are bound to be more patrols out, the radio detectors will be out in force just waiting for us to pipe up on the air and I won't risk having two wireless operators together at the same time, the Gestapo would have a field day if they were to burst in on us!"

"That makes good sense, Pierre, so what do you want us to do?" asked George.

"I need you to move the boat to somewhere where we can join it unobserved once the 'package' has been delivered to us, once we are all aboard, we can make the next move to join the submarine and get this damned fellow the hell out of the country."

"Do you know where the submarine will be meeting us, Pierre?" asked Alice as she became a little excited at the prospect of possibly getting a hold of the Professor within the next couple of days and if she could find out where the rendezvous with the submarine would take place all the better, she might be able to get a message to her brother and he would surely be able to intercept it if she hadn't been able to get the professor away from the group before that.

"No, Mary had a cypher concerning that, but I haven't been able to talk to her about that part of things yet, so George, any ideas?"

"I've a small cottage that I use as a safe house, it's about thirty feet on a bluff above a cove, it was used by smugglers for years before this damned war started and has come in handy a few times, I've used it for the aircrews so I know it's safe and Danny can take you to it as he has been there a few times."

"That's good, George, alright Alice, I'll leave you here with George. The package will be with us tomorrow so let's say we'll meet you at the cove at about midnight, if anything changes between now and then, you can give me a call at Danny's farm."

"Right Pierre, we will see you tomorrow"

"Thank you, Pierre, I don't know what I would have done if I hadn't been able to contact you," said Alice sincerely as she did mean that for everything seemed to be progressing nicely.

George led the way out and Pierre was back in his van in a couple of minutes heading back towards Danny's farm, in the cottage George was showing Alice to a room she could use and told her to get some sleep as they would have to go to the fishing boat in a couple of hours and as she lay down, she was trying to think of a way of getting a message to her brother without arousing the old man's suspicions but if she couldn't then she would just have to eliminate him!

It was tempting to shoot him now and get her brother here with his men so that they could catch the rest of the Resistance and the Professor in one fell swoop but to do that, she would need to know where the cove was and she had the feeling that the old man wasn't going to tell her that even if she asked him point blank; no, he seemed too wary and experienced for that, he knew that you only told people what they needed to know to get the job done and now that the Doctor had been arrested, he wouldn't trust anyone that he hadn't known for a long time. She sighed heavily as she lay down on a bunk, she would get some sleep and see what would happen next.

****

"It's alright, Mary, it's Pierre," called Danny from the window as Pierre's van pulled into the yard, the sound of the approaching vehicle had given them quite a shock as they weren't expecting anyone at this hour and Mary with Margite's help had quickly pulled the kitchen table aside and had just pulled open the hatch in the floor when Danny had called out to them, both Women gave a sigh of relief and replaced the hatch then as Pierre entered the farmhouse they pulled the table back into place.

"You gave us quite a turn, man, couldn't you have called to let us know you were coming?" said Danny as Pierre entered the room.

"Sorry Danny, I didn't know I was coming but something has happened," said Pierre as he entered the room and crossed over to the kitchen table.

"Oh, something up?" asked Danny as the two women sat at the table and Pierre shook his head.

"A few hours ago, I got a frantic call from Alice, you know her, Mary, she was working with Doctor Reeves and his group out of Delpeche?" he said, and Mary's ears pricked up as the mention of Alice.

"Earlier today she had just finished a routine contact with London and had left the Doctor's office when she saw the Gestapo arrive and arrest the Doctor, then she called me, I met her and took her out to George, I've just come from there."

"Oh no! Pierre, you…you have to go back, that old man is in danger if she is with him!" Mary had gasped and put a hand up to her mouth as Pierre had spoken. As soon as he said that the Doctor had been arrested, she knew that Alice was to blame and after what London had told her, she had probably planned it all.

"Danger…what the Hell are you talking about, Mary?" asked Pierre frowning.

"Pierre, I tried calling you earlier, but you must have gone to meet Alice. Yesterday, I received a long cypher from London, they informed me that Alice is an imposter, they believe she is an Abwehr Agent that was infiltrated into SOE. She had managed to get a hold of information that she passed onto the Gestapo, that was why we were ambushed in that field. London believes she has been sent after the Professor, they want me to arrest her and if I can't then I am to eliminate her!"

"Bloody hell! I'm getting sick and tired of London not telling us everything, Mary, this woman was inserted into France at the same time you were, that's over three months ago. Surely, they knew this then?" he said hotly, and she shook her head negatively.

"No, I don't think so, Pierre. The cypher I received was in an emergency code so I'm guessing they only found out recently, I think it would have come as quite a shock for them to know that an enemy agent had infiltrated SOE, to my knowledge it is the first time that this has ever been done!"

"Bloody hell, what a mess!"

"That explains your colour yesterday, Mary," said Margite and Mary smiled at the old lady.

"I'm sorry I couldn't tell you, Margite, and…and I think you must have slipped something into my milk as I slept like a baby, am I right?" she asked, and the old lady nodded.

"Yes Dear, I thought that you needed the rest, I see now why you went pale, that message wouldn't have been pleasant to receive?"

"No, it wasn't. Pierre, you have to go back to George, if she is alone with him then anything could happen, I believe he is in danger from her!" she said as she looked imploringly at Pierre, but he shook his head.

"No, I don't think so, Mary. If she is after the Professor, then she now knows that he is going to be delivered tonight, we were to join George at his cottage at the cove, Danny he said that you knew where this was?" asked Pierre looking at Danny who nodded.

"Yes, I have been there a couple of times but why don't you believe that George is in danger like Mary said, surely if this bitch is an enemy agent, then she will probably already have had him arrested?"

"No. Think about it. The Doctor has been arrested we know that, whether she organised it or not doesn't matter as it has happened. So, she gets to me and come to think about it, I never questioned her on how she had my number, I just assumed that the Doctor must have given it to her."

"He probably did, Pierre, in case something went wrong; we all have a contact number to get the word out if someone is arrested, after all!" said Margite and Pierre nodded.

"I suppose you're right. So, she gets to me and I think that she was hoping that I would bring her straight here to Mary, she told me that London had told her she would be joining this group to help Mary with her cyphers!"

"Yes, London organised that to get her to me, it was then up to me to try to arrest her if I could or—"

"Yes, I know, Mary, Jesus, I don't believe what they expect us to do sometimes!" And Pierre brushed his hand over his head as she said this, something he did when he got frustrated with things.

"So, she knows that the Professor is being delivered to us tonight, I then got her to be with George on his boat and have organised a rendezvous at this cottage, I don't think she will do anything to him until she knows she has a clear shot at getting the Professor."

"Can we bypass George, Pierre, if she is with him then we could get the Professor out of it without him having to go anywhere near her surely?" asked Danny but Mary shook her head before Pierre could say anything.

"No, we can't do that, George, if we do then every Resistance member that she has had contact with over the past three months is in danger, as soon as she realised that she had no chance with him then she would denounce the lot of them, no, it is imperative that we get her out of the way as soon as we can!"

"I really don't like the way this is turning out, Mary, but I see your reasoning!"

"So, what can we do. We have to deliver the Professor safely to England, but we also have to eliminate Alice to protect the Resistance Groups?"

"Then we will do just that. As soon as the Professor has been delivered to us, George will drive him and you to the cottage at this cove. I will go back to George and Alice now and will join them on the boat which we will then take around to the cove to meet up with you, you'll just have to be ready there, Mary!"

"Alright Pierre but on one condition?"

"Oh, what's that?" he asked frowning again.

"I want Danny and Margite out of the picture, I want them to get Mark and then they can all get out of the area, I want them SAFE, Pierre!" she said hotly, and Pierre nodded and held up his hand as Danny made to interrupt.

"I was going to organise that anyway, Mary, I just haven't had the time."

"What do you mean 'you were going to organise that anyway'?" asked Danny hotly, Pierre was about to answer when Mary spoke.

"Danny, I was recently arrested, and I was bloody lucky to have been able to escape, now Doctor Reeves has been arrested and there is an enemy agent in our midst, you must see that you and Margite are no longer safe here, I…I'm just sorry that I can't get you to England." Mary was close to tears as she said this as for, they had both become very dear to her, it was a miracle that they hadn't been discovered for this long, she would never forgive herself if anything should happen to them.

Danny raised a hand as he gestured around at the room in general. "I…I just never thought that we would actually have to leave this place someday," he said quietly and Margite leaned over and hugged him.

"It's better if we do go, my love," she said, and he nodded sadly.

"Thank you Margite, and I really am sorry," said Mary as she patted the old lady's arm and Margite nodded.

"Thank you, Mary, but it isn't your fault, Dear, it is just the way things have turned out."

"I'll go around and see Mark now, I'll let him know what has happened and that he should also leave before anyone gets the chance to denounce us. Then I'll go back to George and Alice, Danny, you will need to get a hold of the Citroen, alright?"

"Alright Pierre, but do you think that Alice might get suspicious with you going back so soon?"

"No, I'll tell them that the Germans were sniffing around my garage, so I thought it best to go now. Mary, once the Professor has been delivered, get a signal off to London and tell them that 'the package has arrived' then destroy the radio and your cyphers, alright!" he asked, and Mary nodded.

"I was going to do that anyway, Pierre."

"Good, oh by the way do you know where the fishing boat is supposed to rendezvous with the submarine yet?"

"Yes, I have the coordinates for George, I'll give them to him when we meet at the cottage."

"Good girl. Right, I'm off then, I'll meet you at the cottage at midnight tonight." Pierre stood up and extended his hand to Danny.

"I will miss you, my friend," he said simply as Danny stood up to shake his hand warmly.

"Take good care of yourself, Pierre, I know we will meet again soon, eh?"

"You can count on that, Danny." Pierre then turned and hugged Margite warmly as he was going to miss the loveable old lady.

"Take care of you both, Margite."

"I will, you take care, Pierre, and please be careful as I have a bad feeling about all of this."

"I will," then before he could see the tears well up in her eyes he hurried out of the farm and a couple of minutes later he drove off.

"I'd best go and fetch the Citroen," said Danny as he turned to leave.

"Be careful, Danny."

"I will, my love," then Danny hurried out and Mary turned to the old lady as Margite wiped her eyes.

"I'll help you pack some things, Margite?" she said, the old lady nodded, and they left the room.

****

For Professor Linus, the day had been long and very uncomfortable as he was once again squashed into his small hiding place in the back of the van, three times he had cowered down as they had been stopped at road blocks and he had sweated it out as the driver had shown his papers and had answered questions before they had been allowed to move on, then thankfully the van was stopping then the rear doors were quickly opened.

"Jump out! Quickly Professor!" Linus scrambled painfully out of the van and groaned as he stretched his cramped muscles then looked up as the driver held out his hand to him.

"This is where I leave you, my friend, Bon Chance!" said Gabin as they shook hands and an old man stepped out of the shadows.

"Thank you for everything, Gabin, keep safe, eh?" The man nodded before getting back into the van which quickly pulled away and disappeared into the night.

"This way!" the Professor followed the old man into the farmhouse then as the door closed the lamps were turned up, he found himself looking at an old man who was holding a pistol pointed at him, an old lady was sitting at the kitchen table and next to her was a young woman who was tapping rapidly on a Morse key which was connected by a long cable to a wireless set, as she finished tapping she turned the set off, removed her headset then looked at him steadily for a moment.

"Professor Linus?" she asked as she stood up.

"Yes, are you Lilly?" he asked as he had been told that an SOE Agent with the code name of 'LILLY' would be meeting him at some stage although he hadn't known exactly where or when he would be meeting her, he just knew that when he did that he would getting near to the end of his journey across the country.

"That's my code name, you can call me Mary. This is Danny and his wife, Margite," said Mary as they all shook hands.

"I'm very pleased to meet you and I must thank you all for what you are doing for me, I know the risks that you are taking, and I am grateful," said Linus as he shook each of their hands in turn.

"We don't have much time, Professor, as we have to leave, the toilet is through there if you need it and Margite has some coffee in a thermos for you."

"We are leaving so soon?" asked the Professor as Mary began taking the radio apart and she nodded.

"Yes, things have happened, we have to leave."

"I need the toilet if you don't mind as it has been a Hell of a long day?"

"I'll show you the way," said Margite leading the Professor off.

"I'll do that, Mary, if you could take care of the codes?" said Danny as he came over to the radio set.

"Thank you, Danny." As Danny continued to take the radio apart, Mary quickly burnt her cyphers and codes, it seemed a funny thing to have to do but they couldn't risk being caught with any of them on their person, it would be hard enough getting through any patrols that may be out and she just hoped that they wouldn't as she didn't want any firefights just now but knew that she wouldn't let herself be caught again.

"Alright, take him out to the car and I'll be right behind you," said Danny as the Professor returned with Margite.

"Don't be long, Danny!" They went out of the farmhouse and Danny went about setting up a couple of boobytraps for anyone that came into the farm, he had no intentions of leaving this place to those pigs, anyone they knew wouldn't be coming back to the farm, so he had no worries of hurting any friends! He quickly went around with his silenced pistol and shot all his pigs then with the explosives set and wiping the tears from his eyes over what he had just had to do, he hurried out to the waiting Citroen; within a few minutes, they were underway.

Having to stay on the backroads to avoid any possible patrols meant that it took them just on three hours, the last part was down a bumpy dirt track just wide enough for the car, it was a rising road and when they finally came up to the small cottage Mary could see why the smugglers had used it for it was well concealed, had a small stone wall about three feet high around it and there was only one way in and out as the rear of the cottage was three feet back from the edge of a thirty foot drop down to the cove with the entire place being shrouded by small shrub like trees and bushes, it was a well-hidden little cottage with a clear view out to sea. Danny pulled the car up outside the small wall.

"I'll have a quick look around, be ready to get out if you hear any shots, alright?" he said as he got out of the vehicle.

"We are ready, Danny!" Danny quickly hurried into the cottage then after a few minutes, he hurried back out.

"All clear, Mary, I don't think you should light any lamps just to be safe, but you have a good view out of two windows. There is a backdoor leading to a small pathway along the edge of the bluff, I'll rig a couple of trip wires at both ends of this so if anyone tries to come up from behind, you'll know, alright?"

"But what about Pierre or George, they might set them off?"

"No, George knows this place better than anyone, he wouldn't use that pathway at night as it is too dangerous, it's very crumbly and not much of a path and Pierre will be with him so it should be alright, and it might give you a couple of minutes warning."

"Alright Danny, you do that, and I'll get us set up inside."

"Right." As Danny set off, Mary led the Professor and Margite into the small cottage, this had three rooms, a kitchen, tiny dining area with a large heavy wooden table and three chairs and a single bedroom, there was also a very tiny bathroom with a toilet and sink at the rear, it was very small but rather homely and as there was a three-quarter moon, it was easy to see your way around.

"Do you think it would be alright to light the stove, Mary?" asked Margite as she looked around the cottage, putting a Sten gun and a bag containing spare ammo magazines on the table.

"Not yet, Margite, the smoke may attract attention, but we might be able to in the morning, I'll see what Pierre says when he gets here."

"Alright, if you're sure." Mary moved to the windows and looked out trying to see what was around so that she knew where she might have danger come from, there was about a six foot gap between the side of the cottage and the stone wall that surrounded the place which had a gateway in the centre, the vehicle was parked near this so she had a good view out, she checked the other window and saw that this also gave a good view of any possible approaching snoopers, whoever built the place obviously had military training of some kind or perhaps they had been smugglers? Then Danny came in wiping hands on his handkerchief.

"All done Mary, I've put a trip wire attached to a hand grenade at both ends of the pathway at the rear of the cottage, if they are set off, you'll have a couple of seconds to react, alright?" he said as he looked around.

"Thank you, Danny, now you had better leave, you've a long way to go before it gets light, eh?" she said trying to smile but there was a large emotional lump forming in her throat, she was going to miss this old man and his wife; to her surprise, Danny stepped forward and hugged her warmly.

"You're a very brave girl, Mary, and it has been my pleasure knowing you," he said which made her tears start to flow.

"Thank you, Danny, I shall never forget you." Then Margite was hugging her as well and both women were crying.

"Take good care of yourself, my dear," said Margite as they hugged.

"I will Margite, take good care of Danny and be careful."

"Bonne Chance, Mary!" Then with a brief nod to the Professor the two hurried out to the car then in a few minutes they were gone and for the first time since she had escaped from Major Schrandt, Mary felt very alone and scared.

"What happens now?" asked the Professor, Mary wiped her eyes and turned to him.

"Now we wait, we had better get ready just in case we get unwanted visitors." She went to the table and opened a canvas bag, pulling out a Sten gun which she checked before holding it out to him.

"I...I've never used a gun," he said hesitatingly.

"Well let's hope that you won't have to but if we get company then I will need your help until Pierre and the others get here. If we are attacked, then we need to make them think that there are more of us here than just you and me otherwise they could rush us. Now, this is a Sten submachine gun, it will fire an automatic burst every time you pull the trigger, try to use only short bursts if you can so you don't use too much ammo too fast as we don't have much."

"Alright." He took the weapon gingerly, and she couldn't help smiling a little.

"It has a twenty-eight round magazine, when the mag is empty the bolt will stay back, you push this little button here to release the magazine, insert a new one then push the bolt forward with your thumb and keep firing and this is the safety catch, its set to safe now so just move it like this to fire, alright?" she said as she showed him how to use the safety catch and he nodded rather dubiously.

"Right, can you help me move this table?" The cottage door was the split barn type, she put the catch on the bottom half then opened the top half and latched it open then he helped her move the old and heavy wooden table which they then up ended at the doorway.

"That should provide us with some cover if anyone shoots at us, you stay here by the door, don't stick your head out, Professor, and let me know if you see anything at all, alright?" she asked as she moved back to where the table had been and took up her canvas bag from which she took three hand grenades before going back to him.

"These are hand grenades, Professor, you hold this little arm down, pull the pin and throw. When you do that, they will go off in four seconds so drop down flat if you must throw them. Now put them in your pockets, use them as a last resort if you must, alright?" Again, the Professor shakily took the hand grenades from her and careful put them into his trouser pockets, he hoped to God that he would never have to use them as he was scared to death just having them on him.

"You…you think that the Germans are going to find us, Mary?" he asked nervously but she shook her head.

"No Professor, I'm just being cautious. What you don't know is that a member of a neighbouring Resistance Group has just been arrested so when that happens, the Germans get jumpy, there are more patrols out now, so I am just getting us ready should the worse happen, that's all."

"Did you know them, Mary?"

"Know whom?"

"The person that was arrested, did you know them and were they arrested because of me?" he asked her as she crossed over to one of the windows and peered out as she cocked her own Sten gun.

"Yes, I knew them, we get to know a few of the other Resistance Groups from time to time, we had worked together before, but it wasn't because of you, Professor; unfortunately, we have a traitor amongst us!" she said, and he could hear the bitterness in her voice.

"Do you know who that is, Mary, the traitor I mean?"

"Oh yes I know her, Professor, I also know that if she wasn't preoccupied trying to catch you then she would have denounced a lot of the Resistance Groups that she has come into contact with, so in a way you have done us a favour."

"All I seem to have done is cause a lot of people a lot of trouble," he was glad that there wasn't the best lighting in the place, so she wouldn't be able to see the shame on his face, he knew that he had caused a lot of people a lot of grief, he was just hoping that no-one had been killed because of what he had done.

"Well, you are doing the right thing now Professor and that is the main thing isn't it, that for whatever reason you have decided to get your information to the Allies so that we can defeat whatever it is that you have been working on?" said Mary but he shook his head negatively.

"I should have done something about this sooner, if I had then maybe my…" The Professor stopped as the breath caught in his voice as he thought about his wife, mother and father, if he had been brave enough to have acted sooner then maybe they wouldn't have been killed, maybe they would have been here with him now!

"Whatever happened in the past, Professor, you must leave that behind you, if you don't it will tear you apart. Right now, you have an opportunity to make things right. Does that make sense to you?" she asked, she didn't really know what it was that he had been working on but whatever it was had to be important otherwise SOE wouldn't be trying so hard to get him to England. Linus looked at her but could see that she was genuine in what she was saying, he didn't know her and yet here she was setting up a defence of this small cottage should it be needed without the slightest signs of any doubts about what she had to do to keep HIM safe, he thought that was remarkable for such a young woman.

Mary moved away from the window, crossing to the wall where she had placed a canvas bag holding a few simple supplies and the coffee thermos, which she took out, pouring a cup of coffee for them both.

"Here Professor," she said passing the small mug over to him.

"Thank you, Mary." The Professor took the mug and looked out of the doorway again as he sipped it, it was only just hot but tasted very nice after a long day but then he stiffened as he went to take another sip as he thought he had seen some movement off to the side but then he relaxed again as a seagull took off squawking into the night.

****

At the fishing boat harbour, on the small stone jetty Alice reached up from the deck of the fishing boat and took the canvas bag from George which she took into the wheelhouse before going down into the boats small saloon, this held a bench seat forming an L shape around a wooden table, there were two bunk beds one over the other to one side and in the opposite corner was a small paraffin stove which provided meagre cooking facilities and the heating in winter, all in all the saloon was small but cosy.

As she dumped the bag down onto the table she had a quick look around the saloon for anything that would show her the location of the cove that they would be moving to shortly but there was nothing here, she knew she was running out of time if her brother was to be able to get some men to the cove so that they could arrest the professor and also capture Mary and rest of her Resistance Group.

She went up into the wheelhouse and started poking around, then her heart seemed to skip a beat as she spotted a rolled up navigation chart stuffed into an overhead shelf above the helm, quickly checking to make sure that the old fisherman wasn't going to stumble across her looking at the chart she unrolled it and then smiled broadly for there was a neatly pencilled line running from their present location along the coast to the cove, she quickly scribbled down the name of the cove on a piece of scrap paper which she put into her pocket then stuffed the chart back into its place, as she did so she heard a thud as George jumped down onto the deck, she left the wheelhouse and met him as he came along the deck.

"All stowed, Alice?"

"I put the bag onto the table, George. Should I get the stove going so I can boil some water for coffee for when we get to this cove?" she asked wondering how on earth she was going to be able to get word to her brother.

"Oh damn!" said George as he put a hand up to his forehead.

"What's wrong?"

"I forgot the paraffin for the damned stove!"

"I'll get it for you if you like; if you could tell me where it is?" she asked as her heart started racing in anticipation, if she could get away for a few minutes then she might be able find a telephone and she had to stop herself from smiling as he nodded.

"Would you mind? It's in a tin by the kitchen table in the cottage. If you can get that, I'll get the engine warmed up, then we can get going."

"Alright George, I'll be back shortly."

"Be careful, the night watchman has been paid off, so he will be out of the way tonight, but you never know if you might run into someone."

"I'll be careful." She quickly jumped up onto the jetty and hurried towards the small gate in the fence surrounding the fishing boat jetty. Then as she approached the gate, she spotted what looked like a wooden shed off to the side but as there was a door with windows she thought this might be some sort of office so hurried over to it, it was indeed a dock office so she went to the side and breathed a sigh of relief as there were window that pulled upwards, she took a knife out of her trouser pocket and after working it in the centre of the window the catch finally gave and she was able to pull the window up.

A quick look Around showed there was no one about so she pulled herself up through the window into the small office which smelt like wet paper and dead fish but her excitement mounted as she spotted a telephone on a table, moving over she quickly snatched up the receiver and getting a dial tone she dialled the number that her brother had given her.

"Hallo Posey Police Station, Major Schrandt's Office," said a rather stiff female voice.

"This is Blackbird, I've a message for Major Schrandt and Major Meyer, do you understand?" she said and hoped that the person on the other end of the line had been briefed for she didn't have much time.

"Understood! Go ahead, Blackbird." Alice gave a sigh of relief.

"Lilly and the package will be in a cottage on the bluff above Sonte' Cove at midnight, did you get that?" Alice waited anxiously as the woman on the other end of the line repeated the information back to her, as she finished, Alice replaced the receiver then hurried to the window and climbing out, she shut it then started running for George's cottage and the paraffin.

At the police station in Posey, the Luftwaffe Secretary who had taken the message hurried along the corridor to Major Schrandt's office where she knocked before hurrying in, the Major was sitting at his desk going over some paperwork and looked up as she entered.

"We just received this message from Blackbird, sir," she said holding out the message which Schrandt took and quickly read.

"Show this to Colonel Brehmner then inform Major Meyer that he is to organise a platoon of twenty men and meet me at that location, got that?"

"Yes sir." As the woman hurried out of the office Schrandt picked up his telephone and dialled a number.

"Sergeant Tolbek." It was Kurt on the other end of the line.

"Kurt, we have Mary's location, get a vehicle and driver then have Conrad meet us out front now!"

"Yes, sir. I—" CLICK, the line went dead before Kurt could finish speaking as Schrandt replaced the receiver before he smiled, he could feel his excitement mounting. He was close to not only getting the Professor but also of capturing 'Mary' then his smile broadened as he thought about what he would do to Mary before he shot her! Then he jumped a little as his phone jangled.

"Schrandt!" he snapped as he grabbed the receiver.

"Schrandt, Colonel Brehmner, I've just been told about the message from Blackbird. What have you done so far?"

"Myself and three me will go straight to the location and Major Meyer will organise a reserve of twenty men and will join me as soon as he can, sir."

"Good, I'll put a call through to the Navy and see if we can't get some sort of patrol boat out to that cove; don't mess this up, Schrandt!" And the line went dead. The major replaced the receiver then hurried out of the office and outside the station, as he did so an open-topped Volkswagen pulled up at the curb with Private Koln driving with Conrad next to him and Kurt was in the back who opened the door for the Major.

"You have the location?" asked the Major as he got into the vehicle next to Kurt.

"Yes, sir I know where it is, and it will take us a couple of hours to get there," said Private Koln.

"Alright, get going!"

"Sir."

"Shouldn't we wait for the Reserve force sir, that way we can surround the place as soon as we get there?" asked Kurt.

"No, that will take time to organise even if this Major Meyer does know what is going on. No, I want us there as soon as possible, we will make sure no one gets the chance to leave before the Reserve gets there."

"Sir." The Major leaned back in his seat and just hoped the information from this Blackbird was correct.

****

On the fishing boat Zeraph, George anxiously looked at his watch, if Pierre didn't hurry up, he would have to leave without him for if he didn't leave at his logged time then the Germans would start asking questions, they might even stop him leaving.

"Here he comes!" called Alice from just outside the wheelhouse, she was standing on the jetty with a mooring line in her hand, this was wrapped around a bollard then led forward to a bollard on the foredeck, the stern line was tied around a bollard near the wheelhouse that George could release easily. Then he was breathing a sigh of relief as Pierre jumped down onto the deck.

"Let go that line, Pierre—Alice, let go!" called George, Alice released her line from around its bollard, jumped down onto the deck and started hauling in the line as George had shown her earlier. Pierre also released the line from the bollard and hauled it aboard and by the time he had done so, they were underway.

"What the hell kept you?" asked George as Pierre entered the wheelhouse.

"Sorry George, I got a bloody flat tyre and had a hell of a job getting the damned wheel off, have you had any trouble?"

"No, everything has gone smoothly."

"Hello Pierre," said Alice as she came into the wheelhouse and Pierre had to force himself to keep his face impassive for with his friends having to leave their farm and with the doctor having been arrested he would have liked nothing better than to be able to get his hands around this bitch's throat, but he couldn't let on that he knew about her being an enemy agent, no, he would do his best to help Mary arrest the bitch and if she couldn't do that then he would shoot her himself!

"Hello Alice, everything alright?" he asked trying to sound friendly and she nodded.

"Yes, but what happened to you, I thought that George was going to have to leave without you.?"

"So did I for a while there, I had a flaming flat tyre."

"Ah well, all good now. I'll go down and make us some coffee, eh?"

"Yes, good idea." Alice nodded and went down to the saloon, Pierre moved over next to George at the helm.

"Do you think that you could take the wheel for a couple of minutes, Pierre? I need to tidy up those lines in case anyone gives us the once over."

"Alright, what do I do?" Pierre moved over and took the wheel as George stepped aside.

"You see this line on the compass?" asked George as he pointed out their heading on the compass.

"Yes."

"Just keep that line on that heading. You won't have to worry about any navigation marks as we have cleared the entrance, so you don't have to worry about anything else, alright?"

"Alright George." The old man nodded then left the wheelhouse leaving Pierre nervously clutching the wheel, ten minutes later Alice came up into the wheelhouse with two mugs of coffee.

"Where is George?" she asked as she handed Pierre a mug.

"Thanks, he's on deck tidying up the mooring ropes, I don't think he was very impressed with our efforts," he said, and she smiled.

"Let's hope that no-one else gets close enough to see them, eh?" Alice put the second mug onto a shelf near the wheel before she turned and went below again, Pierre sipped his coffee and just hoped that everything was going well for Mary and the Professor, he wouldn't be able to help her for another couple of hours if anything had gone wrong.

****

It had taken the Major three hours to get to the cove then they turned off the main road and stopped about a mile short of the cottage's location, as the vehicle stopped the Major inserted a magazine into his Schmeisser Submachinegun.

"Alright, remember that we want these people alive, especially the Professor, so take your time, we'll head for the cottage and keep your eyes open for any sentries that may be posted, keep it quiet. Move out!" He got out of the vehicle and led the way into the low scrub heading for the cottage, he wanted to get his men in place quietly, he would look the place over and decide whether or not to wait for the Reserve force to join him, with any luck he would be able to get the lot of them himself.

Twenty minutes later, he motioned for his men to stop and join him as they neared the cottage. He had seen signs of movement at one of the cottage windows but there had been no signs of any sentries posted which probably meant they didn't have enough men to mount a guard, he decided he wouldn't wait for the Reserve force to join him as they were still about two hours away, no, surprise would be the key here.

"Conrad, Koln, make your way to that gap in the wall, do it slowly so as not to attract attention, Conrad, when I give the signal, lob a grenade at the door, that should burst it open and when it does we will rush the cottage, remember all of you that I want them alive if possible so only shoot to wound, understood?" he said as he looked at each of them in turn.

"Understood Major!"

"Right. Move—quietly!" Slowly and carefully the men moved forward to their positions then the Major signalled to Conrad who raised himself a little as he unscrewed the cap on the bottom of his stick grenade so as to be able to pull the toggle to set it off, then as he moved his arm back to throw the grenade, a

Sten gun rattled at the cottage window, the rounds stitching across Conrad's chest, he cried out as he fell and two seconds later, the grenade went off shattering the peace of the night.

A few minutes earlier, Mary had returned to her position at the window, she had gone to use the toilet and to check that the windows were bolted, as she looked out the window, she caught a movement out of the corner of her eye.

"Professor, we have company!" she whispered harshly as she reached down to retrieve her Sten that was leaning against the wall, the Professor looked up a little startled as she did so.

"What—?" he started to ask.

"Sssshh!" Mary moved her Sten into position in the open window, she had caught sight of two figures moving slowly towards the stone wall surrounding the cottage.

"What's happening?" Linus had felt his heart start to race as Mary reached for her Sten, now he was really worried for if she was going to open fire, it meant that the Germans had found them, and he felt his hope of freedom slipping away rapidly. At first, Mary thought the approaching figures may have been Pierre and the others coming up from the cove but if it was then he would have let her know by now, then she caught sight of a figure crawling towards the gap in the wall where there was a small wooden gate.

"Professor, get ready; when I—Oh Shit!" Mary swore loudly as she saw the man who had been crawling suddenly come up onto his knees as he drew back his arm to throw the grenade, she fired a short burst that caught him across the chest, he cried out as he fell back.

"Fire Professor!" she called, and Linus squeezed his trigger.

KARUMPH! The grenade exploded by the cottage wall with a bright flash and a resounding crack throwing rubble from the wall and dirt through the window shattering the glass and framework, Mary shook her head to clear the ringing in her ears; shaking off the glass as she peered through the dust and smoke.

The Professor had ducked involuntarily as the grenade's explosion scared the hell out of him, he had seen Mary duck as the window shattered and she was showered with dirt and splintered glass, then he looked back out of the door and squeezed his trigger again, the Sten stuttered and a figure that was about to jump over the low wall changed his mind and jumped back as the Professor's rounds sent chips of stone flying from the wall next to him. Linus jumped a little startled as Mary had quickly crossed the room and had put her hand onto his shoulder.

"Change places, Professor, go to the window and remember to use short bursts only as we have to save ammo, alright?" she said, and he nodded surprised that she could talk so calmly.

"S…sorry," he said before he hurried over to the shattered window.

Mary knelt behind the table at the door, she had changed positions with the Professor so that she would have a better field of fire and view from there.

"Professor, left-hand side of the gate, see him?" she whispered urgently as she saw two men, one by the left-hand side of the gateway who was too obscured for her to get a good shot in, there was a second figure just back a little from the wall.

"Yes, I…I see him," called Linus in a hoarse whisper as he moved a little until he could see the figure that she had pointed out to him.

"Short burst—NOW!" she called as she squeezed her trigger, the two Stens stuttered together, the Professor's rounds shattered the woodwork of the gates left side making the figure there move back for cover, Mary's rounds blew the top off the wall directly in front of the figure she aimed at, making him jump sideways for better cover, the bolt on Mary's Sten gun clunked as it stayed back as the magazine was empty, she pulled out the empty mag and rammed in a new one then flicked the bolt home but the attack seemed to have stopped for the moment.

****

The fishing boat Zeraph had dropped anchor in the cove, they dragged the boat's small lifeboat alongside from where it had been on its chocks behind the wheelhouse, Pierre helped Alice over the side then passed down the canvas bag that held their weapons, she moved to the rear as she would be manning the tiller, he then lowered himself into the boat and moved a little shakily to the thwart in the centre and fitted one of the two oars into it rowlock, George stepped nimbly down from the fishing boats side, cast off the painter and moved to the thwart all in one seemingly easy movement then pushed the boat off before fitting his oar and within a couple of minutes and with his whispered guidance they were underway heading for the shore, they were roughly hallway between the fishing boat and the shore when Pierre jumped involuntarily and spun to look towards the shore as a hand grenade exploded somewhere onshore followed closely by the unmistakable stutter of a Sten gun.

"Jesus!" said George as he stopped rowing.

"Come on George, we have to get ashore, quickly!" snapped Pierre as he turned around and picked up his oar again, then he gasped as Alice took a pistol out of her jacket pocket and pointed it at them.

"I think not!" she said, and George looked up in surprise as she raised the pistol threateningly.

"What the Hell!" he said looking at Pierre in disbelief.

"We will return to the fishing boat!" said Alice as she pushed the tiller over.

"What the Hell are you on about, our friend is over there and obviously needs our help!" said George but she shook her head negatively.

"We will wait for my companions who will shortly have everything under control!" Alice gestured towards the shore as she said this as the gunfire started again.

"My GOD! You're a bloody German!" said Pierre with disgust in his voice, he didn't want to let on that he knew precisely who she really was, there could still be time for Mary to arrest the bitch but first they had to get ashore to help her!

"I'm Dutch actually but my companions are German," she smirked as she said this.

"Jump Pierre!" shouted George as the old man suddenly stood up, making the boat rock violently; instinctively, Alice grabbed for the side of the boat to steady herself as she raised the pistol again, sensing what the old man was trying to do, Pierre half lunged and half stumbled as he launched himself at Alice as she pulled the trigger, the pistol barked with a bright flash and Pierre gasped as the round ripped through his jacket and grazed his shoulder with a searing heat as he fell on top of Alice, grabbing her arm as she struggled to raise her pistol to fire again.

She started thrashing about frantically trying to break his grip and shoot at the same time, then he caught a blur of movement as George snatched up the small wooden bailing pail from the bottom of the boat and swung it with all his might, catching Alice a blow to the side of the head, she cried out then fell into the bottom of the boat unconscious.

"Bloody hell!" breathing hard, Pierre grabbed her pistol as he fell back onto his seat.

"You alright, Pierre, you're bleeding," asked George as he pointed to a patch of blood on Pierre jacket as Pierre got himself back under control.

"I am thanks to you, George, that was bloody well-done, mate!"

"What the Hell happened! I assume this bitch is a collaborator?" asked George as he pointed to the prostrate form of Alice in the rear of the boat.

"Something like that. Do you have some rope, so we can tie her up, George, we have to get ashore to help Mary as quick as we can?"

"If she is a collaborator, why don't we just shoot the bitch and toss her over the side, good riddance if you ask me?" asked George as he gave the unconscious girl a hefty kick.

"No, Mary has orders to arrest her if she can, we'll tie her up and leave her in the boat until we know what is happening with Mary." George nodded then quickly found some rope and none too gently he tied Alice's arms behind her back.

"Do you have anything we can gag her with, George, we don't want her yelling the place down once we are ashore?" George reached into his pocket and pulled out his handkerchief which he passed over.

"Let's hope she bloody well chokes on it!" George stuffed the handkerchief into the girl's mouth.

"You take the tiller, Pierre, and I will row us in, alright?" asked George as he took his place at the oars, Pierre nodded and moved to the rear of the boat, he was glad of the old man's suggestion as his shoulder was burning like hell and he doubted if he would have been able to row, as they got underway once more Pierre swore loudly as another grenade exploded ashore.

"Koln, try to make your way to the rear of the cottage, see if there is a back way in, we'll keep them pinned down while you do and sing out once you are inside," said Major Schrandt after getting the two men to come over to him and the Private nodded.

"Right sir." Koln started crawling off to the left and Kurt moved over a little closer to the Majors position at the gate as he watched Koln's progress.

"He's in position, Sir," he whispered hoarsely a couple of minutes later as Koln signalled to him.

"Open fire!" the Major aimed his Schmeisser over the wall and started firing short bursts at the cottage window to cover the Private with Kurt doing the same. At the door of the cottage, the Professor ducked as he saw the muzzle flashes as the firing started and then cringed as the rounds thudded into the woodwork of the doorway and table, showering him in wood splinters and dirt, he raised his Sten and squeezed the trigger, returning their fire with short bursts although he had no idea as to where his bullets were going as he couldn't see anything and was too scared to lift his head up too high as the bullets still thudded into the woodwork and brought plaster and dust off the walls behind him in the cottage. Over at the window Mary also ducked as rounds started thudding into the walls around her, she caught sight of a figure heading towards the rear of the cottage and got in a short burst at him before he disappeared from her sight.

KAARUMPH! As Koln disappeared from view, he snagged the trip wire that Danny had set before he had left, he yelled out as the grenade exploded with a loud rapport in a cloud of dirt and dust, the shrapnel tore his chest open and the blast blew him over the side of the bluff; he was dead before he hit the shingle below. The gunfire ceased as the grenade exploded as it took everyone by surprise. Kurt moved a little closer to the Major as he whispered harshly to get his attention.

"Major?" Major Schrandt looked around as he inserted a new magazine and cocked his weapon.

"What?"

"Koln is dead, and I only have two magazines left, sir."

"Shit!" the Major checked his own weapon; he was also running low on ammunition. "See if you can get over to Conrad and Koln, get their spare clips!"

"Koln is gone, sir, that grenade blew him down the bluff, but I can get to Conrad." Swearing softly to himself, Kurt started crawling toward Conrad's lifeless body a few yards away, he managed to retrieve a couple of magazines and one stick grenade before a burst of fire from the cottage window made him pull back, so he made his way back to the gateway.

Down in the cove as the small boat hit the shingle of the beach, George pulled in his oars, jumped over the side and pulled the boat a couple of feet higher up onto the shingle, Pierre jumped over the side and started pulling a Sten from the knapsack that he had pulled out from under the thwart, he inserted a magazine cocked the weapon and held it out to George along with three spare magazines.

"You know how to use this, George?" he asked, and the old man smiled at him as he took the weapon.

"I do, what now?"

"Use only short burst as we don't have much ammo, alright?" As Pierre said this there came a short burst of fire from the cottage.

"Sounds like your friend is doing the same, Pierre." George looked up the buff and wandered what they were about to get themselves into, he found to his surprise that he was quite calm and steady.

"From what I could hear, I don't think there are many soldiers up there, George, not yet at least so we will have to hurry before reinforcements can get here, are you ready?"

"I am but I'm not a very good shot with these things!" said George and Pierre smiled, he hoped that the old man wouldn't have to be.

"You just keep their heads down, alright let's go!" Pierre started moving up the track that led up to the top of the bluff hoping that Mary could hold out until he was able to help her.

Up on the top of the bluff Kurt moved a little closer to the Major so that they could concentrate their fire on the cottage.

"Use only short bursts, Kurt, we'll keep them bottled up until our men arrive; when they do, we will rush the cottage and get this over with."

"I have three grenades Major, I could lob two, we could move up under their cover, then I could blow the door with the third and we could rush them now, what do you think, sir?" asked Kurt as he looked up at the cottage, he knew the person on the doorway was the better shot, the one at the window had been firing fairly wildly but had been close a couple of times but he thought they would stand a good chance of being able to rush the cottage under the cover of two explosions, they could keep their heads down with their remaining clips then if need be they still both had their pistols with a couple of spare clips.

The Major thought it over for a couple of seconds, he decided it was worth a try, if it failed then they could just sit and wait for their reinforcements to arrive, after all the people in the cottage couldn't get out past them if they kept some of their ammunition.

"Right but we will need a better position. Move over to that gap in the wall." The Major fired a short burst to cover Kurt's move then crawled after him.

Inside the cottage, the Professor had ducked as the shots chipped brick and dust from the wall behind him, Mary could see the two men moving towards a low gap in the wall caused by the earlier grenade explosion and knew they were about to try something, she had only been firing short bursts when she thought she had a chance to hit her target but she only had a few rounds left in the magazine in her Sten, after that she would only have her silenced pistol and she only had three clips for that then it would all be over, as she looked over at the

Professor, she suddenly remembered that he had a couple of hand grenades and an idea started forming.

"Professor—your hand grenades, pass them to me quickly!" she whispered harshly, shakily Linus pulled two grenades from his pocket and quickly moved over to pass them to Mary, he had hated having the horrid things in his pocket and was only too glad to be rid of them.

"Give me a hand to move that table away from the door!" she said as she took the grenades and he frowned at her.

"Why, that table is giving you cover surely?" he asked, and she shook her head as they moved to the table and dragged it out of the way.

"I think they are about to rush us; I don't have enough ammo to beat off a determined attack." As they moved that table, she went back to the door and peered out to see how much time she might have.

"Go over and unlock the back window on the left, I think it was shattered by that grenade we heard. When you hear me call now, I want you to jump out of that window and get yourself down to the beach, find Pierre, he shouldn't be far off but don't go to the right as there is still another trip wire there, alright?"

"No, you can't—you'll—" he started to say but she cut him off angrily.

"Don't argue! I don't have time—Please Professor you have to do this for me?" He could see the look of desperation on her face, and he swallowed hard as he nodded, he crossed to the rear window and unbolted the catch and opened the window before returning to the door which he also unbolted for her.

"Sorry Professor, I didn't mean to bite your head off," said Mary as she pulled the pin on the first grenade.

"Thank you, Mary, Bonne Chance!" Mary nodded and took a deep breath as he opened the door for her before he crossed back to the rear window.

"NOW!" As Mary threw the first of her grenades out of the door and started firing her Sten, the Professor threw himself out of the window and as he landed, he started running for his life with tears streaming down his face for he felt sure that the young woman that he had only so recently met had just committed suicide to save his life.

Major Schrandt had scrambled to his knee and had raised his sub machinegun intending to cover Kurt as the man raised up to lob his two grenades but at the same time Mary had come bursting out of the cottage doorway, her grenade landed a few feet away with a dull thud and he threw himself sideways.

KAARUMPH! Mary's grenade exploded with a dull roar followed closely by two others as Kurt's exploded nearby, he had been caught across the chest by a burst from Mary's Sten as she had burst out of the doorway. Mary saw her burst take the man on the right, she had seen his two grenades fall and had thrown herself to the ground just before they went off in a double flash and bang that showered her in dirt and debris momentarily deafening her, shaking her head hoping to get rid of the ringing in her ears and with her heart racing she madly scrambled back to her feet hurrying to the wall where she stopped dead in her tracks for lying there on his back was Kurt, half his side had been blown off by the explosion of three hand grenades close together, his right leg was missing and his entrails were pooling on the ground, Mary turned aside and was violently sick.

"So, you are here!" Mary jumped startled as the quiet vice spoke behind her, she turned her world spinning momentarily as she saw Major Schrandt. He was lying there partly propped up against the wall, his left leg was shattered lying at an odd angle as was his left arm, there was blood on his chest and he was breathing with difficulty, but he was holding his Schmeisser submachine gun in one hand and it was pointing directly at her.

"Not bad for a schoolteacher, Mary, or should I call you Lilly?" he asked as she straightened up, she could see he was badly wounded, the question was would he shoot before he lost all his strength from the loss of blood?

"Does it really matter now, Major?" she asked as all the fight suddenly drained out of her.

"I don't suppose that it does really, but I would like to know even if it is only for my pride?" he said then gasped in pain as he coughed hard a couple of times.

"I will tell you if you tell me where you got the information about me from, Major?" she asked, and he grinned.

"SOE aren't the only ones to play with spies, Lilly, the Abwehr does also."

"You mean Alice?"

"It would appear so although if those Gestapo idiots had confided in me earlier, I could have doubled my efforts and I would have extracted the information from you!" Mary shook her head, she knew the man was dying, he was ebbing away even as she watched but he was stubbornly holding his weapon on her, at this range he couldn't miss, but she shook her head negatively.

"No! I would have died before denouncing my friends."

"I knew I should have drowned you when I had the chance!" The Major went to raise his weapon then Mary cried out as a weapon barked loudly close to her but the Major jumped and spasmed as six bullets thudded into his body and he slumped sideways as he died, although she thought that he had fired.

"You won't be drowning anyone now, you bastard!" said Pierre as he hurried over to Mary who looked as though she was about to faint.

"I…I thought he had me! Why didn't he shoot?" Pierre pulled the Major's weapon from his hand, pointed it away from them and pulled the trigger, there came a loud 'CLICK' as the bolt went forward, but the magazine was empty as was the chamber. Mary turned aside and was violently sick again. Even though the man had been dying, he couldn't resist tormenting her one last time.

"Mary—the Professor, where is he?" asked Pierre as he put his arm over her shoulder then gasped as he did so as pain shot through his shoulder making Mary look up at him.

"Pierre, you're hurt, there is blood on your shoulder?" she said as she straightened up looking at him concernedly.

"That bloody bitch Alice shot me. George has her tied up in the boat."

"I…I'm so sorry, Pierre," she said, and he shook his head.

"Not your fault, Mary, now where is the Professor?"

"I…I told him to run down to the Cove when I decided—" Mary stopped and took a deep breath to steady herself, she had been about to say when she had decided to commit suicide for that was what it would have been if she had failed and only fate had deemed otherwise as it was by sheer luck that she had decided to throw her grenades at the same time that Kurt did, now she just felt close to collapsing from exhaustion now that the fight was over.

"I told him to run down to the Cove to find you."

"Right, anything in the cottage?"

"Just my knapsack and some empty magazines for the Sten."

"Get them quickly, we need to get the hell out of here before any patrols turn up."

"Alright, don't go to rear of the cottage on the right-hand side, Danny set a booby trap before he left," she said as she hurried off.

"Did he by God, well thank you, Danny." Pierre quickly checked the German bodies, but they were all dead so all they had to worry about now was any patrols or reinforcements that might turn up so the faster they got out of the cove the better he would feel.

"Pierre, all clear on the roadway," called George as he came running up, Pierre had told him to cover the road when he had approached the cottage, he didn't want to risk the old man unnecessarily as he needed him to run the fishing boat if they were to have any chance of escaping.

"Thanks George."

Mary had hurried into the cottage, she scooped up the empty Sten magazines and stuffed them into her knapsack before hurrying back outside to where Pierre and an old man were waiting.

"This is George, we are using his fishing boat, George, this is Mary," said Pierre as an introduction.

"Quite a party you had here, young lady," said George as he nodded respectfully to her, Mary just nodded not sure of what to say as it felt a little surreal to her just then.

"This way!" called Pierre then they started running down the pathway leading down to the cove, as they drew closer to it, they could see a figure leaning in over the boat and Pierre saw that it was the Professor and with a start he realised that he was untying Alice.

"Professor—NO!" he shouted but it was too late for as they started running onto the shingle, Alice jumped out of the boat and spun a startled Professor around, holding a knife to his throat, they all came to an abrupt halt about ten feet away from the boat.

"It's all over now, Alice, Major Schrandt and his men are dead!" said Mary stepping forward.

"I don't give a damn about that idiot, throw your weapons down or I will slit his throat!"

"And if we do, what then, Alice?" asked Pierre, he knew it was too risky to take a shot at her, he might hit the Professor.

"The Professor comes with me, and you can all disappear quietly!" Alice started moving back up the beach as she said this making sure that the man was between her and them, so they wouldn't have a clear shot at her. The Professor was staring at them wide-eyed knowing full well what would happen to him if this woman handed him over to the Germans, he cursed himself for being a fool, he should have known something was wrong when he found her tied up in the boat, but he had thought that the Germans had done that, not his companions.

"Put your weapons in that knapsack and throw it into the water over there!" demanded Alice as she indicated the water off to her side.

"Alright but the Professor is of no use to you, his information has already been sent to England!" Pierre was trying to buy some time as he thought of what he might be able to do, he began putting the weapons into the knapsack as he edged slowly towards Mary, he knew she had her pistol, he had seen her trying to slide her hand into her skirt pocket unobserved.

"Stand still, Pierre, and toss that bag into the water!" snapped Alice as she was getting inpatient.

"Alright." Pierre made to toss the bag towards the water, then at the last second he tossed it directly at the Professor who flinched instinctively bringing his arms up to protect his face which had the effect of moving Alice's arms up as well, as he did so the Professor caught sight of Mary removing the pistol from her skirt pocket, remembering how this woman had bravely charged out of the cottage facing imminent death without flinching stiffened his resolve, he swung his arm up, catching Alice a glancing blow to the side of her face making her flinch back, he broke free of her grip and ran off behind the boat as Mary raised her pistol.

"Stand still, Alice, or I WILL shoot!" Mary snapped this out, she was a little shocked to see that her hand was rock steady as she felt as if she was shaking like a leaf all over, but she was determined not to let this woman escape, there were too many lives at stake, she was even more surprised when Alice gave a short barking laugh.

"Why, Mary? So, you can take me back to England where they will torture me for information before they shoot me for being a spy or hang me for being a traitor, I think not!" As Alice made to bring the knife up to slit her own throat rather than being captured, Mary's pistol jumped twice.

PHLAAT! PHLAAT! Alice staggered back a couple of paces as the two bullets took her squarely in the heart, her mouth opened and closed a couple of times as she dropped to her knees then a smile appeared on her face as she fell sideways dead onto the pebbles. Pierre reached up and took the pistol from Mary as she started to cry quietly.

"It's alright, Mary, it's better this way."

"I…I'm sorry Pierre, but I couldn't let her suffer even if she was a Traitor!" Mary knew that Alice had been right, if she had of taken her back to England, they would have tortured her for information, then after putting her through all of that they would have hanged her for being a traitor, even though she didn't agree with what she had done and how much harm she could still have done, she knew that she couldn't let her go through all of that.

"It's alright, I understand but we must go, Mary!" Mary nodded and let herself be led to the boat, she climbed aboard and sat at the stern while the men pulled the boat out into the water pushing it out a little before climbing in, the Professor sat next to her as Pierre and George started rowing the boat towards the fishing boat, she flinched a little as the Professor put his hand gently onto her shoulder.

"What you did was right Mary, so don't reproach yourself," he said quietly but she pulled her arm away.

"I know you mean well, Professor, but please, leave me alone!" The Professor nodded as Mary wiped the tears from her eyes, she knew she had committed a terrible sin by killing Alice in cold blood, but she also knew that she couldn't have taken her back to England to be tortured. She wouldn't have talked, she would have suffered needlessly before they executed her, she couldn't have let that happen. She tucked her left hand under her armpit as she thought about Kurt and his 'little pins'. As the boat bumped alongside the fishing boat, the men scrambled aboard then the Professor and George reached down to help Mary as Pierre's shoulder wound prevented him from helping, George ushered them all down into the saloon.

"I'll get us underway, Pierre, I've an idea where we can hide up before tonight's rendezvous, I just hope we can get there before being discovered," said George quickly as he wanted to get them underway, they had to be out of the area before first light or before any patrols stumbled onto them.

"I'll give you a hand, George," said Pierre and George chuckled.

"No offence, Pierre, but you couldn't help yourself right now, you need to rest, my friend!"

"He's right, you need to take care of that wound. I don't know much about boats, but I can take orders so if I can be of any use, George?" asked the Professor and George nodded.

"Follow me." As the two men left the cabin, Pierre sat down at the bench seat around the table.

"I really should go and help," he said as Mary came over to him.

"You can't help anyone until we take care of that wound, take your jacket and shirt off while I see if George has a first aid kit on this boat." Pierre didn't argue as his shoulder was hurting like hell, even removing his jacket was agony.

Mary searched around the cabin returning with a bowl of water, some bandages and what she thought was a bottle of some sort of disinfectant which she poured into the bowl and soaked a reasonably clean cloth before she turned to look at the wound. Pierre's shoulder was badly bruised and there was an angry looking furrow across the top of the shoulder as if someone had laid a hot iron across it, but he had been lucky for the bullet could have done much worse.

"This is going to hurt a little," as she said this the fishing boat's engine fired up. Pierre clenched his teeth sucking in a breath as the disinfectant entered the raw wound, bringing tears to his eyes.

"Sorry—sorry." Mary bathed the wound then dressed it as best she could before helping Pierre to put his jacket on.

"You should rest, lay down on the bunk." As she made to move away, he caught her arm.

"I'm so sorry Mary, I shouldn't have left you with the Professor in that cottage." Mary shook her head as he said this, and she forced a smile.

"It wasn't your fault, Pierre, it just happened. Now get some rest eh and I'll see if I can get that stove going to make us some coffee." Pierre nodded and moved over to the bunk where he laid down with his shoulder throbbing dreadfully, Mary started prodding at the stove and by the time she had it lit Pierre was asleep. The fishing boat was underway by the time Mary had made some coffee so poking around in some cupboards she was able to find some tin mugs, pouring the black coffee into these she took three mugs up to the small wheelhouse where George was at the boats helm and the Professor was in one corner.

"How is Pierre?" asked George as he took the coffee.

"He's asleep. I cleaned up the wound as best I could. It had only grazed the shoulder; he was lucky, George." George sipped the coffee and looked at her in the dim light.

"You did well, Mary. This whole thing could have worked out a lot worse, you know?"

"Yes, I know." Mary looked around at the Professor. "Are you alright, Professor?"

"Yes, thanks to you Mary. I…I shall never be able to thank you enough for what you have done, I owe you my life and saying thank you just doesn't seem to be enough." Linus felt totally inadequate as he said this for he knew that he owed his life to this young woman who was the bravest person that he had ever met, twice today she had risked her own life saving his and she hadn't hesitated to do it both times and just saying thank you didn't seem nearly enough.

"Don't thank me yet, professor, we are by no means safe. When they find those bodies, all Hell will break loose!"

"I've been thinking the same thing, Mary, we need to get to the next cove before daylight, I'm pushing the old girl a bit, but I think we will make it," said George between sips of his coffee.

"So, we can hide in this Cove until we have to move out to rendezvous with the submarine, is that right, George?" asked Mary but the old man shook his head negatively.

"No, for us to be able to stay out of sight means that we have to blend in with the local fishing boats, the boats are out fishing now and will go back to the Cove in the morning, that's why we have to be there then but they won't be able to go out again until the following night!"

"Christ! Is there no other way, George, I don't know if the submarine will be able to hang around for another night?"

"Can you get off a signal to find out, Mary?" asked the Professor, he could see the concerned look on the girl's face and could understand why for if they couldn't make the scheduled rendezvous with the British submarine then their chances of escape were slim indeed.

"No. We destroyed my transmitter when we had to leave Posey, along with my code books."

"So, my transmitter would be no good then?" asked George with a mischievous smile.

"What! You have a wireless set, George?" she asked as her hopes started raising again, if George could keep them safe until they could arrange another rendezvous with the submarine then they might still get away yet.

"I do. Professor, can you take the wheel for a few minutes?" asked George and the Professor nodded hesitantly.

"If you show me what to do, I can." The Professor stepped forward and George showed him their heading on the compass.

"Just keep that line on that heading until I get back and don't worry if you are a couple of degrees either side, alright?"

"Got it!" The Professor tentatively put his hands onto the wooden spokes of the boat's steering wheel, he had never steered a boat in his life but he was determined to help these people in any way that he could, he owed them that much; he just hoped the old man wouldn't be away for too long. George led Mary below to the saloon, he went over to the stove and pulled open a concealed panel in the bulkheads woodwork revealing a cubbyhole from which he withdrew a wireless transmitter which he took to the table then with a few deft moves he connected the aerial lead from the set to a socket in the deckhead next to a light fitting, plugged in the wire for the Morse key and then the one for a set of headphones before turning to Mary.

"Be careful, Mary, as there are Direction Finders on the coast here, they will try to triangulate your position as soon as you start transmitting. Can you put the set away once you have finished as I want to go back to the Professor, he didn't look too comfortable at the helm."

"I can and thank you, George." The old man nodded and hurried out. Mary turned the set on to warm up then fiddled with the frequency dial. Not being able to send a coded message was a major risk, London could totally ignore what she was about to send but she still had to try for if they couldn't alter the rendezvous with the submarine, they wouldn't get out of France but she had no intentions of ever being caught by the Germans again so she held her breath as she sat down put the headphones on and started tapping the Morse key.

At the SOE camp in England, the Duty Radio Operator was startled from his daydreaming as he heard Mary's call sign in his headphones.

"Sarge! Call sign 'LILLY' sending," he called, and the Duty NCO picked up his phone and dialled Major Scott's number.

Major Scott had just finished a mountain of paperwork and was pouring himself a small brandy when the telephone jangled, he quickly snatched up the receiver and swallowed the brandy.

"Major Scott?"

"Major, this is the Duty Wireless Office, we are receiving an Emergency Plain language signal from call sign 'LILLY', sir."

"Tell her to standby, I'll be there in a couple of minutes."

"Right sir." As the line clicked off, the Major dialled Beth's number.

"Captain Simms?"

"Beth, meet me in the Wireless Office, Mary is transmitting!"

"Right sir." CLICK—as the line went dead the Major hurried out of his office making his way across the lodge, as he entered Beth walked in from the other side of the room.

"You sure it is Lilly?" she asked the operator and he nodded.

"Yes Ma'am, I've dealt with Lilly a number of times and I know her 'hand'. I would say that it is her." Every Agent had a distinct way of using a Morse key and the operators got to know the way they transmitted, it had come in handy a few times when an agent had been captured and 'turned' being forced to work for the Germans, they had been able to let London know they were being forced to transmit so that their bogus information had been ignored.

"Is she under duress, do you think?" asked Major Scott frowning, he hoped by everything that he held dear that Mary hadn't been captured again and 'turned' there was just too much at stake for her mission to have gone sour, but the Operator shook his head negatively.

"I don't know why she is sending in plain language sir, but I would say that she isn't under duress, if anything she is sending really carefully."

"I would say she is making sure that we know it is her and she's letting us know that she is in trouble!" Beth hoped that whatever was causing Mary to send this way wouldn't prevent her from getting out of France, things were getting too hot for her there now and it would only be a matter of time before she was captured again.

"Right, so we need to keep this brief for her, what's your challenge, Beth?" asked the Major as he looked at her, as Mary's handler she and Mary would have organised a safe word that would be used in just this sort of circumstances, it would be her way of proving that she was who she claimed to be and that she was transmitting under her own free will.

"Send—INTERROGATIVE—BETH?"

"Ma'am," the Operator tapped his key then they waited.

On the fishing boat Zeraph, Mary had anxiously awaited after establishing the initial contact with London, she knew the routine and knew that Major Scott and Beth would have been sent for, now they would either believe who she was and would continue the communications or they would ignore her and if they did that then she was as good as dead for once the German bodies had been found she had no doubts that they would be hunted down and there would be no mercy this time, then she jumped as the Morse started cheeping in her earphones and her heart started racing.

"INTEROGATIVE—BETH?" asked the Morse in her ears, Mary relaxed a little as she knew that Captain Simms was by the Operator.

"MARY—MARGARET," as she tapped out her reply, she couldn't help smiling a little for this was Beth's full name—Elizabeth Mary Margaret

Simms—they had agreed that if she was being forced to send a signal that she would only send 'MARY', so this was proof to Beth that she was genuine.

In England, Beth felt her excitement and relief mounting as she heard the reply coming in.

"It's genuine, Major, that's Mary."

"You're certain?"

"Yes sir, I have no doubts."

"Bloody marvellous! Right, find out what she wants. Something must have stuffed up badly for her to be sending in plain language!" The Major had been holding his breath as he had waited for that authentication, he had been hoping that it was Mary, he just hoped now that they would be able to help her.

"Tell her to send!" said Beth and the Operator started tapping his key. On the fishing boat, Mary could have jumped for joy when she received that single word for it meant that they understood that she was in trouble and they were willing to help so she started to reply.

"PACKAGE MINUS ONE RECEIVED—PICK UP PLUS 24 URGENT," all the while that she was tapping her key, she knew that the shore Detection stations would be trying to triangulate her position, she just hoped that Beth would understand what she was trying to get across to them as she had to keep the bursts of Morse as short as she possibly could.

In England, Beth looked up at the Major as they received the signal, it didn't sound good and was very vague.

"Package minus one? Does she mean the Professor or Alice, do we risk asking her to clarify, Major?" she asked, and the Major shook his head.

"No! Whatever has happened must be bad for her to risk sending in plain language and I don't want to put her at further risk. No, tell her to standby while I talk with the Navy, we have to see if that submarine can hang around for another pickup."

"Right sir." As the Major hurried out Beth told the Operator to tell Mary to standby.

On the fishing boat Zeraph, Mary sat back as she received the 'standby' signal. Looking at her watch, she knew they only had a couple of hours before dawn, then they would be in this Cove where George hoped they could mingle with the other fishing boats but she knew that she wouldn't be able to transmit then so she just hoped that London wouldn't take too long to reply, she sat staring at the frequency dial for forty minutes before the tweeting of Morse in her ears made her jump a little.

'PICKUP PLUS 72'; she sat bolt upright as she received this for it meant that the pickup had been delayed for 72 hours—three days—were they totally insane!

'PICKUP URGENT—REPEAT—URGENT!' She tapped out mainly because she was frustrated and couldn't say what she needed to say without a code book, she desperately wanted them to know what their situation was, but she couldn't send any of that in plain language.

'PICKUP PLUS 72—ENDS'—Mary swore savagely before she acknowledged the signal then she took her frustration out by not too gently dismantling the wireless set and replacing it in its cubbyhole, then she poured herself a cup of lukewarm coffee before heading up to the wheelhouse.

"Well?" asked George as she entered the wheelhouses, and he could see by the look on her face that she wasn't happy.

"The pickup has been delayed for 72 hours, George."

"Oh Christ!" He could see why the girl had looked upset, 72 hours! What the Hell had caused that, he wondered.

"Did they say why?" he asked but Mary shook her head.

"No, but I was using plain language, so they didn't want me transmitting for long in case the shore DF picked us up, bit of a sod, isn't it?"

"Well, there isn't much we can do. Is the pickup in the same place, Mary?"

"As far as I know," she looked at him hard, his calm manner was helping ease her nerves a little.

"I'm sorry, George, I didn't mean to snap at you," she said, and he smiled.

"That's alright, you'd best wake Pierre, tell him we should be up with the other fishing boats in an hour or two."

"Alright, thank you George." Mary went below, she shook Pierre's shoulder gently to wake him.

"Hmmm—what?" Bleary-eyed, Pierre looked at Mary before he sat up blinking rapidly to clear the sleep from his head.

"Oh, sorry Mary, what's happening?" he asked yawning.

"I've managed to establish contact with London, our rendezvous has been postponed for seventy-two hours and Gorge said to tell you that we will be up with the other fishing boats within the hour." Pierre nodded and winced as he sat upright.

"How did you manage to contact London when we don't have a wireless transmitter?"

"George has a small set, but I don't have any code books, so I had to keep it brief as I was using plain language!"

"I bet they loved that!" he said with a broad grin which made her relax a little.

"They had me confirm everything three times before they were satisfied that it was me, Pierre!"

"I should bloody well hope so! Anyway, that's standard routine. So, what did they have to say for themselves?" He knew that transmitting in plain language was normally a massive no-no, but this was an emergency situation, after all if they weren't delivering a 'package' for those idiots in London then they wouldn't have been in this situation in the first place.

"The pickup is in the same place Pierre, but it has been put back for seventy-two hours and with us using plain language—well they could hardly tell me why!"

"Damn! Let's go and see George, see what he has to say." Mary then followed Pierre up to the wheelhouse.

"How's the shoulder?" asked George as they entered.

"Could be worse. Mary tells me the rendezvous with the submarine has been put back for seventy-two hours, what do you think?" asked Pierre as he went to standby the open door where the fresh salt air helped to clear his head and wake him up.

"I'm hoping to join up with some of the boats out fishing in this area, if we can do that then we should be able to get into Taliard Cove."

"Can you do that, just join a group of fishing boats, I mean, George?" asked the Professor, he had been trying to keep out of the way in the wheelhouse, making small talk and being ready to help in any way that he could but he was worried, the postponement of the rendezvous with the British submarine really had him concerned, now it seemed that they were just going to join a group of fishing boats out in the middle of nowhere, it just seemed to be a risky thing to attempt.

"Normally no, but I have an arrangement with the boys here as I have been smuggling in this area for years."

"What about the Germans? I am sure that they would have patrols out surely?"

"Not always. You see, Professor, there are a lot of fishing boats that operate all along the coast, after all, war or no war the population still need to be fed and like most navies the Kreigsmarine have a major shortage of patrol vessels, or at least they don't have enough to have a boat with each group of fishing boats, so what they do is a kind of roving patrol, hopefully our group will be safe when we join them."

"But how will you know if it is safe to join these other boats, what happens if a patrol boat shows up?"

"The boats let each other know if there is a patrol boat in their area. As for you people, well I will need one person to act as my deckhand, the rest I will have to hide and that brings me to another point, Pierre!"

"What's that, George?" The old man pointed towards Mary.

"She will have to act as my deckhand!"

"What! Why?" asked Pierre a little surprised by the suggestion as for the last few days he had been trying to hide Mary, now the old man wanted her out in plain sight?

"Because I had to register Alice as my deckhand before we left. One thing the Germans are hot on is paperwork, if a girl is registered as a part of this crew then a girl there must be."

"That does make sense, Pierre, and with the Major and Kurt dead, there isn't anyone else that knows me by sight, at least not anyone that is actively searching for me." Mary could see the concerned look on his and could understand why, they were taking a major risk by being on this fishing boat and being dependant on someone else for their safety, but it had to be done if they were going to stand a chance of delivering the 'package' to London.

"You still have your pistol, Mary?" asked Pierre and Mary nodded as she touched her jacket pocket.

"Yes, with a couple of spare clips as well."

"Alright George, looks like we are in your hands from here on!"

"Mary, in the Saloon, you'll find some old trousers and a shirt, would you mind changing into those as it is very unusual for a deckhand to be wearing a skirt?"

"Of course, I will do that now," she said then turned to go.

"Could you prod that stove back into life so I can make some coffee?" asked Pierre and she nodded as she left the wheelhouse.

"What's on your mind, Pierre?" asked the old man before Pierre could speak.

"Was I that obvious, George?"

"Only to me but I have been doing this for a long time, don't forget," said George smiling and Pierre nodded.

"If we do run into trouble, George, how are we off for weapons? Their Stens are out of ammo and I'm pretty low myself."

"In the paint locker in the bows, I have an ammo box and a box of grenades, if you'll take the wheel, I will fetch them."

"Thanks George."

"I'll give you a hand, George." As Pierre moved over to the helm George and the Professor left the wheelhouse. A few minutes later, they returned each carrying a small wooden box which they took down to the Saloon before George returned to the wheelhouse.

"Right oh, Son, I'll take her!" George moved back to the Helm.

"Thank you." Pierre made his way to the Saloon where for the next half an hour, he helped Mary load some spare magazines for their Sten guns before priming half a dozen hand grenades. Mary then cleaned her pistol; she had already changed into an old pair of blue trousers with an old shirt and a short jacket which thankfully had large pockets where she could conceal her silenced pistol.

Pierre lifted one of the bench seats on one side of the table where they stashed the Stens, Mary noticed that he had slipped a hand grenade into his pocket, so she did the same before the bench top was replaced.

"I'll take some coffee up to George," she quickly filled two mugs and hurried out.

"What do you think our chances are, Pierre?" asked the Professor as Mary hurried out.

"To be honest, Professor, if you had asked me that question a couple of days ago, I would have said slim to none! Now with Mary having killed that bastard Schrandt with his henchman, well now I think we stand a fair chance." Noticing the man's concerned look Pierre put a hand onto the man's shoulder and smiled.

"Don't worry, Professor, we'll look after you." The Professor nodded and they both went up to the wheelhouse where it was starting to get light with the approaching dawn, as they entered the wheelhouse George was lowering a pair of binoculars, he had been studying a dark shape on the horizon.

"Mary, go forward to the mast, on the right you'll find a line, it's attached to a blue Bargee, haul it up then make it fast, would you?"

"Alright George." Mary hurried out and a few minutes later a small blue flag ran smoothly up the mast to the yardarm and George nodded, suitably impressed.

"Don't look so surprised, George, Mary was in the Royal Navy before she became an Agent, after all," said Pierre as Mary came back.

"How did you know that, Pierre?" she asked as she entered the wheelhouse.

"You told me, back in Posey."

"Oh yes—sorry Pierre I…I must just be tired." She actually felt totally exhausted, her entire body was aching badly, she knew that if she did sit down for any length of time she would go straight to sleep, Pierre nodded as he looked at her, he could see the strain in her eyes. He cursed himself for being a fool, he also felt a little guilty as she had made him rest earlier when she had dressed his wound.

"I'm so sorry Mary, I didn't even think about it. You must be exhausted, why don't you go and get some rest, I'm sure George won't need your help for a little while yet?" he said, and the old fisherman nodded.

"Good idea, you get your head down for a while, young'un, I'll call you when I need you!"

"Are you sure, George?"

"Yes lass, off you go."

"I…I think I might," with a nod to them Mary headed for the Saloon.

"I should have damned well thought of that earlier, she must be exhausted."

"Well, she's been busy that's for certain."

"You might as well turn in too Professor, the next couple of days might be a little hectic."

"Alright Pierre but call me if I can be of any use, alright?" Pierre nodded and the Professor left the wheelhouse.

"He feels incredibly guilty, you know, Pierre," said George as the Professor left.

"Oh, why's that?"

"We were talking earlier, Pierre, did you know that his mother, father and wife were all killed a couple of months ago?" asked George quietly.

"No, I didn't."

"Apparently, they were all under some kind of house arrest, the Germans' way of getting him to do their bidding I suppose anyway his parents' home was near some airfield or other and one day some idiot trainee pilot lost control of his aircraft and crashed into their home, they were all killed at the same time."

"Bloody Hell! This damned war has a lot to answer for, George!"

"It has that."

When the Professor reached the Saloon, he saw Mary laid out on the bunk, she was lying facing the bulkhead with her knees drawn up, she was indeed asleep but she was also sobbing quietly, he pulled the blanket up over her, he felt ashamed for what he had done working for the Germans; as he watched her sob quietly, he swore to himself that he would make it right no matter how long it might take.

****

At the Cove, Major Meyers men rapidly spread out from the track leading up from the main road, they approached the cottage cautiously, the Major held up his hand as one of his men came across the body of Major Schrandt.

"Two more over here, Major!" called one of his men and the Major hurried over.

"Check the cottage! Looks like they have gone but check it anyway, I'll take half of the men down to the cove, let me know if you find anything."

"Yes sir." The Major took half of the men and hurried down the pathway that led down to the cove, as they reached the shingle of the beach they suddenly looked around as there came an explosion from up at the cottage, the Major hesitated for a moment but as there was no sound of any gunfire he continued on to the beach.

"Major—over here sir!" the Major hurried over too where one of his men was kneeling over the prostrate form of a woman and his heart sank as he recognised his sister, kneeling he lifted her shoulders from the shingle, she had been shot in the heart at close range but strangely, there was a smile on her face.

"Oh Greta, I knew this wasn't going to end well for you," he cradled her for a few minutes, he was just thank full that their mother had died a few years before the war so that she wouldn't have to bare this loss, as he knelt there with tears in his eyes he felt his anger mounting, he knew who Greta had been chasing and why, he now swore by everything that he held dear that he would find this traitorous bastard professor and the English agent that had taken his beautiful sister and he would make them pay dearly!

"We can continue with the search if you would like some time, sir?" said Lieutenant Brems as he waked over to the Major but Meyer shook his head as he lay his sister gently down onto the shingle.

"No! I want you to help me find the bastards who did this."

"There are drag marks in the shingle sir, looks like they had a boat waiting." Then they both looked up as a soldier came running up the beach.

"Did you find something?" asked Meyer.

"There was a booby trap set up at the rear of the cottage sir, luckily one of our men spotted it and we managed to set it off with no casualties. From the looks of the cottage, there were at least two shooters inside sir."

"Right, get everyone back to the vehicles, we will head for the next town and find a phone so I can call the Colonel, hopefully he will be able to get a Navy Patrol going along this coast. Could you have a couple of men stay with my sister, Lieutenant, until I can arrange to have her collected later?"

"Of course, sir." They returned to their vehicles then tore at breakneck speed along the coast until they reached the next military post where Major Meyer put through a call to the Colonel.

"I'm sorry about the loss of your sister, Major, from what I hear she was a very good Agent, the Abwehr will miss her."

"Thank you, sir," the Major swore softly under his breath as he didn't give a stuff about the bloody Abwehr, but this wasn't the time to grieve, he could do that later in privacy.

"But you will have to grieve later, for now we have to concentrate on finding that damned professor!"

"I understand that sir, so I thought that I would see the Navy and try to organise a Patrol along the coast here, we have indications that a small boat was taken off the shore so they must have had a larger vessel waiting."

"Leave the Navy to me. Get yourself to Caldace, there is a small port there, I'll arrange for you to join one of their Patrol vessels so you can start your search from there."

"Yes, sir but if they got off the beach then surely—"

The Colonel cut him off, "Don't argue with me, Major. We know they were to have made a rendezvous with a British submarine but we think that was damaged in an attack so I don't think there will be any pickup tonight so get moving and contact me once you have arrived in Caldace!"

"Yes sir." The Major slammed down the telephone as he swore savagely, he wanted to hunt those bastards down himself but now he was tied to the flaming Colonel and he dare not cross him, swearing again he joined his waiting men and they set off for Caldace.

****

Phillipe Brenton was a hunchbacked old man of seventy, he was the master of the fishing boat gypsy and he had fought in the first world war alongside old George of the Zeraph, these days he helped old George whenever he could be it smuggling or helping move downed Allied aircrews to escape from France, now he boarded the Zeraph carrying a string bag holding a bottle of milk, some bread, sardines and tomatoes.

"I hear you lost your nets last night, old friend?" he called out loudly to George as he boarded the fishing boat which was tied up alongside a wooden jetty in the small port of Poldie.

"Yes Phillipe, we lost the bloody lot, snagged on a wreck I think." George held out his hand to his old friend who had been deliberately talking loudly to warn him of the presence of a couple of German soldiers who were walking along the jetty.

"Good to see you again, George, let's go below away from prying eyes eh?" said Phillipe as they shook hands warmly, George nodded and led the way down to the saloon.

"When is the next rotation, Phillipe, I need to hide out here for three days, will that be possible?" asked George quickly as they entered the saloon, he led the way over to the table and Phillipe looked up as Mary entered the saloon.

"Hello—who do we have here then?" asked Phillip as he nodded politely to Mary.

"This is Mary; Mary, this scruffy old bugger is Phillipe."

"Enchante Mademoiselle," the old boy gave her a wink as he said this which made Mary smile.

"Pleased to meet you, Phillipe."

"Well?" asked George a little irritably.

"Normally I would say yes not a problem but about an hour ago, the dock office was told to suspend the fishing for tonight."

"Damn! Did they say why?"

"There are two armed trawlers based at Caldace, that's a larger port about three miles further up the coast, they normally patrol the fishing grounds every couple of days, today for some reason they were sent out on a Patrol, one east the other west and we can't go out until they return."

"Damn!" George looked really worried as Phillipe told him this for it could seriously jeopardise their ability to make the rendezvous with the submarine.

"Is it you they are after, George?" As Phillipe asked this, George turned as Mary had put her hand into her jacket pocket, he knew she was reaching for her silenced pistol as she thought the man might be some sort of threat to them, but he held up his hand, stalling her.

"Easy Mary! Phillipe is a trusted friend; we are safe with him and he has helped me many times with the aircrews." As George said this Phillipe raised a quizzical eyebrow, he saw her relax a little as she removed her hand from her pistol.

"Sorry," she said a little sheepishly and Phillipe smiled broadly.

"It isn't often these days that such a pretty woman considers me a threat, Mademoiselle," he bowed to her, and Mary couldn't help laughing a little as the tension was eased.

"If they hold to their normal form, George, I will say we will probably go out again the day after tomorrow. They can't delay us too long as it interferes with the rationing."

"Well, that might be alright then, don't you think?" asked Mary as she looked at the old man.

"Possibly," George just shrugged his shoulders.

"I will see what I can find out, do you have a lookout posted, George?"

"No but we have a very good view from the wheelhouse."

"Well keep your eyes open, my friend, the Boche seem a little jumpy, eh?"

"Thank you for the bread and milk, Phillipe."

"My pleasure." Phillipe turned to leave then nodded to Mary again with a small wink.

"Mademoiselle." Phillipe left the saloon and Mary waited till he was well out of earshot before she spoke.

"Can he be trusted, George?" she asked, and the old man smiled.

"With your virtue, probably not," and George did a small chuckle at his own joke. "But with our safety, certainly. Phillipe is one of the biggest racketeers in these parts and is known to many crooks, I trust him with my life, Mary."

"We are doing just that, George, I don't want to sound as if I'm doubting you, I just feel very uneasy being in this town." Mary could understand the logic of what they were doing, they were hiding in plain sight as it were, trying to blend in with the other fishing boats in this small port banking on the fact that with the Major and Kurt dead no one else knew what she looked like, they just had to hope that no one took any real notice of them.

"I understand your feelings but there isn't anything that we can do until we can get out of here with the other fishing boats, until then our hands are tied."

"Well, I suppose we had better let Pierre know what is happening, and I am sure that we could all do with something to eat."

"Yes, I'll get the stove going if you could let them out, please?" As George crossed over to their meagre little stove Mary nodded, she walked over to the bunkbed by the bulkhead where she flicked a locking catch before swinging the bunk up on its hinges against the bulkhead, then she reached down to a pull ring set into the deck, pulling this lifted a square hatch cover revealing a three foot wide hatch in the deck which led down into a store room that was approximately ten feet wide and eight long, there was a single bunk on one bulkhead on which were sitting Pierre and the Professor, Pierre had stood up as the hatch cover was raised, he doused the single oil lamp that was their only source of light and smiled at Mary as she stood looking down at him.

"Everything alright?" he asked as he moved to the steel-runged ladder that led up out of the hatch.

"Yes, come up and have something to eat," she moved aside so that they could climb the ladder out of the storeroom, George made them some coffee and they had some bread and cheese as they did, so Mary filled them in on the situation.

"Not much we can do until they let the boats go out fishing again, I suppose," said Pierre as he munched on some cheese, he was glad that George's friend had been able to supply them with some food as he hadn't realised how hungry he had felt.

"Isn't there any other way, Pierre, I think we are taking too big a risk being in this port, I think we should try something else." Mary was getting very anxious just sitting around in this port, she felt sure that someone was bound to get curious about them and that could only lead to trouble.

"What Mary? You have no code book so we can't contact London reliably as plain language is just too risky, I know it is hard, but we just must sit it out and wait for George to get us out safely."

"I suppose you are right. I'm going to the wheelhouse where I can keep a lookout!" With that Mary got up and walked out of the Saloon."

"I can understand her feelings, Pierre, as I don't like this waiting either!" The Professor refilled his coffee cup as he spoke, he had been having a hard time understanding why they had come to this port, it seemed as if they were now bottled up, he couldn't see them being able to get out at all.

"Don't worry Professor, we will get you to your rendezvous with the Submarine come what may. Now I think I will go and give Mary some coffee." Pierre poured a mug of coffee and went up to the wheelhouse where Mary was sitting on a stool by the helm, she looked around as he entered.

"I brought you some fresh coffee, Mary."

"Thank you." Mary took the coffee and took a sip before she looked up at him. "You think I am being stupid, don't you, Pierre?"

"No, I understand your concern."

"I…I won't be taken by them again, Pierre, I…I know I couldn't go through that again." Mary felt stupid as she was close to tears as she spoke, but Pierre could see the fear in the girl's eyes and his heart went out to her.

"Don't worry Mary, I won't let anything happen to you, I promise!" he said sincerely, and Mary nodded as she took a sip of the coffee, she wanted to believe him but as she looked out of the wheelhouse window she had a bad feeling that something was going to go horribly wrong for them.

****

In the small port of Caldace, Major Meyer had just been handed a clipboard by a Naval Lieutenant.

"This is a list of all the fishing boats in this area sir, there is a group that is due to go out fishing tomorrow afternoon, we must let them go out or we start interfering with the fishing quota for rationing purposes."

"And how many Patrol vessels do you have in this area, Lieutenant?"

"We have two armed trawlers, and we have the occasional use of a light aircraft from the local Luftwaffe airfield, sir."

"There is a search plane available?"

"Not always sir but we have been able to use it in the past."

"I want that aircraft in the air at first light Lieutenant, if they argue tell them to contact Colonel Brehmner!"

"Yes sir."

"Meanwhile, have the men split into teams, I want all of these fishing boats checked and accounted for as per this list, make sure they are each searched thoroughly before they are allowed to go out fishing, is that understood?"

"Yes sir." As his men hurried out to their vehicles the Major slapped a fist into the palm of his hand, he would get that bastard professor if it was the last thing that he ever did along with that British agent bitch.

****

On the fishing boat Zeraph, Mary sat at the table with earphones on her head, she had set up George's small wireless set, she was monitoring the London frequency, she didn't think they would try contacting her while she didn't have any codes but it was routine to monitor the frequency and it was keeping her mind off other things. She looked up as the Professor came over carrying a plate on which there was a small omelette, and she raised a quizzical eyebrow.

"How on earth did you manage that, Professor?" she asked as she sat up a little smelling the hot omelette appreciatively as it was something that she hadn't had for some while and the Professor smiled.

"Phillipe managed to send a few eggs over with some other supplies, so I was able to make two of these, one for the boys and one for you. It's my way of saying thank you for what you have done for me, Mary," the Professor looked a little embarrassed as he said this as it felt a totally inadequate thing to say but Mary smiled at him as she picked up a fork.

"You don't have to thank me, Professor, as I was really only doing my job but thank you, this really looks lovely," she smiled then started eating.

"How on earth did you get yourself tangled up in all of this, Professor?" she asked him between mouthfuls.

"Vanity! Pride! My own ego! You see, I was the top in my field before the war, then when the Germans invaded, they put me in charge of a Research Facility where everything was going well for a while," he smiled at a memory which faded quickly.

"When the Gestapo removed two of our top planners because they were Jews, we all protested and refused to work, that's when they showed their true colours, they put our families under house arrest threatening to send them to concentration camps if we didn't 'cooperate'; too late I started to realise that I wasn't as important as I thought I was." He gave a small, embarrassed smile before going on.

"Then they married the pulse jet engine that we had been working on to a pilotless aircraft and before I realised, we had designed a 'flying bomb'!" The Professor paused again to wipe the tears from his eyes.

"Then came the training accident at the Luftwaffe airfield near my parents' home, a plane crashed into the house killing them all, my mother, my father and worse of all my wife!" He pulled a handkerchief from his pocket and wiped his eyes.

"It was then I decided I had to do something about this terrible weapon that I have helped design." Mary could see the hurt and despair in the man's face, and she felt sorry for him.

"Well Professor you are making amends now by taking this information to London, this will help us defeat these weapons," she said but he only shook his head.

"That's just it, Mary, there is no—" The Professor's words were cut off by the ringing of a bell, Mary jumped to her feet as it was an alarm buzzer that George had rigged to warn the passengers that he occasionally smuggled of approaching danger!

"Back into the hide! Quickly!" she called as he jumped up and she started dismantling the wireless set which she stuffed back into its small hide.

"Mary—soldiers! Get up to the wheelhouse quickly," called Pierre as he came bounding into the room, he helped the Professor get down into their hide before Mary slammed the hatch down over their heads, she lowered the bunks then had a quick look around the Saloon making sure there was nothing incriminating in the Saloon before hurrying up to the wheelhouse where Phillipe was talking to George.

"What's happening?" she asked.

"Trouble—the dock office has told us that we can go out to the fishing grounds today, but soldiers are searching every fishing boat in the port." Phillipe was anxiously looking out of the wheelhouse windows as he spoke.

"Is that just routine?" she asked, he shook his head.

"No—they have a list of all boats in the area which they are checking before they search the boats and Zeraph isn't on it, Mary!"

"What do you think we should do, George?" she asked as she felt her heart give a skip.

"There are only two men searching each boat, Phillipe thinks we have about five minutes before they reach us so if I can get them to come down to the Saloon, do you think you can take them out with your silenced pistol?"

"Take them out?" She was a little shocked that the old man could talk about killing two men so casually.

"It's the only way, Mary! Phillipe will get his boat moving shortly and we need to accompany him out of the port to make it look like just two boats going out early to the fishing grounds; now we aren't on this damned list so these soldiers will probably arrest us once they realise, we aren't supposed to be here, I can't think of any other way, can you?" Mary could see his logic and realised that there wasn't an alternative for once these men started searching and realised that they weren't on this list then they would detain them until they were checked out and that wasn't good.

"Should we tell Pierre?" she asked, and the old man just shrugged his shoulders.

"I'd best get going, George." Phillipe turned to leave then turned back quickly.

"Damn, they are already here!" he said as he had spotted two soldiers getting off the nearest fishing boat just along the jetty, he turned to Mary and shook her hand warmly.

"Bonne Chance, Mademoiselle," then he turned to George. "I'll try to delay them a little, George," he said as they shook hands.

"Thank you for everything, old friend!"

"You owe me a bottle the next time I see you." Phillipe hurried out of the wheelhouse, Mary went back to the Saloon and sat at the table, she pulled her pistol from her jacket pocket, checked the magazine, cocked the weapon, she then clicked off the safety catch, she held the pistol out slightly beneath the table then swallowed hard with a mouth that had suddenly gone bone dry as her heart started racing, then she jumped as feet thudded on the deck overhead, she heard muffled voices, her heart started racing faster as she followed the footfalls.

On the deck overhead, George had met the two soldiers as they boarded his boat and was leading them towards the wheelhouse.

"You are not on this list, where are your papers?" asked the leading soldier.

"I suppose you were given that list in the Dock Office, am I right?" asked George as he tried to buy some time as he led the way.

"What difference does that make?"

"Well, I'm not surprised that I'm not on the list because the clerk is a lazy bastard and is never up to date with his paperwork, this happens every time we come to this damned port! So, what is this all about, do you think I'm smuggling or something?" grumbled George but the soldiers weren't laughing.

"How many people are on this boat?" asked the leading soldier as he raised his submachinegun and George raised his hands as he took a step back.

"Take it easy lad, I am unarmed as you can see!"

"How many on board, old man, I won't ask again!"

"Th…there is just the two of us, my deckhand and myself, she is below in the Saloon," George pointed to the hatch leading down to the Saloon.

"And your papers?"

"Their down there in a drawer."

"Show us. You lead the way!"

"Alright lad but I don't see what all the fuss is about!" Cursing to himself because he had wanted them to led the way down to the Saloon, George turned and made his way down the companionway then made his way slowly down the steps into the Saloon, he was hoping that Mary had heard what had been happening and would be ready.

Mary had heard them talking, she realised that she wasn't in a very good position, she quickly moved to the bulkhead near the steps leading up to the wheelhouse where she pressed herself flat up against the bulkhead, no-one would be able to see her until they had stepped off the companionway steps, George was taking his time and had just given her enough time to change positions, then she held her breath as George entered the Saloon.

"DOWN!" she called harshly; George threw himself to the deck.

'Phlaat!' 'Phlaat!' 'Phlaat!' 'Phlaat!' The two soldiers had stopped dead in their tracks as George threw himself to the deck at Mary's call, the next thing they knew was the silenced pistol coughing rapidly four times then the bullets were thudding into their chests as she stepped out from behind the bulkhead. The first round took the lead soldier squarely in the heart throwing him back into his companion before he dropped to his knees, the second soldier jerked back as a round took him in the shoulder as his companion fell back into him, then as he cried out a second round hit him in the head spraying blood and brains onto the steps as he fell back dead before his weapon hit the floor.

Mary stood there staring wide-eyed at the two men as they lay slumped awkwardly on the steps with the barrel of her pistol still smoking, she swallowed hard to clear the bile from her throat as she lowered her weapon.

"Bloody hell!" gasped George as he scrambled to his feet swallowing hard as he looked at the blood pooling on the steps, he couldn't believe how fast that had happened.

"Get Pierre, we need to get underway—MARY!" George's harsh tone seemed to shake her back to reality, she turned and hurried over to the bunks which she latched up before lofting the deck hatch.

"What's going on?" asked Pierre looking up as the hatch opened.

"Trouble—come up quickly!" Mary stood aside as Pierre and the Professor came up from below, Pierre moved over to where George was standing at the bottom of the companionway.

"Bloody hell!" Pierre looked aghast at the two dead soldiers and the blood on the companionway, then he noticed Mary was holding a pistol that he hadn't seen when he came up through the hatch.

"I…I had no choice, Pierre, they were searching each boat and when George wasn't on their list, they…they were going to arrest him!" Pierre nodded as he looked at her, she was as white as a sheet and the hand holding the pistol was shaking badly and he wasn't surprised as she was a wireless operative, she didn't usually get into action like this and not close action at that.

"We need to get underway, Pierre, before those two are missed!" said George anxiously.

"Mary, you help George get us underway while the Professor and I deal with this."

"Right, come on Mary!" Mary swallowed hard then nodded, she gingerly made her way around the two bodies as she followed George up the companionway, she was glad that she had to help George, if she had stayed there much longer, she knew that she would have thrown up, she knew that she had to kill those two men, indeed their freedom may have depended on it but she still felt totally disgusted and sick.

"Mary—your pistol!" said George as they entered the wheelhouse.

"What?" Mary looked down and felt totally stupid as she saw the silenced pistol in her hand, she hadn't realised that she was still holding it.

"I know it is hard, Mary, but we must act normally while we are on deck or we will attract attention, alright?" Mary jumped as George placed his hand on her shoulder, she felt as if she was wound up as tight as a spring, she took a deep breath as she nodded tucking the pistol back into her jacket pocket.

"I…I'm alright, George."

"Good girl! I've already singled up the bow and stern lines, take in the two breast lines while I start the engine, would you?"

"Yes, alright George." While George headed for the engine room, Mary hurried out on deck hoping the activity might take her mind off the horrid things that she had just done. Down in the Saloon Pierre picked up the submachine gun and rifle that had been dropped by the two soldiers, he removed their spare ammunition and bayonets then turned to the Professor.

"Time to get your hands dirty, Professor!" The Professor swallowed hard as he looked at the pool of blood that was congealing on the steps, it was a sickening sight for anyone, but he had to help so he nodded.

"What do you want me to do, Pierre?"

"We will move them out of the stairway and lay them out by the bunks for now. We should be underway shortly so I doubt if we will be boarded where these two might be seen, so once we are out to sea, we will put them over the side." The Professor didn't trust himself to speak as he was feeling a little squeamish, so he just nodded, then he moved over and grabbed the first soldier's legs, Pierre lifted the body under the arms then they moved the man over to the bunks where they laid him on the deck then went back for the second man.

"Once we have moved this one, Professor, would you put the kettle on, I think that Mary could probably use a hot drink. While you do that, I will clean this lot up for George."

"Alright, thank you Pierre." The Professor knew the man could have asked him to clean up the blood and gore on the companionway, he knew he would have thrown up if he had, the boats engine shuddered into life as the moved the second body. Up on deck Mary had just finished pulling in the second breast line when George called out to her from the wheelhouse.

"Let go the fore line!" She waved by way of acknowledgement then hurried along the deck, she released the fore line from its bollard then rapidly hauled it in, as she did so the boats bow eased away from the jetty, as the gap widened Mary hurried back along the deck.

"Do you think we stand any chance at all, George?" she asked quietly, the old man altered their course slightly before he answered her.

"Phillipe will also get underway shortly so it will look like two boats moving out to the fishing grounds, he will alter course away to draw off anyone who might follow. I'm hoping it might be a couple of hours before those two soldiers are missed, so yes, I think that we stand a good chance, Mary." Mary moved into the wheelhouse then looking behind them she just hoped that the old man was right.

****

Major Meyer sat on the edge of a small desk next to the Navy Lieutenant in the dock office at Caldace, he had a telephone receiver in his hand waiting impatiently while the Lieutenant looked through a list of fishing boat names on a clipboard.

"The boat Zeraph is certainly not one of our boats, sir." The Major nodded as he spoke to someone on the other end of the line.

"And you're quite sure that was the name of one of the boats that left here just over an hour ago?"

"Yes sir, our men were searching the nearby boats and a Private remembers that name, it was the first boat to leave—wait sir!" The man on the other end of the line put his hand over the mouthpiece while he spoke to someone making the line crackle badly.

"Sorry about that sir but I have just been told that two of our men, a Corporal and a Private, are missing, we believe they may have gone onboard the Zeraph sir."

"Alright, don't let any of the other boats leave, I'll get a search started from here."

"Right sir." As the line went dead the Major turned to the Navy Lieutenant, "How long will it take you to get a boat searching along the coast and can you get me onto it?" he asked.

"Let's see," the Lieutenant crossed over to a Naval Chart that was pinned on one wall near his desk and made a quick calculation.

"It'll take our nearest boat at least five hours to get here sir, we have a launch that can get you out to it while it's still coming, sir."

"Good, arrange that then call the airfield. I want an aircraft searching for that damned fishing boat as fast as they can arrange it."

"That's already been done sir, we alerted the aircraft as soon as we heard that the boat had left sir."

"Well done. Now get me out to that damned trawler, I want to be there when they catch up to those bastards!"

"Right sir, this way," as the Lieutenant led him out of the office Major Mayer could feel his excitement mounting, he was going to catch those bastards, he would make them pay dearly for what they had done to his sister.

****

Pierre entered the fishing boat's wheelhouse carrying a bottle of brandy with four mugs, he gave a mug to each of his companions then pulled the cork from the bottle before pouring a good measure into each mug.

"I think we could all use a little 'pick me up'," he said as he handed out the mugs, the Professor had an appreciative sniff of the brandy before raising his mug.

"Prost!" he said before taking a sip.

"Cheers Professor." Mary sipped the brandy and felt the warmth explore her stomach, she was about to say something when she froze, her smile fading as a small aircraft roared low overhead.

"Shit!" Pierre ran out the wheelhouse door as the single engine Storch light aircraft banked steeply as it turned to the right.

"Do we shoot at it, Pierre?" asked Mary anxiously as George spun the wheel putting them into a tight right-hand turn.

"No, our Stens aren't heavy enough to do any damage besides he might not know who we are, it could just be a routine patrol."

"No Pierre, the normal search aircraft are Heinkel One Fifteen float planes, this one is too small to be a normal patrol, I think the buggers have found us!" George looked a little resigned as he said this for, he knew that it would only be a matter of time before that aircraft whistled up a patrol boat, then they would be in real trouble.

"How long till dusk?" asked Pierre.

"Till that thing loses sight of us, four maybe five hours!"

"Damn!"

"I've altered course, he'll probably radio our heading to the Patrol boats, so I'll stay on this course until it's dark enough to lose him then I'll return to our original course but—"

"Yes, I know George."

"But what?" asked the Professor anxiously, he had been listening to their conversation, he had seen the look on the old man's face, he knew they were in trouble, but he needed to hear it from them.

"That aircraft will radio our position and heading to his base, then they will whistle up a Patrol boat to intercept us, Professor."

"And the but?" asked the Professor again.

"This old girl doesn't have the pace to outrun a Patrol boat, if I push her hard, we might make eleven knots, but I risk damaging the engine if I push it too hard."

"No George, don't do that, don't risk damaging the engine, just do what you can, alright?" said Pierre and George patted the wheelhouse woodwork sentimentally.

"She'll see us through," he said, and Mary smiled at him.

"She will that, George."

Bbbrrrrrrrrrrrrrrrr! Bbrrrrrrrrrr! Bbrrrrrrrrrrrrrrrr!

"Down!" shouted Pierre as the aircraft flew over them again only this time its machinegun stuttered harshly and spray burst up as a line of bullets swept towards them; ducking down, Mary yelled out as the wheelhouse windows were shattered, they were showered with glass and wood splinters as the aircraft roared away overhead in a tight banking turn.

"Everyone alright?" asked Pierre looking at each of them in turn as he stood up, Mary nodded, she was covered in glass and wood splinters, her heart was beating wildly but apart from that she was unharmed.

"Go below and get our weapons, we will return fire, might make that bastard keep his distance, eh?" said Pierre as she straightened up.

"Bastards!" growled George as he looked over his shoulder at the circling aircraft, that attack had scarred the hell out of him as the gunfire had been unexpected, he would have to watch that bastard more intently now, he would alter course at the last minute if he made another attacking run, that might upset their aim if nothing else.

"Help Mary, Professor!" As Mary went below with the Professor, Pierre looked at the old man.

"You alright, George?" he asked.

"Yes, scared the hell out of me but no real harm done."

"We will shoot at him if he gets close again George, might make him keep his distance but that's about all."

"I know Pierre. Our heading is Three One Five, that's the course that we need to be on after dark to make the rendezvous, I'll try not to stray too far off it, but you need to know in case—well just in case."

"Christ George!" The old man was being pragmatic; Pierre knew their chances of making the rendezvous were now slim at most. Mary and the Professor came back into the wheelhouse, Mary handed him a Sten submachine gun and some spare magazines which he checked, he noticed that the Professor also had one.

"Pity we didn't have a Bren gun." Pierre sighed, they didn't have much chance of doing any serious damage to the aircraft with their light weapons, all they could really hope to do was persuade the pilot to keep his distance and hope that he would either run out of fuel or nightfall would force him to withdraw.

"Mary, take the Professor up behind the lifeboat behind the wheelhouse, that will give you some cover but wait for my shout before opening fire, alright?"

"Right, come on Professor." Mary led the way out to the small, raised deck behind the wheelhouse where the lifeboat was sitting on its chocks, there wasn't much room up on the platform either side of the lifeboat, but it would give them some cover.

For twenty minutes, they crouched there anxiously watching the aircraft as it circled around them keeping its distance, then it banked steeply turning towards them.

"Get ready, Mary!" called Pierre as he watched the aircraft intently. "I think he's attacking, Mary; we will turn into him at the last second so be ready!"

"Ready!" Mary cocked her weapon then gestured to the Professor who did the same.

"We'll turn into him at the last second, Professor, when you fire aim just ahead to allow for his speed, I doubt if we will hit him but he might think twice next time, alright?" She gave him a reassuring smile, the Professor nodded as he swallowed hard then everything seemed to happen very fast. The aircraft swooped in towards them then as the aircrafts machine gun started chattering

George spun the wheel turning their bow towards the aircraft, Pierre shouted for them to open fire, their Sten guns stuttered harshly, the aircraft banked suddenly as they fired, the Professor kept his trigger pressed until the bolt clunked back as the magazine emptied rapidly, he quickly pulled the magazine out and rammed another one in as the aircraft roared away overhead.

"Mary, come down! Quickly!" shouted Pierre and sensing his urgency, Mary scrambled down from the platform hurrying into the wheelhouse where she found Pierre at the helm, George was sitting on the deck with his back pressed up against the bulkhead, his head was slumped forward as he was unconscious, and his shoulder was a large patch of very wet blood.

"Oh God! No!" she said as she hurried into the wheelhouse.

"When the aircraft attacked, he just seemed to levitate across the wheelhouse, I propped him up there then grabbed the wheel," Pierre spoke quickly as he looked wide-eyed at her, it had all happened so fast, the aircraft had started its attack run, George had spun his wheel then the wheelhouse seemed to explode in shattered glass and woodwork, George had been flung across the wheelhouse in a shower of blood, the old man hadn't even yelled out as he hit the deck, Pierre had dropped his weapon then propped the old man up against the bulkhead before grabbing the wheel.

As Mary knelt next to George and started removing his jacket and shirt so that she could check the wound, the Professor came into the wheelhouse.

"Professor, give me a hand!" snapped Mary, Linus put his Sten down then helped her undo the man's shirt.

"Oh God!" Mary's harsh release of breath as she said this made Pierre look round, George's shoulder was a mass of blood where a machine gun round had gone through, but the worse part was a wood splinter that was sticking out of his chest, he was bleeding badly from the bullet wound and from around the splinter.

"I need a dressing; Professor, hold him for me!" The Professor nodded and took the man's weight as Mary hurried below trying to find something that she could use as a dressing for the wound.

"How is it?" asked Pierre anxiously as he looked over at the wound in George's shoulder.

"I…I think it is a wood splinter!" said the Professor as he looked closer at the wound. "Should we try to pull it out do you think?" he asked then he was looking up as Mary came back into the wheelhouse.

"No! I don't know much about wounds, but I do know that you shouldn't try to remove any objects, I'll bandage it as best I can then let the submarine's doctor remove it." Mary opened a small first aid kit that she had taken from the two dead German soldiers.

"Do you think the submarine will have a doctor, Pierre?" she asked looking up.

"I don't know, maybe not a Doctor but someone with medical knowledge I should think." Mary nodded then set about making a small ring bandage that she would put over the protruding end of the wood splinter after she put a pad over the bullet wound, she hadn't said anything, but she knew the shoulder wound was serious but together they posed a real risk as George was bleeding heavily, then she opened the small brandy bottle.

"He can't drink that, he's unconscious!" said the Professor frowning.

"It isn't for him to drink, I need to clean the wound, and this is alcohol, it's the best I can do," she said as she poured a small amount of the brandy over the wounds.

"Just as well he is out of it as that would hurt like hell!" said Pierre remembering how the disinfectant had burnt like Hell on his own shoulder wound and that was nothing compared to this. With the Professor's help, Mary bandaged the wounds as best she could then refastened George's shirt.

"We'd best take him below Pierre," she said as she finished her handiwork.

"I can carry him, Mary!" The Professor waved aside her protests and gently picked up George carrying the old man over his shoulder, he was a dead weight, but he could manage it, staggering slightly but being careful not to bang the old man into the bulkheads the Professor made his way down to the Saloon where he gently laid the man down onto the bunk, thankfully George remained unconscious.

"I'll stay with him, Mary," said the Professor as he sat on the edge of the bunk.

"I don't mind being with him, Professor."

"Seriously Mary I think Pierre needs you up there more than me, after all I'm not much use with a Sten," he said, and she smiled.

"You've more than held your own, Professor but I will go back up. Give me a call if you need me, alright?"

"I will." Mary turned to leave then stopped as she pulled a small tube from her pocket.

"I took this from the first aid kit that the soldier had on him, Professor. When George wakes if he is in severe pain, you can give him half of this but use it sparingly as it is all we have, alright?"

"Thank you, Mary," the Professor took the small tube then Mary returned to the wheelhouse.

"That bastard is keeping his distance, Mary," said Pierre gesturing to the circling Storch as she entered the wheelhouse.

"Maybe we winged him!" She said hopefully as she moved over closer to Pierre. "We don't stand a chance, do we?" she asked quietly.

"I really don't know and that is the truth!" There was a total silence as they were both deep in their own thoughts.

"I have an idea Mary, can I run it past you?" he asked after a couple of minutes silence.

"Of course!"

"I've been thinking it over and I don't think the submarine will surface while that damned aircraft stays around and I don't think it will withdraw until just after dark, but I could be wrong!"

"I think you are probably right, Pierre." She knew their rendezvous was getting precarious, that aircraft would stay with them until it either ran low on fuel, a Patrol vessel turned up or it got too dark for it to operate, she didn't think it would stick around once night fell but she wasn't sure.

"So, we wait for nightfall. I think we should be in the rendezvous area about two hours after sunset, George gave me a course to steer but I am keeping a little off that because of the aircraft. Once the sun goes down, I will alter course onto a heading of Three One Five but if we haven't met the submarine within two hours of the specified time then I think we should head for the coast!"

"You want us to go ashore?" she asked a little surprised.

"We have the two uniforms from those soldiers, we could go ashore and get some medical attention for George then try to hide out until we can make contact with a Resistance Cell, I know it is a slim chance, Mary, but I think we have to consider the option."

"We can't use the soldiers' uniforms, Pierre, they are too bloody and would arouse suspicion, I also don't think we can risk giving George to any hospital staff whom we don't know, they would just hand him over to the authorities, I…I couldn't do that to him, Pierre!" Pierre nodded as he sighed heavily, he was trying to think of alternatives, but nothing seemed very plausible now.

"Alright Mary, I will keep thinking for now. So how is George?"

"Still unconscious, the Professor is sitting with him and I have given him some painkillers that one of those soldiers had in his small first aid kit, there isn't much more that I can do for him, Pierre."

"You've done marvellously, Mary, you really—Bugger! Here comes that damned plane again!" Pierre swore as he had seen the Storch bank suddenly, Mary snatched up her Sten and moved to the doorway for another attack but it was just a feint, it sheared off after getting close, it did this a number of times making them sweat, then as dusk fell the aircraft made one final attack run before banking sharply heading for the coast, thankfully it had been a token gesture as the machinegun bullets tore up the sea alongside the fishing boat, Mary had returned fire with her Sten more out of frustration than with any hope of actually hitting the aircraft.

"Running low on fuel probably," said Pierre as he watched the aircraft fly off.

"Do you think it would have called up a patrol vessel before it left, Pierre?" asked Mary anxiously as she watched the disappearing aircraft.

"It would have done that as soon as it spotted us, no I reckon it's either low on fuel or can't operate at night, either way good riddance to the bugger I say!" Pierre then turned as the Professor entered the wheelhouse.

"How is George, Professor?" he asked.

"That is why I have come up, Pierre, he asked me to take the helm so that you could go and talk to him."

"Oh! Alright, keep her on this course till I get back, would you?"

"Of course." The Professor stepped up to the helm then Pierre hurried below.

In the Saloon, George looked up as he heard Pierre coming down the companionway, his shoulder wound was hurting dreadfully even though the Professor had given him some sort of painkiller, it had taken the edge of the pain so that it was bearable, but it was still hurting badly.

"How are you feeling, George?" asked Pierre as he carefully sat down on the edge of the bunk as he looked at the old man's pale sweaty face.

"I've been better! Listen Pierre, thanks to this wound I will have to change my plans, I had hoped to have been able to work my way up the coast once we had made the rendezvous with the Submarine, I would have transferred you then would have been on my way." Pierre shook his head negatively, so the old man paused.

"Wound or not that wouldn't have worked anyway, George, that aircraft would have sent a sighting report the moment he spotted us, this boat has been recognised, they now have our rough location so it would only be a matter of time before they would catch up with you." Pierre forced a smile for the old man, he knew that George loved this old boat, she meant the world to him, yet he was about to lose everything.

"I'm not stupid, Pierre! I've been in this game for a long time, and I knew this day was bound to come sooner or later," the old man then gave a crooked grin. "Pierre, I've prepared for it! There is a key on a chain around my neck, could you take it please?" George tilted his head sideways so that Pierre could remove the chain from around his neck, Pierre was then holding a small old-fashioned key on the end of the chain in his hand.

"You know where the wireless set is hidden, Pierre?"

"Yes, in that cupboard." Pierre pointed to the hide hole for the wireless set and George nodded.

"Behind the wireless set is a small panel, lift that and you will find a blade switch that is padlocked open, that key opens the padlock!" George reached out and grasped Pierre's arm fiercely.

"I won't let those bastards get their filthy hands on my girl, Pierre, you promise me that you will throw that blade switch before you leave, when you do you will have ten minutes before this old girl blows up, now YOU PROMISE ME, Pierre!" The old man's eyes blazed at him fiercely as he said this, Pierre eased him back onto the bunk gently.

"I will be the last to leave, George, and I PROMISE that I will throw your switch for you."

"Thank you—thank you!" The old man lay back and closed his eyes, he felt calmer now knowing that Pierre wouldn't let his beloved Zeraph be taken by those bastards. Pierre watched him for a couple of minutes, he had to fight down the emotional lump in his throat for the old man's desperate plea had moved him deeply, as George fell asleep Pierre made his way back up to the wheelhouse.

"Is he alright, Pierre?" asked Mary as he entered the wheelhouse.

"Yes, he's resting. I'll take over now Professor." The Professor moved aside as Pierre went back to the helm.

"Mary, do you have a torch ready?" asked Pierre after checking the time.

"George gave me one that I can work with." Mary indicated a small torch that was on the makeshift desk that George used for his chart table.

"Then it's time to switch on the recognition lanterns, are you able to do that or would you like me to do it?" The recognition signal was to be two small lanterns set up in the crow's nest on the forward mast, they would blink a low level light set at intervals and could only be seen over an arc of one hundred and eighty degrees, when the submarine's crew saw this, they would flash a challenge; however, Mary didn't have the coded reply so she would reply with 'LILLY', she just hoped that London had briefed the Submarine's crew in what to expect, then they would either rendezvous with them or alternatively they could just blow them out of the water, it was just a risk they had to take.

"It's alright, Pierre, I'll do it." Mary left the wheelhouse, she made her way to the mast which was forward of the wheelhouse, she just thanked her lucky stars that she wasn't afraid of heights, carefully she climbed the steel rungs set in the mast, she was breathing hard by the time she pulled herself into the small canvas surround of the crow's nest, she quickly unfastened the canvas flap pulling back the shrouds on the two lanterns so that they would be clearly seen, then she reached down flicking a switch, but the two lanterns were still dark.

"Oh god—come on!" she cursed softly sweating as she waited, wondering what she could do if they didn't work as they were supposed to. Then much to her relief the top lantern started to glow feebly but as she watched the light became stronger, she breathed a sigh of relief as the second lantern also started glowing with the light slowly getting stronger.

Five miles astern of the fishing boat Zeraph, Major Meyer paced the bridge of the armed trawler Z52, the crew had gone to their battle stations half an hour before when the radar office had reported a feint contact ahead, the Storch patrol aircraft had given him the approximate position of the fishing boat which had to be the one that had left the cove with the professor and that bastard British agent. Then the aircraft had reported that the fishing boat had returned fire when they had made a machinegun attack, so now they knew that they had the right vessel, but this Patrol boat was only two knots faster than the fishing boat so it was taking a frustrating amount of time to close in to gun range, the Major walked back to where the boats Captain a Lieutenant Commander Reinhart Nagel was receiving an update report from the Radar Office.

"We are within maximum gun range now Major, but I would suggest waiting. At this range, I can't guarantee the accuracy of our main gun!" The trawler was armed with a 4-inch quick firing gun mounted in the bows, they had multiple anti-aircraft weapons plus anti-submarine depth charges aft but their main armament was a piece from 1912 which was well worn with a maximum range of just on four miles.

"I don't want to sink them, Captain! I want to capture them so putting a couple of rounds close by should do the trick."

"Very well," the captain picked up a handset.

"Guns—Captain. Commence firing with Star Shell on them put a couple of rounds as close as you can without hitting them, we don't want to sink them—yet!" The captain replaced his handset and a couple of seconds later there came a warning TING—TING from forward before the Main gun fired with an ear-splitting bang which made the Major jump badly.

On the fishing boat Zeraph, Mary made sure that the two lanterns were glowing strongly before she turned to make her descent down the mast, then she jumped badly in fright as there came a barking BANG! off their starboard side then the night was turned to day in a harsh blue-white light as the Star Shell exploded and the magnesium flare started drifting down beneath its parachute followed a second later by a harsh tearing sound as a shell passed overhead before exploding in a tall column of water off to their right.

Recovering herself Mary scrambled madly down the steel rungs on the mast, then jumping down the last couple of feet to the deck she ran to the wheelhouse.

"Bastards have found us, Mary!" Pierre ducked instinctively as another shell roared overhead.

"Steer into it!" Mary gasped as the round exploded.

"What?"

"Steer for the shell splash, they watch for the fall of shot to correct their aim so steer for the last splash, it might buy us some time."

"Right." He knew that she had been a Royal Navy Officer before she became an Agent so would know more about these sorts of things than he did so he didn't argue putting the helm over, then he was blinking as the Star Shell landed in the ocean and the night went suddenly black momentarily blinding him but this was short lived as another illumination round exploded throwing them into harsh glaring light again before another round roared overhead.

"I saw the flash that time as they fired, over there!" called the Professor as he gestured behind them slightly off to their left side. Mary snatched up the binoculars and started searching the darkness astern, she couldn't see much then she gasped as the vessel behind fired again.

"They're signalling!" called the Professor as a light started winking at them, Mary moved the binoculars until she could see the blinking light, it was Maritime Code letter K—DAH DIT DAH—meaning 'YOU SHOULD STOP YOUR VESSSEL IMMEDIATELY'.

"They are telling us to stop, Pierre!" she called as she read the Morse.

"Bastards!" snapped Pierre as he put the helm over as the Illumination round sputtered out, then another round roared overhead, and another Illumination round POPPED, lighting up the night again.

"Both of you go below and bring George up, I don't want him getting trapped below should we be hit!" Mary and the Professor hurried below; it was a bit of a struggle for both, but they managed to get George up to the wheelhouse.

"Professor, take the wheel! Mary come and help me swing the lifeboat out." The Professor moved over to the helm then Mary and Pierre hurried out to the lifeboat which was on its chocks behind the wheelhouse, it was a struggle for them both in the darkness with unfamiliar gear but they managed to get the boat ready for lowering, while they were doing this five more rounds roared in from the pursuing trawler, each one seemed to be getting closer so it was only a matter of time before they were hit.

"Pierre—Pierre!" called the Professor from the wheelhouse, they hurried back down as it sounded urgent.

"What is it?" asked Pierre as he entered the wheelhouse.

"George asked me to call you." The Professor had propped George up against the bulkhead, he was sweating badly and was weak from the loss of blood as his shoulder wound was bleeding continuously now despite Mary's bandages.

"Pierre, you have to use the key!"

"What are you talking about George, you'll be OK, man."

"Listen, I've had it and we both know it." George shook his head as Pierre made to interrupt him. "Don't go all soft on me, Pierre, we've both seen enough wounds to know I'm done for, so get them on the boat and lower it to the waterline, then you use the key and set the charges. I'll turn side on, Mary can signal that we surrender, that should buy you a little time. I reckon they will stop using the illumination rounds once we stop, probably just use their searchlight and I reckon it'll take about ten minutes for them to reach us, do you understand, Pierre?" Pierre looked at the old man's determined look and felt the emotional lump forming in his throat, even if he was dying, he knew that it was a brave act.

"What's he on about, Pierre, what is he saying?" asked Mary anxiously as she could hear a sort of finality in the old man's voice that was scaring her.

"He's giving us a chance to escape, Mary" he said quietly, Mary could feel the tears start running down her cheeks as the old man gave her a feeble smile.

"You—you can't do that, George! Oh please Pierre, tell him he can't!" Mary wiped the tears from her face as George reached out and patted her arm affectionately.

"It's alright, lass, I'm done for anyway. Might as well go out doing something useful, eh?" he said smiling, Mary leant forward to hug him.

"I owe you my life, George, I will always be grateful so thank you," she said this quietly into his ear then stood up.

"I'll be at the lifeboat!" she said then hurried out of the wheelhouse.

"Professor, go with her, be ready as we will stop in a few minutes."

"Right." The Professor then knelt and took George's hand.

"I'm sorry it has turned out this way, George, but it has been my privilege to have known you," he said as they shook hands.

"Keep safe Professor and look after her!"

"I will." The Professor nodded then grabbing his satchel he hurried out after Mary.

"Help me up, Pierre?" Pierre helped the old man get to his feet then moved him to the helm where he lovingly took hold of the wheel.

"I'll turn to starboard and come to a stop, you get that lifeboat lowered and have Mary flash that bastard a signal telling him that we surrender. Then get below and set that damned fuse boy!"

"Right, I'll be back in a couple of minutes." Pierre patted the old man's shoulder then called for Mary as he hurried out. George waited for a couple of minutes then put the helm over, as the Zeraph began her turn, Pierre with the Professor's help managed to lower the lifeboat so that it was in the water alongside the fishing boat, once this was done Mary used George's torch to flash a signal at their pursuing trawler, as she did so another shar shell lit up the night sky.

"Fishing boat signalling, sir!" called one of the lookouts on the Z52 as he caught sight of the winking light before the star shell lit up the night.

"What are they saying?" snapped Major Meyer, he felt that he almost had his quarry, he would have those bastards in custody shortly.

"Cease Fire! They are surrendering, Major."

"Good, can you keep them in sight, Captain?"

"Yes, we will shortly be in range to use the searchlight then I will send a boarding party over."

"I'd like to go with it."

"Fine, follow the Lieutenant!" the captain gestured to one of his Officers who left the bridge with the Major close on his heels.

Back on the Zeraph, George looked up as Pierre entered the wheelhouse.

"We are set with the boat, George, I...I—"

"Don't get sentimental on me now for God's sake, Pierre, just DO IT!" Pierre looked at the old man's determination for a moment then hurried down to the saloon, he pulled the wireless set out of its cubby hole then pushed the panel behind this revealing the small blade switch, this was securely padlocked so that it couldn't be accidentally set. Pulling George's key from his pocket he removed the small padlock then checked the time, once he set this he would only have ten minutes to get clear of the boat before George's charges went off, he hesitated a moment, once he closed this switch he would be as good as killing George!

"Forgive me, George!" he said then closed the switch, this done he ran to the wheelhouse.

"Bon Chance, my friend, now get off my boat!" snapped George as Pierre came in.

"George, I—"

"GET GOING, YOU BLOODY FOOL!" Pierre nodded, there wasn't anything he could say that would describe the admiration he had for this old man and he was now literally running out of time, nodding he hurried out of the wheelhouse, a minute later he was lowering himself hand over hand down a rope then stepped into the lifeboat.

Mary was sitting at the tiller in the stern and the Professor was sitting on a thwart amidships with an oar already in place, Pierre cast of the line holding them into the fishing boat then pushed them off before sitting next to the Professor, Mary swung the tiller hard over as the two men started rowing, as they pulled away the last of the star shells spluttered out temporarily blinding them as the nights blackness enveloped them.

"Dig deep, professor, we have to get as far away as we can before the next illumination round goes off." Pierre panted heavily as he said this for they were both rowing as hard as they could, the Professor was trying to match him stroke for stroke but it wasn't easy as he had never rowed a boat before, he knew how important it was for them to get as far away from the fishing boat as they could without being spotted, not only to ensure their freedom but also to justify Georges sacrifice!

"Pierre, he's moving!" called Mary suddenly, she had been looking behind them trying to keep the fishing boat between them and the attacking trawler, the fishing boat had been sideways on to them, but she had spotted a flash of white at the stern as the propeller started turning again.

"What the hell!" Pierre wondered what George was up to, had the patrol boat altered course while they had been getting into the lifeboat; did he think the patrol boat was too far away for his scuttling charges to have a chance of doing any damage, he knew that George didn't want his beloved Zeraph falling into their hands but he had been hoping that the fishing boat would be alongside the patrol boat when George's charges went off so they might be damaged by the explosion.

"Can you see the patrol boat Mary?" he called as he pulled on the oar.

"No, the fishing boat is in the way, maybe George was just moving to keep between us, do you think?"

"Maybe." Pierre was panting hard from the fast pace that he had set them but he knew that it was imperative that they put as much distance between themselves and the fishing boat before those charges went off, not only to lessen the risk from the explosion but also because he was hoping that they would be hidden in the darkness when the charges went off, hoping that the Germans would think that they had all been killed on board the fishing boat.

"How long until those charges go off, Pierre?" asked Mary as she moved the tiller slightly, it was hard to know exactly which way to steer as she didn't know the exact location of the patrol boat, she was just relieved that they had stopped firing those illumination rounds, then she jumped suddenly as a searchlight lit up the darkness.

"Down—everybody DOWN!" called Pierre, he pulled in his oar and flattened himself across the thwart as best he could as he turned his head away from the harsh blinding light, the Professor quickly yanked in his oar as he saw Pierre doing then flattened himself as best, he could over the oar panting hard as rowing was very hard work. Mary flattened herself face down in the bottom of the boat as the eerily harsh white light swept over them before suddenly changing colour, then she sat up quickly as she realised the sudden change of colour was due to the shadow being cast over them by the fishing boat.

"NO—OH GOD NO!" she called suddenly as a Sten gun started stuttering from the fishing boat's wheelhouse, within seconds two 20-millimetre anti-aircraft cannons returned fire from the armed trawler that was only a hundred yards away, red tracers arced in towards the fishing boat, the sea erupted around the Zeraph, the wheelhouse exploded as the rounds hit home, George was cut in half as the rounds tore through his frail body then the wheelhouse burst into flames.

WWHHHOOOOMMPPHHAAAAA! The night was suddenly rent by a huge explosion that made Mary cry out in alarm as she grabbed the lifeboat's side, she could hardly believe her eyes as the armed trawler literally lifted out of the water as a torpedo hit it amidships exploding into a huge fireball, breaking in two parts the armed trawler sank rapidly in smoke and flames. The double explosions of the Zeraph's scuttling charges going off seemed tame in comparison but the little fishing boat sank almost immediately as the charges blew her bottom out, tears ran down Mary's face as the boat's mast keeled over as the stern rose up out of the water with the single propeller still turning slowly, then with a final gush of bubbles she was gone. A burning patch of oil showed where the armed trawler had been with the silence being almost painful as the night closed in over them.

"What the Hell!" Pierre looked around in fright at a harsh noise, it was a weird sort of noise, a slight roaring then about sixty feet away the sea seemed to boil but there was no heat or steam, then his jaw dropped his eyes widening as a Submarine surfaced in a welter of foam and spray, there came a dull clanking sound then dark figures were running along the Submarine deck as it turned towards them.

"Ahoy there! Grab the line!" called out an English voice, the Professor ducked as a line landed in the boat, he quickly grabbed it, wrapping it around the lifeboat's stem post a couple of times trying to make it secure, then the Submarine was looming large above them.

"Jump for it—quickly!" snapped out a voice above them.

"Mary, come forward!" called the Professor as he stood up unsteadily holding out his hand to Mary, she let go the tiller then held Pierre's hand as he manoeuvred her past him, the Professor helped her pass him then willing hands on the submarine reached down and just seemed to grab her and haul her up onto the deck.

"This way, miss!" She was led quickly along the deck to an open round hatch.

"Turn around, put your foot onto the rungs then go down the ladder, Miss!" Mary turned around and someone held her arm until she had her foot on the first rung of a ladder then she descended down into a very cluttered Torpedo Stowage Compartment that smelt strongly of diesel fuel, shale oil and unwashed bodies, it was an eerie feeling as the interior was lit in red lighting giving the smiling faces she passed a slightly haunting glow, she was taken along a corridor then in through a curtain into a small compartment that held some bunks, a table surrounded by a bench seat, a sailor holding a rather clumsy looking revolver ushered her into this compartment, a second later she was joined by Pierre then the Professor, the sailor with the revolver then stepped out of the compartment and pulled the curtain across.

"Should we sit down, do you think?" asked the Professor tentatively, then he looked around as the submarine's diesel engines rumbled into life, there came a slight pressure under their feet as the boat started to increase speed, the curtain across the doorway started to sway a little then the lighting suddenly switched from red to white making them blink rapidly then they heard voices on the other side of the curtain.

"Alright Chalky, put the revolver away before you do yourself a mischief then fetch a pot of coffee, would you?"

"Aye aye sir." As the sailor moved off the curtain over the doorway was drawn back, they found themselves looking at two men, one was short and stocky with a round face and a jutting ginger beard, he was wearing grey flannel trousers, a rather large white Submarine jumper but no rank insignia, the second was a tall skinny man with a rather angular face, he was wearing a rather grubby pair of trousers, a green jumper with a reefer jacket on which was the wavy gold bands of a Lieutenant Commander RNVR.

"Uhm, my French is pretty bloody awful so I'm hoping one of you speaks English?" asked the bearded man and Mary felt herself relaxing a little as this was indeed the British Submarine that they had been hoping to rendezvous with, she thought it was very good to be hearing English being spoken again.

"Yes, we all speak English," it was Mary that had answered for them.

"Good, because some silly sod in Whitehall has told me that you would provide me with a code name and if it doesn't match the one that I have been given then I am to shoot you and nip off a bit smartish. I really wouldn't like to do that!" Mary chuckled at the man's pained expression, she hadn't meant to, but she felt herself warming to this strange little man, his manner seemed to ease some of the tension out of her.

"I believe you may have been given my code name, Captain, which is Lilly, and I am with SOE," she said tentatively.

"And if I was to say 'Beth'?" asked the Captain, he was holding himself a little stiffly as he said this for it had been a rather strange patrol so far, they had been pulled off of their normal patrol with short notice being given a time and place to rendezvous with a French fishing boat the location of which had been changed twice on short notice, then he had received strange orders telling him to expect a Dutch Professor who was being aided by a British SOE Agent, then barely six hours before this rendezvous they were told the Agent may have been compromised, he was to challenge whomever came aboard with a simple code word then if he wasn't given the correct answer, without hesitation he was to arrest who ever came aboard with the Agent, something that he had hoped he wouldn't have to do.

Then just before their rendezvous they had detected gunfire on the surface, he had observed the fishing boat that had been showing the correct recognition signal being fired at by an armed trawler, it had taken him some time to manoeuvre the Submarine into a good firing position that would allow him to engage the target without hitting the fishing boat, he had loosed off two torpedoes each costing two thousand pounds, one of which had passed harmlessly astern, he had just been congratulating himself on hitting the armed trawler squarely amidships when much to his surprise and consternation, the smaller fishing boat had also exploded then rapidly sank, he had surfaced with the faint hope of finding any survivors when his lookouts had spotted the lifeboat with its three occupants, which he found to be strange to say the least.

"To 'Beth', I would answer 'Mary Margaret', Captain." To Mary the man seemed to deflate before her as if a great weight had suddenly been lifted from his shoulders as he smiled at her warmly.

"Thank you. I am Lieutenant Commander James Harvey, welcome aboard HM Submarine P211, Miss…?" the captain raised one eyebrow quizzically.

"I am Mary Trumont, Captain, this is my companion Pierre, he was the team leader of my French Resistance group in Posey."

"Pleased to meet you, Pierre," said the captain as the two men shook hands.

"Captain, this is Professor Linus, he is the reason for our mission, he MUST make it back to England!" Mary emphasised the MUST, as she did so the captain noticed that the Professor clutched his briefcase closer to his chest.

"Well, we will certainly do our best. Take a seat, would you?" the Captain indicated the padded bench seat around the table, as they sat down as if on cue, the sailor who had been holding the revolver on them when they arrived entered the room carrying a tray holding a coffee pot, cups, milk and sugar and a plate of toast already buttered with sardines on top.

"Thought our guests might be hungry like, sir," said the sailor as the captain raised a quizzical eyebrow again.

"Thank you, that was a very kind thought," said Mary as the sailor poured them all a cup of coffee then handed out the toast before leaving, as they all sat down Mary sipped the strong coffee and bit into the toast, suddenly feeling very hungry.

"I take it you torpedoed that trawler, Captain?" asked Pierre as he bit into the unusual sardines on toast which at first he thought would be horrible but in fact were very tasty.

"Yes, we were about to surface which is our usual nightly routine when we heard the gunfire."

"Excuse me, Captain, pardon my ignorance but how could you hear the gunfire if you were still submerged?" asked Pierre frowning making the captain smile.

"Water is an excellent conductor, our Hydrophones had already picked up the sound of engines which is what had delayed us surfacing, then we heard the exploding shells. I had a quick looksee through the periscope which usually isn't much cop in the dark, but the trawler was lobbing star shells around like confetti which enabled us to work around into a favourable firing position once we had confirmed your identity."

"So, you had spotted us before the trawler arrived then?" asked the Professor.

"Yes, we had been about to surface once we had confirmed your identification letters when our hydrophones picked up the trawler's engine, you see."

"It wouldn't have made any difference, Mary!" said Pierre quickly as he had seen the look on Mary's face, he knew what she was thinking, if the Submarine had surfaced earlier then they wouldn't have needed to set those scuttling charges, but he knew that George would still have died from his wounds.

"You don't know that Pierre, perhaps with medical attention, he could have—" Mary stopped talking as the tears welled up in her eyes, she knew that Pierre was probably right, George's wounds may have been worse than she thought but she couldn't help feeling guilty over the way the old fisherman had died, it just didn't seem right!

"I seem to have missed something?" said the captain as he saw the look between the two of them.

"Our companion George, he was the fishing boat's skipper, he had been badly wounded during an air attack, you see, a Storch light aircraft spotted us earlier today, it made a couple of machinegun attacks on us and George was badly wounded during one of them, then when that trawler showed up and started shelling us he—well he didn't want his beloved Zeraph to fall into enemy hands, he also wanted to give us a chance to escape so he put us into the lifeboat, then set scuttling charges, he had hoped to have possibly damaged that trawler when they went off, you see." Pierre had to swallow back his own emotional lump as he spoke.

"It sounds like this George was quite a man."

"He was one of the best, Captain." There was a momentary silence as they were each lost in their own thoughts.

"It's going to take us a couple of days to get back to England I'm afraid as we only travel on the surface at night and uhm, we weren't expecting three of you."

"Oh, I thought—" Mary started to speak then trailed off as she realised that London would have told the Submarine only to expect herself and the Professor, Pierre wasn't supposed to have left Posey but then if she had her way then the Entire Resistance Cell would now be here along with the Professor, when she returned to SOE, she would do her best to get the others out!

"Miss?" asked the captain as she trailed off.

"I'm sorry Captain, things have been a little uhm disjoined these last few days."

"Not to worry, your two companions and you, Miss, will bunk here in the wardroom." The captain motioned to one of the bunks near the table.

"Oh, I hope I won't be turning anyone out of their beds, Captain?" she asked, and the captain smiled.

"Our Subby will have a bunk made up in the alleyway there, it won't be for long, so it won't harm him. I'll have our chief explain the working of the heads but if you will excuse me for now, I must go back up to the bridge while we are surfaced."

"Of course, Captain and thank you again for coming to our rescue." The Captain smiled again then hurried out, there was a moment's silence as Mary poured herself another cup of coffee then picked up her toast, it seemed a little surreal sitting there eating sardines after all that had just happened to them, her overriding feeling at that moment was hunger and exhaustion, she felt incredibly tired now that she was sitting down safely onboard the Submarine, her whole body ached dreadfully, then she was looking up as a slightly portly man wearing a pair of incredibly stained overalls entered the wardroom, he had scruffy black hair and was in his late thirties.

"Hello, I'm Oliver Dean the Chief Engineer but everyone just calls me Chief. I'm uhm…to show you how to use the Heads on this submarine," he said a little hesitatingly.

"Heads?" asked the Professor.

"That's navy slang for the toilet, Professor." As Mary said this, the Chief looked at her quizzically for a moment as it wasn't every civilian that knew that.

"Uhm, yes well if you have finished your supper, I'll take you along to the Heads to show you how they work."

"Yes, thank you chief." They then followed the Chief out of the wardroom to the small toilet where he showed them the intricacies of the submarine's toilet.

****

'PING'… 'PING'…'PING'…'PING'…

Mary frowned as she turned over on the bunk as the Morse that she could hear wasn't making sense to her, she had laid down on the bunk shortly after the Chief's lecture on the working of the 'Heads', she had laid down because she still felt incredibly tired but also because she wanted to keep out of the crew's way, the Submarine's crew were being very king to them but she knew that her companions and herself must be incredibly inconvenient for them.

She had been dozing fitfully when the high-pitched 'PING' had started in her ear, she thought that it was Morse, but it wasn't making any sense to her at all.

"Port Twenty—Steer One Four five!" the captain had spoken softly in the Control Room making her eyes open fully.

"Port Twenty—Twenty of Port wheel on, sir."

Mary leaned over and pulled back the curtain on the bunk, as she did so, Pierre looked up from his position on the bench seat around the table.

"What's happening?" she asked quietly.

"Steady on One Four Five, sir," came the report from the control room.

'PING'…Mary frowned again as the sound seemed to be coming from outside of the Submarine.

"A trawler turned up about half an hour ago, that noise apparently is his ASDIC, whatever that is?"

"Anti-Submarine Detection Investigation Committee," she said as she moved out of the bunk to take a seat at the table, this time Pierre frowned.

"Sorry?" he said a little puzzled.

"ASDIC sends out a high-pitched PING into the water, if it hits an object the sound wave is reflected back to the transmitting ship."

"How on earth did you know that?" he asked, and she couldn't help smiling at him.

"We had an ex-Submariner in the Comms Centre and he told us a few things, but I never thought that I would actually get to hear it for myself."

"Would you like a cup of tea, miss?" asked 'Chalky' White, the wardroom steward, poking his head around the doorway.

"If I could please?"

"Miss."

"Doesn't miss much, does he?" said Pierre as the man left.

"That noise seems to have stopped," said Pierre a few minutes later as White returned with the tea.

"Skippers lost him sir, we manoeuvred around a bit till we lost him, hopefully he won't come back over this way."

"And if he does?" she asked a little apprehensively.

"We will move around and try to lose him again, Miss."

"And if we can't, what then?"

"Might get a little noisy if he does come back, but not to worry." With another smile, the man left the wardroom.

"Have you thought about what you will do when we reach England, Pierre?" asked Mary as she sipped her tea, Pierre nodded as he had been thinking about that all day.

"I thought l would ask SOE to send me back, Mary."

"What—to Posey?"

"Well, not Posey for a while but I thought I might be useful somewhere else perhaps."

"I think it would be too dangerous for you to go back to France for some time, Pierre, but maybe SOE could use you as an instructor."

"Well, we will have to wait and see I suppose but I never really thought that I would ever have to leave France, do you know what I mean?"

"I know it was hard for you, Pierre, and I…I am sorry it came to this." Mary looked a little sheepish as she said this, Pierre realised that she somehow thought that it had been her fault.

"It isn't your fault that I had to leave, Mary, if anything it's London's fault, if it hadn't been for this mission to save the Professor then we wouldn't have been in that field in Posey."

"Perhaps." She sat there deep in thought then she was looking up as the captain re-entered the wardroom.

"All quiet now, the trawler has left for a while," he said as he sat down at the table, then the steward poked his head through the doorway again.

"Tea sir?" he asked.

"Yes, thanks Chalky."

"Has the trawler left then sir?" asked Mary as Chalky left again.

"Yes, we stooged around for a while then he bug—uhm…scarpered off," the Captain had been about to swear but thought better of it and changed the word.

"Do you think he will return sir?"

"I think they would have increased the Patrols in the area especially after we sank the other trawler so this one will probably stick around."

"Well, we are very glad that you did sink the other one, Captain," Pierre said, he had hated to think what might have happened if the Submarine hadn't turned up when it had.

"You think that they would have caught you if we hadn't torpedoed that trawler, is that it?"

"Excuse me, I must use the Heads." Mary stood up and quickly left the room, she didn't want to think about what might have happened if the Submarine hadn't turned up when it had.

"I seem to have upset your companion," said the Captain as Mary left.

"Mary has had a very rough time, Captain."

"She was your radio operator, is that how it works?"

"She was a very good Agent, Captain, but things went wrong for us and she was captured by the Germans, they gave her a very bad time before she was able to escape, I hate to think what she would have done if you hadn't turned up when you did, sir." The captain looked at him thoughtfully for a moment wondering if he should ask any more questions.

"I doubt if your friend's scuttling charges would have done any damage to that trawler, they probably would have kept their distance and sent a boarding party, at least that is what I would have done."

"I thought the same thing, but Mary blames herself for George being there at all."

"You said she had been caught by the Germans, did that have something to do with it?"

"Yes, but luckily for us an SS officer wanted to break her, if they had handed her over to the Gestapo then the outcome would have been very different."

"Break her—do you mean…?"

"Yes Captain, Mary was tortured."

"Good Lord, I…I only thought that sort of thing was rumour, I…I didn't actually think it happened."

"Mary was a radio operator agent with SOE, Captain, a very valuable captive made doubly important by her knowledge about the Professor."

"Yes, I was wondering about him, we haven't been told much about you and I suppose I shouldn't really be asking?" The captain knew that he shouldn't really be asking his passengers anything at all but he was intrigued by his passengers but then if they didn't want to tell him anything they didn't have to.

"The Professor was being forced to work for the Germans, apparently he was working on some sort of terror weapon for them when he decided he had had enough, then through a chance encounter he was able to get word to the Resistance who organised his escape."

"That must have been difficult, escaping from the Germans I mean?"

"It was a very brave thing to do, Captain," said Mary as she returned to the Wardroom.

"Sorry Mary, we were just talking." Pierre knew that Mary was still sensitive about her ordeal.

"It's alright Pierre, I will have to talk about it when I get back anyway."

"You don't mind my asking you this, Mary?" asked the captain.

"No Captain, as I said I will have to talk about it when we get back, so I don't mind."

"Thank you, we were talking about the Professor?"

"It was a very brave thing that he did. His family was killed in a freak accident, it was then that he decided to 'change sides' as it were, I don't really know how but somehow he contacted the local Resistance group and they put him into hiding until they were able to arrange for him to leave the country."

"Is that where you came in, Pierre?" asked the Captain, Pierre shook his head.

"Our group was to be the last in a chain of Resistance groups that were to get the Professor out, unfortunately for us when we went to meet a courier that was bringing information for us, a trap had been set, the Courier was killed, and Mary was captured." This time Pierre looked at her as he said this, she nodded.

"Fortunately, I was taken by the gendarmes to a local police station where I met HIM!" Mary couldn't keep the bitterness out of her voice as she said this.

"Major Schrandt of the SS! He and his henchmen took great delight in—" Her voice caught in her throat as she said this being close to tears as those horrors came flooding back to her.

"You don't have to tell me anymore if you don't want to, Mary," said the Captain gently but she shook her head.

"Pierre tells me I was only there for two days, yet it felt like a lifetime! They had plans on moving me somewhere, goodness knows where, and it was a sheer miracle that I was able to escape. You see there was an air raid, most of the policemen were called out so I was able to knock out Kurt then get myself out of the Station, I hid in a disused factory yard overnight then made my way to Pierre's garage, I…I still can't believe my luck!"

"It wasn't just luck, Mary, you see Captain I am a mechanic and own my own garage, it meant that I could move around after the curfew, it came in handy when you wanted to blow things up." Pierre chuckled at his own joke.

"When I managed to get to Pierre, he took me to our safe house," said Mary, the Captain could see the bond between these two people and could understand why as it sounded like they had been through a lot together always being in great danger, he was developing a deep respect for them both.

"Our safe house was a pig farm run by a couple of old friends."

"They are on the run now and have lost everything!" Again, Mary couldn't keep the bitterness out of her voice.

"They will be alright Mary, Danny has relatives in the South of France, they will be safe."

"I hope so, Pierre." Mary swallowed back the emotional lump in her throat before continuing.

"Thanks to a traitor, we had to alter our plans, or I should say that London did. Our group scattered, Pierre and I took the Professor to a house where we were to meet a fishing boat, then we had an encounter with Major Schrandt!"

"You had the encounter, Mary, I got there when it was all over."

"Not quite, Pierre, you killed the Major. We managed to get the Professor to the fishing boat, then that damned Storch plane found us!" This time Mary wiped the tears from her eyes as she thought about the fisherman George and his sacrifice.

"There had been a delay before that as well, something to do with the Submarine?" asked Pierre.

"Yes, we replaced the boat that was supposed to have rendezvoused with you, it had been forced to withdraw from the area after sustaining damage during a Depth Charge attack, you had to wait for us to get over here from our previous billet."

"So that was it, makes sense now." Mary now understood why they had to wait for that seventy-two hour.

"Was that when your friend was wounded?"

"Yes, during one of the machine gun attacks from that Storch George was wounded, he took a large wood splinter in the lung and a bullet through the shoulder, it was much worse than I had first thought, there—there wasn't much that I could do for him as he had lost too much blood."

"Was that when the trawler found you?" the captain could see the anguish in her face as she relived the moment.

"I assume the Storch radioed our position as the trawler found us just after sunset." She took a sip of her tea before continuing, "They shelled us for a while then signalled for us to heave to."

"The shells weren't really close, I think they just wanted us to know that they were there and that it was useless to keep running," said Pierre as he watched Mary, he knew this was a very emotional subject for her but she needed to talk it out, she had been through a lot in a relatively short period of time and it would not do her any good to keep it all bottled up, she needed to talk about it.

"That's when George made us get into the lifeboat, he kept the fishing boat between us and the trawler keeping us out of sight, he—" The breath caught in her throat at the memory.

"He sounds like he was a very brave man," said the captain as she wiped her tears away, then she smiled at him.

"He was a very dear old gentleman, and I shall miss him dearly," There came a moment's silence as they were all deep in their own thoughts again.

"Captain in the Control room!" came the call from the Control Room, to Mary, the Captain seemed to levitate up from the seat then was gone before the call had finished being spoken.

"Goodness, I don't think I have ever seen anyone move so fast!" she said in some surprise.

"Must be important."

"Our trawler friend is back sir" said the Officer of the Watch as the captain entered the Control Room.

"Up periscope!" They heard the periscope wires hissing in the sheaves as it was raised.

"Diving Stations! Starboard Fifteen, steer Two Four five!" there came a rush of feet as the crew hurried to their Action Stations then it went quiet again, Mary looked up as the wardroom steward entered the wardroom.

"Everything alright?" he asked them.

"Yes, uhm—what's happening?" asked Mary.

"Officer of the Watch has spotted that trawler again, Skipper's altered course away from it, nothing to worry about. Now can I get you all some tea?" Not really wanting a cup of tea but thinking that it would take her mind off things, she nodded.

"Could I have some tea as well Please?" asked the Professor as he lowered himself down from the bunk.

"Of course, sir, won't be a tick." As the man left the Professor settled himself down on the bench seat at the table.

"Has that trawler come back then?" he asked.

"I think so although I don't really know how this thing works," she indicated the Wardroom but meant the Submarine.

"It's not hard, Miss," said 'Chalky' as he came back in carrying a tray on which was a teapot, milk jug and some cups, there was also a plate of plain biscuits.

"We are at Periscope Depth now, you, see?" The Steward pointed to a gauge on the bulkhead which Mary had assumed was a clock, she now realised that it was a depth gauge with a black needle that now was resting on the thirty feet mark.

"So, we are now thirty feet under the water?" asked the Professor apprehensively.

"That's right sir, we are at Periscope Depth which is thirty feet, the skipper will alter course and depth keeping the trawler astern of us, you see."

"Can't we outrun them then?" asked Pierre.

"No, our maximum submerged speed is only eight knots, and we can't do that for long without draining the 'Box'."

"The 'Box'?" asked Mary frowning.

"The batteries, Miss, when we are submerged, we run on our electric motors see, so the skipper will only use short bursts of speed when he 'as to but we mostly try to just creep away like."

"All too confusing for me I'm afraid," she said.

"Sixty feet—Group Up, Half Ahead Together!" came the call from the Control Room making the Steward look around.

"The Skipper's going down and increasing speed, excuse me," he said then quickly left. The whirring from the electric motors increased in pitch then the deck tilted down slightly, Mary watched the needle in the Depth Gauge as it moved around to the sixty feet mark before settling down.

"H-E on Red One Eight Oh Sir. Not in contact."

"Very well." The whirring of the electric motors continued to hum for another few minutes.

"H-E altering course, Sir—coming towards…"

"Damn!" For the next two hours the submarine altered course and speed repeatedly to shake off the trawler while the three of them listened in from the wardroom not really understanding what was happening, then the steward poked his head around the curtain at the doorway.

"Skipper said to tell you that the trawler might try attacking shortly so it might get a little noisy like," he said before disappearing again.

"Wonder what he means by noisy?" asked the Professor, then shortly after, they heard it, the ultrasonic 'PING' of the trawler's ASDIC transmissions followed by the returning 'PEEP' which seemed to get closer together as the submarine altered its course and depth a couple of times, then the steward poked his head in again.

"He will be going overhead shortly, you'll hear his engine then the Depth Charges will start, that will get a bit noisy like so hold on," he said then was gone again. Then they heard the trawlers engine as it came closer and closer until suddenly it roared loudly overhead sounding like a steam engine coming out of a tunnel, then Mary cried out as she was startled by a series of massive explosions shook the submarine, making the cups on the tray rattle.

"Don't worry, those weren't close, now he will circle Around to try to pick us up again, alright?" The Steward had poked his head around the curtain again but before they could say anything, he had left.

"They weren't close?" asked Mary as she swallowed hard as the noise of those explosions had scared her to death!

"Well, water is an excellent conductor of sound so perhaps he is right," said the Professor, then he was looking up at the deck head as he heard the high-pitched 'PING' of the trawler's ASDIC.

'PING!'— 'PING!'—'PING!'—'PING!' For another forty minutes the trawler circled them, they listened to the quiet commands being spoken in the Control Room, they sweated it out as they tried to guess the Submarine's movements from what they could hear, then an hour had gone past without any further 'PINGS!'

"Periscope Depth!" ordered the captain and the deck angled up a little.

"Up Periscope!" They heard the periscope wires whirring in the sheaves as the periscope rose then the captain's comments.

"Looks like our square-headed friend has gone off for his dinner—alright, secure from diving stations—patrol routine—down periscope!" Then the crew were filling past the wardroom as the duty watch took over.

"Alright, Number One, if our square-headed friend doesn't come back in an hour, go back to our base course."

"Aye aye Sir." Then the Captain was entering the Wardroom giving them a reassuring smile as he came in.

"Well, the excitement is over for now, I don't think he will be back as that wasn't a very determined attack, I suggest you all try to get some sleep until we surface tonight?"

"Yes, I think I will. Thank you for keeping us informed of what was happening, Captain, it really did help," said Mary as she stood up.

"It was Seaman 'Chalky' White's idea really, but I am glad that it helped, the first attack can always be a little unsettling." Mary nodded to him then pulled herself up onto her bunk, pulling the curtain across, she curled herself up into a tight ball but sleep didn't come easy as it usually didn't these days for when she closed her eyes, the pain came flooding back, that horrid wooden chair in the interrogation room standing out vividly in her mind. The next few hours passed for her in bouts of fitful sleep with nightmares where she woke covered in sweat with her hand and back throbbing dreadfully.

This time it wasn't a noise that woke her but a strange smell of strong ammonia, then she realised that she could hear the submarine's diesel engines rumbling away which meant that they must be on the surface, she reached over and pulled back the curtain on the bunk, the boat's Captain was sitting at the table with Pierre and the Professor.

"What time is it?" she asked as she swung herself out of the bunk onto the bench seat surrounding the table.

"A little before midnight, dinner will be served shortly." The captain reached over and pushed the call button for the Steward, then as if he had been standing outside waiting for the call, Chalky poked his head around the doorway.

"Sir?"

"Another one for dinner, thanks."

"Right oh sir, would you like a cup of tea, Miss?" asked Chalky looking at Mary.

"Please." The Steward nodded then left.

"Does he ever sleep?" she asked making the Captain smile.

"Sleep is of a premium on submarines, I'm afraid," then he leant forward so he couldn't be overheard, "Don't tell him this but I would be totally lost without him." As she smiled, the Steward returned with a fresh cup of tea that he put down in front of her.

"Thank you."

"What's for dinner, Chalky?" asked the Captain as Mary took a sip of her tea.

"Roast beef, tinned potatoes, carrots, peas and gravy sir."

"Sounds good." The Steward left as the captain nodded.

"Do you normally eat at this time of night, Captain?" asked the Professor.

"Our mealtimes are set around our routine, as we spend all night on the surface charging our batteries, our main meal is late at night when the chef can use his ovens, then we have breakfast just after we submerge at dawn, lunch around noon and a couple of snacks in between times."

"So, the crew would normally be resting during the day then?" asked the Professor.

"All the crew have routine jobs that have to be done but when not actually on watch the crew turn in yes, the most sleep they get is about four hours at a time."

"Goodness!"

"So, you had to leave your last billet to come and get us, is that right, Captain?" asked Mary and the Captain nodded.

"Yes, but don't let it worry you as it was becoming a very boring patrol anyway, you gave us a bit of excitement and we are returning early for a refit, so the crew are very happy having you aboard."

"Grub's up, sir," the Steward returned balancing four plates of food which he proceeded to flick onto the table.

"Me 'ands are quicker than the eye, Miss," he said before he disappeared again, now that the food had arrived, Mary found that she was suddenly quite hungry.

"We should rendezvous with our escort late afternoon, day after tomorrow," said the captain as he started eating.

"That's good to know, Captain."

"What's the routine on the surface, Sir, would we uhm be able to get some fresh air, do you think?" asked Pierre; he had been quite surprised by the quality of the submarine's food, he had seen the tiny galley and didn't know how the Chef, as the Captain had called the man, managed to make such good meals for over seventy men three times a day and now also the extra mouths as well.

"Are you a smoker?"

"I am, sir."

"Then while we are surfaced, you can smoke as much as you like and when we have finished dinner, you can come up to the bridge one at a time for a short period as long as you are aware that if we spot anything then you have to nip below a bit smartish, alright?"

"I'm quite happy to smoke down here if I may, Captain" said Pierre, the Captain nodded pointing to a small wooden box on a shelf behind them.

"That's our communal box so please help yourself, you'll find matches next to it."

"Oh, thank you very much."

"How about you, Professor, would you like some fresh air on the bridge?" asked the captain but the Professor shook his head negatively.

"No thank you, I will stay down here if I may?" The Professor had seen how low down in the water the submarine had been when they had been picked up and after being in that lifeboat, well he had had enough of boats and the quicker he was off this one, the better he would feel.

"I'll go up if I may, Captain?" said Mary as she pushed her plate aside.

"You can come with me now if you are ready?"

"Yes, I'm ready, thank you." Mary followed the Captain out of the Wardroom then a couple of paces had them entering the Control Room, to Mary it looked like a very confined space surrounded by pipes, gauges and the two gleaming brass columns of the periscopes for this was the nerve centre of the submarine, in between the two periscopes was a slightly angle steel ladder leading up into the conning tower, she realised that there was a slightly cold draught of air being sucked in through the open hatch by the submarine's diesel engines down aft.

The Control Room seemed a little eerie as it was lit with red lighting instead of the white light that had lit the wardroom, she realised that this was being done to preserve the night vision of those men that had to go up to the bridge, it also explained why the Captain had been wearing a pair of red goggles while in the wardroom which he had now removed placing them on the chart table before moving to the ladder between the periscopes.

"Captain on the bridge!" said the helmsman into the voice pipe after receiving a nod from the captain.

"Follow me and watch your shins," the Captain smiled reassuringly to her then rapidly climbed the ladder up into the Conning Tower, she waited for his feet to clear a little then started to gingerly follow him, the air being sucked in by the diesels howled a little as she blocked the passage, then she had entered the conning tower then started climbing the next ladder up to the crisp night air on the submarine's bridge.

"All clear sir, nothing to report. Oh, hello Miss," said the Officer of the Watch, looking a little surprised as she followed the captain to the front of the bridge.

"Evening, I hope I'm not in the way here, Captain?" she asked as the captain motioned for her to move up to the front of the bridge, she noticed that the two lookouts and the Officer of the Watch hadn't stopped looking around through their binoculars as they had spoken.

"You're not in the way at all, just be ready to dart down below like a rabbit up a drainpipe if I call 'Down', alright?" said the captain as he did a full three-hundred-and-sixty-degree sweep of the horizon through his own binoculars.

Slowly, Mary's eyes adjusted to the darkness surrounding night, luckily the sea was calm with only a slight swell, gradually she felt herself relaxing as she watched the sea foaming over the submarine saddle tanks, it was funny but the diesel engines didn't seem so loud up here with the breeze created by the submarine's passage was somehow relaxing, for the first time in what seemed like a very long time Mary found herself unwinding, she was safe now, the Germans could no longer hurt her, all she had to do now was get the Professor to England.

If anyone asked her why she had started to cry at that moment, she wouldn't have been able to explain it, but she felt happy as the tears ran unheeded down her cheeks. The captain had lowered his binoculars after completing another sweep of the horizon and he had been about to speak to her when he had seen the tears running down her face, not knowing what was wrong, he decided to leave her to her thoughts. An hour later the lookouts were replaced followed shortly after by the Officer of the Watch.

"Bridge—Control Room!" came the call up the voice pipe, the Officer of the Watch leant over the voice pipe lip.

"Bridge!"

"We are receiving a wireless transmission addressed to our passengers, sir."

"Very well, tell them we are coming down," the captain told the Officer of the Watch.

"Control room, Captain's coming down!"

"I thought they would have tried contacting us sooner than this, sir," said Mary.

"They would know that we couldn't transmit while submerged. Shall we?" he motioned to the hatch, Mary turned around awkwardly lowering herself into the hatch then she descended the two ladders, she was relieved that she hadn't had to make that descent in a hurry as she had felt extremely awkward going down those to two ladders, stepping off the bottom rung she turned aft and made her way to the wardroom, blinking rapidly as she entered the white light, the Captain had put on his red goggles as he stepped off the ladder.

"It's addressed to you, Mary," said Pierre holding up a signal flimsy as she entered the wardroom.

"Like some tea, Miss?" asked the Steward poking his head around the doorway as Mary took a seat at the table.

"If I could please?"

"Sir?" asked the Steward looking at the captain.

"Please."

"Sir." As the Steward left the captain sat down at the table next to Pierre as Mary took the signal, it was from Beth and was very brief.

"How many in party, do you require medical assistance?" she read the signal out loud.

"They don't exactly waste words, do they, Mary?" asked Pierre, Mary smiled at him.

"They can't afford to, Pierre, as for me to reply I would have to use the Naval Code, then a third party is involved so we couldn't really say much."

"No, I suppose so."

"Do you want to send a reply, Mary?" asked the Captain as the Steward returned to put the tea on the table before leaving again, the captain held out a pencil to her.

"Thank you." Mary took the pencil, turned the signal over then scribbled a brief reply: 'package plus two—Lilly', then she handed it to the captain.

"Won't take long to code this, excuse me." The captain left the Wardroom, Mary took a sip of her tea before looking at Pierre.

"He must think I am a complete idiot?" she said quietly making Pierre frown.

"I doubt that but what makes you think so?" Mary sipped her tea before sighing heavily, she was feeling a little weird, she was finally starting to realise that she was safe, she no longer had to lead a double life, a schoolteacher by day (she realised that she would dearly miss the children that she had been teaching) then a wireless operator/saboteur by night. Ever since she had been dropped into France, she had been wound up like a tight spring, not being able to trust anyone accept a very small group of friends in her Resistance Cell always living with the fear of being either being denounced by a traitor or discovered by the Germans while out on a mission or while transmitting a signal to London.

But now, when she had been up on the bridge with the gentle swell lapping over the submarine's saddle tanks, she had finally been able to let go, she knew that the captain had seen her crying, she had been grateful to him for leaving her alone. She must have cried for well over an hour, but it had helped her emotionally, it had been a release that she had desperately needed.

"I…I couldn't help it but I…I just started crying, I couldn't stop, stupid, isn't it?" she felt herself blushing a little under his steady gaze.

"No, it isn't stupid, Mary, we all handle things in our own way but I'm glad you were able to let it go, it isn't easy sometimes."

"Thank you, Pierre, I knew you would understand, I…I don't think I could have done this without you," she said, Pierre smiled at her warmly.

"Yes, you would. You probably won't think so, Mary, but you are very good in this field, everything you did you did very well without hesitation, you have more than proved your loyalty to those around you but I…I'm just sorry that you had to suffer under that bastard Major!" Pierre couldn't keep the bitterness out of his voice as he said this as he remembered what that SS swine had done to her.

"Do you think they are safe, Pierre?"

"Who?" he asked frowning.

"Danny, Margite, Mark, we had to leave in such a hurry. I…I only hope they are safe as they are good people, they were very good to me, Pierre."

"Danny and Margite have friends in the South of France who will look after them, Mark will be making his way to Bordeaux, there is another cell there that he will be joining so he will be safe, we always make contingency plans in case things do go wrong so don't worry, Mary, I know they will be safe."

"Thank you, Pierre, that really is good to know." Then she was looking up as the captain came back into the Wardroom.

"Your message has been sent, Mary; we will be submerging soon so we won't be able to transmit but we will be able to receive," he said as he sat down at the table.

"Thank you, Captain, but there won't be any reply."

"Oh, how can you be so sure?"

"Well sir, I don't have my codes, they now know how many are in our group and that we don't need any medical assistance so the rest can wait until we meet in person."

"I see."

"I think you should have told them that you need medical attention, Mary." Pierre knew she wouldn't like what he had said but he had to say it, he knew her wounds were troubling her as he had seen her holding herself awkwardly a couple of times, he was also worried about infection as the submarine wasn't the cleanest place with water restrictions so they hadn't really been able to clean themselves since they had been picked up but Mary shook her head as he knew she would.

"I'm alright, Pierre, really!"

AAUUGGGHAA! AAUUUUGGGGHA! AAUUUGGGHAA! As the submarine's klaxon alarm sounded, the captain shot out of the Wardroom.

"Dive—Dive—Dive! Flood Q—100 feet," called the Officer of the Watch harshly as a Star Shell popped into brilliant harsh light behind them then a shell whistled overhead exploding in a tall column of water as spray burst up from the opened ballast tank vents with the submarine taking on a steep down angle with the klaxon blaring up from below as the two lookouts and the Officer of the Watch scrambled below madly.

"Bloody Hell!" gasped Pierre as the crew hurried past the Wardroom going to their action stations, the diesels had cut out abruptly as the deck had taken on its steep down angle, the needle in the depth gauge on the bulkhead had spun rapidly around to the 100-foot mark.

"Shut Q! Group down—slow ahead together Starboard Fifteen!" the Officer of the Watch called as he stepped off the ladder after closing the conning tower hatch above then turned to the captain.

"Sorry sir, the bastard snuck up on us, first I knew of it was the Star shell going off, I turned directly towards when I dived, I think it was a trawler and there was only the one, sir."

"Very well, David, I have her, well done."

"Sir."

"H-E bearing Green Four five, range four thousand yards, closing sir," called the ASDIC operator.

"For what we are about to receive! Shut off from Depth Charging—Group UP! Full ahead together!" as the captain snapped out his orders the Wardroom Steward entered the Wardroom.

"Hang on tight, it's about to get a little noisy!" as he said this Mary looked up at the deckhead as an engine noise suddenly roared overhead.

'WHAAM!' 'WHAAM!' 'WHAAM!' 'WHAAM!' 'WHAAM!' 'WHAAM!'

The submarine reverberated like a giant gong rocking madly to the thudding explosions, Mary looked up a little startled as what looked like white flecks of paint floated down from overhead like confetti.

"That's cork, Miss, they mix it in with the paint to help absorb moisture. Is everyone alright?" asked Chalky looking at each of them in turn.

"I…I think so," she said licking her suddenly dry lips.

"Bloody Hell, that sounded close!" gasped Pierre as he looked at the Depth Gauge that was now reading 200 ft.

"Nah, not really. you know when they're close as you can hear the double click of the detonators just before they explode, just push that bell if you need me, right?" with that the Steward left again.

"Close or not, they scared the Hell out of me!" said Mary as she brushed the cork chips off her shoulders.

"H-E bearing Red Eight Oh—Closing—Attacking sir!"

"Sod it! Port Twenty—Group Up—Half ahead together!" called the captain, then Mary was looking up at the deckhead as the trawler's engine noise grew louder and louder before roaring away over their heads, Mary found herself holding her breath, waiting!

'WHAAM!' 'WHAAM!' 'WHAAM!' 'WHAAM!' 'WHAAM!' 'WHAAM!'

The noise of the explosions reverberated loudly with the submarine shuddering, but they weren't as noisy as the first ones, Mary breathed out as the engine noise faded.

"Not so loud, do you think?" asked the Professor as he wiped the sweat from his forehead.

"Midships—Steer One Three five--Group Down—Slow Ahead together!" came the orders from the Control Room. For another hour, they twisted and turned as the trawler made repeated attacking runs.

"In contact—Revs increasing—Attacking sir."

"Persistent little sod! Alright Group Up—Half Ahead Together!" Mary swallowed hard as she held tightly to the bench seat as the trawler's engine noise started getting nearer again.

'WHAAM!' 'WHAAM!' 'WHAAM!' 'WHAAM!' 'WHAAM!' 'WHAAM!'

The submarine leaned sharply to the left before righting itself as the sound of the explosions faded, Mary took a sip of cold tea to ease the dryness in her mouth.

"Stand by Tubes ONE, TWO, THREE, FOUR, FIVE and SIX, set running depths of Six Feet!" as the captain called his orders the Steward poked his head into the Wardroom again.

"The Skipper's going to Kipper the bastard!" he said then withdrew.

"Kipper?" asked the Professor frowning.

"I think he means to try a torpedo attack."

"Oh, I see, I think."

"Group Down—Slow Ahead both, Periscope Depth!"

For the next half an hour, they tried to follow what was happening by the orders that they could hear, but it didn't really make a great deal of sense to them, then they heard the captain rapidly give some bearings and ranges.

"Stand by! —Fire One—Fire Two—carry on firing by stopwatch!"

As each torpedo was launched the submarine paused as if it had run into something soft, there was an abrupt change of pressure in their ears, then as the last torpedo was launched Mary had to swallow hard to clear her ears.

"All torpedoes gone and running, sir!"

"Starboard Twenty! —Sixty Feet—Half Ahead Together!" as the submarine dropped turning to starboard, Pierre found himself counting in his head, he stopped himself feeling a little idiotic as he didn't know how long it would take the torpedoes to run to their target so it was stupid to count.

"H-E bearing Green Six Oh—Revs increasing, sir!"

"Bugger! That means he has spotted the bloody—!" the captains words were cut short by a loud 'WHOOOMPAA!' resounding explosion that made the submarine shudder.

"Group Down—Slow Ahead—Periscope Depth Number One!"

Half an hour later, although it seemed a lot longer to Mary, the crew started filing past as they stood down from their action stations then the Captain smiled at them as he entered the Wardroom.

"Scratch one trawler!" he said as he plonked himself down onto the bench sear.

"Uhm, congratulations captain," Pierre smiled broadly now that it was over, he had been quite worried there for a while.

"I'm afraid the Admiralty won't be pleased."

"Oh, why is that sir, I thought it was your job to sink enemy vessels?" asked Pierre frowning.

"I used four torpedoes on that trawler, they're two thousand pounds apiece so I don't think the admiralty will see the worth in the target."

"But you think differently, Captain, am I right?" asked Mary as she caught the tone in the man's voice.

"Yes, they aren't the ones on the receiving end of those Depth Charges, besides which that Captain was a fool, you should never use the same manoeuvres when dealing with a submarine!"

"I don't understand, sir?" she said.

"The only reason I attacked that trawler is because he put you people at risk, I could have spent all day outmanoeuvring him then toddled off after we surfaced tonight, he may have gotten in a lucky shot but we weren't damaged, he made the mistake of turning the same way after every attack then slowing down to reacquire his target, it took us a while but we managed to get into a position where after his last attack, we were able to loose four kippers and Bob's your Uncle!" Mary could see the logic behind what he had told them, she could also see that he had gained no pleasure in having just sunk an enemy vessel.

"Well, I for one am very happy that it turned out the way that it did, and I take my hat off to you and your men, Captain, I can see this isn't easy what you have to endure with on these Patrols, sir."

"Just all part of the job I suppose."

"Well I think I will turn in, thank you Captain." Mary nodded to the Skipper then climbed into her bunk, she laid on her back for a while until the pain became too acute to bear anymore for her body was still in a lot of pain from the beatings that she had taken. She turned onto her side bringing up her knees until the quiet humming of the electric motors had her eyes drooping, then for the first time in a long while, she dropped off into a deep sleep.

Chapter Fourteen
First Mission France 1943

It was a cool quiet night lit by the stars in a moonless sky as Mary pulled up on her bicycle in the yard of Danny's pig farm, she leaned the bike against the side of the shed then walked over to the farmhouse, the door opened as she approached.

"Hallo Mary, come in," said Margite as she held the door open.

"Hello Margite, has Pierre arrived yet?" asked Mary as she entered the farmhouse, Margite closed the door then pulled the blackout curtain across the doorway then turned the lights on making Mary blink rapidly then Margite came forward and hugged her warmly.

"Pierre should be here shortly, would you like some coffee, Mary, I've just made some?"

"Please." Mary went in and took a seat at the kitchen table as Margite went over to the stove to fetch the coffee.

"Thanks, Margite." Mary smiled as she took the coffee, she had only been in Posey for a month now yet this farm felt like home for her, she kept to herself for the most part going to the school for the day during the week (she had only ten pupils in the class that she taught, all between seven and eight years old who she had been accepted by and had great fun with for the most part); she would ride her bicycle into town to fetch supplies when she needed them, then she would ride out to this farm every couple of days to make radio contact with London (she was in contact with Beth at SOE but London called the shots).

Then, she would ride home again or stay the night, especially on the weekends, where she would help the old couple where she could either with the pigs (although she was still a little afraid of them) or in their vegetable garden, this was partly to help with a cover story should she be stopped and questioned by the local gendarmes or Wehrmacht soldiers but also because she genuinely enjoyed helping them out.

A few minutes later, Danny entered the farmhouse carrying a small wooden box and a haversack.

"Evening Mary, all set for tonight?" he asked smiling broadly at her as he put the box down onto the table.

"Hello Danny, yes, I'm all set, I think. What do you have there?" she had kept her answer light but was actually feeling a little nervous for she was to go on her first sabotage mission with Pierre this evening, she knew what she had to do and had trained for this moment in England, although she was excited at the coming mission, she was also a little scared.

"Your supplies for tonight, the explosives and the timer pencils, can you put those in your pocket along with the pliers?" asked Danny as he passed her a short length of canvas inside which was three thin metal pencil detonators which when the ends were crimped by the pliers would set off a chemical reaction leading to the small blasting cap in the end of the pencil being detonated. This pencil would be pushed into a small explosive charge consisting of a couple of pounds of C4 plastic explosive which they would be using tonight to destroy the electrical transformers in the nearby town of Melbec, the transformers provided power not only for the town but also for a small factory that was machining parts for radio transmitters.

She took the canvas roll and put it into her skirt pocket then the pliers went into her shirt pocket, the explosives would be carried in the haversack, then when they got to their target, Pierre would provide lookout and cover while she entered the transformer park, she would place the explosive at the base of the transformer, insert the pencil timer into the explosive, crimp the bottom of the pencil to activate the timer before getting the hell out of it. She jumped a little, startled, as the telephone jangled three times then stopped.

"That's the signal, Mary, Pierre will meet you at the crossroads in ten minutes," said Danny as he closed the haversack.

"Alright."

"You have your pistol?" he asked as he passed her the haversack, she nodded as she had a silenced 9 mm semi-automatic pistol in the right-hand skirt pocket with the timing pencils in the left one.

"Yes, in my pocket Danny," then much to her surprise Danny leaned forward hugging her warmly.

"Good luck, young'un." Margite then led her to the door holding blackout curtain as she switched off the light.

"Bon Chance, Mary," whispered Margite, Mary nodded to her then hurried to her bicycle, mounting it she quickly pedalled out of the farm. The night seemed eerily bright to her as she peddled wobbling slightly down the laneway to the crossroads where she was to meet Pierre, they had rehearsed this a couple of times now so she knew exactly where she could hide her bike, she stopped near a large bush by a fence a few yards short of the crossroads, pushing the bike behind the bush where she cold lean it up against the fence, she then knelt down behind the bush where she peered out at the crossroads, a couple of minutes later she cursed herself for being a fool for she hadn't removed the pistol, it was still in her skirt pocket.

"Some flaming Agent you are!" she cursed to herself as she removed the pistol, this was already loaded and cocked to fire, she simply had to thumb the safety catch to the 'fire' position, this would save the timed needed to cock the weapon which could mean the difference between life and death in a difficult situation, then she was tensing up as she heard the sound of an engine approaching, her mouth had gone suddenly dry as she raised the pistol getting ready in case it wasn't Pierre!

A small van turned the bend, slowed then stopped, Mary found herself holding her breath as she waited for the signal, if it was Pierre, he would flash the Morse letter 'M' consisting of two dashes which he would make using a small torch through the windscreen, of course he may have been captured and made to talk, in which case she could be walking into a trap!

She jumped a little as a small circle of light briefly sent the DAH DAH letter M through the windscreen. Swallowing hard, she forced herself to break cover, hurrying over to the van, she opened the passenger door, and the van was moving as she got in closing the door breathing a sigh of relief as she did so.

"Bring everything, Mary?" asked Pierre as they started picking up speed.

"Yes, it's all here."

"Is your safety back on?"

"Oh damn!" she said as she thumbed the safety back to 'safe' as Pierre chuckled at her.

"Oh Shoosh!" she said but couldn't help grinning hugely at him as he had helped her to relax a little. Then fifteen minutes later they were slowing down then Pierre turned off the road into a small laneway then a few minutes later off this near some bushes, he turned the engine off letting the van roll to a stop.

"Hand signals from here on, Mary, good luck!" with a final smile he quietly opened his door getting out, Mary did the same then moved off to the right at his signal, this time she had her pistol in her hand and had automatically thumbed off the 'safety' as her training kicked in. Five minutes careful and watchful walking brought them to a small laneway at the back of the transformer park, Pierre motioned for Mary to wait while he made his way to the fence surrounding the park, then as he started snipping through the fence. Mary stood tensely on guard watching along the laneway hoping that no one would come along it.

Then Pierre was signalling to her, she had a quick look around then hurried over to the where he had cut through the fence, she squeezed herself through this gap then crouching low she hurried over to the first of three large transformers, kneeling down she quickly unfastened the haversack taking out the first of the prepared C4 charges, she pressed this onto the base of the transformer as they had shown her back in England, then reaching into her pocket she pulled out the roll of canvas then took out one of the pencil timers, her heart thudding in her ears seemed to be very loud as she pushed this pencil into the explosive, then she cursed herself as she dropped the pliers as she took them out of her pocket, picking them up she crimped the end of the pencil thus activating the fuse!

She quickly moved over to the second transformer, setting the charge there then made her way to the last one, then as she crimped then end of the pencil setting the fuse running, she froze as she heard voices, she dropped flat onto her stomach in the shadow of the transformer as she looked around towards Pierre, he had also dropped flat and was motioning for her to stay down.

"Hold up Hans, I need to take a piss!" Mary held her breath as two German soldiers came into her view on the other side of the fence not twenty feet away from her position.

"Well, hurry it up will you, I want to get going!"

"What's wrong, Peter, don't you think she will wait for you?" asked Hans then Mary was having to clamp her jaws tightly shut as she had a sudden inane urge to giggle as there came the sound of splashing as the first soldier urinated onto the ground near the fence.

"Come on!"

"Alright, keep your shirt on!" The soldier laughed out loud as they started walking off, Mary closed her eyes with sheer relief as they moved off.

"Bloody hell—the fuses!" she jerked her head around looking for Pierre, her heart had almost stopped as she remembered that she had activated the fuses, although they each had a one-hour timer they were notorious for going off early! She had to wait for Pierre to give her the all clear signal as he could see those soldiers where she couldn't.

"Come on—come on!" she whispered harshly to herself.

Over at the fence Pierre had dropped flat the second he had heard the approaching voices, he saw the two men turn the bend in the lane then saw Mary dropping flat in the shadow of the transformers, he gave her the signal to stay put and was very relieved when he received a small nod from her, it meant she had seen the danger and wouldn't move. "Of all the times to have to take a piss, you bastards!" he cursed quietly to himself as he knew Mary had set the timers which were now burning down towards detonation, if they went off now Mary would be killed for certain, he could feel the sweat rolling down his neck as he watched the two soldiers.

"Come on—come—on—move!" He was cursing quietly, then the two soldiers were starting to move, he signalled Mary to remain down for if she moved now, they would hear her for sure as they were right on top of her.

As the two men moved off down the lane, he gave them a couple of minutes to make sure that they were well and truly clear then getting up onto his knees he frantically signalled to Mary. Mary had started to sweat badly as she thought about those fuses burning down, then she was almost sick with relief as she saw Pierre coming up onto his knees as he signalled to her, scrambling up she hurried to the fence where Pierre held the wire apart, she squeezed through the gap then they were running for the van, once the engine had started and they were moving up the laneway Mary seemed to breathe out as the tension eased.

"You did good, Girl, you really did! I thought you were going to move when those two bastards showed up."

"They scared the Hell out of me when they turned up, Pierre, and then…" Mary trailed off as she suddenly thought that Pierre would think that she was an idiot for having nearly giggled when the man had relieved himself.

"Then what?" asked Pierre frowning.

"Then I…I had to clamp my jaws shut when he started urinating near me, I…I had an awful urge to giggle, Pierre, I'm sorry," she said looking at him sheepishly but to her surprise, he threw his head back as he started laughing, making her grin.

"Oh, that's classic, Mary! Here you are almost getting blown up by your own charges and all you want to do is giggle because that soldier needed a piss, oh god that's funny!" Pierre laughed again and Mary couldn't help grinning to herself for she felt as if she had now truly been accepted by her team leader; she knew that she would never forget this night.

****

The walls of the small courtyard seemed to be closing in on her as she struggled against the manacles that held her arms pinned behind the wooden post that she was standing against with the wood pressing into her back, a few yards away Kurt grinned evilly at her as he started to slowly raise his pistol.

"Tell me your codes you stupid bitch!" Kurt snarled at her as he took aim.

Mary couldn't breathe as she stared at the gaping muzzle of the pistol, any second now he would fire, and she would be dead!

OH GOD, SHE WAS GOING TO DIE!

"Mary?" someone seemed to be calling her name, but it seemed to be coming from far away adding to the unreality of the scene in the courtyard.

OH GOD—OH GOD! She struggled against the cold manacles, but they seemed to be getting tighter as she did so.

"Mary?" her name was being called again but it couldn't help her, she couldn't breathe! She was going to vomit but she couldn't breathe!

"Mary—you're safe—Mary!" her name being called softly was insistent, but she couldn't understand where it was coming from in the courtyard, then she jumped startled, suddenly awake as a hand was gently placed on her shoulder, she was disorientated, panting hard and covered in sweat, she stared wide-eyed at Pierre for a few seconds before she became fully awake, safe on the submarine's bunk with Pierre looking at her worriedly.

"Oh god!" Mary turned onto her side facing the bulkhead as she drew up her knees and started sobbing into her pillow.

"You're safe Mary, no one will hurt you here, girl," Pierre said this quietly as he pulled the curtain across the bunk to give her privacy with her nightmares, he had heard her starting to moan a few minutes ago, then he had become worried as he had heard her distress becoming louder, he had gently pulled the curtain back, at first he hadn't quite known what to do as he saw her struggling with her nightmare, they said that you should never wake someone in the middle of a nightmare but his was different, he could see the girl was terrified by something and she was getting louder in her distress, she would be waking the others if he didn't do something.

He also knew that she would feel very humiliated if the other men saw her distress so he reached out and very gently laid his hand on her shoulder as he spoke quietly to her but he hadn't been prepared for her reaction for it was as if he had struck her as she jumped badly startled to stare at him totally bewildered, then an emotional lump was forming in his throat as she turned onto her side, drawing up her knees as she started sobbing.

He drew the curtains back across the bunk then sat down at the table, wondering what on earth those bastards had done to this girl.

It took Mary a good hour to regain control of herself; she wiped her eyes as best she could then slowly drew back the curtains.

"I'm sorry, Pierre," she said as she moved down from the bunk taking a seat at the table.

"You don't have to say sorry to me, Mary, not after everything that has happened to you," he smiled at her trying to reassure her, he could see that she was embarrassed, Mary swallowed hard as she reached for some water.

"It was just a nightmare, Pierre, I…I was in that damned courtyard!" she said after taking a drink of water, she did feel embarrassed by Pierre having seen her like this, she was also very grateful as she realised what he had been trying to do by rousing her like this.

"Courtyard?" asked Pierre frowning, he didn't understand what she was talking about, but he was happy that she was willing to tell him what had happened as it might make it easier for him to help her, Mary nodded before speaking.

"It was at the police station Pierre, it was after they had beaten me with a rubber truncheon, they had tried to drown me in that horrid bathtub a number of times then beat me. Major Schrandt was getting frustrated because I wouldn't tell them anything you see." Mary took another sip of water before continuing.

"Then he told Kurt to take me out because he had had enough. I…I thought at first that they were going to hand me over to the Gestapo, but…but it was worse, Pierre." Mary paused as she wiped away the tears that were streaming down her face, Pierre could see the anguish in her face.

"That bastard Kurt frog marched me out to a courtyard at the back of the police station, there was a wooden post set in the ground near the rear wall, I…I realised that the courtyard was used for executions, Pierre!"

"What—they showed you this courtyard to scare you, is that it?" he asked frowning, again she shook her head negatively swallowing hard as she remembered that horrid courtyard with its pockmarked wall.

"No—he manacled me to that post then—Oh God Pierre—he drew his pistol, cocked it then took aim—he—he said that if I didn't answer his questions this time then—then he would fire!"

"My God!"

"I thought I was going to die Pierre, I…I wouldn't answer him then—then he fired!" Mary sobbed out loud as she said this, Pierre quickly moved up alongside her, she flung her arms around his neck and started sobbing hard as she buried her face into his shoulder.

Pierre couldn't believe what she had just told him, he was sickened by the thought of what those bastards had done to this girl, he was also extremely proud of the way that she had stood up to them, no matter what they had done to her she had stood up to it not talking, she had protected them all, he knew he could never repay her for that, he was also extremely glad that he had been the one to kill that bastard Major Schrandt, he put his hand gently on her head and for the next twenty minutes just let her sob it out.

"I…I am so sorry, Pierre, crying like this," she said sheepishly as she sat up wiping her eyes as best, she could.

"You have nothing to reproach yourself for, Mary!" Mary looked around as the Professor said this, he had pulled back the curtain on his bunk while she had been talking to Pierre, now as she looked up, he pulled himself down from the bunk moving over to the bench seat at the table.

"I do not know Pierre or the other members of your Resistance Group, Mary, but I know that they like myself owe you our lives, you protected us all by not talking to those evil men, I have also seen for myself what a brave fighter you are!" Mary was a little surprised by the Professor's outburst, he hadn't really said much since they boarded the Submarine, now for some reason his words didn't embarrass her, she wasn't sure why, maybe it was the look on his face for he genuinely meant every word.

"I…I'm not sure about that last part but thank you Linus."

"I mean it Mary, I owe you my life, I will never be able to repay you for that."

"Yes, you can Professor, by making sure that the information you have gets to the right people and is put to good effect against those bastards!" Mary couldn't keep the hatred out of her voice as she said this.

"Oh, I will Mary, believe me I will!" then they were all looking up as the Captain entered the Wardroom.

"We should be surfacing in just over an hour, then if all goes well, we should pick up our escort tomorrow evening." The captain looked at each of them in turn as he sat down at the table, he knew he had interrupted something but thought it best not to say anything.

"What will you do once we get back? Oh sorry, I suppose I shouldn't really be asking that," he said as he looked at Mary.

"That's alright sir, I can't really tell you much because I don't really know. I assume there will be a major debriefing for us once we have handed over the Professor, but I don't really know." She had been thinking about what would happen when they reached England, she knew that there would be some kind of debriefing and that this would prove painful for her as it would bring back some unpleasant memories that she would rather forger, but she knew that it would be harder for Pierre; after all, she was going home whereas he had lost everything.

"Well, let's hope that it turns out well then." The captain lent over to push the call button; a couple of seconds later Chalky poked his head around the doorway.

"Sir?"

"Could we have some coffee please, Chalky?"

"Right-o Sir." As he left again the captain looked at his passengers, he knew they had had a rough time of it and wanted to ease their discomfort a little if he could.

"Would anyone like to come up onto the bridge when we surface?" he asked.

"I wouldn't mind, Captain," said Mary, she would love to get some fresh air after being cooped up in the submarine all day.

"Good, I'll give you a call once things have settled down after we surface then."

"Thank you, Captain."

"There you go, Ladies and Gents!" said Chalky as he reappeared carrying a tray with a coffee pot, milk, sugar, cups and a plate of biscuits.

"I don't know what I would do without you, Chalky," said the captain as he reached for the coffee pot.

"Neither do I, sir!" Grinning hugely, Chalky left again.

****

"My dear girl, it is so good to see you again!" Mary was a little surprised as Captain 'Beth' Sims hugged her warmly. They were standing in the submarine depot ship's wardroom, they had arrived early that evening after an uneventful day before they had picked up their escort in the late afternoon, the Captain had allowed her to stay on the bridge as they had entered the harbour and she had watched in fascination as they had manoeuvred alongside the Depot Ship, then there seemed to be a mass exodus for once the submarine was secure alongside, the crew had grabbed their belonging before they had left for a well-earned period of leave.

Mary with her companions had waited until the pandemonium had subsided before they made their way up the long gangway to the depot ship's deck where the submarine's captain had warmly shaken hands with them all before handing over to the depot ship captain, he had also then departed. She had winced a little as Beth's hug had hurt her shoulders and back, but it was very good to see her again.

"It's very good to see you again, Beth, believe me I didn't think I was going to for a while," she said as Beth released her, stepping back a little.

"Well, you are safe now, Mary, that's the main thing." Mary nodded then turned to her waiting companions.

"Captain Sims, this is Pierre, my team leader from Posey."

"I am very pleased to meet you, Pierre, I want to thank you very much for everything that you have done for Mary," said Beth as she shook hands warmly with the man.

"Enchante Captain, I want to tell you that Mary is a very good operative, because of her loyalty my compatriots were able to make a clean getaway from Posey."

"We have received word that your group are all safe, Pierre."

"Oh, that is good, Captain, thank you," said Pierre grinning broadly.

"You are sure, Beth, Danny, Margite, Mark, they are all safe, you are certain of that?" asked Mary excitedly for it was very important to her to know that all her friends were finally safe as well.

"Yes, we have received cyphers from the groups that they have joined, they are all safe and well, my dear."

"Oh, that is wonderful, Beth, I was so worried about them, they are very good people, and it really is good to know that they are safe now."

"Well, you needn't worry any more, they are quite safe, I assure you."

"Who's safe?" asked Major Scott as he entered the Wardroom making his way over to them.

"Mary's team from Posey."

"Yes, all taken care of," then much to Mary's surprise the Major also hugged her. "You have done a wonderful job, Mary; I am just sorry that you had to go through what you did, welcome home!"

"Thank you, Sandy," she said as she took a step back.

"You must be Pierre?" asked the Major as he extended his hand to Pierre.

"Pierre, this is Major Scott, my Team Commander at SOE," said Mary as the two men shook hands.

"You need to make sure that you keep this one, Major, as she is a very brave girl." Mary felt herself blushing a little as Pierre had looked directly at her as he said this, but she didn't feel very brave as she remembered how she had screamed when Kurt had used his 'little pins' under her fingernails.

"I can also tell you that she is a very brave fighter, Major," the Professor stepped forward a little as he said this.

"Major Scott, this is—" Mary started to say but the Major cut her off.

"Professor Linus Kruen, you have caused us a great deal of trouble, Professor, I only hope your information is worth it?" said the Major a little firmly as they shook hands.

"I can assure you that it is, Major."

"Then welcome to England, Professor." The Major turned and gestured to two MPs who had been standing waiting by the doorway and who now came forward.

"Professor, these men will take you to a waiting motorboat that will take you ashore, there you will be driven to London, I will meet you at the car shortly."

"Am I under arrest, Major?" asked the Professor raising an eyebrow.

"No, but there are Nazi sympathisers here in England and we want to keep you safe now that you are here."

"Then, I may say goodbye first, Major?"

"Of course."

The Professor turned, extending his hand to Pierre. "Thank you for helping me escape, Pierre, I owe you a great debt!"

"Bon Chance, Professor." Pierre shook the man's hand warmly then the Professor turned to Mary, he made to extend his hand to her then changed his mind, stepping forward he hugged her hard.

"I owe you my life, Mary, I shall always be grateful to you!"

"Make it worthwhile, Professor, help them in any way that you can and take good care of yourself."

"I will Mary, thank you." The Professor then turned to the two MPs, who led him away.

"Mary, Pierre and I will escort the Professor to London, Beth will take you back to camp."

"I'm not going to London, sir?" she asked frowning.

"Not just yet, we need to debrief you first and you need to rest, alright?"

"I…I suppose so, sir."

The Major reached out and patted her arm.

"Don't look so worried, Mary, the debrief is only a chat, alright?" Then he turned to Beth. "I'll see you back at camp as soon as I can, Beth."

"Sir." With a final nod, the Major turned and led Pierre out of the Wardroom.

"We have a boat waiting for us too, Mary." Captain Sims then led the way out of the wardroom up to the depot ship's well deck where they said their goodbyes to the ship's Captain before they made their way down the long companionway to a waiting motorboat which took them to a small landing stage ashore.

"Will Pierre be alright, Beth?" asked Mary as they walked up the wooden steps from the landing stage to the roadway.

"Yes of course, he will be debriefed in London then the Major will bring him out to the camp, sandy wants him to work as an instructor for us."

"He wants to go back to France, but it would be too dangerous for him so soon!"

"He might be able to later but for now we can use his experience for our new agents."

"Yes, I…I suppose so." Mary felt very relieved as she knew that Pierre would be safe for a while, then as they walked up the steps onto the roadway another staff car pulled up near theirs, the rear door opened, and Colonel Winters was looking out at them.

"Good evening, Colonel, I didn't know you were expected here sir?" said Beth as they moved over to the vehicle.

"Evening Captain Sims, I thought I would drive you back to camp, I'd like to talk to Mary on the way, if you wouldn't mind?" Beth thought that this was a little unusual but as she had no ground on which to refuse him, she thought that they had better comply with his wishes.

"Of course, sir." Beth climbed into the staff car with Mary getting in after her sitting on the bench backseat beside her, the Colonel was on another bench seat opposite them, he closed the door then the vehicle got underway.

To Mary it all seemed a little unreal, a few days ago she had been running for her life, yet now she was sitting in the backseat of a staff car in England with no one trying to kill her, it was slightly surreal.

"Mary, I'm Lieutenant Colonel Winters of MI5, you don't mind if we have a little chat while we drive back to SOE, do you?"

"Is this a debriefing, sir?" For some reason, Mary felt herself getting defensive as she tensed up a little.

"No. Captain Sims will do that later, I would just like an informal chat if you don't mind?"

"I…I suppose so sir."

"Thank you. I believe that you had an encounter in France with one Major Schrandt of the SS?" asked the Colonel, he could see the girl had tensed up just at the mention of Schrandt's name, he could understand why as the man had the reputation of being particularly cruel to enemy agents.

"Yes sir, I was unfortunate enough to have been captured during a Courier drop in a field near Posey." Mary swallowed hard as she said this as she still felt incredibly guilty for having let herself be captured.

"Nothing unfortunate about it, Mary, your group was ambushed due to the information that was given to Major Schrandt by Alice's handler. From what Captain Sims here tells me, if it hadn't of been for an overzealous soldier opening fire a bit early then the barricades would have been in place and the Lysander making the Courier drop wouldn't have been able to take off." Mary looked at Beth as he said this, who nodded.

"The Lysander pilot told us about the searchlight being mounted on the back of a vehicle that burst onto the field, he said himself that someone seemed to have opened fire a little prematurely, he also said that he had seen the Courier go down and that you were with him as he was taking off," said Beth and Mary nodded as she swallowed back the emotional lump forming in her throat as she could clearly see the agony and determination on the courier's face as he had passed her the small tin holding information for her group.

"The Courier was a very brave man, Beth; he had been hit in the chest by machinegun fire but he—he made sure that I had the information before he died!"

"I'm sorry Mary, I know this is painful for you, but it is important," said Beth quietly.

"I know, I'm fine, honestly!"

"Good girl!"

"So, this Courier was able to give you the information, but the Germans didn't discover it when you were captured, is that right?" asked the Colonel frowning a little.

"The information was in a small tin; when I left the field during the firefight, I had gone maybe half a mile when I saw a vehicle coming around a bend in the lane, I knew that I couldn't be taken with my Sten and the tin, so I threw them both into a drainage ditch before they saw me!"

"Well, that was very quick thinking, then the Germans captured you, is that it?"

"The vehicle was being driven by two Gendarmes with a Wehrmacht Sergeant, they then took me to the police station in Posey, that's where I met HIM!" Mary couldn't keep the bitterness out of her voice as she said the last part.

"Major Schrandt of the SS, you mean?"

"Yes sir."

"I'm sorry Mary, I know that you had a rough ordeal under the Major, but I have to ask these questions."

"That's alright sir, yes, I did have it rough, but I got the impression that the Major was in a hurry to break me, he kept saying that he didn't have much time, that's when he introduced me to his henchman Kurt!" Again, she couldn't keep the bitterness and hatred out of her voice, the Colonel could clearly see her distress.

"it's alright Mary, we won't go into any more of that now, you can discuss it with Beth later, alright?" he said, and Mary was very grateful at not having to talk more about what they had done to her to a man as it was still very raw and humiliating for her.

"Thank you, sir."

"I will tell you that you were very lucky to have escaped as Major Schrandt had a very formidable record when it comes to dealing with enemy agents, we know for a fact that he is responsible for the capture, breaking under torture and then the execution of three British and two French agents over the last two years alone." Mary nodded swallowing hard as the Colonel said this.

"I can certainly believe that sir, he certainly had very detailed information on me!"

"Yes, that was thanks to Alice, my dear, or I should really say Greta I suppose," said Beth.

"It seems incredible that she was able to infiltrate the SOE, sir?" Mary thought that this whole saga with Alice was incredible, all the time that she had spent training with the woman at SOE she'd had no inkling that she was an enemy agent.

"She was only able to do that because we have a traitor in our midst and also because she had help from the Resistance themselves."

"The French Resistance sir?" Mary asked incredulously as it seemed impossible to her that the Resistance would actively help an enemy agent.

"Yes, they had helped smuggle her to England, in all innocence as it turns out as they thought that she was on the run from the SS, what they didn't know was that it was her own brother that was actually doing the chasing!"

"Good Lord! We had no inkling of that, sir," said Beth who was still acutely embarrassed at how easily Alice had fooled them all.

"She was very good at what she did, Beth. So, Mary, I suppose there was no possibility of her surrendering?" he asked but Mary shook her head firmly.

"No sir, she was determined not to return to England where she would have been tortured for information before either being shot as a spy or being hanged as a traitor. She—she gave me no choice; she had a knife at the Professor's throat then when he managed to break free, she went to slit her own throat so I…I had to shoot!" All Mary could see was the look on Alice's face when she had shot her in the heart, the colonel held up his hand to stop her as he could see the anguish in the girl's face.

"My dear girl, please don't think that I am admonishing you in any way because I'm not, you have acted with exemplary courage throughout this entire mission, and you should be commended for your actions. It's just a pity that we haven't been able to identify the person who has been helping Alice from here in England; as I said, we have a traitor in our midst!"

"A traitor sir?" asked Beth frowning as they hadn't been told anything about a possible traitor at SOE and she wondered if Sandy knew anything about this.

"Yes, thanks to some rather corrupt diplomats at the Spanish Embassy, we now know that we have a traitor who has been working for the Germans for some time and has made a tidy penny from it, he has been passing information on to the Germans while working for us at the same time, it's been bloody frustrating, we know this person has been doing this for a considerable time. We believe he was forced by Admiral Canaris to infiltrate Alice into the SOE which brought him to our attention again, but after three years dedicated work searching for him the only thing, we have to go on is the code name of 'Crockus' and even that is pretty vague!" As the Colonel said this, Beth gasped as she involuntarily put her hand up to her mouth.

"My God! Colonel! Are you sure of that code name 'Crockus?" she asked as she visibly paled.

"Yes, and that has only come to light recently, why, does it mean something to you, Beth?" he asked frowning.

"Yes sir! 'Crockus' was the code name given to two agents that were infiltrated into Spain during their Civil War! The reason I know this is because I was their radio liaison at the time."

"My God, Beth! Are you sure?" asked the Colonel eagerly.

"Yes sir, I can even give you their names, but I can't believe that one of them could be an enemy agent!"

"My dear woman, you may have information that could crack this case wide open for us, we may be able to eliminate a traitor and stop any further Abwehr infiltration into SOE at the same time. So, Beth, who were the members of the 'Crockus' team?" The Colonel couldn't hide the excitement in his voice as he asked this for, he could see three years' work coming to fruition and hopefully, they would be able to capture this traitor.

"The 'Crockus' radio operator was a Corporal Timothy Hollis, he was killed when they were leaving Spain, that just leaves the team leader who at the time was a Second Lieutenant, it's—it's Alexander Scott! But I…I can't believe that he would be a traitor!"

"You are absolutely certain, Beth, that the Second Lieutenant then is now our Major Scott today?"

"I hate to say it, but yes, I am certain sir!"

"You're saying that Major Scott is working for the enemy!" said Mary incredulously as she tried to follow the conversation.

"I…I just can't believe that Sandy would do such a thing!" Beth was quite stunned at this new turn of events, she thought about all the Agents that the Major had infiltrated into France and other occupied countries, but it would explain some of the losses that they had experienced as well, God it made her feel sick.

"My God! He's with the Professor!" Mary gasped out suddenly.

"What! Are you sure?" asked the Colonel.

"Yes sir, he is taking Pierre and the Professor to London, he had another staff car that left a few minutes before you arrived, sir." The Colonel turned and banged on the glass partition that separated the driver from the passengers making the driver look up at the rear-view mirror.

"Davies! Turn around. Head back to the port as we need to chase down that other staff car." The driver nodded then the passengers were holding on as he braked heavily making a rapid U-turn then started to increase speed.

"If Major Scott is indeed our double agent, then we have put the professor in danger, Scott knows that Mary took out Greta, he also knows how valuable the Professor's information is to us, so he will either try to return the Professor to France and hand him over to the Gestapo, or he will kill him, destroy the information then disappear!"

"My God! I can't believe this is happening." Mary was quite stunned by the turn of events, it seemed that all they had been through to get the Professor out of France would have been for nothing if indeed Major Scott was a double agent, she suddenly felt incredibly sick.

****

Professor Linus Kruen thought that it was a pity that they were travelling so late as he would have liked to have been able to see the countryside in the daylight, after leaving the harbour they had travelled along through the outskirts of a large town they had turned right picking up speed as they headed out into the countryside.

"Will it take us long to reach London, Major?" asked Pierre, he was also wishing that they weren't travelling after dark, he was feeling a little lost not being on home soil as it were and would have felt a lot happier if he could at least see where they were going.

'I'm afraid it will take us a little longer than it should as I have to deliver a package to a courier who will be taken to France on a fishing boat. I'm sorry about this delay but this operation came up on short notice, you know how it is, Pierre?" said the major, he was feeling quite elated that everything had just seemed to drop into his lap, Mary had obligingly eliminated Greta so he would have no interference from the damned Gestapo, even the fishing boat with the Courier drop had been a godsend when it had come across his desk, he'd had to tweak things a little so that the boat's departure would coincide with Mary's arrival with the Professor but it had worked out remarkably well, now he expected to have the Professor back in France within a few hours.

"Oh yes, I know how it is, Major." Pierre thought back on the Courier landing in a field near Posey which had started all of the events which led up to his being in England, that little field seemed such a long time ago now.

"We will stop for a short break soon; I have brought some tea along so we can have a cup while we stretch our legs, if you like?" said the major a few minutes later bringing Pierre out of his thoughts.

"That would be good, Major, do you think I would have time for a smoke when we stop?"

"Oh yes I should think so, we have plenty of time before the boat is due to leave," the Major smiled trying to seem unruffled, he had to keep these two relaxed or his plans could backfire, he knew that he had no real danger from the Professor but Pierre was a different proposition as he had been an operative in occupied France for a number of years so that made him a very dangerous man.

Twenty minutes later after they had passed through a town, the car pulled over into a small clearing near a paddock fence gateway.

"All right chaps, you can jump out and stretch your legs while I organise the tea," said the Major as the driver switched the engine off but left the covered headlights on which although masked for the blackout regulations meant that the little clearing wasn't in total darkness. The Professor followed Pierre out of the car.

"I must say, Pierre, it's nice to be able to stretch out a bit after being cooped up on that Submarine, eh?" said the Professor as he stretched his arms out.

'PHLAAT!' 'PHLAAT!'

"What the Hell!" Pierre spun around as he heard the unmistakeable sound of a silenced pistol being fired, he was in time to see the driver dropping to the ground dead, then the Major was turning the pistol towards him!

"Professor—Run!" he shouted as he dived to the side, hoping to get out of the headlights patch of light to make a harder target.

'PHLAAT!' 'PHLAAT!' Pierre grunted loudly as two bullets thudded into him, their impact knocking him sideways onto the ground, he landed heavily turning onto his back, searing pain wracking through his head and right arm, then he was blinking rapidly as the Major was shining a torch at him as he knelt next to him.

"Sorry Pierre, but you are too dangerous to take as a prisoner." Pierre opened his mouth a couple of times, but the words wouldn't come before he blacked out. The Major stood up then turned to a stunned Professor who was looking at him wide-eyed not believing what he had just witnessed as it had all happened so fast.

"We don't have much time, Professor, so I will make this quite simple. You either come with me now—quietly—or I will shoot you!"

"What! What the Hell are you talking about?"

"It is very simple, Professor, I intend returning you to France but if you won't come quietly then I will shoot you before I destroy your information, the choice is yours!"

The Professor stared at him wide-eyed for a few seconds unable to believe what the man was saying. He was scared stiff at the thought of being returned to France where he would be handed over to the Gestapo which terrified him but so too did the thought of being shot by this officer who was obviously some sort of traitor but whom was also not bluffing as he had already killed the driver and possibly Pierre, he hoped that Pierre might survive but he had two bullets in him and wasn't moving! God-he didn't want to die!

"Why! Why do you want to return me to France after all the efforts that your Agents went through to get me out!"

"If those idiots in the Gestapo hadn't infiltrated Greta into SOE, then no-one would have known about me, now my position is untenable, but taking you back to France with your information will be a coup for me and I will make a tidy sum at the same time. So, Professor, what are you going to do—live or die?" The Major waved his pistol threateningly which made the Professor swallow hard. Then he remembered how Mary had been willing to sacrifice her life on that clifftop in France to save him, he nodded as he thought about that brief desperate firefight at the cottage. *Where there is life there is hope*, he said to himself, he owed it to Mary not to give up.

"I don't seem to have a choice, Major; I will do as you want," he said quietly, making Major Scott grin with relief.

"Good! Move to the front passenger door," the Major motioned with his pistol again so with a final look at his friend Pierre, the Professor moved over to the car, there the Major pulled a set of handcuffs from his briefcase.

"You don't need those, Major, I will do as you say."

"Sorry Professor." The Major quickly fastened the cuffs around the Professor's wrists then opened the car door.

"Get in!" Awkwardly the Professor got into the passenger's side of the car, the Major shut the door before hurrying over to the dead driver, he grabbed the man's ankles then dragged the body a few yards away from the road before rolling it into a patch of nettles, he hoped that no-one would find him until well after sun up, he quickly moved over to Pierre pulling him into the nettles in the same way before hurrying back to the car where he got in the driver's side, starting the engine he pulled out slowly trying not to leave any tracks, then once on the road, he started increasing speed.

An hour later the Major's staff car pulled up just short of a stone walled jetty in a small fishing village, as the car came to a stop the Major switched off the engine then took the key for the handcuffs out of his pocket, he unlocked one of the cuffs removing this from the Professors wrist, then before the man could react he had pulled his hand towards the steering wheel where he put the man's hand through the gap in the steering wheel refastening the cuff about his wrist so that he was now securely handcuffed to the steering wheel.

"I'm just going to check on the fishing boat, Professor, you stay still and quiet—or else!" With that threat delivered, the Major got out of the car walking off quickly down the jetty.

When he was out of sight, the Professor tugged and pulled the handcuffs madly but they were secure through the steering wheel and had no intentions of letting go, as he stopped struggling, his gaze fell onto his satchel which the Major had dropped onto the driver's seat, as he looked at it he had a mental flashback to the hill top cottage in France where he and Mary had a brief but fierce battle with the SS Major and his men. Mary had given him some hand grenades before the fire fight had started, she had also given him one to use 'as a last resort'!

She had taken back two of the grenades when she had madly rushed the Major to give him time to escape out of the back window, but he had completely forgotten about this one which he had put into his satchel, and it was still there!

With his excitement growing, he awkwardly turned sideways to use his feet to pull the satchel towards himself as he couldn't use his handcuffed hands, it took him three attempts to be able to work his feet over the bag, then very carefully he started moving it towards himself, he was panting from the exertion by the time he had manoeuvred the bag alongside, but he was still unable to reach it with his handcuffed hands.

"DAMN!" He shook the wheel in frustration before he suddenly thought that he might be able to pick it up with his teeth if he could lean over far enough, it was amazing how flaming helpless you felt when you were unable to use your hands, also it was extremely awkward trying to lean down sideways far enough to be able to use your teeth, by the time he finally managed to get the satchel in a position where he could finally bend over far enough to where he could get a firm grip on the satchel's handle with his teeth.

He was sweating badly from the exertion, he slowly pulled the heavy bag up far enough so that he could get a hold with one of his hands, then he again had to use his teeth to start to pull the strap through the buckle on the flap, then he could finally use his fingers to pull the straps free, then using his teeth again he was able to hold it so that he could use one hand to get into the bag and feel around, the contents in the bag got in the way and it was hard not being able to see what he was doing.

He finally felt the grenade under his fingers, then he froze as his finger was on the pull ring of the grenade, if he pulled this out then the arming arm would fly off and four seconds later the grenade would explode!

Breathing hard and sweating badly, he wriggled the grenade around until he had a firm grip on it then he let the bag go which fell to the floor but luckily, the contents didn't spill out. Then he jumped badly as the driver's door opened.

"What the Hell!" as he got into the vehicle the Major was shocked to see a hand grenade being clutched rather clumsily by the Professor who looked scared stiff, he quickly reached out grabbing the grenade, with his hands being handcuffed to the steering wheel there wasn't anything that the professor could do as the grenade was pulled out of his fingers.

"What the Hell were you thinking?" asked the Major as he pulled the grenade from the Professor.

"I was going to destroy the information that I have here, you as well if I could have!" said Linus fiercely, now that he had said this he knew that he would have pulled the pin on the hand grenade if he had seen the Major approaching, he was surprised to find that he actually felt quite calm about it, as if killing yourself was quite a normal thing to do, he wondered if Mary had felt this way when she had run out of the cottage with her gun blazing.

"So, Professor, you're not as dumb as you look after all." The Major reached into his pocket taking out the key to the handcuffs which he proceeded to unfasten.

"The crew of the fishing boat are not here so we will be manning the boat ourselves, which means that I don't have time to mess around with you!" For a second the Professor thought he was going to shoot him out of hand to save himself the difficulty of dragging him around, but he breathed a sigh of relief as the Major reached down picking up the satchel.

"Right, we will now go to the fishing boat, Professor, and I suggest that you remember that I will have my pistol trained on you all the time, one false move and I assure you that you will be dead before you hit the ground, now get going!" As he got out of the staff car, Linus knew that he would have to do something soon or that fishing boat would have him back in France within a few hours, but WHAT!

****

The rumbling of a truck going past the small clearing near the paddock gate sounded very loud in his ears as Pierre opened his eyes groaning as pain slashed through his head and right shoulder. Sucking in his breath against the pain he moved his left hand up gingerly touching the lived jagged slash in his right temple, his fingers came away very bloody, also in the feeble light of the approaching daw he could see that his shoulder was saturated in the blood that had flowed from the slash in his forehead, also his jacket shoulder and arm were saturated with the blood from where a bullet had gone through his right shoulder which was very numb and ached dully.

He knew that he was very lucky to be alive for if the 9 mm round that had slashed acrost his forehead had been just slightly to the left then instead of a livid gash he knew that he would have had his brains blown out.

Gasping against the pain that slashed through his forehead he tried to sit up but couldn't manage it with only the one arm as his right wouldn't support his weight, going a little dizzy he waited for the spasm to pass before he dug his heels into the ground and pulled himself along with his left hand, he had to get to the roadside if he was to have any hopes of getting any help. He had to stop every few minutes as waves of nausea swept over him but he was able to pull himself out of the nettles and over to the roads edge, he dare not go out onto the road as he knew that he wouldn't have the strength to get himself out of the way of any fast approaching vehicles but he desperately needed to find help.

Lying at the road edge, he fumbled in his jacket pocket until he found his cigarette lighter, he knew it wasn't much, but he hoped that the small light would attract some attention, all he needed now was a vehicle to pass close.

Shortly after they had made the U-turn, the Colonel's staff car had pulled up at the check point leading to the harbour where the submarine had docked, here they were told in which direction the other staff car had gone, then they set off in pursuit again.

"Christ! They could be anywhere!" the Colonel didn't sound happy as he said this.

"Do you think he is actually heading for London sir?" asked Beth worriedly.

"Damned if I know and that's the truth!"

"I still can't believe that it's him, sir," said Mary, she was finding it hard to believe that Major Scott could possibly be a traitor and if he was then he had been doing this for some time and was very good at it!

"Are we completely sure that it is the Major sir?" she asked, she had been thrown completely off balance by these events, it had been hard for her to grasp but it would explain a few things that had happened like the ambush in the field just outside of Posey where she had been arrested.

"We had best get used to the idea, Ladies."

"Stop! Stop! Stop the car!" shouted Beth suddenly, the Colonel reached forward banging on the partition between them and the driver and the driver braked hard as he pulled over.

"What on earth, Beth!" asked the colonel as they came to an abrupt halt on the side of the road.

"Back there sir, I thought I saw a light being waved from side to side, I'm sure it was a signal of some kind but…?" she said as she was looking around out of the back window.

"But—worth checking out, Davies, turn around and go back up the road!"

"Right sir." The car turned around and slowly started moving back up the roadway.

"There sir, I see it—a small light being waved side to side!" called Mary as she suddenly caught sight of a small light low down moving slowly, it could only be a signal of some kind as there was nothing else around here.

"Is that a person?" asked Beth as the car pulled to a stop slightly past the person.

"My God! That looks like Pierre!" called the Colonel as he opened the car door stepping out.

"What! Oh no!" called Mary as she jumped out of the car and hurried over to Pierre who had dropped his arm to the ground as the vehicle had stopped.

"Bonjour Mary," said Pierre feebly as she hurried over kneeling down next to him.

"*Chapeau my god, Pierre Est arrive?*" She was close to tears as she spoke to him for Pierre looked a mess, he was covered in blood with a hole in the right shoulder of his jacket and there was a very livid bloody gash in his right forehead.

"*Ce bastard Scott, Il a tire sur la conductor et a le Professor!*"

"Why is he speaking in French?" asked the Colonel as he knelt down next to the man.

"I think he is in shock; he's lost a lot of blood sir."

"Let's get him into the car; Davies?" the Colonel turned calling for Davies who was coming over with Beth.

"Here sir."

"Let's get him into the back of the car then fetch the first aid kit."

"Right sir." Davies was a large man who seemed to just scoop Pierre up as if he was a rag doll, a couple of minutes later he had laid him on the back seat and fetched the first aid kit which he passed to Mary as she climbed into the back.

"Pierre, can you hear me?" asked Mary as she put a gauze pad over the livid gash on his forehead before starting to bandage it.

"*Oui, je ne suis pas encourt mort!*" (Yes, I'm not dead yet!) again he smiled feebly.

"What happened Pierre—Oh I'm sorry!" Mary said the last part as Pierre had sucked in his breath against the pain as she started moving the bandage around his head.

"Davies, turn the car around, we'll go back to the last town we passed to get some medical attention."

"Non!" Pierre made to sit up as the colonel said this, but he gasped again as he lay back down.

"Easy Pierre!"

"NO Mary! That bastard Scott has the Professor. He's going to a fishing village where there is a trawler waiting, if we don't hurry, he will escape!" Pierre lay back as everything started spinning.

"Pierre, where is this village, did he name it, Pierre?" asked Mary quietly as she finished tying off the bandage, she was close to losing her control as she thought that he was close to death after having lost so much blood, she was scared for him, angry with Major Scott but incredibly proud of Pierre all at the same time, she felt like screaming!

"No—he—he said they used it for Couriers—but—" Pierre started then his eyes rolled back as he blacked out.

"Pierre?" Mary leaned forward as he blacked out.

"Colonel, I know where he means, SOE has a trawler that we use to take Couriers and supplies across to France, its located at North Castor Bay, it's the only place on this coast that I know we use," said Beth excitedly as she realised where Major Scott was heading.

"Colonel, he is going to bleed to death if we don't get some help soon, you can't let him die sir, please!" Mary was almost pleading as she leaned over to remove Pierre's jacket so that she could check the shoulder wound but their small first aid kit wasn't up to the task; Pierre needed a hospital.

"Damn! Alright Davies, get us back to the last town we passed as quick as you can!"

"Right sir." Davies hurried back to the driver's seat then got the car underway turning the vehicle around.

"Thank you, sir," said Mary with some relief.

"Beth, when we get to this Town, I'd like you to stay with Pierre, I'll give you a number so you can put a call through to the Navy. I want any fishing vessel off this coast stopped and searched in case we are not able to stop the Major leaving."

"Right sir, I will do that and when you leave this town the fishing village is straight ahead; you'll be there in about twenty minutes." Beth then leaned forward placing a reassuring hand on Mary's arm.

"He will be alright, Mary,"

"He has to be, Beth, he has done so much for me." Then Mary looked at Colonel Winters, "I know how important the Professor is, Colonel, so thank you."

"I'm not that big a bastard that I would let a man bleed to death for my own ends, Mary, besides, now that we know where Scott is heading, we may yet be able to stop him." Mary nodded turning back to Pierre, he was unconscious, white as a sheet with shallow breathing, she just hoped that they wouldn't be too late getting him to a hospital.

Ten minutes later they pulled up outside of Saint Marks hospital where Davies blew the car horn getting the attention of the staff who hurried out with a gurney, Davies gently lifted Pierre out of the car placing him onto the trolley which the orderlies then hurried off with.

"He'll be alright Mary, you take care!" called Beth as she ran after the orderlies.

"Right Davies, get us to North Castor Bay fast as you dare!" called the Colonel as they got back into the car.

"Right Sir!"

"Are you armed, Mary?" asked the Colonel checking his revolver in his jacket pocket as the car started to move again.

"Yes Sir." Mary pulled here silenced 9 mm pistol from her skirt pocket.

"Goodness, I'm surprised the Navy didn't confiscate that when they picked you up," he said frowning and Mary couldn't help smiling as she remembered the look on the submarine Captain's face when he thought that he might have had to shoot her.

"I don't think they really knew how to search a woman, sir."

"No, I suppose not, how much ammunition do you have?"

"I have two spare clips in my pocket Sir."

"Well let's hope that we don't have to use them, eh?" The Colonel put his revolver back into his jacket pocket then leaned back in the seat closing his eyes, all they could do now was wait as the staff car started gaining speed as they left the town.

Dawn was breaking as they entered the small village moving down towards a small stone wharf where they could see a couple of trawlers moored alongside.

"That must be the trawler," said Mary as the boats came into view then she leaned forward a little as she caught sight of the other staff car that had pulled up alongside a small stone wall at the beginning of the wharf.

"Damn! There he is with the Professor; Davies, put your foot down, try to run him down!" called the Colonel as he spotted Major Scott a few yards away from the vehicle with the Professor a couple of feet out in front of him, if they could get close enough with the car then perhaps it would all be over quickly.

As the car increased speed a few yards further down the wharf, Major Scott spun around as he heard the car's engine.

"Run Professor!" he said as he gave the Professor a shove, Linus felt his heart start to race as the Major gave him a hefty shove in the back, he knew that Mary would be in that other staff car, he didn't know if she knew about the Major being a traitor but by the way the vehicle had increased speed suddenly as it had caught sight of them meant that someone was in a hurry to get to them, he didn't know who was onboard that trawler but he knew that once it got underway then he would be back in France by the morning, then he was as good as dead!

"Get down behind those crates, Professor!" The Major pushed him towards some crats that were stacked near a small stone wall that ran down the side of the wharf above the water.

"Move and you're dead!" said the Major as he waved his pistol under the Professor's nose as he pushed him behind a large crate, Linus stared wide-eyed down the barrel and nodded.

PHLAAT! PHLAAT! Linus jumped badly as the Major raised his pistol firing two shots at the oncoming car, there came a screeching of tyres as the vehicle braked heavily with its front end banging into the stone wall.

"DOWN! Everyone down!" shouted Davies as two rounds starred the windscreen narrowly missing his head, he had ducked involuntarily as they impacted the windscreen as he braked hard sending the vehicle banging into the wall as it came to an abrupt halt.

"OUT! OUT! Get out the right side!" called the Colonel as he threw himself against the right-hand side passengers door, Mary scrambled madly to follow throwing herself to the ground and squeezing up against the rear wheel for some cover, as she did she heard a sharp grunting as Davies jumped out the driver's door, he seemed to slump forward as a round took him in the upper right arm, he slid down by the front wheel.

"Bloody Hell!" he gasped as he grabbed his arm with his left hand with blood pumping around his fingers. Mary pulled a handkerchief from her pocket then doubled over as she inched her way forward to the driver, she quickly tied the rag around his ram then placed his bloody fingers over it.

"Keep the pressure on, try not to move!" she said giving him a reassuring smile.

"Thank you, in my jacket pocket, my spare clips, they won't be any good to me now," he said then gasped in pain. Mary reached in and took the two spare clips.

"Alright, try to keep still now." As Davies nodded, she inched her way back to the rear wheel then looked over at the Colonel who was by the wall at the front of the vehicle.

"What now sir?" she asked, and he shook his head then ducked as another round blew out the passenger side window in a shower of shattering glass.

"Can you see any cover; we need to move from here." Mary peeked around the side of the vehicle, she could see an upturned rowing boat a few yards away with some fishing nets in a heap nearby but it was open ground between her and there, she would be hit if she tried to make a break for it, but there were some small boxes a few yards behind them which would give her some cover, she might be able to work her way over to the boat from there.

"If I can get to that small boat, I might be able to get a shot at him, but I will have to go back there to get over to it sir."

"Right, I'll try to distract him to cover your move, be careful and say when you're ready to go!"

"Right!" Mary nodded swallowing hard, if she made a hash of this the Major would shoot her for sure, she lifted her head to see around the tail of the vehicle and a round shattered the rear light on her side making her duck as she gasped out loud.

"You alright?" asked the Colonel worriedly as he had seen how close that shot had come to hitting her.

"Yes, fine!" Mary sat down with her back against the rear wheel as she wiped her eye, something had flickered over her eyelid as the lights had been shattered making her eye water, she was breathing hard as she knew that had been too damned close.

"Major Scott! This is Colonel Winters. We know what you have done, Major, it's all over for you now so give yourself up!" called the Colonel as he nodded at her relieved that she hadn't been hit.

"Sorry Colonel, but the Professor and I have a little trip to make, you see!" Behind the crate the Major pushed Linus up against the wood of the box.

"In a minute, Professor, we are going to make a break for that trawler, if they are armed, they won't shoot as they won't want to risk hitting you!"

"You don't have to do this Major, there is no way out now you must see that?" Linus jumped as the Major grabbed him by the scruff pushing him up against the crate.

"Shut UP! If you want to live you will do as I say. Got it!" The Major's eyes were blazing into his, Linus just nodded not daring to speak, then they both jumped as a revolver barked a couple of times and splinters flew off the top of the crate as the bullets thudded home.

"Major Scott, if you surrender now, I will do all I can to help you, but you must give this up!" called the Colonel and Scott laughed before firing a couple of shots back shattering the rear window of the car.

"You can't do a damned thing for me Colonel and you bloody well know it, if I surrender, they will hang me!" As Scott shouted this he fumbled in his pocket reaching for the hand grenade that he had taken off the Professor earlier, putting the grenade in his left hand he put his right forefinger through the pull ring he looked at the Professor.

"When I say, you run for the trawler and don't try to deviate or you will be dead before you hit the ground. Right!" The Professor could see the desperation in the man's eyes, he knew there was no way out for him now but he was determined to try, Linus also knew that if he was to avoid being taken back to France or indeed of possibly being killed by this lunatic then he had to do something NOW! Then he suddenly felt quite calm.

He knew that what he was about to do would probably end up killing him, but he had to do it, he had to stop this Man, he also had to help Mary, he owed her that. Then thinking of Mary, he wondered if this was how she had felt back in that cottage before she had made her desperate rush against Major Schrandt to save HIM, yes, he owed her his life!

Back at the staff car, Mary looked over at the Colonel.

"Ready sir?" she asked him knowing that this was not going to end well but they had to try, if Major Scott thought that he couldn't win then he would shoot the Professor, that meant that everything that they had gone through to reach England would have been for nothing.

"Alright, GO-GO-GO!" as the colonel called this Mary took a deep breath, she pushed herself up from the wheel starting to run, then everything seemed to happen at the same time.

Over at the packing crate as the Major pulled the pin on his hand grenade the Professor took hold of one end of his satchel swinging it as hard as he could, the Major staggered back from a blow to side of his face, he had raised his arm to ward off the blow that he had seen as a blur of movement before the satchel hit him, he had inadvertently stepped sideways from the blow which brought him out from the cover of the crates, in reflex he half-threw half-lobbed the grenade towards the staff car as he raised his pistol to shoot the Professor. Mary had started running then skidded to a halt as she saw Major Scott step out from behind the crates, she didn't see him lob the grenade as she quickly raised her pistol.

"Grenade—DOWN!" shouted the Colonel as he fired a shot then Mary's pistol coughed three times.

PHLAAT! PHLATT! PHLAAT! She saw Major Scott stagger sideways as her round hit him then there came an incredibly loud Bang! as the grenade exploded, she cried out as a searing pain took her in the arm as she was blown off her feet by the explosion, then her world went black as she hit the cobblestones.

****

Mary blinked rapidly as the room was spinning, she closed her eyes then opened them again, the room steadied then came into focus, she frowned as she found herself laying in a bed in a dimly lit room that had a funny smell, then she panicked! That smell was the interrogation room, that bastard Schrandt had her again! She started breathing rapidly as her heart raced, then she jumped, startled as a gentle hand was placed on her shoulder.

"It's alright Mary, you're safe!" She turned her head blinking rapidly as a woman spoke quietly to her, then she seemed to deflate as she realised that it was Beth speaking to her, that she was laying on a bed, the smell that had startled her was in fact hospital disinfectant, she was safe!

"Wh...where am I?" she croaked through incredibly dry lips.

"Have some water." Beth held a glass to her, and she took a sip of water through a glass straw which felt incredibly good, then she gasped as pain shot through her left arm as she made to sit up a little.

"Easy Mary, you've been injured, do you remember?" asked Beth quietly as she placed a reassuring hand on the girl's shoulder.

"I…I'm not sure, where am I?" asked Mary as she looked around the room, she felt a little disorientated, the last thing she remembered was an enormous Bang before she seemed to levitate through the air before the hitting the cobblestones of the wharf, then she woke here in a hospital somewhere.

"You're in a hospital in London, you were moved here yesterday after they operated on your arm."

"My arm?" Mary looked down panicking a little as her left arm was swathed in bandages, they felt a little tight, her arm was hot but it didn't really hurt unless she moved too quickly then pain shot along her arm, she also felt another bandage on her side which was also tender and the fingers on her left hand were also wrapped in bandages but they didn't hurt, but it just didn't seem real.

"It's alright, you were hit by shrapnel from a hand grenade, they removed the shrapnel, you have a long gash in the left arm which has just over a hundred stitches, also your left side had numerous pieces of shrapnel which luckily didn't penetrate far, they will be tender for a while but there is no serious damage, you were very lucky, Mary." Beth smiled reassuringly at her as she said this, but she knew just how lucky the girl had been for she had been moving to new cover when the grenade exploded, if she had been a little further to her right she would have been killed.

"What happened! I remember shooting at Major Scott?" asked Mary as she tried to piece things together, but it was all very fuzzy.

"From what Colonel Winters told me, everything seemed to happen at the same time. As you made to move to better cover, Major Scott was about to throw a hand grenade to cover his move to the trawler, the Professor whacked him in the face with his satchel which made him stagger out from the packing crates."

"So that's why he moved, but where did he get a hand grenade from, he only had his staff car, we thought he had no weapons?" asked Mary frowning.

"Apparently, he got it from the Professor who had earlier tried to blow himself up when the Major handcuffed him to the steering wheel of his car."

"Did he, but where on earth did the Professor get a grenade?"

"From you apparently," said Beth smiling broadly at Mary's confused look.

"From me?" asked Mary frowning hard as it was all too confusing.

"Yes, from what Winters tells me you gave the Professor some hand grenades in a cottage at a cove where you had a firefight with Major Schrandt, then when you made a dash out of the cottage you took a couple back but the Professor still had one in his satchel that he had forgotten about until the Major cuffed him to the steering wheel."

"I had forgotten that as well." Mary thought that the Professor must have been desperate to have risked hitting the Major with his satchel, but she was glad that he had found the courage to do it as it had meant that she had been able to ger her shots off when he stepped out from the cover of the creates.

"What happened to the Major?" she asked after digesting this information for a couple of minutes with things slowly starting to make sense to her.

"When he staggered out from behind the crates, the Colonel got off one shot which hit Sandy in the shoulder, you got off three rounds before the grenade exploded, one hit him in the right shoulder but two hit him in the heart, he was dead before he hit the ground, Mary." Mary could see that Beth was a little saddened by the Major's death, she could understand this for she had worked with the man for a couple of years and had built a rapport with him so it would be hard for her, but she also detected a sense of pride in her having hit him so well with her shots.

"I...I'm sorry I had to shoot him, Beth, I know you have known him for some time, I didn't want to, really, I didn't." Mary's eyes started to droop as she said this for, she felt incredibly tired.

"I know that Mary, but he wouldn't have surrendered, you know that?"

"I suppose so, but I still don't understand why he did it, Beth."

"He did it for money, my dear." Both women looked around as Colonel Winters entered the room, Beth made to stand up, but he waved her to stay seated.

"Good morning, Colonel, I didn't know you were here sir?" said Beth as he came over to the bed.

"Had a couple of meetings so I thought I would look in on our Agent here, I hope you don't mind my calling in like this, Mary?"

"No Sir, of course not." The Colonel pulled up a chair and sat down alongside the bed. He could see the girl was still a little groggy, he assumed that she hadn't long woken, there were very dark rings around her eyes, the left side of her face was still a little bruised and now she had a large bandage covering most of her left arm, he had also been told about the shrapnel wounds in her side which although they would be painful for a while would heal completely, all in all the girl had been very lucky.

When he had shouted out about the grenade, he had gotten off one round before the grenade had exploded, he had seen Mary's rounds hit the Major before the explosion had blown her off her feet, when he had seen her hit the cobblestoned he had felt for certain that she had been killed, he had been very relieved to still find her breathing even though she had been covered in blood, his driver Davies, although he was injured himself had hurried over to her, he had confirmed that she was only unconscious then they had both been shoved out of the way by the Professor who had picked Mary up, carrying her to the staff car he had barked orders at them to get the damned car started to get the girl to hospital, the man had stayed by her side until they reached a hospital where he gently laid her on a gurney watching her being wheeled away, then the Professor had breathed a sigh of relief before turning to the Colonel and formally surrendering himself.

"My driver Davies sends his regards and his thanks for what you did for him, Mary."

"I didn't really do much, sir." Mary's eyes were drooping as she spoke, he could see that she was still very tired from her ordeal.

"Well, he sends his regards anyway as does the Professor, full of surprises that one."

"I think she is asleep, sir," said Beth as Mary's eyes closed.

"Yes, we'll let her rest, I will come and see her again tomorrow when she is fully awake then I'll fill her in on what happened."

"Fine sir."

"I'd like you to be here then as well if you don't mind, Captain, shall we say about one?"

"Yes sir."

"Good, I'll see you tomorrow then." With a nod, the Colonel left the room, Beth made sure that Mary was fully asleep before she also left.

The following day Mary was fully coherent, she felt a little better as far as her wounds were concerned as she didn't get the sharp pain in her arm when she moved now just a dull warm ache, she had seen the Doctor that morning who informed her that she wouldn't have any trouble with her arm or the puncture wounds in her left side but she would have a little trouble with the fingers on her left hand which would take a lot longer to heal, her fingernails may or may not grow back fully, only time would tell but she would have full use of her fingers but the nails may not grow back fully.

Mary had just nodded at that information, she really didn't mind if the nails didn't grow back, at least she had the full use of her fingers so no nails was a small price to pay, the Doctor had also informed her that the deep bruising and severe lacerations on her back would also heal in time but there would be slight scarring from some of the cuts across her back, the man had looked a little embarrassed as he had said this but she was just grateful that there would be no lasting effects to her back, she knew that she had gotten off fairly lightly from the beatings that she had endured at the Posey police station.

Just after one in the afternoon, Beth came in all smiles as she entered the room.

"Hello Mary how are you feeling, my dear?" asked Beth as she took a seat next to the bed.

"Hello Beth, very good really." Quickly, Mary explained what the Doctor had told her.

"That is really good news, I'm just sorry that you had to go through all of that, Mary, it wasn't how things were supposed to have happened."

"I know Beth, now tell me, how is Pierre, is he alright?" Mary looked quite anxious as she asked this for it had been playing on her mind, she knew that she hadn't asked after Pierre yesterday, she felt bad about that even though she hadn't been in any fit state to ask many questions, yesterday was still a bit of a blur.

"He is going to be fine, like you he was very lucky. When Sandy shot him it was dark so he missed his mark, one round went into Pierre's shoulder but it was a through and through wound which will heal completely, the other round grazed his temple, we think that because it was dark and because Pierre had tried to jump out of the light from Sandy's headlights, that the round fired only grazed his temple although it was a deep graze, but a little further to the left and it would have blown his brains out, so he was very lucky, Mary."

"But he is going to alright, Beth?" asked Mary anxiously as she was still feeling incredibly guilty for not having asked about Pierre earlier, not after everything that he had done for her, especially after he had risked his life to tell them where Major Scott had gone after he had been shot.

"Yes Dear, he will be fine, I did tell you some details yesterday do you remember?" asked Beth but Mary shook her head.

"Not really, yesterday is still a bit of a blur."

"Well, that isn't surprising as you had a severe concussion from the grenade's explosion and then you were recovering from the operation on your arm and side."

"Yes, I suppose so." Mary frowned again, she knew that she had spoken with Beth and the Colonel, but it didn't really make sense to her, most of it was a blur, then she was looking up as Colonel Winters entered the room.

"Afternoon Ladies," he said jovially as he crossed over to the bed waving Beth down as she made to stand up as he entered.

"Afternoon sir," they said together.

"Well, how is our patient today, a bit more awake then yesterday, hmm?" he asked pulling up a chair and sitting down next to the bed.

"A bit more with it sir, I'm afraid that I don't really remember much about yesterday to be honest," said Mary making the Colonel chuckle.

"Grenades tend to do that I'm afraid, my dear, I know that you were still very groggy yesterday so why don't you tell me what you recall happening with Major Scott and we will go from there, hmm?"

"Well sir, I remember that Major Scott had the Professor bailed up behind some packing crates on the fishing wharf, he was apparently heading for a trawler when we arrived." This part of things was very clear in her head, she could vividly recall their staff car slamming into the stone wall on the wharf when the windscreen had been starred by three rounds fired by Major Scott when he had caught sight of them arriving on the wharf.

They had been very accurate and Davies had ducked involuntarily when the bullets had thudded into the windscreen, all three of them had then made a rapid exit from the car, Davies and the Colonel had been huddled down behind the front wheel which with the crumpled bonnet had given them some cover, she had scramble madly out from the back seat ducking down behind the rear wheel, she had jumped badly each time a bullet had thudded into the vehicle being covered in glass when the rear windows had been blown out.

"That's right, Scott had told the Professor and Pierre that he had to take a package to the crew of the trawler, then they had stopped for a short break on the side of the road near a paddock gate."

"That's when he shot Pierre then sir?" she asked.

"Yes, Pierre heard the silenced pistol cough as Scott shot Phelps the driver, he shouted for the Professor to run as he dived aside trying to get out of the ring of light from the headlights, I've spoken to him and he tells me that he believed the Major was about to shoot the Professor when he saw the driver go down, his quick reactions are what saved his life."

"Because the second round only grazed his temple instead of—" Mary stopped as she thought of how close Pierre had come to having his brains blown out, it was funny, but they had expected things like this to have happened while they were in France literally surrounded by the Enemy, but they hadn't expected anything like this to have happened here in England where they SHOULD have been SAFE!

"His quick reactions certainly saved his life also his determination after having been wounded was what enable us to get to Scott before he was able to leave the country, your friend is a very good man to have in a tight spot, Mary."

"He certainly is a good man, Colonel, he did a very good job of organising the Cell in France, I couldn't have done my mission without him, sir."

"I intend to see that he gets the recognition for his efforts."

"That would be good sir but what I don't understand is why Major Scott did what he did?" she asked frowning as it still didn't make sense to her, what had made Sandy work for the enemy, why would anyone help kill a woman so as to be able to infiltrate another woman into SOE, what possible motivation could there have been to make him betray his country!

"Well, fortunately for us, the Major has explained his reasoning, after returning from getting Mary to the hospital and the Professor off to London we searched Scott's office and home, it took a bit of digging but we eventually found a safety deposit box in a London bank where the Major had deposited a number of diaries, he has kept a detailed account of his actions from the time of the Spanish Civil War."

"Good Lord, but that goes against everything that an Agent is taught sir," said Beth for she herself fiercely instructed her Agents never to write anything down that could be found to give away their identity or location, she couldn't believe that Sandy would have made such an elementary mistake.

"I believe that he wanted to explain his actions should anything happen to him, you see; although he did what he did voluntarily, I think he knew how onerous his actions were."

"But why sir, I don't understand what on earth made him do it, he betrayed his country and everything that he believed in. Why?" asked Mary as she couldn't understand what had made him do the things that he did, things that had led to her own capture and torture by that bastard Schrandt.

"Money, I'm afraid that it all just came down to money."

"Money?" asked Beth frowning for it didn't make any sense to her at all.

"Yes! Money! You see during the Spanish Civil War the Major was inserted into Spain as part of the Crockus cell as you know, Beth?"

"Yes sir, they operated for about four months if I remember correctly, everything went well, there was no sign of trouble or anything," said Beth frowning as she remembered the operation where she had been the radio liaison between the member of Crockus and London, it all been rather sporadic at the time as the wireless sets they were using were notorious for breaking down, in fact now that she came to think about it they had used a diplomatic courier more than anything else but she couldn't remember anything having gone wrong.

"Most of your contact was through a diplomatic courier, is that correct, Beth?"

"That's right sir."

"So, there were many times when you didn't have contact for weeks, is that right?"

"Yes sir."

"Exactly, so you didn't find it unusual to have no contact for extended periods of time?"

"That's right sir, in those days our radios weren't very reliable, and we didn't have the techniques that keep our agents safe as we do now, SOE didn't exist then, Military Intelligence didn't have much to work with, I'm sad to say." Beth knew that in those days putting Agents into the field was riskier that it was now, everything was done ad hoc, they were ill equipped and although there were a few very good outcomes they really had been floundering and trusting to luck, unfortunately, it cost a few lives in the process."

"So not having contact for extended periods wasn't unusual so when our two agents were captured by the Spanish, we didn't know about it, then when Scott returned to England, he had the cover story that his partner had been killed while they had been making their way out of Spain, isn't that right?"

"Yes sir, if I remember rightly there had been some sort of accident, I don't remember what it was exactly, but Hollis had been killed."

"That's right but it now turns out to be all lies! What actually happened was that they were both captured after moving to their second safe house. The Spanish had been about to execute them as spies when German Intelligence stepped in, now I don't know the full story of what happened next obviously but

Hollis was executed within a couple of days but the Major was offered a tidy sum of money to work for the Germans."

"But why didn't he just agree to work for them; then when he returned to England, he could have owned up to what happened then it would have been over surely?" asked Beth still wondering why on earth Sandy would have changed sides.

"Because he knows that he would have been shot as a traitor, his actions in Spain had led to his companion being executed. But the main reason that he 'turned' as it were was as I said because of money, apparently his parents were very sick with some sort of cancer and he need money to keep them in care, as you know a Lieutenant's pay wasn't very much back then so when the Germans offered him a chance to make some serious money he took it, his reasoning was that he could pass over low grade intelligence to them which wouldn't do much harm in the scheme of things, then when the war started he was in too deep to be able to get out."

"So, he was in effect a double agent sir?" asked Mary as she tried to understand what had made the Major change sides, it didn't really make a great deal of sense to her as she knew that she would never have done anything like that herself, no matter what the reasons.

"Yes, as I said by the time the War started, he was in too deep to be able to get out, if he had tried then the German Intelligence would have killed him or he would have been shot by his own side, everything had been going well and he had made a tidy sum before German Intelligence messed it all up for him, they insisted that he help infiltrate Alice into SOE, if that hadn't happened then I doubt if we would have caught him, and the rest you know."

"It—it still doesn't seem real somehow," said Mary as she was still shocked at the story, it meant that everything that she had gone through had been caused because one man had changed sides for money! There was a silence for a couple of minutes as they were each lost in their own thoughts.

"So, Mary, do you intend to stay with SOE as an Agent?" asked the Colonel making Mary come out of her thoughts.

"I'm still an Agent sir although I…I don't think that I could go on another operation for a while." Mary hadn't really thought about her future with SOE as it was a little early, she had only just managed to escape from France and her wounds were still a little raw to contemplate going on another operation; in face if she was honest with herself, the mere thought of that terrified her; she didn't know if she would be able to operate successfully in France undercover, everything was still too raw.

"Mary needs time to recover from her ordeal, Colonel, she would be working as an instructor until she feels ready for operations." Beth wondered why the Colonel had brought this up, he knew the girl had only just escaped from France with injuries, he knew her mental state precluded her from going on operations until she had been thoroughly cleared by a medical team and that her experience would make her a very useful instructor for new agents as would Pierre's.

"I'm aware of the procedure, Beth, but what you don't know is that Major Scott has left us some very useful information on other enemy agents working in the United Kingdom, but what I need is some Agents who have experience in the field who would be able to help us round up these enemy Agents, what I also need is help to find the Major's handler who has…uhm…disappeared."

"Major Scott had a handler sir?" Mary was quite shocked to think that the Major actually had someone handling him here in England, it seemed incredible that German Intelligence had managed to infiltrate people into SOE, at least she assumed that they were in SOE.

"Are you sure, Colonel, I thought Sandy had been acting on his own?" asked Beth as she too was shocked to hear that Sandy had been 'handled' by someone, she could understand him having been working on his own, but it seemed incredible to think that someone else had been calling the shots.

"We thought the same but thanks to his diaries, we now know that he had a handler, someone who had been working inside the Admiralty since the early thirties!" The colonel couldn't keep the bitterness out of his voices as he said this, as the infiltration of enemy agents in the United Kingdom was worse than they had at first thought but thanks to Major Scott's detailed diaries they now had information that would lead hopefully to the capture of a number of enemy agents and one agent in particular who had turned traitor in the early 'thirties'.

"Commander Harris!" said Mary thinking out loud, the Colonel smiled as he nodded.

"Exactly!"

"Who is commander Harris?" asked Beth frowning as she tried to follow their reasoning, but they obviously knew things that she didn't.

"Commander Harris is the Operations Intelligence Officer at the Admiralty; he was the one who recommended me to Major Scott." Mary thought that this seemed like years ago but was in reality only a few short months ago when she had first gone to the Commander's Office.

"Exactly, he also disappeared from that office the day that Major Scott was killed, at the present we have no idea as to where he has gone. That is one reason that I would like you and Pierre to work with me, we need to seal this breach in our security, we need to round up these agents that Scott has named, and we need to find Commander Harris!" Mary nodded as the Colonel said this for it made sense to her for him to use Pierre and herself, after all they were both experienced Agents who knew how the other Agents would think and act, she also knew what Commander Harris looked like having met the man herself, but she had one reservation!

"If I agree to help you, Colonel, and I am sure that Pierre will, I would like to know one thing before agreeing, sir," she asked and much to her surprise the Colonel nodded as he smiled again.

"I can assure you, Mary, that there would be no torture used by my department, any enemy agent captured will be given a choice, they either agree to work for us or they will be executed as enemy spies, that much I cannot change." He looked at her hard for a moment as if trying to read her reactions to this, Mary knew that any enemy Agent caught in the United Kingdom would be shot as a spy, that much she couldn't change nor would she want to as any Agent knew the risks they took, she herself would expect no less, the only differences being that the Germans did torture people to get their information before executing the agents concerned, but with everything that she had gone through she would not be a party to any type of torture, no matter what the cause.

"Then if it is alright with Beth, Sir, I would like to help if I can," she said as she looked at Beth who also nodded.

"I don't like you poaching my Agents, Colonel, but I can see the sense with this, so I have no objections, sir."

"Good. Well Ladies, I will leave you to it for now. Mary, I will be in touch in about a week or so once your wounds have had a little more time to heal." With that, the Colonel stood up.

"Thank you, Colonel, I only hope we can be of help."

"I have no doubt about it, my dear." The colonel nodded to them both before he strode out of the room.

"Well, that is a turn up for the books, I must say," said Beth as she also stood up.

"I'm sorry, Beth."

"What on earth for?"

"I kind of feel like I have let you down a bit."

"Nonsense Mary, you have done no such thing. You have been given a chance to help with counter espionage and would be silly not to accept it. No, I think you will do very well with the Colonel, just don't be a stranger, eh?" said Beth as she smiled warmly at her, making Mary feel better.

"I won't and thank you Beth, I know I owe you a lot."

"You don't owe me a thing, my girl, you just take care of yourself and give my regards to Pierre when you see him, alright?"

"I will."

"I'll stop by tomorrow," with that Beth left the room. Mary lay back on the pillows, she was still a little dazed at how things had turned out but she was glad that she wouldn't have to go on any other Operations into France, she knew that she wouldn't be ready for that for some time, she only hoped that she would be able to help the colonel, she lay further back on the pillows and a couple of minutes later, she had drifted into a deep and—for the first time in quite a while—very restful sleep.

Ingram Content Group UK Ltd.
Milton Keynes UK
UKHW020033060423
419711UK00006B/162